FOLOVOI

ISOVOI

THE GRAY WASTE

DRAGOVOI

THE VINE

THE MAROVAR

Fallow Vale

LUMILAR

Iron Mine

TRIKOVOI

THE HASSURA PLAINS

◆ Livabai

THE FAN

Quarry

GERBANYAR

◆ Zirevasi

Sea of
Beasts

THE ASP

◆ Chalbora

◆ Zareshoma

Spindle
Bay

THE EMERALD COAST

Sabor

THE MERCIFUL CROW

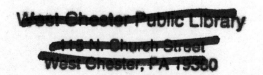

THE
MERCIFUL
CROW

Margaret Owen

Henry Holt and Company
New York

Henry Holt and Company, *Publishers since 1866*
Henry Holt® is a registered trademark of Macmillan Publishing Group, LLC
120 Broadway, New York, NY 10271 • fiercereads.com

Library of Congress Cataloging-in-Publication Data
Names: Owen, Margaret, 1986– author.
Title: The merciful Crow / Margaret Owen.
Description: New York : Henry Holt and Company, [2019] | Summary: Fie, a sixteen-year-old
chieftain from a lowly cast of mercy-killers, must rely on her wits and bone magic to smuggle
the crown prince of Sabor to safety.
Identifiers: LCCN 2018038716 | ISBN 9781250191922 (hardcover) |
ISBN 9781250211903 (cd) | ISBN 9781250211897 (audio)
Subjects: | CYAC: Fantasy. | Euthanasia—Fiction. | Plague—Fiction. |
Witches—Fiction. | Kings, queens, rulers, etc.—Fiction.
Classification: LCC PZ7.1.O89 Mer 2019 | DDC [Fic]—dc23
LC record available at https://lccn.loc.gov/2018038716

Our books may be purchased in bulk for promotional, educational, or business use. Please
contact your local bookseller or the Macmillan Corporate and Premium Sales Department
at (800) 221-7945 ext. 5442 or by email at MacmillanSpecialMarkets@macmillan.com.

First edition, 2019 / Designed by Rich Deas and Sophie Erb
Printed in the United States of America

1 3 5 7 9 10 8 6 4 2

To everyone whose mercy is demanded, and who dreams instead of teeth.
And to my parents: No, you're not in this one. The cat had first dibs.

One way or another, we feed the Crows.
                              —Saborian proverb

On nights you burn sinners, sleep with your sandals on.
                              —advice for a young Crow chief

CASTE

{ **PHOENIX**
Birthright: Fire }

{ **SPLENDID CASTE** } ------------------

{ **HUNTING CASTE** } ------------------

{ **COMMON CASTE** } ------------------

{ **CROW**
Birthright: None }

LEGEND

{
PEACOCK
Birthright: Glamour

SWAN
Birthright: Desire

DOVE
Birthright: Artistry
}

{
HAWK
Birthright: Blood

CRANE
Birthright: Truth

OWL
Birthright: Memory

VULTURE
Birthright: Hunting
}

{
GULL
Birthright: Wind

PIGEON
Birthright: Luck

SPARROW
Birthright: Refuge
}

PART ONE

SINNERS

— AND —

QUEENS

THE EMPTY THRONE

PA WAS TAKING TOO LONG TO CUT THE BOYS' THROATS.

Near ten minutes had run dry since he'd vanished into the quarantine hut, and Fie had spent the last seven of them glaring at its gilded door and trying not to worry a stray thread on her ragged black robe. Taking one minute meant the Sinner's Plague had already finished off the boys inside. Taking three meant Pa had a merciful end to deliver.

Taking ten was taking too long. Ten meant something was fouled up. And from the whispers sweeping the pristine tiles of the courtyard, their throngs of onlookers were catching on.

Fie gritted her teeth until the queasy pinch in her gut retreated. Pa knew what he was doing. Twelve hells, just yesterday morning he'd led their band of Crows to answer a plague beacon, collected corpse and coin, and had them all back on the roads before noon.

That town had no shortage of gawkers either: a man slipping looks through his loom threads, a woman steering her goat herd past the sinner's hut to steal a better view. Children had twisted from their parents' grasp to stare at the Crows and ask if monsters hid under the beaked masks and black robes.

Fie reckoned the answer changed depending on whether a Crow was in earshot.

But Fie had seen gagglers and worse near every day she could recall. As the only caste untouched by the plague, the Merciful Crows were duty-bound to answer every summons.

And as Pa's chief-in-training, she hadn't the luxury of a faint heart. Not even here. Not even now.

The boys they'd been called to take tonight were no different from the hundreds of bodies she'd helped burn in her sixteen years. No matter that few had been this high-caste. No matter that Crows hadn't been summoned to the royal palace of Sabor for nigh five hundred years.

But the needle-sharp stares of warriors and aristocrats told Fie the plague mattered to the high castes tonight.

Pa knew what he was doing, she told herself again.

And Pa was taking too long.

Fie yanked her gaze from the door and searched for trouble in the crowds packing the walls of the royal quarantine court. She'd kept the habit since the first time an angry next-of-kin had trailed them out. From the looks of it, the latticed galleries were all Peacock courtiers, fluttering in mourning paints and ornamental woe as they gawped from a safe distance.

Fie grimaced behind her mask as she caught whispers all too familiar: "*. . . such disgrace . . .*", "*. . . his father?*", and the pestilent "*. . . bone thieves.*" An old, tired kind of trouble. The scandal-thirsty Peacocks were transfixed by the spectacle of thirteen Crows below, awaiting a show.

Hawk trouble was wholly a different beast. King Surimir fancied the war-witches as his palace guards, warriors who healed wounds just as easily as they tore their foes apart from within. Double as dangerous and, since the Hawks knew it, thrice as easy to vex.

These war-witches' hands had anchored on their sword hilts the moment the Crows dragged their cart through the gate. They hadn't budged since.

Fie found no grief in their stony stares. The Hawks weren't waiting on a show. They were waiting for the Crows to foul up.

She caught herself rolling another thread betwixt two thin brown fingers. The queasy pinch slunk back; she nailed her gaze to the door. It stayed damnably shut.

There was a slip of a movement to her left. Hangdog, Pa's other trainee, had shifted by the cart. Torch-flame charred his silhouette, edging it in vivid orange where the light caught tattered robes and the long curve of his beaked mask. From the tilt of his head, he was eyeing the patchouli burners squatting about the hut.

Fie wrinkled her nose. She'd stuffed a fistful of wild mint into her own mask's beak to ward off plague-stink. She couldn't fault this fine palace for trying to daub it over as well. She could, however, fault them for their terrible taste in patchouli.

Hangdog's sandal idly inched toward the burner.

Anywhere else and she'd have *accidentally* punted the patchouli herself. Hangdog was likely itching under so much high-caste attention, and the sneering arcades of gentry above were begging for some nasty surprise.

But not here, not now. Fie tugged at the hood of her robes, a sign only the other Crows would ken. *Don't make trouble.*

Hangdog's foot slid another toe-length toward the burner. Fie could all but smell his grin behind the mask.

They'd both been born witches, and for Crows, that meant they were born to be chiefs, too. Fie's gut gave a hard little twist every time she thought on it . . . but she doubted Hangdog thought on being a chief at all. Pa called him "two-second clever": too bent on making fools of others to catch his own purse getting cut.

Fie looked at the soldiers, then at Hangdog, and resolved to scalp him if the Hawks didn't do it for her first.

There was a squawk from the hut's rare-used hinges as Pa finally stepped outside.

Fie let the loose thread go, head and heart steadying. Damp red streaked down the front of Pa's robes. He'd dealt a mercy killing, then.

Wretched slow mercy, Fie reckoned.

Her relief lasted half a heartbeat before metal rasped, dreadful, from the wall behind them.

Any Crow knew the song of quality steel being drawn. But Pa only turned toward the sound, torchlight flashing off his mask's glassblack eyes. And then he waited.

A hush iced over the courtyard as even the Peacocks froze.

In the city streets, in sorghum fields, anywhere from Sabor's western merchant bays to its cruel mountains of the east, a higher caste could cut down Crows for any invented slight. Brothers, aunts, lovers, friends— every Crow walked with the scars of loss. Fie's own ma had vanished down a dark road years ago.

But for now, the Hawks kept to their walls. The Sinner's Plague spread swift once its victim died. One body could rot a town to stone before year's end. Here in the quarantine court, with two dead boys guaranteed to bring the palace down in less than a half moon . . . here was where the Crows could not be touched.

There was another rattle as the blade returned to its scabbard. Fie didn't dare look back. Instead she fixed on the rumble of Pa's rough voice: "Pack 'em up."

"I'll handle the dead moppets," Hangdog said, starting forward.

"Not on your own." Pa shook his head and motioned for Fie. "They're bigger than you."

Fie blinked. The steward had called the sinners "boys" when he led the Crows in. She'd expected tots, not lordlings ncar grown.

Pa caught her shoulder just as she reached for the door. She cocked her head at him. "Aye, Pa?"

The mask hid his face, but she still caught a hitch in his breath, the way the beak tipped less than a fingerbreadth to point clearer to the Hawks.

"Just . . . bring them out," said Pa.

Fie stiffened. Something was fouled up, she'd swear it on a dead god's grave. But Pa was the chief, and he'd gotten them out of worse.

Most of them, at least.

She nodded. "Aye, Pa."

The second the door swung shut, Fie cuffed Hangdog upside the head.

"What in twelve hells were you thinking?" she hissed. "The Hawks near gutted Pa for walking out a *door*, and you're aiming to try their patience?"

"Aiming to make you mad." This time she heard Hangdog's grin in the hut's thick darkness. "Those scummers won't gut the chief. Or they'll all rot with us if they do."

"You're the only one keen to test that," she snapped, then stopped cold.

Her eyes had adjusted to the little torchlight filtering through the hut's canvas window screens. The lordlings were already tightly cocooned in linen shrouds on their red-stained pallets, a blot of blood seeping through the fabric at each throat.

Bundling up the dead was their job, not Pa's.

"Maybe chief didn't trust us to get it right." Hangdog didn't sound like he was grinning anymore.

That was nonsense. The two of them had handled shrouding for five years now, ever since Hangdog had come to her band for chief training.

"If Pa's got reasons, he'll tell us," she lied. "Sooner these scummers are on the cart, sooner we clear the damn patchouli."

There was a short, muffled laugh as Hangdog picked up one body by the shoulders. Fie took the feet and backed through the door, feeling every gaze in the courtyard alight on her—and then dart to the bloody shroud.

Quiet shrieks ruffled through the Peacock courtiers as Fie swung the body up onto the cart. Hangdog gave it an extra heave. It toppled onto heaps of firewood with an unceremonious thud, knocking over a pile of kindling. A collective gasp swept the galleries.

Fie wanted to kick Hangdog.

Pa cleared his throat, muttering pointedly, "Mercy. *Merciful* Crows."

"We'll be nice," Hangdog said as they headed back inside. He'd just picked up the remaining body by the feet when he added, "Wager someone faints if we drop this one."

Fie shook her head. "Pa can sell *your* hide to a skinwitch, not mine."

The second body was met with another round of sobs as they loaded it. Yet once the Crows began to haul their cart toward the courtyard's gateway, the Peacock courtiers miraculously overcame their sorrow enough to jostle at the lattices for a better look.

The spectators' enraptured angst grated like a broken axle. The dead boys must have been favorites of the royal Phoenix caste if this many Peacocks battled to out-grieve one another.

Fie's skin crawled. Of all the bodies she had ever dragged off to burn, she decided she hated these two most.

To reach the quarantine court, they'd been all but smuggled down cramped, plain servant passageways; now a stone-faced Hawk hustled them straight through the belly of the palace. The longer the bodies lingered, the greater the odds the plague would pick a new victim.

Fie's spite grew with every marvel they passed. Their cart clattered over ceramic inlays in mesmerizing whorls, past gardens of amber-pod wafting its perfume through the damp late-spring night, and into arching corridors of alabaster and bronze. Every pillar, every alcove, every tile paid some tribute to the Phoenix royals: a sun, a gold feather, a curl of flame.

The Hawk threw open a set of enormous ebony doors and pointed her spear inside. "You'll know your way from here."

Pa motioned them on, and the cart creaked into what could only be the fabled Hall of the Dawn. They'd emerged at the head of the hall, which was crowned with a dais; the way out waited far, far down a grand walkway bracketed in more galleries. Great black iron pillars held up an arched ceiling, each cut like a lantern into the likeness of a dead Phoenix monarch. Fires burned within every column, hot enough to cling to Fie's arms even from the door.

Most of the hall was lacquered in deep purples, scarlets, and indigos, but frothy gilt laced the railings of each gallery, and at the dais, a grand disc of mirror-polished gold sat on the far wall above a pool of fire. Gem-studded rays of gold fanned all the way to the roof. Every facet hoarded up firelight until the dais hurt to look at straight on. The whole mess made a sun that rose behind the Phoenix thrones.

The *empty* Phoenix thrones.

Fie sucked in a breath. No king, no queen, and neither the older prince nor the new one here to mourn the dead lordlings, yet the gentry wailed as if their fortunes depended on it. It didn't make sense. But whatever this was, whatever had fouled up, Pa would get them out as he had every time before.

They rolled onto the walkway and began to march.

She hated the way the hall's slick marble tiles whined against the nails spiking her sandal soles, dulling them with every step. She hated the perfume oils besmirching the stagnant air. And most of all, she hated the galleries of Peacock gentry, who shuddered daintily in their satins as if the Crows were no more than a parade of rats.

But behind the Hawk guards stood a silent legion in the brown tunics of Sparrow-caste palace servants, near outnumbering the courtiers above. Harrowed expressions said their grief was more than decorative.

The pinch in Fie's gut returned with a vengeance. Nobody liked Peacocks *that* much.

This was bad business, treating with castes too high to fear the plague. At this rate Pa would be throttling their viatik fee out at the gate. At this rate, maybe they wouldn't get paid at all.

Then, halfway to the door and ten paces ahead of the cart, Pa stopped.

At first Fie didn't understand. Then her eyes skipped to the colossal palace gate, the final landmark betwixt them and the capital city of Dumosa. It had been built large enough for parades of dignitaries and mammoth riders alike; it would swallow the thirteen Crows and their cart easy enough.

And sure enough, a lone sentry stood at the gate, waiting to pay viatik for the dead.

The woman was a glittering specter, from her unbound cascades of silvery hair to the silk white gown that barely rippled in the sluggish breeze. Even from so far off, the telltale shatter of moonlight and torchflame on her finery promised enough gems to feed Fie's whole band of

Crows—twelve hells, maybe the entire Crow caste—for her lifetime. But one thing carried more weight than the sum of her jewels: the collar around her neck.

Two hands of gold, cradling a sun that dawned below her collarbones. It was the royal crest. Fie had seen those hands stamped into every Saborian coin and woven into every flag, and now she could say she'd seen them wrapped around the neck of a queen.

Marriage had made the woman a Phoenix, but she'd been called the Swan Queen even before she left the courtesan caste's pavilions. One of those empty thrones Fie'd passed belonged to her.

And in that moment, Fie kenned what part of tonight had fouled up.

It had been five hundred years, or somewhere near it, since the Sinner's Plague had touched the royal palace. Five hundred years since Phoenixes had lit that plague beacon. Five hundred years since they'd called for Crows.

But if Queen Rhusana was here to pay viatik for these sinner boys, Fie knew sore plain who was under one of their shrouds.

The Crows were hauling the crown prince of Sabor to his funeral pyre.

CHAPTER TWO

─── THE MONEY DANCE ───

A DEAD PRINCE LAY IN THEIR CART LIKE ANY OTHER SINNER, NOT an arm's length away. Fie could scarce believe it. A prince. A *Phoenix*.

Some morbid part of her wondered if Phoenix boys burned like any other sinner. Maybe slower. At least they had the poor bastard beside him to compare.

But Pa didn't move, still fixed to the spot even as the rest of the band pulled the cart nearer. And then Fie saw why.

The queen at the gate meant to pay them, to be sure; the steward at her side held the viatik in plain view. A viatik's worth fit the family's means, that was the rule. A Sparrow farmer might pay them in a sack of salt or dried panbread; a Crane magistrate might offer panes of glass-black. Viatik for royalty, though . . . Fie didn't even know what would be proper.

She did know, however, that it wouldn't be the dirty tabby squirming in the steward's arms.

The night blistered with sudden, furious tears. A stray cat. Fair pay for a beggar at most. Not for two gold-sucking palace boys they'd marched seven leagues to burn.

Every frayed wisp of Fie's patience twisted into a taut, angry wire.

The palace had leered at them, drawn steel on them, all but spat on them, and now they'd made a mockery of payment. Queen Rhusana didn't care about sending her family into the next life with the barest scrap of dignity. All she cared for was flaunting the brutal truth: as queen, she could give Crows naught but contempt, and every time, Crows would have to take it.

No chief would abide this, not even one in training. Not even one facing a queen. Something had to be done.

The Crows were merciful, but they weren't cheap.

The cart had near caught up to Pa. Fie leaned forward, blinking sweat and tears from her eyes. "Pa," she whispered. The beak of his mask dipped. "Money Dance?"

For a long moment, he didn't move. Then the beak dipped again.

For the first time that night, Fie grinned.

She jammed her nail-studded sole into the ground and stuffed every grain of spite into a long, satisfying scratch, the marble screaming for mercy. And then she screamed back.

Around her, the dozen Crows wailed in answer to the call, jolting to a halt. Thirteen torches clattered to the ground.

For the second time that night, the galleries above went silent.

The Crows shrieked again, Fie loudest of all, her pitch climbing at the end. The others took her signal and waited, stock-still. She counted out the quiet in her head: *Four. Three. Two. One.*

Another bloodcurdling cry tore through the hall from thirteen throats, its unmistakable anger echoing off distant archways. Another silence crashed in its wake.

On the third round of screams, the noble sneers were gone. All eyes hung on the motionless cart.

On the fifth round, half the gallery looked ready to cry.

Most fine lords and ladies had never been this close to Crows or plague-dead. To them, the plague was a poor man's problem.

They didn't understand that there were rules. That the plague cared naught for silks or jewels. That it left when the Crows said it could.

But by the thousand dead gods of Sabor, Fie wagered they were starting to catch on now.

She decided they'd stewed enough, and trilled the marching order.

Stamp. The thirteen Crows stepped forward as one, but the cart stayed in its place, its drag-ropes coiling on the marble like asps. *Stamp.* Hunting Castes, Splendid Castes, Common Castes—it didn't matter. The Crows would teach every Saborian in this hall to remember. *Stamp.* Before, their threadbare black rags and long-beaked masks had made them look a superstitious joke. *Stamp.* Now she saw nightmares in the eyes trailing the corpse-cart. *This* was the fear they'd learned at their father's knee.

Fie trilled again.

The footfalls picked up pace, ending in a sweep that carved hellish curls into the tiles. Another stamp. Another guttural scream. Another two paces away from the cart. The gallery recoiled.

Stamp-scrape-scream. Fie huffed under her mask. That was for their ugly palace.

Stamp-scrape-stamp. That was for drawing steel on them.

She trilled again, and the Crows stopped just shy of the threshold. A sick tension clung to the gallery, knuckles whitening on gemstones and silk.

The Crows snapped about and spun into a weaving, vicious pattern back to the cart. Nervous relief wound through the galleries, then wavered when the Crows didn't immediately take up their ropes and torches again. Fie took her place at the cart's front-right corner and waited until the nearest Peacock looked likely to piss himself.

Fie let out a murderous whistle. The Crows snatched up torch and rope, exploding down the hall and into the last courtyard like a hurricane, howling with the gods' own wrath.

Courtiers scattered, tripping over satin trains and painted leather slippers. From the corner of her eye, Fie saw Hangdog had got his wish: at least three Peacocks had fainted.

That, she thought, *is for trying to pay us with a damn cat.*

Pa liked to call it the Money Dance. Fie just liked that it worked.

Their cart slowed near the gate, yet the dance carried on. The queen had not fled like the others of her court, her steward still quaking by her side. From ten paces off, Fie could see all too clear who they intended to shake down.

Queen Rhusana bristled beneath the arch, pale eyes glittering like two hard moons. Under the intricate whorls of white mourning paint, her face was a few shades lighter than Fie's own terra-cotta, her brown complexion nearer to polished bronze. Everywhere Fie looked she saw wasted coin: a diamond-studded headdress wrought like a phoenix of white gold; ropes of pearls and diamonds dripping from her arms to drag on the ground; a white tiger pelt draped over her shoulders. The black-striped tail coiled about her arm, one hind paw fastened to clutch at her hip, and its stuffed head lolled on the tiles, eyes blank with more white gold. To Fie's disgust, even the dead thing's claws were crusted over with diamonds.

The silent demand of tradition had brought Rhusana to pay for her husband's dead son. But it was clear as day that the queen had her own unspoken demand: every eye would stay nailed to her glory alone.

It had never been about the coin. But by every dead god, Fie hoped Pa would make it about coin now.

Then Pa gestured to Fie, jerking his head at the gate.

He wanted *her* to deal with Rhusana. To name the viatik price.

Fie froze. Sweat rolled down her backbone. Calling the Money Dance was one thing. Making demands of a queen was another. She wasn't a chief, not yet—it wasn't proper—what if she fouled it up and cost them all—

She didn't even know *what* to ask for.

Torchlight glinted off steel as Hawks shifted at the wall, a sign their indulgence ran thin. A paper threat with plague bodies heaped in the cart, but a threat all the same. Enough to make a few Crows flinch. Enough to strike lightning through Fie's gut.

Only a paper threat, yet they made it because they could. Because they liked seeing Crows jump.

Fie's anger was a curious thing, sometimes tempered and unwavering as cut steel, sometimes raw and unstoppable as a cut vein. Now an old, sharp kind of rage climbed up her spine, forged of every blade pointed at her for a jest.

And it was that old, sharp rage that told Fie her price.

The screams and footfalls of the Money Dance rose in fury as she stepped forth.

Rhusana had deliberately daubed her face over with boredom, clicking her own diamond-cluttered claws a breath faster than the beats of the dance. Fie knew the signs of impatience: the queen still didn't think she'd answer for this insult. The steward, however, had gone near as gray as the tabby in his arms.

The cat was offered tremulously. Fie didn't take it. She had a chief's price in mind.

She wanted to look the Splendid Castes in the eye without fear. She wanted to make the Hunting Castes think twice before flashing their steel for laughs. She wanted her ma back.

But since the queen couldn't give her any of that, she'd take the next best thing.

"I'll have the teeth," Fie said.

Rhusana glared at the steward. He looked ready to vomit, eyes locked on the bloody shrouds in the cart. "Chief, I cannot—it is not your place to ask—"

"The teeth," Fie repeated, stone-cold. She squashed down the odd little jolt in her chest at being called "chief." *Not yet.*

Behind her, the Crows wheeled and roared. Both she and Rhusana knew they could keep terrorizing the court for hours while the dead sinners steeped the palace in plague. The Swan Queen might wear the royal crest, but here and now, Fie ruled the courtyard.

Rhusana did not answer.

Nor did Fie budge. The longer this went, the worse the queen looked for letting Crows drag her about.

Sweat beaded the steward's face. A pity that Fie needed the queen to crack, not him.

"You have a count of a hundred," said Fie, turning her beaked mask square on Rhusana and mustering every scrap of old fury. "Then we leave the boys at your gate and come to your city nevermore."

"But—" the steward sputtered, "the king—"

"One," said Fie.

"Please—"

"Two," said Fie.

"Enough," Rhusana snapped.

Fie waited. A passing breeze plucked at her robe, then settled.

"Fifty naka." Rhusana's lip curled, her diamond talons clicking faster. "And we will overlook your insolence."

The steward wheezed a sigh of deliverance. "Thank you for your immeasurable generosity, Your Ma—"

"Three," said Fie.

Rhusana's claws went still, digging into her silk-clad thigh.

At the count of ten, the queen's servant was sent running. By the count of seventy, he was back, thrusting a heavy brocade bag into Fie's hands.

If the heft didn't give the contents away, the quiet, echoing hum of magic in her bones did. Every family in Sabor saved their teeth for the day they might call on Crows empty-handed. Each tooth was near good as gold, if only for the Crows who heard their whispers. Some were worth more, a scrap of Pigeon luck or Sparrow refuge when a Crow called for it.

No royal had paid a viatik in centuries. But tonight, Fie had come to collect.

A rare harvest of teeth clicked and rattled inside that brocade bag, entire Phoenix dynasties of teeth, thousands of milk teeth and even teeth pulled from the dead.

And now her band of Crows owned each and every last, priceless one.

A smile sharper than steel cut beneath Fie's mask. There was a reason they called it the Money Dance.

Razor-thin lines had appeared at the corners of Rhusana's perfect, thin-pressed mouth, and Fie took that as a personal victory. She gave a mummer's grand sweep of a bow, stepped back, and handed the bag to Pa.

He raised his fist. The dance stopped; the courtyard rang with aching silence. Ropes were collected, feet reshuffled into a march, and a sigh swept through the crowd as the cart at last began to roll toward the gate.

Fie paused, then doubled back.

The queen whirled, eyes flashing.

"What *more* do you want?" Rhusana flicked her hand at the guards. Every Hawk snapped to attention, spears at the ready.

One of the queen's bangles caught Fie's eye as it flashed in the torch-light: a clever work of silver and pearl, crafted to look like a string of white oleander blossoms.

For a moment, Fie felt like those diamond claws had wrapped around her throat.

She sucked a breath down and let the mint settle her bones. Anyone could wear oleanders. It didn't have to mean aught, not on a queen. And if it did . . . well, the Crows were already on their way out of the palace. Fie'd just make sure they left faster.

She plucked the cat from the steward's arms. "I'll have this, too."

The cat didn't fight as Fie scurried back to the cart, only burrowed its face into the crook of her elbow with a grumble. By the time they cleared the gates, it had begun to purr.

Fie decided she liked the cat. Anything happy to leave the royal palace had good taste.

———— ◆ ◆ ————

It was a long, hushed walk out of the capital city of Dumosa, lit only by their torches and the occasional Dovecraft lantern in a mansion window. Fie wagered the rest of the Crows felt the same tight-throated impatience to make it past the city walls before Hunting Castes rode them down. Every single Crow knew what carrying a bag of Phoenix teeth meant. Every one of them wondered if they'd truly be allowed to carry it out of Dumosa.

Fie felt eyes spying from behind lattice screens or through knot-holes every step of the way, past the fine pavilions of the Swan-caste courtesans, through the granite-pillared Magistrate's Row, even in the Pigeon commons, where dirty faces cowered behind cracks in shanty walls and spat in the Crows' wake to ward off ill fortune.

She kept a sharp eye on the shadows, and more than once she caught Pa tapping his sternum slow, just below the string of teeth about his neck. If the dead gods were kind tonight, he'd have no call to use them.

But if Fie had learned aught over the years, it was that the dead gods skewed miserly with kindness when it came to Crows.

It was nigh midnight before they set foot on the League-High Bridge over the Hem. The great river thundered only a few hundred paces below, but for murder's purpose, it worked near good as a league. Fie minded her step during the ten minutes it took to cross.

The moment her nail-studded soles touched gravel instead of cobblestone, Fie held her breath. If the royals meant to claw back their teeth, this was where the Hunting Castes would strike.

All of them strained to catch any hint of company. The long, terrible silence stretched thin and treacherous as young ice while Fie scoured every flicker of leaves for an ambush.

None came.

Maybe—just maybe—they'd done it.

Someone inhaled sharp. Then a deafening cry broke out:

"OH, I ONCE KNEW A LAD FROM ACROSS THE SEA, WITH A MOST PARTICULAR SPECIALTY—"

Madcap's voice split the night like an axe, swinging into the bawdiest walking song Pa'd let them sing in Fie's presence. The rest of the band broke into wheezing laughter, near weeping with relief.

"Twelve *hells*, Fie!" Wretch clung to the cart for dear life, slapping a knee. She had near as many years as Pa and twice as quick a temper, one of the few who'd known Pa when he was still called Cur, not yet Chief. She took the cat from Fie and scratched its brow. "I thought you'd ask the queen to throw in a crown for all that trouble!"

"What good's a crown?" Swain drawled from behind Wretch. A flash of mirth leavened his perpetually dour voice. "She could have just asked to slap the king. Probably would've gone over better with Her Majesty."

Madcap, a Crow allergic to dignity, snatched up Fie's hands and wheeled her about the road in a giddy whirl, belting yet another lewd and anatomically improbable verse of "The Lad from Across the Sea." Fie couldn't help but throw back her head and laugh. Aye, they still had leagues to walk and bodies to burn, but—but she'd done it.

For once, she'd made the palace pay.

"Stop, stop," Madcap wheezed, laughing as they clutched their stomach. "I'm like to barf!"

The two of them slowed to a drunken tilt near Pa. By all rights, he ought to be reeling with glee like the rest of the band.

He hadn't even taken off his mask, staring straight back at Dumosa.

"Come on, chief—" Madcap started, but Pa cut them off.

"It's not done yet. Save your dance for when the bodies burn." Pa fired off the whistle-order to march.

Wretch passed the cat back to Fie, shaking her head at Pa's back. An unease draped over the Crows once more. Madcap still hummed under their breath, and Swain muttered along after a few steps, but otherwise silence clung to the cart as they dragged it on.

The scattering of huts and god-grave shrines by the road eventually yielded to the twist-trunked, lichen-shawled forest. "The Lad from Across the Sea" wound down, another song rising in its wake, louder and steadier. Soon the only marks of Dumosa were glimpses of a gilded crust over dark hills, sometimes sparking through the trees.

"Here."

Pa's voice cut through the night, snipping off the walking song's last verse. He thrust his torch into the soft dirt by the roadside. The cart creaked to a halt as Pa shucked his mask and nodded at Fie and the tabby. "No strays we can't eat, girl."

"Not a stray, she's mine," Fie returned. "My share of the viatik."

Pa huffed a short chuckle. "Covenant's crap she is, Fie, but we'll talk your share later. What's her name, then?"

She thought of the steward's queasy face and Madcap's dance and grinned. "Barf."

"That's proper." Pa ran a hand over his bald crown. All his hair had migrated south to his short salt-and-pepper beard long years past. "Now let's see about these boys, eh?"

Fie leaned on the edge of the cart and studied the two shrouds lying among splits of kindling. "Big," she said. The prince had been near a year her elder, and clearly both boys had been better fed. "Dunno if we have enough firewood for both."

"Will if we douse 'em in flashburn," Hangdog suggested, lounging over the cart's other side.

Fie's beak was only in the way now. She set Barf down in the cart and pushed back her hood to loosen the mask's straps, letting it hang about her neck as she ran a hand through her chin-cropped tangle of black hair. It was a blessing to breathe clean night air and not the palace's incense or her mask's stale mint.

She had naught to fear of contagion. It was said that every Crow had fouled up something grand in their past lives, bad enough for the Covenant to strike them down with plague and boot them directly to a life of atonement in containing the disease. That Crows were born already in debt to the Covenant's measures of sin. That it would not take them to their next life before that debt was paid.

So it was said, at least. Fie didn't know how much of that rang true to her ear. But it was truth hard as iron that the Sinner's Plague left only Crows untouched.

Death-stink hadn't settled on the boys yet, but she still flinched at the crimson stains on their shrouds. Of all a chief's duties, cutting throats was the one she dreaded most.

She reached into the cart, prodding what seemed like the nobler of the bloody heaps. "They really royals, Pa?"

"Just the one. Other was his body double."

Fie tugged back the linen until torchlight landed on a boy's rust-flecked face, looking for all the world like he was sleeping. Maybe a little afraid. Maybe he'd been awake when Pa's blade touched his throat.

She pursed her lips. "So that's what a sinner prince looks like."

The dead boy sat up.

"Well, no," he said, "but I've been told I'm fairly close."

A COVENANT OATH

FIE DIDN'T INTEND TO PUNCH THE BOY, BUT SHE DID ALL THE SAME. Fie didn't intend to scream, either, but that happened, too, and with enthusiasm. As did tripping over her feet as she bolted back, landing on her rear in the damp grass. Hangdog's curses and Pa's roaring laughter only muddied her panic.

The dead boy yanked his left hand loose from the bindings, wincing as he felt his jaw. Gore on his plain long-sleeved tunic made it impossible to tell if any of the blood was new. Fie scrabbled about to arm herself with a rock as the other shroud also began to stir.

"Here, here," Pa said, wiping tears from his eyes as he reached into the cart to help free them. "You've gone and spooked my girl."

"There's an understatement," the boy said, dry. He glanced down at the wiggling shroud beside him. "Jas, as your personal guard, I feel obligated to warn you"—he pointed at Fie—"*that one* is easily startled."

Fie's mind was a fly in her hollow skull, buzzing in fruitless circles. The dead boys were moving. The dead boys were *talking*.

The dead boys weren't dead.

"Yech." The bodyguard slid out of the cart, wincing at the crackle of his blood-stiff shirt. "Is pig blood always this vile? Next time I fake my death, I'm picking something more glamorous. I hear poisoning's in vogue."

"Pa." Her voice came out strangled. "Did we just kidnap royals?"

Pa grinned ear to ear. He loved a good jest, but Fie wasn't sure the Phoenix caste would find abducting the heir all that amusing. "Told you, Fie, just the one. And only on account of them asking kind."

A prince and a guard. A Phoenix and his Hawk, then. Fie didn't know if she wanted to scream or laugh. Perhaps this was all one garish nightmare. If they were lucky—

"You're *certain* we weren't followed?"

The quiet voice belonged to the boy the bodyguard had called "Jas."

Jasimir. Everyone knew the crown prince's name. As the prince untangled himself, neither he nor his guard seemed to note how every mutter had died like birdsong before a storm. The Crows eyed the lordlings as if twin serpents had slipped from the shrouds. By torchlight the two blood-soaked boys were nigh identical in their wide, sharp-jawed faces, sleek black topknots, and loose linen shirts and trousers. Where his Hawk guard was all good-natured ease, though, the prince was as grim as if he were truly at his own funeral.

But it took more than a crown and a frown to faze Pa. "Oh aye, we were followed." He pried a tooth from his string and tossed it aside. Fie couldn't believe he'd burned a whole Sparrow tooth without her catching on. "Pair of the queen's trackers. They tailed us to the bridge and no farther."

"Cur."

The prince, the Hawk, and Pa all looked up. Wretch's mask was off as well. Fie knew when she called Pa "Cur," they were in for a spectacle.

"I see you're busy ministering to the needs of the royal louts here," she cooed, voice rising, "but I don't suppose if, perchance, when it suits your fancy, you might share with your kin what nonsense, suicidal, *scumbrained* scheme you've just dragged us into?"

The Hawk bodyguard moved first, striding toward Wretch. "Of course, I apologize. We've been quite inconsiderate." He tapped his right fist to his lips and held it out in greeting. Wretch, taken aback, did the same, and they clasped hands briefly. "My name is Tavin. I'm sure you've figured out who my friend is."

"We've a notion," Hangdog drawled, leaning on the cart. There was a nasty edge in his voice, the kind he got when he hungered for a fight. "Got bored of your palace, *cousins?*"

The prince's face darkened at the slantways insult. Before he could bite back, his Hawk guard flicked his hand, dismissive. "I don't typically commit wide-scale blasphemy out of boredom. Repeat assassination attempts tend to motivate a man, though."

Wretch scowled. "If someone doesn't start talking sense, I'm getting as far clear of here as possible."

"Then I'll rephrase," the Hawk said. "Rhusana wants us dead."

"She wants *me* dead," Prince Jasimir corrected. "She's wanted it since she used Father to marry up into the Phoenixes, and she wants it even more now that she's birthed a prince of her own. First it was just a hunting accident, then a viper in the bathhouse, then ground glass in the wine . . . and it won't stop until she's gone. Or I am."

Wretch flung her arm at the road. "Well done, then! You've given her square what she wants. So now that we've dragged you to freedom, we'll be taking our leave, aye?"

The Hawk—Tavin, he'd said he was Tavin—didn't answer, instead holding out a hand to Fie. "I'm sorry for scaring you, by the way."

She let him pull her back to her feet before yanking free. "Well, I'm not sorry for punching you."

"That's probably not the last time you'll say that." His teeth flashed in a grin. "Jas and I need to tag along with you for a few days."

Pa stiffened, crossing his arms. "That wasn't our deal."

Tavin and the prince traded looks. Tavin's mouth twisted. "It's complicated," he began.

"It's not. I kept my word. Our business is done." Pa's tone had turned a chill sort of civil. Fie snorted. Typical high castes, thinking they could twist the terms of a deal as they pleased. They'd picked the wrong Crow chief for that.

"You don't understand." Prince Jasimir's voice rose. "We're—"

"Out of Dumosa," Pa answered, even and immovable. "And we have our viatik. That was the deal. No more, no less."

The Hawk guard scowled. "You *have* to hear us out."

Fie contemplated punching him again.

"This isn't your palace, lads." Pa bent to pick up a drag-rope. "We don't *have* to do aught."

"They're going to try to kill you," Prince Jasimir said, abrupt.

A moment's hush dropped, then ruptured in laughter. Madcap wheezed so hard, they had to lean on the cart. Both the prince and the Hawk looked taken aback.

"Oh, they'll try to kill us?" Wretch cackled. "That's new. That's bold. Oh, I like that."

Prince Jasimir's brow furrowed. "How could you possibly find that amusing?"

"They've *been* trying to kill us. There's always some 'they.' Reckon *they've* been at it a few centuries now." Fie swept him the same mocking bow she'd given Queen Rhusana. "My deepest of sorrows, Your Highness, but if you mean to frighten us into helping you, you'll have to think bigger."

"Are the Oleander Gentry big enough?"

Fie snapped up straight to stare at Tavin as the laughter died. The Oleander Gentry were more than a "they." The Oleander Gentry were a fist to the windpipe of every Crow.

"It's a funny story, you see," the Hawk guard continued, the sudden razor edge in his words suggesting it was anything but a jest. "Turns out the queen's been making lots of new and horrible friends. Right now I'd give it a month before she tries to take the throne for herself. And when she does, she'll owe most of her success to her greatest allies: the Oleander Gentry."

Part of Fie wanted to hit him again. Part of her wanted to run clear from Sabor.

Every Crow carried scars from the Gentry. They were the reason Crows didn't stop near many a village after sundown. That was when the Gentry would ride, bearing white oleanders on their breasts, faces hidden in pale paints and undyed cloth so they couldn't be traced to kin or caste.

Most of Sabor believed Crows to be dead sinners reborn, sentenced to repent through a hard life of containing the plague. Oleanders believed the part they liked—that the Covenant meant to punish Crows for their misdeeds—and claimed the Crows spread the plague themselves. Then they took it upon themselves to dole out that punishment. The Covenant was one more mask for them, and Fie kenned too well the monsters that rode beneath it.

They were rich and poor, nameless and infamous, many and merciless. Their hunts were only called murder when they were caught. And since they only hunted Crows, the regional governors were in no great hurry to catch them.

When the Gentry took Crows, only the lucky few walked away.

Fie's mother hadn't been lucky.

Fie thought of a road in the dark, one that stretched over a dozen years behind her, when she'd scarce reached Pa's knee. Yet she still remembered the trail of fingers the Oleander Gentry had left to point the way.

She caught up her robe's loose thread again and twisted it hard.

"I won't demand your obedience in this." Torchlight danced over Prince Jasimir's bloody face. "But with Rhusana on the throne . . ."

". . . the Oleander Gentry will ride where they please, when they please," Fie finished. Hangdog was gripping the cart so tight, his knuckles looked near to burst through the skin. She could only guess what he saw in his own terrible memory.

Tavin nodded. "And they'll get an armed Hawk escort to help."

Fie didn't have to guess at her own memories: far away and long ago, a little girl picked up a crooked, fleshy caterpillar in the cold and dusty road, then found nine more in a red-tipped trail.

Ma had hooked that finger through Fie's small hands enough times for her to know every scrape, every callus, every bump of the scar down one joint. And when Fie had fumbled, and the broken stump of fingerbone scraped against her palm, she'd known the spark singing to her from that bone. She'd know Ma's song anywhere.

The road had caught Fie back then, in the peculiar way that only roads could. Chief—not Pa to her, not yet—had strode that bloody path, blade in a shaking fist, knowing he had mercy to deliver to one of his own. And Fie—not a chief-in-training, not yet—had stayed frozen in place, wanting to see her ma but knowing that every time that blade came out, Ma had covered Fie's eyes.

That cold road had trapped her there until Wretch bore her away, for even then, Fie had known her choices were to either walk down the chief's way, or to run from it.

And on this road now, in the torch-lit dark, Fie still could not say which way was worse.

But if the queen gave Oleanders command of her Hawks—if not even daylight gave Crows refuge—Fie knew sore how all their roads would end.

The lines in Wretch's face seemed to carve a little deeper than they had a moment before. "If you boys are fixing to have us Crows storm the palace and fight off Her Majesty, I got hard news for you about how that will turn out."

"The Oleanders only have sway." Prince Jasimir seemed steadier on political ground. "And the people still call Rhusana the *Swan* Queen for a reason. She can rule through her son's claim to the throne, but she still needs support from the regional governors to keep the kingdom united. My cousin Kuvimir is the lord-governor of the Fan region. He's sworn to take us in and rally the others behind me, which should force Rhusana to back down. If we move fast, we can reach his fortress in Cheparok before she deposes Father."

"So we smuggle you to your kin in Cheparok, they make a big, ugly show of liking you over the queen, and you remember us rosy on your throne someday." Fie nodded to the wagon's load of firewood. "Reckon you forgot how most of Sabor thinks you and your Hawk here are charcoal in a pyre right now."

The prince hesitated to answer; the Hawk pounced. Tavin's teeth flashed wolfish as a gambler who knew how his loaded shells would land. "That's my favorite part, actually. I'll have to lie low for a while, but Jas . . . Let's just say Queen Ambra set a precedent for Phoenixes miraculously returning from the dead."

Fie's jaw dropped. Of all the things she had heard this night, what Tavin proposed was the most rattle-brained of all.

In the entire history of Sabor, only one soul had ever burned bright enough to survive the Sinner's Plague: the invincible Ambra, matriarch of the Phoenix caste, Queen of Day and Night. Legend said she rode tigers into battle, a spear in each hand; that she walked in wild-fire unscathed; that the sun came at her beck and call, so greatly did it love her. Legend said that her rebirth in the Phoenix caste would herald another era of prosperity and peace.

Legend hadn't much to say about shamming her reincarnation for political gain, but somehow Fie couldn't imagine it landed on the right side of the Covenant. Nor could she conjure a vision of the willowy prince before her riding aught more spirited than a poppy-addled pony.

Tavin must have read the doubt on her face, for his hand flapped once more. "We can't *really* sell Jas as the King of Day and Night. But bouncing back from the Sinner's Plague is a good argument that Ambra's bloodline is strong in him. That alone will win over half the country."

"The idiot half," Wretch muttered.

"If there were another way out, we'd take it." Prince Jasimir's gaze traveled from Crow to Crow. What he was searching for, Fie couldn't say. "But Rhusana will give every one of you over to the Oleanders if she reaches the throne. I'm asking for your help to stop her. Otherwise none of us has a chance."

"If you're speaking true . . ." Pa rolled a tooth strung at his neck. Fie would've gone for a Crane-caste tooth, one that could sift out lies from the lordlings. Instead Pa's hand dropped. He looked at the rest of the Crows. "We've only got one rule. Strikes me we'd best follow it."

Look after your own. Fie had heard that rule near every day. As a chief, she'd need to live it soon. But even if she could keep her own band of Crows safe, the whole caste was scattered across Sabor.

If the Oleanders could ride free, road after road would end like her ma's had.

Her jaw stiffened. It was a chafing thing: even filthy with pig blood, the lordlings still looked like they belonged in a palace.

There was no real bargain here, just make-believe benevolence of offering the Crows a choice. It was written in the imperious tilt of the prince's lips, in the jut of Tavin's chin, the way they both drummed their fingers as they waited for an answer they were sure they'd get.

Just like Rhusana, with her damned oleander bangle. Even if the lordlings were bluffing about her ambitions, the Oleander Gentry still had her favor. Of course the Crows had no choice.

Of all the bodies Fie had ever dragged off to burn, she most *surely* hated these two the most. For all their talk, the lordlings treated with the Crows as if they were back in that miserable gilded hall, forcing them to dance for fair pay—

An idea carved through her thoughts like her sandal-nail on marble, and left a trail like a bloody finger.

"No," Fie said. "I say no deal."

Surprise flashed over every face on the road. Hangdog's snort followed. Prince Jasimir's dark eyes narrowed. "We want to help—"

"Oh, *you want to help*," she mimicked. "Does His Highness have another servant to shovel up all the crap falling out of his mouth, or is that *his* job?" She jerked a thumb at Tavin. To his credit, the guard only raised his eyebrows, but that razor edge danced in his gaze again. "You faked your deaths. You tried to go back on your deal with Pa. And you just told us your whole plan is to lie to everyone in Sabor. Why would we trust you?"

"Because your lives depend on it," Prince Jasimir snapped, panic sparking in his voice. "Do you truly think the Oleander Gentry will treat with you?"

Fie smothered a laugh. "Awful convenient how your heart only bleeds for Crows now that you need us. Spent your life weeping on the inside, did you?"

"That's not fair," Tavin started.

That same old rage whipped the words from her. "Fair? *Fair?* You want to tell me what's fair, palace boy? You want us to choose betwixt letting the Oleanders run us down by day or making sure they still have to do it by dark so *your* castes can keep pretending you don't see?" She spat at their feet. "Call that help if you want. Your Hawk'll pick it up with the rest of your crap."

If any Crow thought Fie had overstepped, she'd hear their grumbles. Instead, the roadside was wired in taut silence, all eyes on her.

They knew a Money Dance when they heard it.

Tavin moved first, rubbing his hands together. Somehow the gesture still looked deadly. "You're not wrong," he admitted with a shrug. "At least, not about your options. It'd take another ten years in service of the palace for me to make it all the way to royal dung collector. I'd recommend you take our word on the Oleanders, though."

"What's your word worth when you're good as dead?" The rot in Hangdog's voice said this was more than the Money Dance. "When we're *all* good as dead?"

"Fine." Prince Jasimir pinched the bridge of his nose. "Gold? Jewels? Lands? What's your price?"

Fie mimicked Tavin's dismissive hand flick. "Flash and trash. If the Oleanders don't loot those from us, your other gentry will."

"Then what *do* you want?" Prince Jasimir asked.

This time, Fie already had a chief's price in mind.

Look after your own. She had one foot already down this road, and every eye was on her. She couldn't go back; she couldn't give her ma mercy or keep Hangdog from screaming in his sleep. But she could keep any Crow from having to walk that way again.

She took a deep breath and looked Prince Jasimir dead in the eye. "I never want to see the Oleander Gentry again. The Hawks that Rhusana promised the Gentry? They'll guard us instead. I want your Covenant oath that with you as king, every caste will know we Crows are worth protecting. *That's* my price."

The prince's face turned as gray as the steward's had.

Pa, on the other hand, had the tiny wrinkles under his eyes that only showed when he was beating down a smile. Fie took that as a good sign.

"Crows," Pa called out before either lordling could speak. "Do we favor those terms?"

Another twist of her dance. There was a chorus of ayes. Another twist of the knife. Tavin's glare could have cut through stone.

"You know what you're asking?" Prince Jasimir asked. "No caste has ever had special protection like this before."

Swain coughed. "Suppose your palace Hawks are just highly trained, well-armed houseguests, then?" One more whirl and stamp, one more scratch in the floor.

The prince opened his mouth, then closed it, thinking. "It's different," he said slowly. "Royalty are prime targets for coordinated attacks and internal violence—"

"Aye, and we actually die from those." Fie folded her arms. "*You* said you wanted to help. Rhusana seems to think she's got Hawks to spare. We've named the terms, prince. Cut your oath or leave us be."

Fie's favorite thing about the Money Dance was that it always, always worked.

Tavin ran a hand over his dark hair. "She's got a point, Jas. Several, in fact. Enough points that I'm starting to think she's mostly thorns."

"Some bone in there, too," Pa added, his grin little more than lacquer over an unspoken threat. "Y'know. For structure."

Prince Jasimir scowled, eyes darting from Fie to Tavin. After a long moment, his shoulders drooped. "Fine. You have my word."

Fie caught her breath. A ripple shifted through the Crows; it might as well have echoed down the road, all across Sabor.

The prince had just sworn to tell his country that Crows were worth protecting.

But they only had his word. Fie knew how flimsy a Phoenix's promise was. "I said a Covenant oath."

The prince shrank back. Hangdog laughed cruelly. "Oh, the wee princeling's afraid of cutting an oath, then?"

Pa shot Hangdog a dark look. "No harm in it, lad. I'm the chief. You'll bind it with me." When Jasimir didn't move, Pa slowly drew out a jagged stump of a sword from under his robes. Some long-past battle had sheared the blade in half, leaving a length of steel no longer than Pa's forearm, but its broken point still gleamed wickedly as Pa jabbed it into his palm.

He held up his hand, showing a small, bloody gash. "Naught to it, see?"

"Tav . . ." Jasimir's voice had withered like a raisin. Fie knew that fear, the trap of a road that only went two bad ways.

"Isn't his word good enough?" Tavin slid between Pa and the prince. A line in his brow said the casual façade was like to split a seam.

"No," Fie answered, cold. Tavin's diplomacy caved as he frowned at her. She scowled back. "What's the matter? Afraid your king-to-be might have to keep his deal this time?"

Prince Jasimir flinched and shook his head. "I . . . Fine. You're right."

"Jas—" Tavin put a hand on the prince's shoulder.

"A king doesn't get to make empty promises. This is just a formality." Jasimir shrugged him off, walked over to Pa, and grasped the sword's broken end. His fingers came away bloody.

He and Pa clasped hands. The air round them fried with a cold heat, like the moments before a lightning strike. The ring of torches burned higher, washing the roadside in red light.

"In flesh and blood do I make this oath," Pa said. "Me and mine will see you safe to your allies, prince. To the Covenant I swear, may my soul not rest until it be done."

"In flesh and blood do I make this oath," echoed Jasimir. "As king, I will ensure the Crow caste's protection as payment for their service to me now. To the Covenant I swear it."

A breeze stirred Fie's hair, dragging the torch-flames sideways. The very ground seemed to hum beneath her toes.

Pa still held steady. "By the Covenant, we bind this oath. I swear to keep it in this life and, if I fail, the next."

The wind only grew stronger.

"With the Covenant as witness, this oath shall be kept." Jasimir's voice was louder now. "In this life or the next."

Firelight seemed to catch round their joined hands a moment, flaring brighter as it wove through knuckle and skin.

There was a brief, furious blaze of light, and then it was done.

The Covenant had heard them, Pa and the prince and even Fie.

The breeze died, the dim torchlight suddenly paltry in the wake of the oath. Fie swayed in place, trying to snatch whole thoughts from a whirlwind in her head.

She'd sworn the prince to a Covenant oath. No more Oleanders; no more riders in the night; no more fingers in the road. So long as they kept their end of the deal.

But if it went bad, Pa would pay the price.

The notion coiled about her throat like a collar on a queen.

If Pa or Jasimir failed in this life, they would still be sworn in the one after, and after, and after. Until their oath was kept, Pa would be bound to the prince.

And a royal Phoenix would be sworn to protect the Crows.

Hate the boys or no, Fie had to admit that extorting royalty had its sunny side.

"Pleasure doing business with Your Highness," Pa said, cheery. He let the prince go. "Now I believe we've got some bodies to burn."

CHAPTER FOUR

—— TOOTH AND NAIL ——

"**M**AKE YOURSELF USEFUL OR MAKE YOURSELF SCARCE, HAWK."

If Tavin kenned the salt in Wretch's tone, he didn't show it, swaying by the cart as he tried to balance a split of kindling on his head.

"I heard this is how Sparrow farmers carry their burdens," he answered with a grin Fie was already sick of. "Don't you want me to blend in?"

"Wrong caste," Fie snapped, pulling another armful of firewood from the cart and loading it into the sling she'd made of her cloak. At least Prince Jasimir had the sense to stay out of their way as the Crows built up the pyre. "The only way you'll pass for a Crow is if you keep your fool mouth shut."

"That's a lost cause," Tavin admitted with a shrug. "I couldn't even keep quiet as a corpse." At Fie's baffled look, he plucked the stick of kindling off his head and pointed it at her. "At the quarantine hut? You said something about the incense, and I laughed. And then your grumpy friend nearly broke my neck tossing me into the cart."

She'd thought the laugh was Hangdog. And she'd thought wrong. Again.

The prince fidgeted, flexing the hand he'd cut. The Covenant had healed him with the sealing of the oath, but that didn't seem to ease his nerves. "That incense has been the ceremonial—"

"*The damn patchouli*, that's what she called it." Tavin laughed, balancing the kindling on a fingertip. "Three solid days of that mess. I told you it was foul, Jas."

Fie swiped the kindling from him, swung her bundle of firewood over a shoulder, and stomped away.

"*She* agrees with me," Tavin added in her wake, unperturbed.

The Fan. She only had to put up with the lordlings' nonsense until they made it to the Fan. Well, to the governor's city of Cheparok. Then Pa's end of the oath would be kept, and she could forget about them and the Oleander Gentry both.

Hangdog was turning a band of earth for a firebreak round the growing stack of wood as Fie approached. At the sight of her, he stuck the spade into the ground and muttered, "His Highness giving you grief?"

"Just his guard dog," she grumbled back.

"Seems they trained him a few tricks." Hangdog jerked his chin behind her.

Fie snuck a glance. Tavin had perched on a wobbling log by the cart, balancing more kindling on each palm and the crown of his skull. Half the Crows were rolling their eyes. The other half were laughing.

Her lips pursed. "Thought Hunting Castes were born with a stick up the arse."

"Turns out the prince is a piss-baby and his guard is a clown." Hangdog spat and resumed digging. "Waste of brains, the both of 'em."

Fie chucked her load of firewood onto the heap, itching with distrust. This was square why Pa called Hangdog two-second clever: Tavin had already gone to work winning Crows over for his prince. The Hawk was no clown. He was walking trouble.

And trouble incarnate was rummaging through the bloody shrouds on the ground when she returned to the cart. He fished out first a dagger that he tossed to the waiting prince, then two short swords that he belted at his hips with a swift, practiced ease. The scabbards of every blade looked rich enough to feed the whole band for a year.

Fie turned to the prince. "Do Phoenixes even burn?"

Prince Jasimir blinked. "Are you speaking to me?"

"Aye. Do you burn?" Fie waited, gathering up more firewood, but Jasimir seemed wholly confounded. She sighed. "Should we be faking a funeral pyre for a boy with the fire Birthright?"

Fie had wondered more than she liked about the day the dead gods handed out Birthrights. She wondered what drove the Sparrows' gods to bless their caste with the gift of refuge, letting them slip from notice when they pleased. What inspired the Cranes' gods to give their children the Birthright of truth, so they could spot lies like stains.

She wondered, too much, why the Crows' gods had left them no Birthright at all.

And she reckoned that when the Phoenix gods gave their children the Birthright of fire, they hadn't had funeral pyres in mind.

Tavin spoke for the prince. "It's fine. Phoenixes burn when they're dead." He stood and dumped the bundled shrouds atop the firewood in her arms. "Here, this should go in the pyre, too."

Something slipped free of the linen. Fie caught it by habit.

A jolt shot up her arm, stampeding into her brain before she could stave it off. For a moment, Fie's vision went blank and the world was mud and sour slop, squeal and grunt, bristle and—

"Pig bones."

The torch-lit night returned at the sound of Tavin's voice. Firewood lay scattered about Fie's feet, her hands still tangled in linen. Tavin was clearly fighting down a grin; likely he thought she was disgusted, not dizzy.

"They're pig bones," he laughed, kneeling to gather up the spilled firewood as her mind scrambled back into a more human tongue. "We figured the pyre wouldn't be complete without some bone fragments."

She hadn't fouled up with animal bone in months. The power in human bones and teeth, *that* she could draw out or stuff down at will, but beasts . . . beasts had a nasty way of running wild.

Fie's hands shook now more with rage than shock. "You listen, Hawk boy, and you *ken* me." She threw the linen bundle back at Tavin's chest. "Don't you ever, *ever* surprise a Crow with bones like that. *Never.*"

"Especially not one like Fie," Pa said from behind her with a brief pat on the shoulder.

"She's a bone thief?" Prince Jasimir asked, eyeing her sideways.

Most every Crow in earshot flinched at the slur. So did Tavin. The prince didn't seem to notice. Pa dug round in the cart's lower cargo hold before answering, prompting a mew of protest from Barf the cat, who had holed up beside a sack of millet.

"Every Crow chief is," Pa said at last, stowing a jug of flashburn under his arm. He rolled his right sleeve back to show a black witch-sign swirling on the wrist, same as the one Fie bore. "Bands don't last long without a witch. I'm chief for this band, and I'm training Fie and Hangdog to lead their own someday. But with Fie, the witch part's not your trouble. It's her temper that'll leave a mark."

Pa winked at Fie, then twitched his fingers at the blades the boys had strapped at their sides. "You'll wrap those scabbards and hilts in rags tonight, and you'll keep them out of sight. Hunting Castes don't abide Crows with whole blades."

"What do you mean?" Prince Jasimir clutched the jeweled hilt of his dagger. "Saborian law allows everyone to bear steel."

Pa shrugged. "And that's well and fine, but the law doesn't weep much for Crows. Most we're allowed is a broken blade for the chief. Your blades stay hidden, or they go in the pyre." He didn't wait for a response before walking off.

After that, Tavin's stupid grin made itself scarce.

Fie couldn't help kicking about the memory of grieving servants in that reeking, gaudy palace. Perhaps they truly had mourned for the lordlings. But if the last hour was any measure, she couldn't for the life of her see why.

Once the pyre sat crowned in shrouds and bones, Pa uncorked the flashburn jug. Thick, clear ooze drizzled out as he turned back to the boys. "I'll take your shirts, too, lads. Best leave some scraps in the coals. Fie, Hangdog, give 'em your robes and masks."

Prince Jasimir seemed to have resigned himself to preserving the fragile truce, for by the time Fie shook the wood scraps from her cloak, he and his guard were already pulling off their bloody tunics. She could read a history of training in their clean-healed scars, a map of every time they weren't quick enough to beat the blade. Torchlight also snagged in the whorls of a burn crawling round Tavin's left knuckles. It looked old, and not the work of any training Fie knew.

"The old queen didn't think much of royalty who were useless in a fight."

Tavin had caught her staring. Fie flushed. He just took her cloak and mask. "Jas and I won't be a burden if we meet trouble."

The first queen had been born a Markahn, the oldest, proudest clan of Hawks in Sabor. It sounded like marrying into the Phoenix caste hadn't changed her much.

Hangdog seized Tavin's unburnt wrist. "Hold—"

In an instant, the fragile truce shattered.

There was a breath, a tumble of mask and black rags, an adder-swift twist of flesh and torchlight and steel, a startled curse.

And then there was Hangdog, standing stone-still as a sword point strummed the skin beneath his chin.

Any hint of amity had vanished from the Hawk, one hand thrown in front of Prince Jasimir. Tavin's eyes stayed on Hangdog, but when he spoke, it was to them all.

"I'm tired. I haven't eaten in three days. And I don't take kindly to being dragged about. So let's have another accord, yes? *We* will follow your bidding on passing for Crows, whether that be hiding blades, keeping quiet, or, Ambra help me, warning you about *animal bones*." His scoff grated even more than his grin had. "And in turn you, all of you, will not lay one unbidden finger on myself or the prince. Not once."

The pulse jumped in Hangdog's throat, perilous close to the point of the blade.

"Do we have an understanding?" Tavin asked, cold.

A muscle in Hangdog's jaw twitched, like he aimed to spit in the Hawk's face. It was clear as day how that would end.

Fie stepped between the boys, pushing Hangdog back. "Understood," she said, matching ice for ice in Tavin's glare. The sword's point hovered not a handspan from her eyes.

"He's a war-witch," Hangdog muttered behind her. "I thought I saw the sign."

Sure enough, black lines adorned the Hawk guard's unburnt wrist.

"Hear that?" Fie spoke loud enough for Pa to catch, trying not to think how close, how sharp the sword's tip loomed. "He was just look-ing at your witch-sign."

She counted one breath, then two, then three, never breaking Tavin's stare.

Then the blade vanished in a hiss of a sheath, as swift as it had appeared. Tavin nodded, curt. "Of course I can hear him now. He's fig-ured out how to use his words."

Fie dragged Hangdog over to Pa before he figured out words the prince or his guard dog found more offensive.

Pa shook his head as the last few globs of flashburn oozed from the jug onto cold wood. "Near one," he said under his breath. "Hawk fools are still Hawks. Let's not forget the claws, aye?"

"Aye, Pa." Fie hated the shake of her hands, the old wrath curdling her veins. Oath or no, Hawk boys still liked to see Crows jump when they flashed steel. She wouldn't forget twice.

Pa pressed something small, hard, and familiar into Fie's palm. His voice rose. "You two will stay back to mind the fire. No call to salt it without sinners. Meet us at the haven shrine once it's burned low. Every-one else, we're clearing out."

"Flint," Hangdog called as the other Crows grabbed their cart-ropes. "It's still in the cart."

Pa shook his head, pointing at Fie. "No need."

She uncurled her fist. A single milk tooth waited there, gleaming bright against her fingers. Startled, she looked to Pa.

He just nodded. "Go on, girl."

Fie set her other hand over the Phoenix tooth, rolling it betwixt her palms like a gambler about to throw a shell. It only took a moment's focus to find the spark of old life buried deep within, a ghost slumber-ing in bone. This was unlike any spark she'd dug up before—but Pa wouldn't give her aught she couldn't conquer.

Closing her eyes, Fie pulled her hands apart. The spark broke free.

She saw silk and gold, sandstone courtyards, a fist thrust into fire before a cheering, jewel-dusted crowd. No hunger, no fear, only the weight of terrible ambition. Then, like the beast before, it vanished— all but a flickering heat still in the palm of her hand.

She opened her eyes. The tooth was burning.

Fie felt no pain, even though the rag strips wrapped about her palm had begun to char. Fire wouldn't harm a Phoenix, nor, it seemed, the witch who called royal ghosts. The small flame burned bright, pure gold, as if Fie held sunlight itself. She rolled her shirtsleeve from elbow to shoulder and focused on the spark once more. Fragments came to her: archery practice, a lover waiting in the amber-pod gardens, a ceremony committing the teeth of a dead uncle to the viatik stash . . . then, at last, what she'd sought. Candle-flame, winding round fingers like a purring kitten.

Fie clung to the way the dead Phoenix had threaded the fire with his will, then sought the answering hum in her own bones. One rattled up her spine. She'd called out the spark, joined it to her own power. Now it was time to make it sing.

With her head and her heart and all of her bones, Fie pulled.

The tooth erupted in her outstretched hand. Heat blasted through the clearing, gasps turning to awed curses as too-bright flames clawed at the stars.

The first time Pa had spoken to Fie of being a witch, he'd started with the gods.

Eons ago, he'd told her, when the thousand gods had founded their castes and chosen their graves, they'd left one final blessing before they died: a Birthright for every caste.

Every caste, that was, save the Crows.

The gods who begat the Crows had a bad sense of humor. Crows came into the world with no blessings, but their witches had a gift all the same. It was why other castes called them bone thieves: their gift was stealing Birthrights.

In the years after, she'd learned the ways of a Crow witch under Pa's watchful eye. She could call any Birthright from the cast-off bones of the living or the dead, as long as its spark lasted for her.

But why, she'd asked long ago, *did the thousand gods have to die?*

And Pa had answered: *Everything has a price, Fie. Especially change. Even Phoenixes need ash to rise from. Do you know how many witches there are in Sabor?*

She'd shaken her head.

One thousand, Pa had told her. *We had to rise from something.*

She'd never wholly believed it. She'd never once felt like a god.

But with fire, the Birthright of royals, howling in the palm of her hand, Fie felt like one now.

She took a breath and reeled the fire back to a respectable blaze, but a prickle on her neck said eyes still lingered on her. Sure enough, the Hawk's thin squint was one she knew too well. It belonged to someone adjusting how they'd first sized her up.

The prince, on the other hand, looked appalled. Fie reckoned he didn't like the sight of divine Phoenix fire in her low-caste hands— then she saw that no witch-sign adorned either of his.

The dead gods had left their graves as havens for their castes, sites where Birthrights were heightened to rival even a witch's power. The royal palace squatted atop every single Phoenix god-grave in Sabor, less a haven and more a show of strength. Within its walls, any of Ambra's line could call some measure of fire, witch or not. But outside Dumosa— perhaps for the first time—Prince Jasimir was powerless.

She glanced to Pa. He was beating down a smile once more. He'd made his point loud and plain: the prince had his steel and his pet Hawk, but the Crows still had his teeth.

Fie tossed the tooth to the pyre. It would burn as long as she willed it, until its spark burned out. The flashburn caught with a crack, white flames chasing out a swarm of sparks. Fie dusted her hands off, took a few steps back, and shot a sideways look at the lordlings. Perhaps now they would bury their high-and-mighty nonsense.

But Tavin was peering into the beak of the mask. "Why is there mint in here?"

Pa just whistled the marching signal in answer.

"We're moving out," Wretch translated for the lordlings. The cart creaked an affirmation.

Fie turned back to the pyre and kept her eyes there. Soon enough, the footfalls and wooden groans faded down the road, into the night beyond the fire.

Her palm itched with the memory of tickling flame. The tooth had been so old, the spark so small—its owner had been dead for decades, maybe centuries. And yet for that brief moment, it had burned fierce enough to light Sabor ablaze from mountain to coast if she'd let it.

Part of her wanted to.

That was false. The thought rolled round her head like a tooth in her hand. It wasn't that she wanted to burn the world down, no. She just wanted the world to know that she *could*.

"It's a bad deal."

Hangdog's voice broke above the hiss of flashburn.

Fie shook her head, stuffing down thoughts of blazing tyranny. "It's always a bad deal."

"Not like this it isn't."

With neither Pa nor lordlings to puff up for, the ache of the long, long day clipped her temper even shorter. She might have softened her tongue for Hangdog long ago, when the two of them still slipped away to more private groves. They'd had an understanding of their own: Crow bands only had one chief in the end, so for their time together, they shared little more than short-lived need. But moons and moons had passed since they last reached for each other, and her patience had worn threadbare in more places than one.

"What would you have done?" Fie snapped.

Hangdog's face turned harsh as the flashburn began to fade out, yielding to the bloody orange of wood-flame. One hand grazed his jaw. "I would've cut their throats back in their ugly palace."

"And let the Oleanders run loose?"

He spat on the fire. "Does it matter? That piss-baby prince can't keep that oath." His eyes turned hollow. "If they knew a damn thing about the Oleanders, they'd know better than to try scaring us with them."

Fie bit her tongue. For all his talk of cutting throats, she saw the way Hangdog pinched his ragged sleeve between a thumb and forefinger. The question was which was stronger: his fear of the Oleander Gentry, or his hate of the actual gentry.

"They should know better," he said again, and his voice pulled distant and furious all at once.

She held out her hand. He took it, holding tight enough for his pulse to drum against her fingers where Phoenix fire had burned moments ago.

The false pyre raged and roared before them, devouring its empty shrouds. If they'd been full, Pa would have tossed salt into the fire and welcomed them to the Crow roads in the next life. The lordlings hadn't even had to die to start walking Crow ways.

Fear crept up Fie's spine, whispering that they would be caught, whispering that Pa would be bound to the oath forever, whispering the worst of all: that Hangdog was right.

She held his hand, minded the pyre, and tried not to think of Phoenix teeth.

———◆———

Morning came too soon and found Fie too quick. She hid her face from the slashes of sun through reed screens as long as she could, curling deeper into her thin blanket. In the end, it was the smell that pried her up from the sleeping mat: fresh panbread sizzling on a griddle. She sniffed again and caught fried soft cheese and honey, her favorite.

Only Pa cooked panbread that way, and when he did, it meant one of two things: either she'd earned a treat, or he needed a favor.

Curiosity and hunger rolled her to her feet, and she stretched in the empty haven shrine. It had been halfway to dawn before she and Hangdog had finally made it to the camp. The handful of hours she'd slept weren't near enough, but they'd have to do.

Fie peered about the small room, trying to remember which god had been buried here. Urns of teeth huddled about a central idol's base, but those sat in every shrine to a Crow god. Fie's bones hummed with the drone of hundreds of teeth at work: lowly Sparrow to keep the shrine unnoticed, lordly Peacock to weave an illusion of trees in its place.

No Oleanders would find them here, nor in any other haven shrine. Pa said nigh two hundred of them were stashed about Sabor; he also said the Crows would be lost without them. Only shrines gave them a safe place to raise tots until they were old enough to walk the roads, or to tend the sick and wounded, or to leave spare goods for another band short on luck.

Crude, flaking murals stained the clay walls with dead gods everywhere she looked, scrawling out the crafting of the world. In one corner, the first gods made their thousand god-children; in another, the thousand gods struck the Covenant, bringing death, judgment, and rebirth into the world. Until that moment, humans had been naught but the gods' playthings, with no will of their own.

Fie wasn't sure they'd improved much since.

A few Crow gods loomed in the murals: Loyal Star Hama guarding sleeping Crows, Crossroads-Eyes leading them away from treacherous roads, Dena Wrathful and her hundred-hundred teeth. Pa had left Fie and her ma in Dena Wrathful's own ruined temple for Fie's early moons; Ma had told her that they'd known Fie for a witch when, soon as she could crawl, they'd found her giggling among the shrine's bones night after night.

This shrine's idol splayed six worn hands, clasping a compass, hammer, staff, blanket, basket, and crow. A cart wheel made her crown.

Maykala. Patroness of weary travelers. Proper to be sure. Fie bowed to her ancestor and pushed through the doorway's faded crowsilk curtain, scooping up her sandals from the threshold.

Hangdog slept yet in a heap beneath the shrine's eaves. The other Crows shuffled about the clearing, rolling up sleeping mats and shaking out cloaks. They gave a strange wide berth to the fire, where Pa tended to a smoking griddle and a growing stack of panbread.

A *rasp-rasp-rasp* drew Fie's eye to the culprit: the lordlings sat across the fire from Pa. One of them dragged a whetstone along an unsheathed blade; the other stared, grim, into the flames. They'd changed to mismatched crowsilk shirts and trousers from the shrine's viatik stash. Both wore the castoffs like ill-fitting costumes.

Beside them sat Besom, the shrine's keeper and maybe the oldest Crow Fie had ever known, with Barf the tabby curled in her lap. Not many Crows lived long enough to feel the ache of old bones. Those who did spent their elder years keeping the teeth-spells of a haven shrine alight, passing rumors and warnings from band to band, and pointing them down different roads so no one region wound up glutted with Crows. Besom's hair had grayed long before they'd met, her brown hands stained night-purple from picking and weaving the crowsilk lichen that bearded the tree boughs. Though her fingers were gnarled as old vines, they worked a web of thread nimbly enough as she mumbled to Pa.

"Three?"

"Three, aye. We'll stretch them as long as we can."

Fie headed over as Besom fished in a bag lying in the sun-yellowed grass. No doubt the old keeper was knotting Phoenix teeth into a chief's string for Pa. Neither lordling glanced up from fire or sword-whetting. It was a blessing in disguise, for even by daylight Fie couldn't mark which of the two was the prince.

As soon as Fie sat, Pa plucked the puff of panbread from the griddle, dropped it into a clean rag, drizzled it with honey and a pinch of salt, and handed it to her. "Here."

One lordling paused the scrape of stone on steel. "Oh, are we eating now?"

That amiable act could only be the Hawk boy. Both lordlings eyed the stack of panbread like tax owed to the crown; Fie recalled them saying they hadn't much to eat for three days.

She looked the Hawk boy square in the eye and bit off a chunk of panbread.

"Aye, we can eat now." Pa twisted about to call to the rest of the Crows, and likely also to hide his grin. His voice carried across the clearing. "Breakfast time, you lot."

Tavin flicked his hand at her. "Pass a couple for me and Jas, will you?"

"Can't. Hands're full." Fie took another monstrous bite.

The Hawk muttered a curse and scrambled to reach the panbread heap before the others. Pa scarce had time to dash salt over two rounds before Tavin snatched them away. Prince Jasimir shot Fie a dirty look over the campfire, waiting while Tavin bit off a scrap of each, chewed them over, then tore off the untouched halves and handed them to the prince.

There was a moment's peace as Pa salted panbread and passed it to Crows. Then Prince Jasimir spoke up. "Your glamour's wearing off."

Tavin swallowed with a grimace. "We can leave it for a few days."

"Don't they have Peacock teeth? They can fix it." The prince jerked his head at Pa.

Pa raised his eyebrows. "You've a Peacock glamour, then?"

Tavin nodded. "For my face. I mean, I'm Jas's double for a reason, but you can still tell us apart without one."

Fie pursed her lips. So far, the only difference she'd spotted betwixt the lordlings was which one mummed at liking the Crows.

"Sorry, lads. We don't have enough spare Peacock teeth to glamour you all the way to Cheparok. And on that notion . . ." Pa dropped a wheel of dough onto the hot griddle, then pointed his tongs at the lordlings' fraying topknots. "Those? They have to go."

He was right. Both lordlings had inherited a gold cast to their brown skin from the northern Hawks, but it'd take a close study to pick them out from Crows, and their dark hair and eyes only helped. The topknots, though . . . those would mark them for royals on sight.

"Absolutely not." Prince Jasimir recoiled. "I'll just keep my hood up. I'm sure you have long-haired Crows."

"Only ones that fancy lice," Wretch chipped in as she nabbed a piece of panbread and held it out for Pa's salt.

Behind her, Swain let out an unvarnished laugh. "Madcap bet me two naka these boys would blow their own cover by the end of the day. I bet we wouldn't make it to a league marker. At this rate I'm bound for fortunes."

"Because I won't cut my hair?" the prince asked, stiff.

Fie prayed the boys wouldn't be this tedious the whole way. "Because you'd fuss the chief over it."

"I'm sure you don't follow his every little suggestion to the letter," Tavin said with the slick assurance of an unscathed blade.

Pa scratched at his gray-flecked beard, but his face stayed mild. "Aye, Swain. You're bound for fortunes."

"Be serious." Prince Jasimir's lip curled as Swain and Wretch retreated. "You can't truly expect us to obey your every command until we reach the Fan."

Pa flipped the panbread. "You're smart lads. I expect you'll do what's needed."

Tavin stood and cracked his knuckles. "How much longer until we leave?"

"The Fan's a province, not a debtor," Pa answered, watching the dough. "It won't be running out on us anytime soon."

"If Rhusana takes the throne, she'll want to do it on the solstice, two moons from now." The prince's face had frosted over. "My father could be dead before the end of Peacock Moon."

"Chief swore to find people who like you," Hangdog sneered over Fie's shoulder. He'd risen at last. "No surprise that'll take a while."

Tavin's expression stayed sharp but polite. "How much longer?" he asked again.

"An hour, if that, 'til we're on the road." Pa scratched a rough map in the dirt with one finger, tracing the route to come. "The walk from here to Cheparok . . . I say it'll take a week, if we're lucky."

"'Lucky'?" Tavin picked up his sword. "A crone could walk there in four days."

Besom swatted him on the shin.

Fie froze. Tavin had been beastly clear about not being touched by Crows.

But he just laughed and sheathed his blade. By Fie's eye, it hadn't needed sharpening in the slightest. "Apologies."

Pa flipped more dough as Barf the cat stretched and climbed from Besom's lap. "Lucky means we only have to answer one plague beacon, and it's close to the road. *Unlucky* means that beacon's a day's walk out, and there's a day's work there and a day's walk back."

"That's unacceptable." Tavin was more sharp than polite now.

Fie had had enough of the Hawk's paper threats. She got to her feet. "Take it up with the Covenant."

"Don't speak to him like that," Prince Jasimir snapped.

"Don't speak to Pa like that," she spat back.

Tavin turned his glass-hard stare on her, and a warning glinted in his tone. "You're addressing the crown prince of Sabor."

"Funny," Fie hissed, "could've sworn that prince is dead."

The Hawk opened his mouth—then looked down. Barf had rolled onto his sandals, purring.

"Fie." The tongs scraped on iron as Pa flipped the panbread. Like it or not, she knew her chief's signal when she heard it. She sat.

"Crows go where we're called," Pa said. "A beacon's a beacon. Hawks run those stations, and they don't take kind to Crows ignoring their calls."

"I'll deal with the Hawks," Tavin said.

Pa didn't look at him. "That's only the half of it. We answer every beacon we see, or we answer to the Covenant later with scores of dead on our account. If we don't take a sinner in time, plague takes the whole town—every animal, every seed, every babe. Can't do aught but burn it all to the ground before it spreads. You ever listen to a child die by fire?"

Prince Jasimir swallowed and shook his head.

"Then let's keep it that way, aye?" Pa drew wavering branches on the dirt map. "Direct, it's two days southeast to reach the Fan region, and another two days to Cheparok. Count on at least one detour. But we'll have His Highness to safety by week's end, well before Peacock Moon is up."

Prince Jasimir shifted, uneasy. "For all we know, Rhusana's already set Vultures on our trail."

Fie flinched, one palm sliding over the black curves of her own witch-sign. A Vulture-caste skinwitch had put it there years ago, when Fie had registered as a witch as required by Sabor law. The woman had been a northerner like most Vultures, sour and pale as bad milk, and her clammy fingers had glued so tight to Fie's wrist that it stung when she let go.

The best skinwitches could track flesh like a hound. Fie had felt the tracking magic when she'd practiced at Vulture teeth: the long-dead skinwitch saw every footstep, every thumbprint, everything her prey had touched, all spinning a trail plain as thread. If skinwitches like that came looking . . .

Pa patted the nubby string of teeth around his neck. "I'll know when they come, lads. You're with three Crow witches now. We'll keep the Vultures busy."

Fie slipped her hand from her witch-sign and tried not to think on how Pa had said *when*, not *if*.

"Hm." Tavin pried his foot from under the tabby and scuffed Pa's map out of the dirt.

"Wee over-fearful, boy?" Besom asked.

"No." Tavin didn't elaborate, just held his hand out to the prince. "Jas, give me your knife."

Prince Jasimir passed his dagger over, jeweled hilt twinkling in the sunlight. Tavin stuck it through his sash, then started to undo his topknot.

"You can't." The prince straightened. "How are you supposed to pass for me?"

"I already won't pass for you once the glamour wears off. If Rhusana is looking for us, two needlessly hooded Crows is a little conspicuous. Besides, if there's an emergency, they can spare a tooth to fix it."

Fie tilted her head and donned her most cloying smile. "Who's 'they' now, Hawk boy?"

Tavin rolled his eyes, twisted his dark hair about his knuckles, and began to saw. "You know what I mean."

A tense quiet fell over the clearing as he hacked through all but a few wayward strands. Whether he kenned it or not, the Hawk boy had just chopped off his rank. And he'd done it because a Crow chief had asked him to.

Tavin caught the stares and gave a sheepish grin, hair falling in an uneven black curtain. "That bad?"

"I'll tidy it for you," Wretch offered, and that was when Fie knew Tavin had won the old Crow over. Her belly sank. Was it naught but one more ploy to charm the Crows?

"Thank you." Tavin started to toss the hair in the fire, then thought better of it, wrinkling his nose. "Is there a place to wash up?"

"Hangdog." To Fie's shock, Pa lifted a string of teeth from the grass and handed it to him. "Anyone who wants to wash, follow Hangdog to the creek."

Strings were for proper chiefs. Fie hoped Hangdog was closer to a chief than she wagered.

Tavin stuck the dagger back in his sash. "Creek it is. Jas? Coming with?"

"Once I'm done eating." Prince Jasimir picked at his remaining pan-bread and didn't look up until Tavin was out of earshot. Then he mumbled to Fie, "Was my father upset?"

"What?"

Jasimir ducked his head. "When you took us through the Hall of the Dawn. Could you see if my father was all right?" Fie shook her head. "He wasn't all right?"

"He . . ." She didn't know why it felt so sour to say. "King Surimir wasn't there."

Jasimir stopped tearing at his panbread.

"The thrones were empty," Fie said. "Rhusana paid us at the gate."

Jasimir went still. Then he stood, dropped his panbread in the fire, and stalked off after Tavin without another word.

"Hmph." Besom raised her eyebrows. "Waste of good bread."

Fie supposed she ought to feel sorry for the prince. She might have if the king's throne hadn't been good as empty for every Crow, long as she could remember.

And she had other matters on her head. Apart from her, Pa, and Besom, only Swain lingered, tallying inventory by the cart.

She could talk plain. "*Hangdog* gets a string?"

"So do you." Besom wiggled her string-netted fingers.

"I'm no chief." For that matter, neither was Hangdog, but Fie kept that to herself.

"It's time you carry your own. Things are a-shift." Pa prodded another wheel of panbread with a pair of tongs, testing whether the puff of dough was ready to flip. "We're rolling fortune-bones, Fie. They land right? We're rid of the Oleanders, and by my ken, that more than earns you a chief's string. But if the bones land wrong . . ." He paused to pry the panbread off the hot iron. It was still too raw in the middle, splitting in twain. One half landed in the coals as Pa cursed.

"That'll be us," he grumbled, turning the remaining half. "Either way, I want you wearing a string."

Fie watched the burnt half shrivel, thinking. Most chiefs-in-training had to wait until the ceremonies in Crow Moon to take up a chief's string. Carrying one was an honor, naught she needed a bribe for.

Unless—

She stared at Pa, aghast. "I'm to inherit the oath."

Besom cackled as her fingers danced around thread and tooth. "Clever, clever. Told you she'd sniff it out."

"No call for a fuss," Pa said, firm, but his eyes were fixed on the fire, not her. "It's only if the deal goes bad. You've got the steadiest head of any of us. If something happens and I can't keep the oath . . . well, I won't be looking to Hangdog to finish it for me."

Fie's pulse rattled in her ears. It shouldn't have shaken her so; she trusted Pa. And though they'd never spoken of it, she and Pa both knew who would lead their band when his time came. But if aught happened to him now . . . the prince, the oath, the weight of every Crow alive— they'd fall to her alone.

Fie checked over her shoulder, then asked, "Did Hangdog get Phoenix teeth?"

Besom shook her head. "Sparrow, Owl, Pigeon, a few Crane."

Refuge, memory, fortune, and honesty. Birthrights that couldn't hurt anyone. That wasn't happenstance. "You think he'd try to jump the lordlings?"

"I think he'd jump the king himself if he had a chance," Pa said, grim. "We need this deal." He plucked the puff of panbread from the griddle. "That's why I'm trusting you to see it through if need be."

Fie's belly knotted up like the string in Besom's hands. Pa was right. No matter how the prince called her a bone thief, no matter how his pet Hawk rattled his steel, they needed the oath. They'd needed the oath for generations.

Fie's ma had needed the oath.

Fie'd just never thought she'd be the chief to barter it. And there was no running from the chief's bloody road for her now. Not anymore.

"Done." Besom passed the string to Fie. It was heavier than she expected. Teeth of all twelve castes dangled in dull clusters, more than Fie could count. Familiar sparks flickered in each one, a promise and a burden.

Once she tied it on, she'd be duty-bound to bear a chief's string until the day her road ended.

She'd asked for this, back at the palace. Demanded it. And she had danced Pa into this mess. By every measure, by every dead god, she was bound to help him make it out.

———— ◆ ————

True to Pa's word, he whistled the marching order to send them to the roads before the hour was up. Madcap launched into a loud and lewd walking song once they reached the flatway, a wider, busier road that the kingdom's Pigeon and Sparrow laborers kept smooth and even. Barf resumed her post inside the cart, though Fie reckoned that would last only as long as they stayed to the flatway. Besom had claimed she'd miss the cat more than the lot of them combined.

Then, halfway to the next league marker, the demands of the Covenant called.

Madcap's song dried up. The cart drew to a halt.

"Why are we stopped?" Prince Jasimir demanded, sweating beneath his hood.

Wretch spat in the road and pointed to a string of deep-blue smoke rising over the treetops.

"I say let 'em rot," Hangdog grumbled.

"Aye, and then the farmers rot, and their fields rot, and our *pay* rots, lackwit," Fie shot back. She'd watched Swain tally up their supplies. Duty to the Covenant was the pretty side of it. The hard truth was that they also had two more mouths to feed.

"But what *is* that?" the prince asked.

"*Really?*" Hangdog gave him a look of disgust. "When was the last time your powdered ass set foot off palace grounds?"

"Enough." Pa cleared his throat, scowling at the sky. "It's a plague beacon."

CHAPTER FIVE

—— FEED THE CROWS ——

T HE SUN HUNG AT AN HOUR PAST THE NOON MARK WHEN THEY
reached the village. They had followed the beacons down a twisting eastbound roughway, passing first the blue smoke beacon, then the
violet. Both beacons snuffed out in their wake. Pa, Hangdog, and Fie all
used the walk to wrap their hands and forearms in clean rags, the better to keep blood off their sleeves.

Now Pa rang the bell at the base of the village's signal post, where
black smoke smeared a charcoaled thumb into the clear sky. A Hawk
guard peered over the edge of the platform, found fifteen Crows in fifteen masks and cloaks (and one grumpy gray tabby), and nodded before
vanishing again. The smoke began to choke out.

Barf had fled the wagon once they'd turned down the narrower,
bumpier roughway, but Fie stowed her back inside the hold now. "You'll

thank me later," she muttered over outraged mewls. There was no telling how the village would receive them, but Fie had an educated notion. She couldn't chance they'd take their spite out on the Crows' pet, too.

Pa looked over Fie's head and picked out the prince and his Hawk. "We'll handle the heavy lifting, lads," he muttered. "You keep clear of the body."

Behind Fie, Tavin grumbled into his mask, "How do you people even tell one another apart like this?"

The answer was the way Swain rolled up his sleeves so neat in the damp warmth. Or Wretch's habit of swaying in place, never wholly still. Or how Hangdog's fingers dug into his palms every time the lordlings spoke.

But all Fie said was "You two are the only ones who walk like we should get out of your way."

And then she followed Pa into the village common.

The locals clustered near the communal oven, huddled like their round-shouldered thatch houses. Most doors bore the mark of Common Castes; the one beside the town's god-grave brandished a Hunting Caste crest and the painted border of a Crane arbiter.

The silver-haired Crane stepped forward as Pa approached. Her eyes were red-rimmed, her faded orange smock marbled with faint blood-stains that soap-shells couldn't break. As the village arbiter, she served as their judge, doctor, and teacher. Likely she'd known the sinners since birth.

She pointed a shaking oak-brown finger to a nearby thatch house. "They're in there."

"More than one?" Pa asked.

The woman's lined face crumpled a moment before steadying. "Two—two adults. A husband and wife."

"Naden and Mesli," a man spat. "They have names."

Had, Fie thought, grim, studying the onlookers. No crying mop-pets, no wailing family. Anger still simmered below the surface. They hated the Crows for being here. And they hated themselves for calling them.

But if the corpses didn't burn by their second sunset, plague would spread faster than rumors through a Swan pavilion. Fie knew too well what happened after that: By week's end, no one in the village would be left untouched. Two weeks in, the dead would be piled up, the crops blackening in the fields. By moon's end, only rotten timber, ruined earth, and bitter ghosts would remain.

Pa led the cart as far down the path to the thatch house as it could go, stopping before mud could glut the wheels. The nearby field stretched half-tilled, its mossy sod a green island in the sea of dark earth. Pigeon Moon was for sowing; Peacock Moon would be for waiting.

That field wouldn't be touched again until the thatch house had been burned down and built anew. This time, as they walked up to the door, Fie caught the true, familiar stench of plague and death.

"Hangdog. Watch the cart." Pa crooked a finger at Fie. "You come with me, girl."

Fie swallowed. Pa had cut throats in front of her before, but only when he couldn't shield her from the sight. It felt like one more final handoff, another chief's string, another oath to carry; the teeth hung heavy round her neck.

When, not if.

The door swung open into stinking dim, and she followed Pa inside.

Two bodies coiled together on a pallet at the far end of the single room. One rash-mottled hand sagged atop the wooden water pail. A blanket had been tossed aside in the throes of fever still lingering in the room's clingy warmth.

To Fie's surprise, Pa unstrapped his mask and set it on the low table beside a clay plate of molding panbread. "Gets in the way," he explained, rubbing his nose.

The whispered question bubbled up before she could gulp it back: "Why didn't you bring Hangdog?"

Pa glanced over his shoulder as Fie shed her own mask. His voice lowered. "That boy doesn't need practice cutting throats."

A whimper pierced the small quiet before Fie could scrub at that answer.

Pa strode over to the pallet, Fie in his shadow. He knelt in the dirt and hooked a careful hand round the nape of the woman's neck. Sweat plastered her dark hair to her skull, her face and arms purpled with the unmistakable Sinner's Brand. A yellow rind around her eyes crumbled as they cracked open.

"*Hurts*" rattled out from dry, bloody lips.

Pa had fair many voices. He had a Chief voice for steering their family of Crows as best he could. He had his Cur voice for needling Wretch or playing a jest on Swain. He had a Pa voice for teaching Fie how to use teeth, how to deal fair in a dispute, how to treat with Peacock gentry and gutter-born Pigeons alike.

But he had another voice, the one he'd used when he'd first adopted Fie as his own. When nightmares of her mother still made her cry herself sick. When she cowered at every flicker of white fabric in the markets. When hoofbeats sent her scuttling into the roadside hedges for fear of Oleanders.

He'd used the Safe voice to quiet her sobs, steady her nerve, coax her from the thorns before she scratched herself worse.

And at that moment, Fie learned that he used it to cut throats.

"Shhh," Pa said, gentle, reaching for the half blade at his side. "We're here."

A drop of blood welled and trembled on the woman's mouth. "Please," she gasped, ". . . burns . . ."

"Fie." That was his Pa voice. It was time to study.

"Aye." She knelt beside him.

"Hold her head."

Sticky hair crackled under Fie's palms. Her eyes squeezed shut at the glint of Pa's sword.

"You have to keep your eyes open." Pa's voice landed somewhere between reprimand and apology. Fie ground her teeth together and obeyed.

"Crows," the sinner mumbled. The red bead spilled as her lips waxed to a shallow smile of relief. "Mercy. No more . . ."

"No more." Pa leveled the blade across her throat. "Sleep, cousin."

There was a savage jerk. The sinner died smiling.

When the body had stilled, Pa handed Fie the broken sword, hilt-first. "For the husband."

She tried not to stare. The blade slipped a little in her hands. Watching had been hard enough, but this—

When, not if.

Mercy was a chief's gift. Inflicting it was their duty.

She reached for the other body—then pressed two fingers to where neck met shoulder. The flesh was cooler, salt flaking from a long-dry sweat trail.

No pulse.

She pried his mouth open and touched a tooth. If he yet lived, the bone-spark would've sung for her, double as loud as any on her string. Instead, it sighed and hummed.

"He's dead." A reprieve. The knot in her gut loosened.

Pa reached for her shoulder, then caught himself. His hands were yet a gory mess. He plunged them into the water pail, then dried them on the cast-off blanket and stood.

Whatever he'd wanted to say had gone stale. Instead, he donned his mask and said, "Pack 'em up."

With Hangdog's help, the bodies were bundled and loaded on the cart within a quarter hour. The rest of the village waited for them in the commons, shifting with unease and muttering among themselves.

No viatik in sight. Fie bristled.

The Crane arbiter stepped forward once they were in earshot. "Thank you for your . . . services," she said, brittle. "We've left two pyres' worth of firewood at the gate in payment."

"And?" Pa turned his head toward a fenced pasture crowded with goats and cattle.

"That's all we can spare."

Cranes commanded the Birthright of honesty, but just because they could catch lies didn't mean they never told them. Fie counted at least three iron bells collaring livestock in the pasture—three beasts marked for slaughter. For Common Castes, the villagers looked well enough, no one skimping on meals or garments. They could spare a bolt of cloth or the smallest cow for proper viatik, or even just a bag of salt, easy.

Fie caught a mumble of "*feed the Crows*" from the cluster of towns-folk. The Crane's jaw stiffened.

"That's all," she repeated.

The full proverb was less charitable: *One way or another, we feed the Crows.* The Covenant did not look kind on skinflints. Shorting the Crows now only made it likelier they'd have sinners to collect later.

Pa waited, giving the Crane one final chance to put it to rights. No one stirred. Only the clank of an iron slaughter bell punctuated a long silence.

Pa went to a compartment in the wagon's sideboard and removed a pair of pincers as the lordlings fidgeted. He passed them to Hangdog. "Take the teeth."

Tavin's hands curled to fists.

"Aye, chief." Hangdog reached for the first shrouded corpse. Fie hoped it wasn't the woman whose throat they'd just cut.

She turned her mask back to the villagers before she could find out. Most of them had gone gray. Families like theirs stashed milk teeth for viatik, having neither the desperation nor the belly to pull teeth from their dead. Their buzz of anger wound even tighter with every rustle of the shroud.

"Here?"

Of course the prince would get squeamish.

The villagers glanced his way. Prince Jasimir coughed and lowered his voice. "Do we have to do this here . . . *chief*?" He dropped the title like a redjay rolling its rival's eggs out of the nest.

"Aye." That was Pa's Chief voice.

Behind her, metal scraped on bone as Hangdog went to work.

The Crane arbiter flinched with the steady *click, click, click* of every tooth hitting the wagon boards. Behind her, villagers traded darkening looks that boded ill to Fie. The sooner they got out and on the road, the better.

At last the clicking stopped. A moment later, Hangdog handed a knotted rag to Pa, little red sunbursts blooming in the cotton.

"Are you done?" the arbiter demanded.

Pa weighed the rag in his hand. "Aye, cousin, this'll do." He whistled the marching order. "We'll be back when you call."

When, not if.

The wagon creaked into motion. They rolled to the gate, only to find the signal post's Hawks had descended to hurry them along, waving at stacks of firewood beside the trough for their mammoth mounts.

To Fie's surprise, Tavin followed Swain to the wood. Maybe he was ready to be back on the flatway as swift as possible. For once, they were of the same mind.

Tavin loaded up an armful of firewood, but as he straightened, one of the Hawks let his bronze-tipped spear slip, just enough of a twitch to make Tavin jolt back. A log fell from his arms and landed on the guard's foot. The guard swore.

"I think you owe my friend an apology." The other Hawk guard laughed.

Tavin stiffened with indignation, an indulgence no Crow could afford. The only thing saving them all was his mask.

Swain looped his arm through Tavin's and bobbed a hasty bow. "No disrespect, guards, none. The boy doesn't speak. Nasty accident. Terrible sorry about that." He steered Tavin back to the cart as Pa signaled for the others to collect the firewood. Soon enough, the Crows rolled on their way.

For a while, only their footfalls and rattling wheels broke the forest's birdsong-speckled hush; not even Madcap dared a walking song this far off the flatway. Then Pa stripped off his mask and tossed it into the cart. Fie followed suit, dragging fresh air through her teeth. Soon a pile of masks rested atop the shrouds and firewood.

The Hawk kept both his mask and his prince's, one slung over each shoulder, as over-fearful as he'd been with Pa's dirt map.

"Was that really necessary?" The prince's chin was set proper mulish beneath his hood.

"How do you mean, Highness?" Pa asked, not looking back.

"They left you payment. And you ripped their friends' teeth out in front of them."

"Firewood isn't a real payment." If Tavin noticed heads turning his way, it didn't show. "You can't hire a smith to make a sword, then pay her only enough steel to forge it. There's no compensation for the labor, let alone walking three leagues for the job."

Jasimir's cheeks darkened. "That's no excuse for mutilating bodies. The dead should be treated with honor."

"*Honor?*" Fie asked, heat creeping up her own neck. "That village wanted to spit in our faces. And they wanted that more than they wanted their dead friends to leave with dignity. They got what they wanted. Why shouldn't we?"

"And who decides if you want too much?" Clearly Prince Jasimir was still sore from cutting the oath. "What if you demanded half their cattle? Or a year's wages? Or the rest of the bones, while they're still warm?"

Fie glared. "The Oleanders would gut us all before sundown—"

"Perhaps if you didn't give them a reason—"

"Jas." Tavin cut him off. "Taking the teeth was a message. A harsh message, yes, but that village will think twice before trying to cheat Crows again. It's no different from our court games."

Either the Hawk was starting to ken their trade, or now that half the Crows liked him well enough, he was working double-time to woo the other half. Fie snuck a look out of the corner of her eye, wondering if a Crane would smell a falsehood from him. All Fie saw was a lordling with a haircut and a new scar—

She blinked. It was a tiny thing, a thin line through the Hawk's right brow, but it was a mark the prince didn't carry.

The Peacock glamour would keep breaking with her every blink. With his hair shorn to his ears and a face almost his own, soon no one would mistake him for the prince.

The Hawk boy had cut his hair for Pa, he'd had the sense to not push the guards, and he'd reined in the prince. Fie didn't trust him as far as she could shove him, but perhaps he'd earned the benefit of the doubt.

Tavin flashed a broad, too-pretty grin at her. "Besides, taking whole bones, *that's* just impractical. Or do I have it wrong? You strike me as someone who would tear a man's spine out if she fancied it for a new necklace."

Fie's newfound goodwill withered.

She narrowed her eyes at the road ahead. "You got one part awry," she said. "I don't truck with jewelry."

"What *do* you truck with, then?" Tavin's grin hadn't faded one bit; if anything, it curled wider. "Flowers? Poetry? I know I can rule out patchouli."

The prince pulled a face like he'd found a hair ball in his sandals. It was plain he'd seen this dance before, and that told Fie all she needed to know.

"Silence," Fie answered. "I truck with silence."

"And punching corpses," Tavin added. "I'll concede I have that effect on people. So you've a shine for silence and violence. What else?"

"People who can take a hint," Hangdog gritted.

Tavin remained undaunted. "And?"

"And I think I'm starting to fancy a new necklace," Fie said, cold.

"So you *do* truck with jewelry."

Behind him, Madcap made a crude gesture that suggested exactly what they thought Fie trucked with. Swain snorted and waggled his eyebrows at her.

Fie's temper ran thin. His charm was a ruse; the Hawk had no intent of courting her. He just aimed to see what could knock her off-balance. Two could play that game.

"I truck with people I can trust," she returned, direct as a warning shot.

It did the trick. Wretch and Swain traded looks, and Tavin straightened, donning mock-innocence.

"Now that's hardly reasonable," he jested, "when all *we* did was use you to help fake our deaths and commit blasphemous fraud on the entire nation of Sabor for personal gain."

That got a round of chuckles. He'd wanted them to laugh it down. Fie mummed along, cracked a humorless grin herself, but her voice stayed sharp. "Aye, but that's not why I don't trust you."

The laughter dried up.

Tavin gave her the same look as when she'd kindled Phoenix fire last night—measuring.

Now who's off-balance?

"Is there just the one reason, or did you draw up a list?" A good parry. He meant to paint her as shrewish, petty.

And Fie meant to remind her Crows who he really was. "We don't even know who you are. Or who might be looking for you. You never told us your whole name."

He shrugged. "Is that all?"

The look the prince gave her could have kindled her own funeral pyre. "Tav, you don't have to—"

"It's fine," Tavin said, but that warning line in his brow was back. Fie had hit the nerve she'd dug for. "My full name is Taverin sza Markahn. Does that answer your question?"

It did. *Sza* meant "son of." A clan like the Markahns, high enough to whelp the crown prince, should have flaunted Tavin's own parental pedigree in the name that followed. Instead, he only had the broad clan name.

Or, as Hangdog summed up: "So your pappy was good enough to rut a Markahn, but not good enough to give his name?"

"That's no business of yours," Jasimir snapped.

Tavin shrugged again. "No, that's about right, and I'll give my father your opinion if I find out who he is. But all things considered,

MARGARET OWEN

my bastardry is probably the least of our problems." He tried another patronizing smile on Fie. "Got anything else?"

Fie wondered how many times the lordlings would just wander direct into her traps. At this rate she could dance her way onto the throne herself.

"Oh, I was just curious about your name, Hawk boy." Fie mimicked his shrug, then went for the throat. "I mainly don't trust you because you like flashing your steel."

"*What?*"

"You saw the only blade we have is broken. You didn't need to pull your sword on Hangdog last night and you knew it. You just did it because you could."

That rustled up hums of assent. He could cut his hair and mum at diplomacy, but when it mattered, he still acted the Hawk.

"So I'm not allowed to defend myself."

"Pray, cousin," Fie crooned, "when was the last time you pulled steel on the Splendid Castes?"

"You don't know what you're talking about," the prince broke in. "Drawing a blade on the wrong noble could start a civil war."

"Right. Best stick to Crows, then."

Prince Jasimir scowled. "When they attack us—"

"She has a point."

The prince's head snapped around to stare at his guard.

Tavin's mouth opened, then closed. He sighed. "So do you, Jas. Everyone's right. Gods, I'm tired of talking about this."

"Oh aye, *you're* tired," Fie scoffed.

Tavin tipped his head back. "Yes. I'd much rather address the fact that we've been followed for the last quarter league."

"Aye." Pa didn't turn about, but one hand rested on his string of teeth.

72

Fie swore a silent oath. She ought to have been minding her roads, not dancing about with the Hawk. She snuck a glance down the trail. Sure enough, three distant figures hovered at the road's bend, just far back enough to haunt them unheard. Weak sunlight glinted off their hand-scythes.

"They won't trouble us long as we still have the bodies," Pa said. "And they'll leave off once we hit the flatway, it's too open."

That was half the truth. Fie swallowed a sigh. Followers could be an omen of Oleanders. That meant the Crows had to drag the bodies double as far before making camp tonight, and hope the distance put off any Gentry.

"So you'll allow them to trail us as long as they please?" Prince Jasimir asked.

"What'd you have us do, Highness?" Wretch scowled. "This is squarely why scummers like them don't let Crows carry whole blades. They don't chase fights they won't win."

Jasimir only rolled his eyes.

In that moment, Fie knew that for all his talk of murderous plots and ruthless assassins, the prince had never once known the true fear of a stranger in the dark.

You need this deal, part of her whispered.

But another ugly voice hissed back: *Only if the prince is good to keep it.*

Barf posted herself atop the pile of masks, but leapt off to catch her dinner once they pulled over for the night a couple leagues down the road. Fie let her go. The lurkers had vanished after they'd reached the wide-open flatway road an hour ago, and the cat seemed able to look after herself.

Unlike the eve before, the Crows had true sinners to burn. Pa, Hangdog, and Fie left their arm-rags in the budding pyre, then took turns washing up in a nearby stream, first with soap-shells for any lingering blood, then with salt for any lingering sin. Fie returned to the pyre in time to hear Pa send the sinners on with a fistful of salt in the fire and a rumbled, "Welcome to our roads, cousins."

The Hawk kept one eye on the proceedings as he aided Swain with the cooking fire, staying out of the Crows' way for once. The prince exiled himself to the far side of the clearing, sneaking looks Fie couldn't trace until they landed on Hangdog changing his shirt. She couldn't begrudge Jasimir that, at least: Hangdog had problems aplenty, but looks weren't one.

When Swain set out a pot of boiled soap-shells, both lordlings all but lunged for it, anxious to wash up before the Crows soiled the water. That Fie *could* begrudge. And if the lordlings caught stares when they ate before Pa salted the food, they still didn't so much as slow a single bite.

Barf returned after dinner, smugly sauntering into their roadside camp with tail aloft as Fie unrolled her woven-grass sleeping mat a safe distance from the fire. It was early yet, but Fie'd needed the rest ever since waking up in Maykala's shrine. The others rolled gambling shells, mended masks, pounded fresh nails through their sandals' soles; all of them kept one eye on the flatway as dark fell. Barf herself just jumped back into the wagon hold and curled up among their sacks of millet and rice.

The prince hunched by the campfire, curling flame round his fingers, until Swain sat to his side. "Would His Highness like to see the rarest scroll in the kingdom? You'll not find its like anywhere, not even in His Majesty's own library."

Jasimir's brows rose.

Fie settled down on her mat. Swain had worked at his scroll long as she could remember, setting down all the songs and tales Crows carried in their heads. She'd never been able to read a single letter, but she supposed it mattered to him.

When Fie's eyes at last drifted shut, Swain's and Jasimir's heads still bowed over the scroll, intently conversing by the fire.

Then Fie's dreams dragged her from the dark of empty sleep, fast and vicious and red.

She held Hangdog's hand in front of a pyre in broad day.

It was no pyre; it was the village they'd left behind, and it burned with phoenix-gold fire.

She'd wanted to burn it to the ground. No, she'd wanted them to know that she could.

Teeth spilled from her open palm, bloody and new, bursting into flame as they fell.

We need this deal, Pa said, nowhere to be seen.

The village changed: Now she saw a vale far to the north, burning end-to-end, all a massive black plague beacon. Screams for mercy filled the air.

No one answered, Pa said, shaking his head, much too close to the fire. *And now we all will.*

It was not Hangdog at her side; it was Tavin's hand in hers, and he took her measure once again.

She yanked free—

"Fie."

She woke to a sea of flames.

The campfire. It was naught but the campfire. Fie tried to catch her breath.

"Fie, get up."

That was the Chief voice.

"Pa?" She sat up, rubbing her eyes. It was too dark yet to pack out.

The prince rolled to his knees, drowsy and scowling. Hangdog stood frozen nearby.

Then the answer came with the faint rumble in the earth beneath her thin pallet. Her own gut frosted over.

They never should have taken the sinners' teeth.

"Get the prince and grab what you can." Pa was a blur in the night, rushing from one Crow to the next, then dragging the prince to his feet. The rumble only grew. "*Up*, Highness. The Oleander Gentry are coming."

CHAPTER SIX

THE CAT AND THE KING

T HE PRINCE WAS BAREFOOT.

In her sixteen years, Fie had learned many a hard lesson when it hit her right in the teeth: Always watch the crowd. Always know your way out. Never go into town alone.

And on the nights you burn sinners, sleep with your sandals on.

Jasimir's toes slipped on a mossy tree trunk as Fie struggled to hoist him to the nearest branch, choking down a frustrated scream. Thunderous hoofbeats welled in the ground beneath them; Crows darted about camp, scrambling to cover their tracks. Though the prince's heel was braced on Fie's shoulder, his hands shook too bad to find purchase on vine or bark. But Pa had said to get the prince out of sight—she had to get them clear—

Tavin pulled the prince from the trunk. "Fie, you go first—pull him up—"

Up. The word was a shackle breaking.

Nails in her sandal soles chewed through bark and moss as up she went, easy as walking a stair. The strap of her loose mask cut into the flesh at her throat, the heavy beak banging against her spine. From the corner of her eye she saw other Crows scaling the trees as well. Wretch had strapped the rolled-up pallets to her back. Swain bore their meager stash of maps and scrolls, the cooking pot bouncing at his side.

She didn't see Hangdog at all.

Up. If she lost the prince, she lost the oath.

Fie crawled onto the first branch. She whipped her robe over her head, twisted it into a rope, then looped it where branch married trunk. The prince seized a handful of crowsilk and began to climb.

"Fie!" Pa stood below. He threw a tooth up to her, then dashed away once she'd caught it.

The tooth sang in her fist, so loud and clear that she near dropped it when she kenned what she held.

Orange torchlight pinpoints glittered far, far down the road.

Up. Fie knotted the priceless tooth into her waist-sash, then yanked the cloak to hurry the prince.

But this bough wouldn't hold her, Prince Jasimir, and Tavin as well. Once the prince sat steady, she scuttled up to a sturdier branch.

"You can't leave me!" Jasimir hissed, wide-eyed.

He was panicky, he was learning a new kin of fear. She had to remember that. But some Crows were more merciful than others.

"Bring up your Hawk boy, lackwit," she shot back, "*then* you pass me the cloak—"

Tavin's forearm curled into view. He'd climbed up on his own. A moment later he straddled the same branch as the prince. It shook and creaked under his weight, as she'd feared.

Up.

Hoofbeats whispered through the leaves.

Below, she spied Pa handing Hangdog a fistful of hemp ropes, each leashed to a spiky, weighted block of wood carved like a crude foot. Hangdog took the ropes in both hands and ran into the dark, away from the Oleanders, blocks tumbling behind him to cut up the road with Crow tracks.

Pa didn't send out a runner unless things were dire. They'd near lost Madcap to a run last year, and Swain's wife had vanished into the night two years before, no trace of her or the wooden feet ever found. But if anyone was guaranteed to run far and hard from the Oleander Gentry, it would be Hangdog.

Fie's robe-rope slapped up to her. She winched it about the bough as first the prince, then his Hawk, climbed to either side of her. Tavin stayed on his feet, toes curling around the thick branch, one hand catching another bough for balance. Jasimir pulled the robe up behind him.

Individual hoofbeats rattled the air now. She knew what came next.

But this time, Pa had given her a witch's tooth.

Like all the Common Castes, Sparrows birthed scant few witches. Their teeth were good as gold but sore harder to come by. The refuge Birthright let any Sparrow turn unwanted gazes away as they pleased, softened their footfalls, let them slip away from a threat unnoticed. For Oleander raids, Pa burned two teeth at a time, sometimes three, a trick Fie had yet to learn.

But the sole Sparrow witch-tooth he'd handed her—that would wipe her and the lordlings clear out of sight.

"Get steady and keep your mouths shut, cousins," she warned under her breath, working the tooth free from her sash. "I'm hiding us."

It warmed against her fingers as she called its spark, eyes closed, searching for a song. Instead, the world went silent. Flickers of the

Sparrow witch's life slipped through her: The Hawk who'd found the witchery in his blood as a boy, years bound to serve the Splendid Castes, solace in a loving husband. A thousand-thousand times he faded from the notice of a Peacock lord, a Dove craft-master, or a Swan courtesan, occasionally to gather secrets, but more often so they didn't have to think on who served their tea. The thousand-thousand times they forgot he was there. The thousand-thousand times he couldn't forget.

And at last: the noblewoman who paid the Sparrow witch for his secrets and service, and then one year, paid Fie's pa with his teeth.

The Sparrow witch's life passed in the beat of Fie's heart. Then his Birthright woke in the hum of her bones.

When she opened her eyes again, the boys' weight still pressed the branch, but they were nowhere to be seen. Her own hands looked solid enough, but she'd be as good as a ghost to the others.

Across the clearing, two more Sparrow sparks kindled in her senses. Pa had gone to work. Fie blinked, and her gaze skidded off the other Crow-laden trees. It'd take a fight to look at them head-on while those Sparrow teeth burned.

"Put out the fire," Tavin said under his breath.

"And how do I do that from a *tree*, pray?" she demanded.

"Use a Phoenix tooth."

Her grip tightened on the branch. So far she'd only called a fire, not banished one. But it was worth the risk. Maybe if the Oleanders thought the camp was abandoned, they'd pass by.

The boys reappeared as Fie let the Sparrow witch-tooth stagnate. One of her three Phoenix teeth lit up, searing against the hollow of her throat. She found the spark of the owner—an old princess from centuries past—and tried to bend it to her will.

The bark under her fingers began to smoke.

No. Fie bit her lip. *Take the fire. Take it away.*

She tried to sense the campfire. It was wild and wicked, dancing from her mind's grasp. *Go*, she willed. *Go away.*

The fire leaned and cowered—

"It's not working," said the prince. Her focus splintered.

The campfire spat a fountain of sparks, crackling higher than before, calling to the torches now strung along the road like a garland.

The bough trembled as Tavin shifted, uneasy.

Fie sucked in a breath and pushed at the campfire with every ounce of command the dead Phoenix princess had in her. For a moment it held, relentless, roaring its fury—and then collapsed. The flames huffed out, the logs cooling to black. Even the coals darkened to a sullen gray.

She let the breath go. The Phoenix tooth simmered yet, its spark far from expired. *Be quiet*, Fie ordered, smoke still threading her fingers as she returned to the Sparrow witch-tooth.

The boys began to vanish again. There was a scrape to her left as Jasimir adjusted his perch. Then a startled curse—a flash of steel—

The prince's dagger slid free from its scabbard and landed on the branch below them, a swaying silhouette, ready to drop and betray them at the slightest breeze.

And as the camp flooded with mottled torchlight, Fie saw Jasimir hadn't wrapped the gilded, jewel-scabbed, gods-damned hilt in rag after all.

"Can you make it disappear?" Tavin whispered.

Fie pushed the Sparrow tooth's range beyond their branch, but near the dagger, her bones buzzed a warning. She wasn't about to foul their cover by straining too far.

"No," she wheezed. The dagger would have to stay as it was. And they'd have to pray the thousand dead gods would, for once, be kind.

The Oleander Gentry circled below, sending tremors up through the branches as they mangled the turf where she'd lain just moments earlier. They were as the coils of an enormous, pale serpent, white sweat frothing from their horses' flanks, white chalk dusting hands and manes and bridles, undyed veils and cloaks hiding their faces. Only the torch-flame burned hues into their edges.

Fie's breath glued in her lungs, her heart pounding faster. The Phoenix tooth sizzled on its string. Its surly princess lingered yet. And the princess said she should give the Oleander Gentry a taste of fire.

Steady. Steady. Fie was no princess, she was a chief. She'd never have the luxury of a faint heart again.

Their leader slowed and halted his mount, his silvery sandpine mask turning from the campfire ashes to the forlorn wagon. "Is this it?"

"That's their cart." Fie thought she recognized the voice of the Crane arbiter from the village they'd just left. There looked to be near two dozen others, one of the largest Oleander parties Fie'd seen yet, with sabers and clubs and hand-scythes strapped at their sides, even a bronze-tipped Hawk spear.

The leader dismounted. Unlike the others' mismatched cloaks, his pale silk robe looked tailor-made for nights riding after Crows. Only Peacocks had coin and time alike to waste so. He held one immaculate hand over the darkened coals. "Still warm."

A thousand obscenities galloped through Fie's head. It seemed the dead gods were not in a kind mood after all.

"So's the pyre." Another man jerked a thumb over his shoulder. "But warm means it burned down mayhap hours ago. Wet or sandy means it was put out in a hurry."

The leader's sneer carried through his mask. "Thank you, *Inspector*, we've all seen fires before. But there's no reason they'd simply abandon their cart."

"They're damned animals, they don't need a reason." No mistaking the Crane arbiter now, even under a layer of white paint and another of coarse-woven veil. She swung down from her horse and stalked over to the wagon to peer inside an open panel. After a moment she tore a strip from her veil and reached in.

"Well?" demanded the lordly Oleander.

The Crane held up Pa's pincers, wrapped in her rag. "It's them all right." She spat at the ashes and slammed the panel shut, casting the pincers aside. "The wagon's still full of their trash. They have to be hiding nearby."

Fie dug her fingers into the bark.

Give them fire, the dead princess urged. *Give them fear.*

Fie could burn Sabor down from mountain to coast if she wanted to. Her and that bag of Phoenix teeth.

"That fire's been dying since sundown," the other Oleander man protested. "They must've set the pyre and run, they knew we'd come—"

"Don't be absurd." The genteel Oleander ran an idle finger over his mask, pacing slow about the camp. "These are *Crows*. They're as dull as they are lazy."

Heat simmered in Fie's throat, in her belly, in her spine. *Teach them to burn.*

Smoke trickled through her fingers.

Then the Oleander lord snatched a torch from a rider and strode to the edge of camp, staring out into the dark forest.

He stopped dead beneath their tree. Beneath the prince's trembling dagger.

The spark in the Phoenix tooth fell silent.

"They're *filth*," the lord said loud, thrusting his torch out into the night. He meant to taunt them, shake them from their cover. If Hangdog had stayed, that might have worked. "You hear me? *FILTH.*"

The plain, hard wooden face turned this way and that, scanning the trees. Torchlight oozed around the blade above.

Light puckered over the dagger's jeweled hilt as it rocked on the bough. One end dipped. Fie's eyes darted from the man to the dagger and back. *Dead gods be kind.*

"They're the true plague of Sabor!" the man screamed behind his mask. "They extort us for our hard-earned property, then steal our children, our spouses, even our prince!"

The dagger slid a finger-width, then tipped swiftly back the other way. One branch above, the prince sucked in a breath.

"The gods weep for every breath we *allow* a Crow to take! And there will be no peace, no *purity*, until this blight is purged from our land!"

With a flash, the dagger slid off the branch.

Three things happened at once:

The Oleander lord turned on his heel.

Fie poured every ounce of her strength into the Sparrow tooth clenched in her fist.

And the dagger vanished in midair.

There was a tiny thud, and a razor-thin line where the point of the unseen blade jabbed into the dirt. The Oleander stopped, back to them.

Fie's skull pounded, the camp swimming in her sight. Every bone rattled and whined. A copper tang singed her throat. Too far, she'd stretched the tooth-spark too far—but she couldn't let go, not now—

The Oleander lord strolled over to the wagon.

"'Feed the Crows,'" he drawled, disgusted. "Better to starve the damned leeches."

With a flick of the wrist, he dropped his torch on the wagon's top.

Fie cringed, her grip on the branch going white-knuckled as she fought to stay upright. Flames spread like a blanket over the dry wagon wood. If they were lucky, someone in the trees had smuggled out a stash of food. If not, they were in for a lean few days. Even a sack of rice . . .

A horrible thought near felled her from the tree then and there. No, there had been such a commotion before they took to the trees, for sure—

Her heart sank as a confused mew pierced the night.

Barf was still in the wagon's hold. And the Crane arbiter had shut the way out.

The Oleander lord walked away.

"What now?" asked the Crane.

He mounted his horse and turned to the trees. "We wait."

Flames began to lick down the wagon's sides. Another cry rose from inside, unmistakable. The Crane hesitated, stretched a hand out toward the side panel, then jerked back at the heat. After a moment she, too, mounted her horse.

Another plaintive mewl wound around the camp.

The ghost of Pa's voice scratched across her skull: *You have to keep your eyes open.*

Fie fought down vomit as her bones screamed, holding on to the Sparrow witch-tooth, holding her own panic back even harder, clinging to the only truth that mattered: she had to see Pa's oath through. She had to keep the prince safe. She had to look after her own.

Tears burned salt tracks down her face.

Look after your own.

Blood trickled from her nose.

Look after your own.

The Oleanders waited.

Look after your own.

Barf's wailing rose, desperate, fearful. Flames streaked higher into the dark.

Something seized Fie's elbow. She near fell off the branch.

"The tooth," Jasimir muttered in her ear. "Give me the tooth."

"Wh—"

"Will it still work if I'm holding it?"

"Aye, but—" Her whisper faded, another wave of dizziness splitting her sight.

The prince's hand found hers. He pried the Sparrow witch-tooth loose. "Don't let them see me."

And before she could say another word, he slid down her robe-rope and dropped from the tree.

Tavin reappeared at her side for a split second as the Sparrow witch-tooth strained to cover them all. Then, mercifully, Pa kindled a third tooth. The Hawk didn't vanish, but Fie found her eyes glazing right over him. Pa must've felt Fie's own Sparrow tooth drop.

Even better, Tavin hadn't yet kenned that Jasimir was gone. Instead, his hand settled on Fie's shoulder. Whether he meant to comfort or restrain her, she couldn't say.

Fie twisted the witch-tooth's spark so she alone could see the prince. To his credit, he had landed with scarce a sound; his mother had trained him well before she died. Not a single Oleander looked his way, still hunting the dark for any sign of Crows.

Barf's mews climbed to a frantic howl.

Jasimir plucked his dagger from the ground, and the Sparrow tooth's range shrank even farther. Relief near brought tears to Fie's eyes.

The prince's bare feet were useful after all; he left nary a track as he picked a path across patches of moss and grass. But closer to the wagon, there was only open dirt. And two Oleanders idled nearby, their horses' eyes rolling at Barf's shrieks.

Fie studied Jasimir's options from above: He could try to weave round the Oleanders. Or he could inch across the dirt and chance the horses startling at his scent. Both would take precious time.

Barf went quiet.

Prince Jasimir stiffened, then smacked one of the horses on the rump.

The horse whinnied and reared, its rider swearing. Jasimir darted across the dirt, ducking flying hooves, and rounded the wagon until it stood betwixt himself and the Oleanders. Fie had to allow that he'd been clever there: from that angle, the riders couldn't see the side panel crack open.

Jasimir's arm vanished into the flames, then reappeared with a fist around the scruff of Barf's neck. He yanked her out swift and stepped back from the fire. Barf wriggled and buried her face in the crook of his arm.

And not a single soul had witnessed it save Fie.

"Get your beast under control," the Peacock lord barked.

The rider who'd near been bucked off patted his horse's neck. "Apologies, m'lord. She'll settle once we're away from the fire."

Another man gave a shout, waving his torch to the road. "Tracks over here. Nail-marks on 'em, like their sandals. Headed south."

The Oleander lord stared at the burning wagon. Jasimir took another step back. Sparrow witch-tooth or no, he wasn't accustomed to going unnoticed. But the sandpine mask only turned to the road and then back to the camp.

"*YOUR DAYS ARE NUMBERED,*" he thundered, loud enough that Fie flinched. "*LONG REIGN THE WHITE PHOENIX.*"

Tavin's fingers tightened on her shoulder again. This time she knew it had naught to do with her.

The Oleander Gentry spooled from the clearing like a weft of burning wool, all white and dust and flame.

Once the hoofbeats sank from earshot, Pa let his own Sparrow teeth go and whistled the all-clear signal. Crows rained from the trees, flocking to put out the burning wagon.

"I'm sorry about your cat," Tavin said, and let her go.

Fie smirked up at him, a little jump-drunk from swinging betwixt fear and relief. "Well, I'm not."

She cut her Sparrow witch-tooth free, and Tavin's eyes flashed with panic as he realized the prince was gone. Then a muffled cheer rose from the Crows below, drawing his attention to where Jasimir stood, still cradling the groggy tabby.

"His idea," Fie said, smug. "Royal command, even. Can't disobey that."

Tavin studied the prince for a long, long moment, a muscle jumping in his jaw. Then he crouched to better look Fie in the eye, face inches from hers.

"Jas is a good person." His voice was a dangerous breed of quiet. "He's going to be a good king. Better than the one we have. And by every dead god, I will do whatever it takes for him to sit on that throne." His eyes narrowed. "I would have been sorry about your cat. But you would have been sorrier if anything had happened to my king."

"Is that a threat?"

"Call it what you want. But you're going to be a chief, and he"—Tavin jabbed a finger at the prince—"is the Crows' *only* hope at not reliving this night, *every* night, for the rest of what will consequently be a very short life."

He was right.

She gave him her coldest, nastiest smile anyway.

"Joke's on you, bastard boy: they're all short lives. Wager I've spent more nights ready to die for my kin than you've spent rolling palace girls."

Something haunted shot through the razor hum of his anger. She hadn't dug for a nerve this time but she'd rattled one all the same. He tilted back, his stare dropping to her mouth, and when he found words after a long moment, all he said was "You're bleeding."

Her nose. Fie tasted salt and copper tracks flaking on her lips. She scrubbed them away with a sleeve. "It doesn't matter."

Tavin nodded, still oddly off-balance, but a heartbeat later, humor glossed over his face once more.

"As for how I spend my nights . . . you might win that wager, you know." Tavin rolled off the branch, effortless, dangling from his fingertips as he flashed that damned grin up at her. "If you're counting *only* the girls."

He dropped. The branch sprang back and near flung Fie off. She swore and flailed for a handhold.

Tavin landed and gallantly stretched out his arms. "Let go, I'll catch you!"

"Get scummed," she spat, and made her own way out of the tree.

By the time Fie touched ground, Jasimir had gone to work fishing out any goods that could be salvaged from the still-burning wagon, ducking his head with embarrassment as Wretch and Madcap lauded each rescue.

Tavin in turn had commandeered the cat. He shook his head when Fie stalked over, frowning at Barf's bloodied paw.

"Give me a bit," he muttered, distracted. "Looks worse than it is. At least, now it does. She tried scratching her way out."

Fie watched a torn toepad slowly knit together and swallowed her spite. Perhaps the Hawk witch had some usefulness to him yet. For all his pompous nonsense, the prince had proven as much for himself.

And from the drawn look on Jasimir's soot-streaked face, he'd learned the fear of strangers in the night after all.

But one Crow still hadn't returned from the dark. Fie thumbed a certain Crow tooth in her string, worry gumming in her belly. The milk tooth gave off a sullen but welcome simmer, kin to the one knotted beside it. One tooth from Pa, one tooth from Hangdog, both burning bright in her mind. Crow teeth had no Birthright to conjure, but they carried a spark if their owner yet lived. Either Hangdog hadn't crossed the Oleanders yet, or they'd passed him by.

Half a weight lifted from her shoulders. The rest stayed as she and the other Crows bundled up their meager surviving supplies into make-shift packs.

Then, at last, the light of the still-burning wagon carved Hangdog from the dark of the road, fake feet coiled around one shoulder, eyes hol-low. A long scratch left red trails across one cheekbone, the only wound Fie could spy.

"Did you see them?" Pa asked.

Hangdog blinked, then nodded. After a moment he cleared his throat. "Rode by."

"How far?"

Hangdog didn't answer, eyes on the fire.

When he'd first come to their band five years ago, he'd not spoken for nigh two moons. Another Crow chief had found him the dawn after an Oleander raid, the only survivor. That chief wouldn't repeat what she'd seen in the ruined camp, aside from a silent scrap of a witch-boy still clutching a fistful of spent Sparrow teeth. But she did let one thing slip: what had happened to Hangdog's kin, what Hangdog had witnessed that night . . . it was all in full sight of the finest Peacock manor in the region.

"Far," Hangdog said after a heavy silence. Another dark bead welled in his bloody scratch. "They won't be back."

Tavin shifted the cat to tap his own cheek. "I can fix your f—"

"No." Hangdog sat by Fie, setting his false feet in the dirt beside them.

Fie glanced back to the Hawk. He raised his eyebrows at her. She ignored him and returned to the heap of supplies.

"Did you hear?" she asked Hangdog under her breath, knotting a bit of twine in one corner of the grass mat she was fashioning into a pack. "The riders. They said our days were numbered. They said—"

"'Long reign the queen.'" Hangdog tried to help her fold the pallet over its contents, but it slipped from his shaking hands. "Aye. I heard."

"The lordlings spoke true," she whispered. "The queen—"

"*I know.*" Hangdog swore under his breath as he fumbled the mat again.

Fie hadn't seen him this shaken in years. Ever, perhaps. She couldn't blame him. The threat was real. They'd been sold to the Oleander Gentry for a throne.

And if she couldn't get the prince to his allies, every Crow in Sabor would pay the price.

This road had trapped her, trapped Pa, trapped them all in the way only roads could—no going back now. For her ma, for her kin, she would walk it to the end.

Or, part of her whispered into the night, she was bound to die trying.

CHAPTER SEVEN

TWELVE SHELLS

PA KEPT MORE PIGEON TEETH THAN THEY COULD EVER HOPE TO use. After all, teeth were the easiest and cheapest viatik at hand, and city folk of any caste seldom parted with anything valuable without a knife in their face to encourage them. With the Birthright of luck, Pigeon teeth could bend fortune in the smallest ways: a timely look to catch a pickpocket, a spare three-naka coin in the gutter, a solid guess on six out of twelve gambling shells.

Pigeon witches, though, could play fortune like a flute. They wrought havoc or blessings as they willed, inviting a flush harvest as easy as a city-wide scourge of rats. Lucky for Sabor, witches of the Common Castes were among the rarest, and their wayward teeth even rarer.

And at dawn, Pa hoisted the only Pigeon witch-tooth he had into the clammy air, knotted his fist around it, and closed his eyes.

Fie saw no change, but after a moment Pa lowered his arm. "Done."

Hangdog just shook his head and began walking down the road. He'd called it a waste; he'd been the only one. The rest of the band knew that with half their supplies burned up in the ruined wagon, they were sore overdue for good fortune.

"What comes now?" Tavin asked, standing behind Jasimir.

The prince knelt in the packed dirt of the flatway, face turned to the east and the rising sun, lips moving in a silent prayer. Barf sat beside him, tail flicking in the dust. Fie had heard the Phoenix caste kept rituals to honor the dawn. At the moment, she would have rather honored some breakfast.

"No telling," Pa answered, rubbing a hand over his beard. "But we'll know when it finds us."

His eyes locked on the empty road behind them, where naught lurked but dirt washed in dawn-gray shadow. Then he slung a weighty sack from his back and fished inside, emerging with two teeth.

"Fie." His hand twitched toward her.

She took the teeth. Twin Pigeon sparks burned inside—not witch sparks but the plain kind.

"It's time you learned to use two at once. That was too close last night." That should have been his Pa voice. Instead it was his Chief voice, quiet, immovable—unsettling. It rose as he turned to the rest of the band. "Swain. How far left to go?"

The lanky Crow tweaked a rolled-up map jutting from his pack. "We're near the coast. One day until we walk the Fan region proper. From there, two days to the Cheparok fortress."

"I sent a message-hawk to our contact in Cheparok before we were quarantined." Tavin helped Prince Jasimir to his feet. "He's a Markahn stationed in the markets. His commanding officer will alert the governor to light the fortress's plague beacon once I give them the signal. That gives us an excuse to walk right up to Governor Kuvimir's front gate."

Pa nodded and whistled the marching call, casting one final look behind him. "Then let's hope our good luck holds out awhile."

———◆———

Good luck came swift, wearing the face of ill fortune: a black finger of smoke beckoning over the treetops an hour later. Hangdog sulked the entire short walk to answer the beacon, and Fie couldn't help chewing over her own doubts.

When they returned to the flatway with a flush viatik of two river oxen, a new wagon, and all else they fancied from the dead sinner's abundant property, Fie's doubt was naught but dust in their trail. She hadn't even had to cut the sinner's throat.

"How many villages are like that?"

Fie looked up from the twin teeth in her salt-lined palm. She was allowed to ride in the wagon with the prince as long as she practiced her toothcraft, but thus far the two Pigeon canines only squabbled in her grasp like fussy toddlers.

"Like what?" she asked.

The prince leaned on the wagon's railing, watching the vine-laced cypress reel past as he rubbed Barf's ears. The tabby hadn't strayed from his side all morning, save to beg attention from Tavin. "Friendly. Generous. Was that just the tooth at work?"

"No." She leaned back against a sack of rice, then hissed as a splinter from the wagon's rough planks slipped into her thumb. "The Covenant marked that sinner long before we used the tooth. Likely the village wanted him gone. That skinflint sucked up all their wealth and squatted on it. Luck didn't do any of that. Luck just made them wait to light a beacon until we were the nearest band of Crows."

"I see." Jasimir pursed his lips, tugging on the hood that hid his top-knot. A walking song from Swain seeped in over the rumble of the wagon.

Fie picked out the splinter and sucked on her thumb, grimacing at the whisper of salt beneath her nail. "What's Your Highness really after?"

"I . . . I suppose I'm wondering why the Crows are still here if it's all that bad." Jasimir unfurled the words slow and careful. "You have no home. I don't know why you would stay in a place that doesn't want you."

Fie's fist closed around the teeth a little too tight, thoughts skittering around her head like water off hot iron.

It was the same as Jasimir calling her *bone thief*, as leaving his dagger hilt unwrapped. He didn't know better. He didn't mean hurt by it. To a prince, this was all a week's mummery before he paraded, glorified, back to Dumosa.

But that did naught to lessen the damage.

Fie's hand shook as she pointed to the road. "That is my home, cousin." She pointed, again, this time to the rolling hills due north. "That is my home." The thin blue rag-edge of sea to the southern horizon. "That is my home." And last, she pointed to the Crows scattered around the wagon as Swain's walking song wound down. "*This* is my home."

Wooden wheels ground against the sand-grit road, scraping at the silence that stretched betwixt Fie and the prince. Finally she trusted her voice enough to continue.

"We stay in Sabor because it's our home. Aye, the villages don't want us, but the sinners always do. Every plague-fearing soul sleeps easier knowing we'll come when they call. So you ask why we stay? Because the plague stays. Because someone out there needs mercy. And because this is our damned home."

"I didn't mean to offend—" the prince began.

"You've been good as dead for two days and no one cares," Fie interrupted. "Why don't *you* leave? Ask a village with a live plague beacon if they want Crows or kings more, and you'll know which of us the country can do without."

The wagon rocked as Tavin swung himself up to peer at them over a railing. "Do we need a healer in here?"

"What?" Fie asked, startled but not surprised. The Hawk seemed to have a sense for when the prince's pride risked a puncture. Barf chirped at Tavin until he scratched her chin.

"Do we need a healer?" he repeated, giving an exaggerated wave of his witch-sign. "Because it sounds like someone's getting skewered."

Jasimir's cheeks darkened. "We were . . . having a discussion."

"Of course." Tavin rested his own chin on a forearm. "You know, you two are almost making the exact same face right now."

Fie hadn't known what to expect when his Peacock glamour ebbed away, but pretty-boy blood ran plain strong in the Markahns. By daylight, he still looked the prince's kinsman but more the Hawk, one the world had gnawed at like a mutt gnawed a bone. He tilted his head at Fie. "I'd pay good Saborian coin to watch you have that *discussion* back at the palace. You'd tear half the court to shreds."

Hangdog sent a foul look their way.

"Only half?" Wretch asked from the road.

For once, Fie caught no whiff of schemes in Tavin's grin. "I'm hoping the other half would figure out to run for their lives. If they don't, that's entirely their fault."

Fie couldn't stopper up a laugh. This time, Hangdog wasn't the only one to shoot her a look.

She ducked her head, ears burning.

Pa cleared his throat from the driver's bench. "How's that practice, Fie?"

"Coming along," she snapped, and unfurled her fist. The teeth had bit two hollows into her palm. Beyond the wagon, Wretch set on a new walking song, a marching hymn to the dead god Crossroads-Eyes.

"Lord Hawk." Pa patted the bench. "A word."

Tavin clambered over to Pa. Jasimir hunched into a sulk disguised as a nap, but Fie paid it no heed, glowering at her Pigeon teeth. Wasn't her fault if nobody else had cut him a slice of hard truth before.

"How may I be of service?" Tavin asked, settling beside Pa.

When Pa spoke, Fie had to strain to hear over the cart's rattle. "Tell me about the queen's Vultures."

Fie caught her breath.

The bench creaked as Tavin shifted. "Are they on our trail?"

"Something is." Pa flicked the reins. "They won't catch up unless they're riding devils themselves, but . . ."

When, not if. No wonder Pa had stared at the road so.

Fie stole a glance at Prince Jasimir. He'd traded the fake nap for a true one, eyes shut against the noon sun, head lolling against the railing.

"Rhusana keeps five skinwitches in her pay," Tavin muttered low. "Four are just trackers. Damned good trackers, but you, me, or Fie could easily drop them in a fight."

"And the fifth?"

Tavin paused. "Greggur Tatterhelm," he said at last. "The queen's favorite. Biggest northman I've ever seen. You'd swear his father had a deviant shine for mammoths. He cuts a notch in his helmet for every mark he brings in, one if they're alive, two if they're dead."

"Tatter-helm," Pa drawled. "Quaint."

"He's not the best skinwitch, nor the fastest. But he's all twelve hells to cross."

"Hm." The bench creaked again under Pa's weight. "And this lord in Cheparok, he's sound and true, aye?"

"What?"

"You boys trust him to hold to your plan?"

"Of course," Tavin said a little too loud. Pa let the unanswered silence speak for itself. Tavin lowered his voice. "The governors of the Fan have been the crown's strongest allies for centuries. Besides, Cheparok sits on the biggest trading bay in the south. No country will do business with a nation on the brink of civil war. Kuvimir's been very clear who he stands with."

"I see."

The last time Fie had heard Pa use that tone was just yesterday, when the Crane arbiter had told them their viatik was only firewood.

"It's all been arranged," Tavin said. A wiry strain of conviction twined about his words, the kind that said you'd draw blood trying to pull them loose. "He'll take Jas in once we get to Cheparok, and then Tatterhelm will have to go through the governor." He stood. "Let me know if the Vultures get closer."

"Aye." Pa waited until Tavin had jumped clear of the cart, then half twisted round. "You catch all that, girl?"

"Aye, Pa," Fie answered, quiet, eyes on the road behind them. The wagon rolled on.

"Then keep practicing."

"Aye, Pa."

———◆———

"There. Harmony."

Fie tried to brand the moment into her memory: the rosy campfire against the dark, the cool, sandy earth pressing against her crossed legs, and most of all, the two teeth humming in her hand.

"Harmony's the key," Pa said, nodding his approval. "They don't wake up the same, they don't burn the same, but they'll burn together if you strike a balance betwixt them."

Using one Pigeon tooth always felt like stepping on a loose paving stone: an odd, sudden tilt, and then it was gone. Calling on two was wholly different. Now fortune flowed like a river around her, eddies coiling about her fist. Whorls also bloomed round Pa, likely from the lingering witch-tooth's pull.

Fie gave one coil an experimental tug with her mind. It lit up . . . then sputtered out as the teeth's harmony frayed. Both sparks flared and died as she swore.

Pa chuckled. "First step's the hardest. Just a matter of practice from here."

"I've been practicing all day," she grumbled.

"Do you want to take a break?"

Fie looked over her shoulder. Tavin stood on the other side of the fire, stretching an arm. "If you want, I'll teach you to play Twelve Shells." He waggled his fingers at Jasimir and Hangdog. "Oh, look at that—twice in one day. Now *you* two are making the same face."

"Because you *always* do this," the prince grumbled, just loud enough for Tavin and her to catch.

Hangdog was less subtle. He ran a thumb down the scratch across his cheek, thunder in his brow. "Keep your own business."

"You keep yours," Pa rumbled. "Go on, Fie. You've earned a rest."

Fie reckoned anything that riled the prince was worth doing. She rocked to her feet just as Hangdog's snarl echoed across the clearing. "Just because he can't rut his own women out here doesn't mean he's welcome to ours."

She froze, an angry flush clawing up her neck, as the camp went quiet. Every Crow eye stuck on her.

Pa's voice cracked across the clearing like a whip. "You'll keep a civil tongue, boy, or you won't use it at all."

"I didn't mean to cause you trouble," Tavin whispered close behind her. She started. *Damn* if the dead Hawk Queen hadn't trained the boys well. "We . . . we can forget the game."

That settled it. Fie'd be cinders in a pyre before she let Hangdog say who she could sit at shells with.

"You need a whole set of gambling shells, aye?" she asked, a little too loud. "Madcap? Can we use yours?"

Madcap tossed their small leather bag over Swain's head, then followed it with a less-than-discreet wink. Fie ground her teeth and stalked to a clear patch of sandy dirt big enough for both her and Tavin.

He sat a moment after she did, glancing sidelong at Hangdog, then dragged a line in the dirt between them. "It's a fairly simple game. We both start with six shells." Fie handed half the bag over. He dropped his shells into two rows of three, and she followed suit.

"There are twelve rounds," Tavin continued. "Each round, you can either take a shell from my side . . ." He reached for a shell on her side of the line. She seized his wrist out of habit. He snorted a laugh. "Or try to stop me from trying to take one from yours, just like that. Once you touch a shell, it's yours. After twelve rounds, whoever has the most shells wins."

She let go of him and blamed the flush up her neck on the campfire. The one a solid dozen paces off. "That's all?"

"For the basic game. At court we play a couple different variations"—his voice hitched for the briefest moment—"but those are more . . . complicated. Any questions?" She shook her head. "Then on the count of three. One—two—*three.*"

He tried for the same shell as before. She caught his hand before it came close.

"Well done," he said, and drew a tick mark to the side. "Round two."

This time she caught him again, reaching for an outside shell.

"Beginner's luck," he huffed, the corner of his mouth tilting up even as he sat back.

"You're easy to read," Fie returned. That was a half-truth. She'd sorted a handful of truths about the prince's Hawk by now, though most ran as deep as the line in the sand between them. Yet one was clear enough: she'd met holy pilgrims who put less effort into getting to their dead god's tombs than Tavin did trying to make it onto her good side.

Time to sort out an uglier truth, then.

"Round—"

"It wasn't right," Fie interrupted. "What Hangdog said about you."

About us, that ugly voice whispered. Fie kept that to herself.

Tavin blinked at her, wordless. She'd managed to throw him off-balance once more. The question was if that meant Hangdog had the truth of it.

"Thank you," Tavin said quietly. "If you're concerned I'm going to hurt him—"

"He shouldn't have said it," she said, cutting him off again. It'd take a harder push to crack the Hawk. "We have two more days to Cheparok. He's going to keep saying things he shouldn't."

"And I'm going to keep ignoring them." Tavin glanced across the fire to the prince, then back to her. "My . . . the old queen, Jasindra, had a favorite Hawk proverb: 'When you act in anger, you have already lost your battle.'"

Fie reckoned that hadn't worked out too well for the dead queen. She also reckoned she'd best keep that to herself as well. Instead, she asked, "Did you see her much?"

"Every day." Tavin's voice roughened at the very edges. "She raised me like her own, though . . . King Surimir made sure Jas and I remembered who was the prince. But you could say the queen and my mother were close."

He'd not mentioned his mother before. Not with the prince in earshot. "Is she with the palace Hawks?"

A shadow slipped across his face. "No. She's a mammoth rider in the Marovar."

Fie whistled under her breath. Mammoth lancers had to be hammered of stern stuff. Only the sternest guarded the ancestral Hawk stronghold of fortresses scattered about the northeastern Marovar mountains. "Sure it's a proper holiday, riding for the master-general."

Tavin cracked another honest smile. "You want to know a secret?"

"Aye."

"My mother once told me Master-General Draga just wants to be left alone with her spears, her mammoths, and her husbands and wives. But she'll bring all twelve hells down on anyone who takes her away from that." Tavin tossed a shell from hand to hand. "In retrospect, maybe that contributes to the 'don't get angry' philosophy."

Fie wrinkled her nose. "Reckon 'don't get angry' is a lot easier to say from the back of a mammoth, too."

"The mammoth probably helps," Tavin admitted. "Round three."

Fie came away with a shell this time, snatching it before he could stop her.

"You know what else helps?" Tavin asked, grimacing as she added the shell to her side. "A bag of Phoenix teeth. Round four."

"Teeth burn out. Phoenix witches don't."

"One. Two. Three."

They both seized shells. Tavin stayed silent as he placed his stolen shell in the gap she'd made in his rows. Something was amiss; he always had a parry to every strike.

"There *are* Phoenix witches, aren't there?" Fie asked.

His mouth twisted. "Right now? Only King Surimir. If Rhusana kills him before another witch appears . . ."

Fie filled in the blanks herself. With all of their dead gods buried under the palace, any Phoenix stood near as good as a witch on its grounds. But outside of their palace, and outside of their witches, there was only one way to call down that terrible fire.

The bag of Phoenix teeth that now dangled at Pa's belt.

"Round five," Tavin said.

He won that round, stealing a shell faster than she could stop him. Her mind was only half there, scrubbing at notions of teeth and royals. A question chipped loose. "That why the prince's so fussed to save the king?"

"I don't even know that the thought's occurred to him." Tavin rolled the shell in his fingers. "Jas cares about the welfare of his country, and he looks up to his father. And generally, he frowns on coldblooded murder, which is something *I* look for in a monarch."

Fie didn't decide to ask the question; it just seemed to fly out on its own: "Do you really think he'll be a good king?"

"You don't?" Tavin looked up, brows raised. She let her silence answer. That same taut-wire edge crept back into his voice. "It's been my job to die for Jas since we were seven. I'm not about to die for a bad king."

"Must be nice to have a say in dying on a bad king's account," Fie muttered.

Tavin didn't seem to hear her, rolling the shell around scar-dappled fingers. "Dumosa loves him. The Peacocks are practically catapulting their sons at him for suitors. The king's council thinks he's the sharpest heir in generations. And his aunt is master-general, so the Hawks won't be a problem."

"For him."

"For *anyone*." Tavin had slipped wholly off-balance now. "We're bound to protect every Saborian. You know, if we'd camped nearer a league marker last night, the Hawks on duty could have run the Oleanders off."

Fie tensed, wondering if this was a road she could go down with a Hawk witch, even one trying to make it to her good side. "You didn't see it?"

"See what?"

"At least one Oleander carried a Hawk spear last night," Fie said. "Bronze-tipped, for the village outposts. They aren't running off the Oleander Gentry, Hawk boy. They're riding with them."

Tavin stared, silent, at the void in his rows where the gambling shell in his fist belonged. Fie waited for the inevitable denial. Of course he hadn't seen it; of course he believed no Hawk could do such a thing.

"Jas . . . Jas can fix it once he's king," he said instead. "You swore him to that."

Fie sat back, startled. But if they were digging into ugly truths, she carried more than her share. "This morning, hours after an Oleander raid, your king-to-be didn't ask me how he can better protect the Crows. He asked me why we don't just make it easy for him and leave. So I ask you again: You think he'll be a good king?"

"Fair enough." Tavin sighed and at last dropped the shell in place. "If it helps, you two are more alike than you'd think."

"I'm——" Fie's voice came out louder than she wanted. She tamped it down to a hiss. "He and I are *nothing* alike."

"Oh? Round six."

"He's spent his life having everything handed to him, with a roof over his head, all the food he wants, and the best guards in the nation." She seized a shell from his side, scarce caring as he swiped one of hers. "Reckon it slipped your ken that I haven't."

"No, but he'll fight to the death for what he believes in, like you. And he lost his mother, too, just a few years ago——"

"Who told you about my ma?" Fie demanded.

Tavin looked pointedly at the campfire, where Pa knotted new teeth into his string.

Pa? When did Pa trust outsiders so?

Fie bit the inside of her cheek. "I've no duty to like him because both our mas are dead."

"You don't have to like him at all," Tavin said. "I just suspect it'll be easier to carry out that oath if you two find common ground. Both of you have been raised to lead your people since birth, for example."

"Don't care."

"And neither of you are looking forward to it."

Any scorching reply died in Fie's throat, gutted on that notion.

Half of her wanted to slap him. She didn't know why.

The other half of her could only think of the moment Pa had handed her his broken sword and told her to cut the Sparrow man's throat.

"I want to be chief," she said.

Another half-truth.

"Round seven," said Tavin.

She wanted to be chief.

When, not if.

She had to be chief. She wanted—

There was a line there, as clear as the one drawn between her and the Hawk. She wanted to flash her own steel the next time a guardsman tried to make her jump. She wanted to tell off the next village that tried shorting them on viatik, and punch herself a new tooth string if anyone pushed back. She wanted to light every Oleander ablaze until fire turned the night to sunrise.

But the cost of all that wouldn't come out of her hide alone.

Look after your own.

Crows had one rule. And she had to be a Crow chief.

He won the next five rounds, played in silence but for the countdown. Fie didn't care. The sooner this damned game was over, the better. She'd learned her lesson for digging into ugly truths with pretty boys.

"Round twelve."

The shells caught the firelight, studding the sand. Tavin was winning. On "three," she made a halfhearted grab for his side.

He caught her, of course. Fingers landed on her wrist, then let go—but not wholly, the tips trailing across the back of her hand, following ridges of vein and bone.

"What do you want, Fie?" he asked.

She'd been asked what she wanted before: her price from the prince, which branch of a crossroad she favored, what to leave in a shrine's viatik stash. Matters for a chief, matters of business, matters of surviving another day.

Tavin didn't mean survival. He meant the way she wanted steel, and fire, and games with pretty boys. She couldn't remember the last time someone had.

And she had no good answer, only a bitter true one. "It doesn't matter."

"Doesn't it?"

Heat crept up her neck again, and a little anger—but not at him, at herself, for not wanting to pull away.

She did anyhow, swiping all of his shells in one fell swoop. Then she stood and dusted herself off. "I win."

"Beginner's luck," he said with a shrug and a smile.

A thousand thoughts clamored for attention as Fie strode across the camp, tossing the bag of shells back to Madcap and ignoring their surprised yelp.

"Where you headed, Fie?" Pa asked as she passed.

"Washing up," she said, short, and stopped at the wagon for a fistful of soap-shells. "I'm on watch tonight, aye? It'll wake me up some."

"Aye." A lilt said he knew that was only half the reason. True, she did need to keep sharp tonight.

She also sore needed to cool her head. The burn of Hangdog's glower did naught to help as she marched out of camp.

They'd used this site a few times before, enough that she could pick her way down to the nearby creek easy by the light of the dwindling moon. Sandy earth yielded to hard, sticky mud by the water, mosquitos whining in her ear as they skirted the tongues of yellow-eyed skinks.

Fie rolled up her leggings and waded to where the stream ran fast and clean, sucking a breath at the chill.

What do you want?

She splashed cold water on her face and bare arms, then paused. Sometimes she caught her reflection in panes of glassblack or polished brass, and sometimes in streams like this. She'd seen her own face well enough to know it now even as a silver-edged shadow in the water: a rounded nose, broad mouth weighed in a frown, wide black eyes. Hair near as black, pin straight only after she washed it, the ends always bristling up where the mask strap left a crease. Sometimes a smudge of road dust on the point of her middling-brown chin. She couldn't say if anyone called her pretty; outside the Crows, most everyone only looked her way when she wore a mask.

Now her eyes threaded her silhouette in the brook, searching for a hint of whether she'd been pretty playing shells by firelight.

Then she kenned her own folly and ground the soap-shells betwixt her palms until their hulls split, ears burning. The sharp-smelling sap foamed into suds once she worked it into her face, arms, and hair, wishing she could go deep enough for a proper wash. Maybe once this was all over the prince's cousin would spare a bit of hospitality.

The thought of *over* made her pause.

Over meant a Covenant oath kept. It meant no more fear of the Oleanders, not with an armed guard of the Crows' own. *Over* also meant no more lordlings.

Fie's stomach gave a mutinous twist.

Enough.

Gritting her teeth, she splashed deeper until the water reached her waist, shuddering at the chill. Then she sat and plunged her head below the water.

The cold shocked her skull mercifully empty, even if she could only take it a scant moment before bolting to her feet. Annoyance set in a moment later. She ought to have stripped out of her clothes first, even if she'd dry off quick enough keeping watch by the campfire. But her head was in a twisted way tonight, and it didn't seem she could think straight for the life of her. She turned to slog back.

A shadow waited on the bank.

"You reckon that bastard's shining to you?" Hangdog's sneer slid across the water.

Something in his voice said she was better off staying in the creek. Fie didn't answer. When Hangdog got himself in a temper like this, she knew better than to try aught but look for a way out.

"You reckon he'll take you away and polish you up so much that the gentry forget what you came from?" he continued. "Don't fool yourself. That oath's trash. You're only good to his kind on your knees."

The angry simmer flared fierce. "Oh aye, and I was never that to you? Us fooling about moons ago doesn't give you a spit-weight of say in who I talk to."

"I didn't know you were just practicing until you found a lordling to lie with," Hangdog shot back. "You think he wants aught more from you than an easy—"

Footsteps crunched toward them. Most of Fie prayed it was a Crow. A treacherous part of her wanted someone else.

Wretch stepped into a patch of moonlight, hefting an armful of empty water skins. "You fall in that creek, girl?"

Relief tumbled down Fie's spine. She wrung out her shirt's hem. "Something like that."

"Help me fill these, will you?" Wretch tossed a water skin to her.

Hangdog looked from her to Fie, then stomped back toward the camp.

Wretch didn't speak until his footfalls faded. "He corners you again, you call for me, all right?"

"I can handle him on my own," Fie mumbled, surprised when her eyes burned. The anger had boiled down to mortified spite. "I just . . . All I did was play a damn game."

Wretch dropped the water skins on the bank and waded out to Fie, shaking her gray-streaked head. "Aye, all you did was play a game. And with a pretty boy. And if it were fair, that's all there'd be to it."

Wretch wasn't much for sentiment, but she gripped Fie's shoulder anyhow. "I would have left you to handle Hangdog. We all know you could trounce him twice with your eyes shut. But when he followed you? The only reason that pretty boy didn't come haring after was because I beat him to it. And we both know where that road would have led."

Fie did. And she hated it. All this mess over a stupid game.

"We're two more days off Cheparok. Then you're clear of all this nonsense, and we'll have a Covenant oath to cash out and no more fretting over Oleander rides. That's a mighty thing, Fie."

"Aye," Fie said softly. Two days and it would all be over.

"They'll come up with a fancy name for you," Wretch teased. "Tell stories for centuries. Fie Oath-cutter. Fie the Cunning. Fie, the Crow Who Feared No Crown."

"I'll settle for Fie, Who Never Saw an Oleander Again." Fie rubbed her eyes.

There was less jest than truth when Wretch said, "So would we all."

That night passed, and two more, without Fie looking at Hangdog or the lordlings if she didn't have to. Instead she huddled in the wagon, practicing her toothcraft as the road turned from sand to rocky clay, and bristling pines shifted to copses of stout palms. Each field they passed seemed lusher than the last, a distant thin ribbon of green broadening into the Fan River, which gave the region its name. That ribbon pointed straight to a hard, jagged line against the coin-bright sea: Cheparok.

And that river marked their way, flashing coy as Fie fought to strike harmony with pair after pair of teeth. As Cheparok neared, Pa looked over his shoulder less, but a telltale creak of the wagon seat still gave him away each time. At least the Pigeon witch-tooth had kept any plague beacons at bay until after they'd passed.

By the time they drew within half a league of the city's western gates, Fie's shirt clung horribly to her skin, half from the choking air and half from the murderous sun overhead. Cheparok's towering walls didn't even have the decency to cast a long enough noontime shadow to offer respite.

Pa whistled a stop and guided the oxen to the side of the road, then twisted in his seat to face her and the prince. Tavin climbed up into the wagon bed a moment later, prompting a disgruntled mew from Barf as she peered out from behind a sack of rice. The other Crows gathered round.

"Hold up a moment." Pa cast his gaze about and waited until a band of Owl sojourn-scholars had passed down the flatway. "All right, here's the pinch: they'll have Vulture witches at the gate."

"Why?" Prince Jasimir frowned.

"Checking for witches, mostly unregistered ones from the countryside. That'd be no trouble, but . . ."

"They'll spot me for a Hawk witch," Tavin finished. "One who's supposed to be dead. So how do we get past?"

"Can't hide you in the wagon. Odds are we'll be searched." Pa continued even as Prince Jasimir tilted his head at that. "We burned our only Sparrow witch-tooth on the Oleanders. We can sneak you through with two plain Sparrow teeth . . . but the Vultures will pick up on any spell I'm casting when they test my witch-sign. So that leaves Fie."

Fie's stomach dropped. "What?"

When, not if.

"It's time." Pa held out a fistful of Sparrow teeth. "How's that practice?"

CHAPTER EIGHT

—— WHEN ——

"STEP IN THE FOOTPRINTS."

"What?" the prince whispered to Fie's left.

"Don't make new footprints. Step in Hangdog's prints. Or Swain's."

"Good thinking." Tavin's voice drifted too close behind her.

Hair stood on the back of Fie's neck. She ignored it, focusing on the Sparrow tooth in each fist. One burned already, humming steady with her bones. The other waited yet for her call.

Fie picked her way through Wretch's tracks behind the wagon as they headed for where the flatway split five ways. Each path led to a gate in Cheparok's sturdy walls, just like those on the eastern side of the Fan River. Blue-green roof tiles flashed just behind the city walls, crowning towers that flew the banner of the Floating Fortress. The lord-governor's palace had earned its name by squatting direct over the Fan and the reservoir it filled.

At least, that's what she'd been told. From this side of the walls, all she got was fancy roofs and bright flags. She'd have her chance to see it up close soon enough.

A trio of Hawk guards sat at the root of the branching roads, rolling gambling shells and sweating in the brutal sun. The one with a corporal's copper armband eyed the Crows, spat, and jerked his thumb over a shoulder. "Fifth gate."

He didn't look up from the shells even once as Fie and the lordlings passed.

Each gate before them sat lower than the last, dropping from east to west like a stair. The first gate was meant for Phoenixes, and it stood empty save for its guards. The polish on their armor glittered nigh as bright as the green tassels on their spears, and just as eye-catching even from hundreds of paces off. Less flashy Hawks milled in and out of the second gate, stepping around Splendid Caste palanquins festooned in fringe and bead. That gate yawned the largest, its arch stretched high for visiting mammoth riders, though the heat made no such accommodation for the beasts. The third gate bustled with Hunting Castes, from melon-orange open carriages of Crane magistrates to the tiered lavender wagons of proud Owl scholars.

The fourth gate rambled even more chaotic, strewn with Common Castes. Sparrow farmers waited with strings of goats and cattle; Pigeons had set up shop at the roadside with their goods spread about the ground, peddling anything from clay luck charms to meat that Fie judged extremely untrustworthy. A few Gull sailors wandered from vendor to vendor, some haggling with Sparrows for livestock.

The line for the fourth gate was long, but it crept along with a slow, steady order. The same could not be said for the fifth gate. The muddy road sloped down, down, down, to the lowest point in Cheparok's walls. There the fifth gate gapped, teeming with beggars, bloodflies, and the brands of Common-Caste convicts. It hadn't a line so much as a mass that slid down the hill and pooled at the gate, some trickling through, others turned away to plead sanctuary elsewhere. The mud itself gave off a damp reek, one part ox dung, one part plant decay, and one part a musk Fie didn't care to speculate on.

Her Sparrow tooth held as they waited their turn, humming patient in her mind. The second one stayed buried in her sweating fist until, bit by bit, they trudged down to the bottom of the hill.

Two Vulture skinwitches hunched together by the gate on rickety wood stools, the yellow of their thin cotton robes clashing against their fish-flesh-pink hides. Meager boastings of valor marks were scattered over their arms. One eyed the creeping shadow of the city wall and scooted his stool a little farther into its shade as a Hawk behind him laughed. The other Vulture rattled off a halfhearted oath and beckoned the Crows' cart forward.

Pa whistled and flicked the reins. To other castes, it'd sound like a marching order. Fie knew better. In the Money Dance, that whistle meant "pair up."

"Keep quiet," she told the lordlings, "keep close, and move when I say."

Harmony, she told herself, and kindled the second tooth.

The two Sparrow teeth grated against each other a moment, then settled into grudging cooperation. As with the Pigeon teeth before, her senses shifted, drawing new trails in her mind. Before, she'd kenned the prickle of eyes trained on her; now each person nearby cast a beacon of a gaze. And with two teeth in hand, any time that gaze turned near Fie and the boys, it rolled away like water off a greased cloak.

The first skinwitch leaned to look behind Pa, scanning the rest of the Crows. Fie held her breath, held the teeth, held off that gaze. After a moment, the skinwitch leaned back. "I count two bone thieves," she called. "Treggor?"

"I got two, Inge," the other Vulture confirmed, pressing farther into the shade.

Fie let her breath out.

"Witches to me," Inge said. Pa climbed down from the driver's seat and walked over, rolling up his sleeve, Hangdog a step behind. Two Hawk guards twitched their spears at the other Crows to step away from the wagon.

"Move with them," Fie whispered, and slid along at the back of the band.

The Hawks strolled over, lips curling. "What's your business in Cheparok?" one asked.

Pa's eyes darted back. "Restocking," he answered, loud enough to bounce off the walls and echo back to the guard. "We're out of flash-burn and low on soap-shells—"

"Don't need a list," the guard snapped. "Those're pricey goods for a Crow. How are you planning on paying for those? You bring any coin?"

Pa flinched. "Aye. Last job gave us ten naka for viatik."

The guard rounded the back of the wagon while his partner planted herself between it and the Crows. "Ten naka," he mused, prodding the crates and sacks with a spear tip. The blade sank too far into one bag. Rice spilled across the wagon bed as Barf climbed out from behind the ruined burlap, yowled in disdain, and stretched. She seemed wholly untroubled by the spear point now inches away.

One of the lordlings shifted behind Fie. "*Don't,*" she hissed under her breath.

"Hey Kanna, you remember how much the fee is to pass the fifth gate?" the guard asked, spear point following Barf.

His partner turned to laugh at him. "Eight naka."

"Eight naka," he echoed.

Both Hawks faced away now, and both Vultures were fixed on Pa and Hangdog. "Follow me," Fie whispered, and slipped away from the rest of the band, slinking toward the gate.

Pa's shoulders slumped a little. "As you like," he said, and pulled back his over-robe.

The guard loped around the side of the wagon, suddenly close. Fie yanked the boys to crouch behind the oxen as the Hawk swung his spear to point dead at Pa. "You carrying a sword?"

"It's broken."

"Drop it."

Pa nodded and made a show of reaching for his other hip, where the buckle sat. The half sword hit the mud, sending a cloud of bloodflies into the air.

The skinwitch called Inge chortled behind Pa. "All that's good for is mercy, to be sure."

"The purse." The guard jerked his spear at Pa.

Pa untied his purse and tossed it to the Hawk. The Hawk dumped it onto the wagon's driver's seat and slid coins around until he was satisfied. "Your change is on the seat," he laughed, and nodded to the skinwitches. "Go ahead, Inge."

The skinwitches seized Pa and Hangdog, fish-flesh fingers pale against their bare arms. Inge's and Treggor's eyes squeezed shut a moment.

"Move," Fie whispered, and crawled for the gate.

Inge's gray eyes cracked open. She let go of Pa and spat to the side. Her spittle landed on Fie's sleeveless arm.

Fie gagged in disgust, and the Sparrow teeth slid out of tune for a terrible instant. She yanked them back into harmony, swearing a silent litany, and froze in place.

Inge straightened up, her beacon-like gaze drifting in Fie's wake. "Treggor?"

The other Vulture blinked. "Aye?"

Harmony, Fie prayed into the reeking muck, wringing the twin Sparrow teeth for everything they were worth. *Harmony*.

Inge squinted around, then slumped back. "Nothing."

When she turned to Pa, Fie whispered, "Move."

She reckoned that when the prince had thought to come to Crows for help, he hadn't banked on crawling through the lowest gate of Cheparok on his hands and knees.

"Their witch-signs are good," Inge croaked behind them, tweaking a fold of her yellow robe. "Ken me, you two. You're marked men. Any spells you use now can and will be traced to you. We take the tag off when you leave the city."

"So don't make trouble," the female Hawk sneered. "And don't stay long."

She jabbed her spear toward the gate just as Fie and the boys ducked round the corner.

Pa retrieved his blade, climbed back into the wagon, and smacked the reins without a word. The oxen lurched forward. Fie and the lordlings fell in with the Crows once they passed the gate, not chancing a look behind them. Nor did Fie chance dropping her stranglehold on the Sparrow teeth.

The wagon creaked into the lowest ring of Cheparok. The city rose above them in circular tiers, each smaller and higher than the last. Buildings lining the mud street down here were little better than walls of lumpy baked plaster and woven palm screens, most clustered near a dirty canal that curved down the road until it bent out of view. Pa followed that canal, then turned a corner, then another, until they'd slipped into a narrow alley away from the busy street.

"You're clear, Fie. Well done."

Fie let the teeth go. Wretch took in their coats of muck and covered a snort, but the lordlings had other concerns.

"They just took most of your money," Tavin said, angry. "I can't—we'll—I'll report them once we reach the fortress—"

Pa waved a hand and reached into his robe. "Fret you not, lad. Aye, they took most of the coin I had"—he drew a long, slim leather pouch from behind his back—"in that purse. Tell them you only have ten naka, and eight is what they'll take."

"They shouldn't take anything at all," Jasimir said. "I won't forget."

The other Crows traded looks. All Pa said was "Let's get you to your cousin first."

Tavin nodded to the city's higher tiers. "There's a Markahn in Second Market waiting to hear from me. He'll pass the signal to the Floating Fortress once we find him, and then Governor Kuvimir will light the plague beacon."

"Second Market? Good luck." Swain pointed at the plaster wall over the wagon, marked with soot-darkened curls and slashes. Easy to mistake for the work of a lazy vandal, but the two crossed black thumbprints made a sign Fie would know anywhere.

The lordlings looked baffled. Fie tapped the thumbprints. "This is a Crow mark. And this"—she waved at the wall—"is a map. Here." She indicated a square capped by a curve on the eastern side of the city. "That's the Crow shrine. And these"—she traced a series of spikes— "are the markets. Second Market is . . ." Fie counted the patches of market in each ring and pursed her lips at what she saw. ". . . bad. Bad for Crows."

"We've got '*No one sells to Crows.*'" Swain ticked off his fingers, reading down the symbols by the market. "Let's see . . . both '*hostile guard*' and '*bribe the guard*,' so be open to a fair number of options there . . . And '*no masks.*'"

"I'll deal with the guards," Tavin said. "But why no masks?"

Fie sighed. "Draws notice. Just keep your hood up instead."

"Fie . . ." Pa started.

"Aye, Pa." Fie unstrapped her own mask from where it hung around her neck and tossed it into the wagon. She should have known her work was far from over. "I'll bring the boys back to the shrine after."

"I'll go with," Hangdog said, abrupt. Pa started and stared at him. "At least to Fourth Market. Buy the flashburn and the soap-shells."

Pa traded a look with Fie. She gave a tiny shrug. She'd already be reckoning with a prince and his fussy pet Hawk. If Hangdog wanted to fuss, too, at least one of them would be useful about it.

The string of naka clinked as Pa slid coins free and passed them over. "Here. Be safe. I'll see you four at the shrine."

⸺◆⸺

"The sign says water-lifts are that way."

Fie scowled, already sweltering under the heat of her black over-robe. But since he'd kept his topknot, Jasimir had to stay covered, so Tavin had to stay covered, and so *she* had to stay covered lest she draw notice. Still, she envied the airy wraps and shaved heads of the Cheparok women around them. *They* were dressed for the muggy heat.

"I don't know what the sign says, cousin," she said. "And I don't care. That mark there? That means Crows aren't allowed. We need to take the stairs. And the stairs are this way."

Tavin blinked at her. "You can't read?"

Something in her shrank at his surprise. "I . . . I know Crow signs," she mumbled. "Swain does the reading for us."

"And the Crow signs say we won't be allowed on the water-lifts," Hangdog chipped in. Perhaps two and a half days of Fie's silence had taught him to keep a cooler head, for no resentment smoldered in his voice, only stiff resignation.

"Well, those signs look old. Let's make sure." The prince set off down the muddy road.

Fie gritted her teeth and followed. She couldn't blame him, not truly. The idea of slogging up stair after limestone stair, all the way up to Second Market, made her want to vomit. The water-lifts used the force of the reservoir's water channels to move cargo and citizens between Cheparok's tiers with considerable less effort.

The lift attendant looked up from a cotton-heaped cart only long enough to snap, "*No.*"

For a moment Fie wanted to stand there anyway and relish the faint relief of mist and water splashing down from Fourth Market. Then she remembered that same water had traveled from the Fan, into the city reservoir, and down four tiers of canals and bathing steps, carrying whatever those tiers' citizens felt like throwing in it. Likely it was as clean as the grime on her arms.

"Come on," she said, wincing, and headed back toward the stairs. This time Jasimir kept his mouth shut.

Hangdog split off once they'd climbed the three-score steps to Fourth Market. "Luck, cousin," he muttered to Fie, and gave her a half grin. She briefly debated pushing him back down those three-score steps, but it seemed like an awful lot of work in this dreadful sun.

Instead she looked for a Crow mark for the stairs. One was carved into a signpost nearby, pointing to the opposite end of Fourth Market.

"Do they even know how hot it is?" gasped Tavin, staring at the crowds packing the market. Fie could scarce hear him over the lowing of disgruntled cattle, shouts of vendors, wailing children, and high-pitched warbling from some unholy horn busker.

Holy texts said the Covenant disposed of irredeemable souls in one of twelve hells. Fie wasn't sure what she'd done to deserve this one.

A mother shoved past, dragging a child on each arm. It gave Fie a notion equal parts distasteful and effective. She snatched one hand from each of the lordlings. "Hold fast."

Then she plunged into the crowd. It was chaos and cacophony, a crush of sweat and flesh and salt-stiff cotton. She lost count of how many people trod on her feet, but she was dead sure that the nails in her sandals repaid that in triple.

At last they reached the end of Fourth Market. Fie staggered to a quiet place between stalls, and the prince yanked free of her, shaking his hand out. She let go of Tavin and swayed in place, catching her breath.

"Let's never do that again," Tavin said, tone dark.

Fie shook her head, wheezing. "The way . . . back."

"I'd rather throw myself down the water-lift." Jasimir started to pull his hood back, then thought better of it. "What now?"

Fie looked at the next hundred stairs and winced. "Third Market."

This stairway led past a set of bathing steps, where one of the green-tiled reservoir channels spilled out over limestone blocks larger than those Fie climbed. People of the fourth tier splashed in the milky water, rinsing laundry or stripping down and bathing as they pleased. Fie and the boys stopped a moment to scrub down their arms; it took more will than she'd admit to not wash up head to toe.

Third Market was mercifully less crowded than Fourth, giving them a moment to catch their breath in the shade of a cool stone wall. An uneven brick street wound between stalls and tents, where merchants dubiously promised the coolest palm screens, the fattest lambs, the brightest lamp oil in Cheparok. Crews of Gulls poled their cargo barges down the canal at market's edge, shouting for buyers in the spice-laden air as they wiped sweat from deep brown faces. A distant smear of orange roof tiles marked a Magistrate's Row, where Crane witches called truths out of witnesses and petitioners alike.

Fie's eyes landed on a pair of Hawks lounging near a water-lift. One squinted back at her and mumbled to his partner. The other Hawk turned to look as well.

"We need to keep moving," Fie said, and stepped back into the sun.

"We're being followed?" Tavin asked, falling in beside her.

"Maybe. Point at the stall on your right."

He did, gesturing to an altogether spiteful-looking sow. A bemused farmer raised his eyebrows. Fie feigned a moment's consideration, then shook her head and moved on.

"Don't look back," she hissed, winding toward a glassblack vendor. The woman's tent glittered with samples of her work, strings of discs fluttering in the breeze. Glassblack only showed through on one side, reflecting the other in nigh every hue imaginable. Fie had seen whole panes of the stuff in the windows of the wealthy. Crows just dealt with the plainest kind, black, to cover the eyeholes in their masks.

The discs spun lazy on their wires as Fie neared, flashing fragments of the marketplace: a reflected tapestry, a slip of an Owl scholar, a brass lamp perched on a windowsill. A blue disc twirled and showed her the two guards, still watching from the water-lift. She stopped, reaching for a disc of black.

"Keep your filthy little hands off," the vendor spat.

Fie flashed her empty palms and stepped back. "Just looking."

The black disc spun to show her the guards again. They'd been distracted by the water-lift's wheels churning into motion.

"Come on." Fie jerked her head toward a signpost. To her annoyance, once they reached it, she found that any Crow signs had long since worn away, if they'd been there at all. Her ears burned. "Can . . . does it say where—"

"This way." Tavin set off across the market.

This time, the steps rose past grand mosaics, their vivid tiles painting the deeds of dead gods and heroes. In one, Lovely Rhensa danced above a field of vanquished foes; in another, Ambra, Queen of Day and Night, stood astride the sun, wreathed in gold Phoenix fire. Jasimir grimaced at that one for a breath before moving on. Most of Cheparok fell below them once they reached the top of the stairs, dropping tier by tier until the last plateau bled into docks and canals. Smaller barges flocked in the shallow bay like litters of puppies, their mothers the great trade ships moored at a crest of islands between Cheparok and the sea.

Fie didn't realize she'd stopped until Tavin tugged at her shoulder. "The view's even better from the fortress."

Second Market was quieter than Third. Fie hesitated to even tread on the flat sandstone slabs, the nails in her sandals grinding in protest. A few stalls flapped banners for imported rarities and the crests of renowned Crane merchant houses, but for the most part actual storefronts made up the tranquil street. Posh silk-gauze billowed everywhere in the breeze, from layered wraps sported by Cranes and Peacocks to drapes tacked over windows and tent frames. Swan courtesans of every shade and gender drifted by in head-to-toe white, trailing filmy veils of their own from wide-brimmed hats meant to hide their faces from the jealous sun. Heads swiveled as they passed. Swans commanded the Birthright of desire, and even the plainest could gather attention like folds of silk, wielding charisma sure as Hawk steel.

One Swan man glanced sidelong at Fie and wrinkled his nose. She wrinkled hers back, reminded too much of Queen Rhusana.

"Well," she said, wiping her brow, "your Markahn lout shouldn't have much trouble spotting us."

"He said he's stationed by an apothecary." Even Tavin seemed reluctant to venture into the market.

Fie peered down the street and saw a banner with a mortar and pestle. "There's one."

"So there is." He took the lead again, sliding seamless into the meandering traffic. Jasimir followed, leaving Fie to bring up the rear.

They wove through the crowd, nail-studded soles rasping on the stone in a way that pricked goose bumps down Fie's arms. She couldn't help but scowl at the boys' saunter. After near a week with the Crows, they still walked like the Peacocks ought to move for them.

No helping the way they'd been raised, she supposed. And it wouldn't be her problem much longer.

A hand locked around her wrist. "What's this?"

Fie's hood fell back as she was yanked around. A Hawk guard had her in an iron grip, his mouth twisting.

"What's a Crow runt doing in Second Market? Didn't anyone tell you there's no bones to steal here?" He jerked his arm up, dragging her to the tips of her toes. "Or are you after something else, little Crow?"

Fie's thoughts whirled about her head in a panic. The guard had picked her on purpose—the boys wouldn't notice her gone—she was walking the city with an untagged witch-sign—

The Hawk must have read the dismay in her face, for he cracked an unsettling smile and stepped back, dragging her away from the street. "That's right, you're in trouble now. So let's talk about how you're going to get out of it."

"*What do you think you're doing?*" A fist shot over her shoulder, closed around the Hawk's wrist, and gave it a vicious wrench. The guard let go with a yelp and reached for the sword strapped at his side.

Somehow, in the last few days, Fie had forgotten how fast Tavin could move. It seemed all she did was blink and the market guard was already crushed up against the wall, Tavin's elbow pushing into his windpipe.

"Easy, cousin," Tavin said tightly, more a threat than a reassurance.

"Think nice and hard about what your next move is, because if you're *lucky*, I'll just settle for letting Aunt Loka strip your hide."

"Tavin?" the guard wheezed, incredulous. His gaze skipped over to Jasimir. "Is that the *prin—*"

Tavin clapped a hand over his cousin's mouth. "Are you a special kind of stupid?" he demanded under his breath. "What part of 'think about your next move' was unclear?" The guard scowled at him. Tavin didn't budge. "I'm going to let you down, and then you're going to do us both a favor and shut up so you can listen very, very carefully to what I want you to do."

The guard nodded, and Tavin stepped back. Fie checked over her shoulder for onlookers, but none of the shoppers nearby had so much as glanced their way.

"I thought you'd come alone," the guard mumbled. "Not with—him. Or your honey rag there. Since when do you suck Crow sugar—"

And back up against the wall the Hawk guard went, face-first this time.

Tavin's voice turned to the razor-sharp calm that warned of thin ice. "I suppose 'shut up and listen' was a tall order, but do it for your country, all right? I want you to tell Sergeant Bernai that you saw Crows in the market—those exact words—at the end of your shift. And then I want you to forget we talked. And if you can't do that, at least keep your miserable mouth shut. Now, what are you going to do for your country, cousin?"

"Tell the sergeant I saw you—"

Tavin cleared his throat.

"—that I saw Crows in the market . . . And tell only the sergeant."

"That's the patriot I know." Tavin let him go again. "You should also tell your sergeant the fifth-gate guards won't let travelers pass without bribes."

"And?" His cousin shrugged. "The third and fourth gates don't, either."

"And that's *illegal*." Jasimir's voice burst over Fie's shoulder. "The law says citizens should come and go as they please. I've never been charged at the first gate. Nobody else should pay, either."

Tavin's cousin eyed the prince, then saluted, face blank. "As you wish, Your—sir. I'll tell my sergeant about the gates."

Fie traded a look with Tavin. Both of them knew plain what that meant: he'd tell the sergeant indeed, and the sergeant wouldn't do a damned thing.

"First tell him you saw Crows," Tavin said, sounding too much like Pa. "Then keep your mouth shut. And stop embarrassing the Markahns." He hiked his hood up. "Let's get out of here."

No one spoke until they'd made the descent back to Third Market. At the base of the stairs, Tavin caught at Fie's arm, drawing her back to an alcove.

"That wasn't the first time, was it?" he asked, face taut with anger. The prince tilted his head, but Fie got Tavin's meaning clear enough.

She met Tavin's gaze, then pointedly looked to where his hand still curled around her forearm, just as his cousin's had.

He let go as if he'd been burned, cursing under his breath.

"Oh." Jasimir's face dropped.

"I keep clear of Hawks if I can help it," she told them. "But it wouldn't be the first time for Crows. What do you do when a Hawk takes what they want? Tell another Hawk?"

"*Yes*." Tavin ran his hands through his hair. "That's what you—what you should be able to do."

"And how do you reckon that ends for people who aren't Hawks or gentry?" she asked.

He looked away, toward the stairs to Second Market. Somehow that made her angry.

Fie grabbed a fistful of Tavin's cloak and gave it a jerk. He blinked at her.

"I reckon," she said coldly, "we all know how it ends."

Then she let go and set off to cross Third Market.

It was a long, silent, stifling walk back to the fifth tier. But as Fie led the way down the final set of grimy stairs, she caught on to how close the Hawk had kept to her, now warding her back each step of the way.

Fie didn't know how she felt about that.

Almost over. In a few hours, this would all be over. The prince would be safe, Pa's oath would be kept, and she'd never again need to fear riders in the night.

A few hours, and then no more roads would end like her ma's had.

They'd just hit the muddy fifth-tier street when murmurs and cries swept down through its straggling crowd. A beggar pointed back behind them. Fie turned.

"Here we go," Tavin said.

When, not if.

Four city tiers above, a black string of smoke trailed from the Floating Fortress's plague beacon.

They left the shrine near sundown, copper sunlight striping shadows down the street as Fie slung her mask about her neck.

"Here." Hangdog held out a fistful of fresh mint leaves. "Found some in Fourth Market."

"Thanks." She shook long-withered leaves from her mask beak and stuffed the new ones in. "Run into any trouble?"

An odd look crossed his face before it blanked. "Nary a bit. You?"

She strapped on her mask, taking a deep whiff of mint as the world narrowed to what she could see through the eyeholes. "Naught worth mentioning."

Yet another half-truth. But she'd have plenty of time to mull it over once the lordlings were gone.

They ran into no disputes with the water-lifts this time. The attendants' ashen faces said the sooner the Crows took the sinners, the better. One tier after another they ascended, market crowds splitting before the Crows' grim procession with a sober, furious hush.

The final water-lift released them into a waiting line of Hawk guards on the tiled lane of the first tier. Walls of snowy marble and iridescent glassblack towered around them, plaited into green-roofed mansions and pavilions where the soft trickle of fountains whispered through stone and shadow. Vivid painted tiles bordered each household's foundations, layer upon layer detailing generations of Peacock-caste achievements.

The Hawks fell into step at their flanks as they marched up the tight coil of the first tier and past gentry mansions, each more absurdly ornate than the last, until at last the great round black eye of the open reservoir drew into sight. The Floating Fortress sat no more than a man's height above the Fan, stilted on thick columns that jutted from the water's surface.

The Fan itself flowed direct under the fortress and into the massive well, and as Fie followed their wagon up a limestone slope, she saw no sign of the reservoir's bottom. Rumor said it reached all the way down to the fifth tier. At the top it fed the canals, spilling out into the blue-tiled chutes that cut down the city's tiers. Tavin had been right: the view was best from up here, a grand mosaic of jewel-toned roof tiles and lush gardens tumbling down the tiers.

The dying sun sent odd whorls across the sea-green walls of the

Floating Fortress as the wagon neared. Fie tilted her head, wondering if it was a trick of her glassblack, until a gold hue burst across one shimmer. The walls had been painted in enamel and gold dust.

A hot lump rose in her throat as she thought of every time Pa had passed his dinner to her. Every time she'd made herself sick on moldered panbread or chewed a fistful of mint just to keep from thinking about the hunger, just to hold out until the next viatik.

"There's Governor Kuvimir," Prince Jasimir whispered, relief flashing through his voice like gold dust.

Sure enough, a man watched them approach from the balcony of a courtyard ahead, his neck and chest glinting with the necklace-plate bearing the governor's fantailed insignia. A peculiar wrench wrung Fie's gut.

Almost over.

She found a stray thread to pick at. The wagon rolled on.

The walkway curled upward, leading to a marble bridge that stretched betwixt earth and fortress, over the rushing water where river met reservoir. Jade statues of the dead Peacock gods lined the railings. Governor Kuvimir still waited above the courtyard at the other end, clutching the balustrade with both fists.

Fie's sandal-nails gave a particular horrid whine as she set foot onto the marble bridge. Wagon wheels rattled after her, the oxen lowing with unease as their hooves clicked and scraped without purchase. More scratching echoed across the water as Crow after Crow marched onto the stone.

Someone tapped her shoulder.

"Fie." Tavin's voice was almost too quiet to pick out. "Something's wrong."

She cast a look about and found the lordlings to her right, still walking like they owned the fortress. "What?"

"The lord-governor should walk out to greet us."

"You think he'd walk out for Crows?" Hangdog barked out a laugh.

"I'm telling you—" Tavin's voice rose.

Fie turned to hush them both—

And froze.

Their Hawk escort had lined up across the bridge at their back, a bristling wall between the Crows and the only way out.

Fie heard a scuffle and whipped around. Hangdog had shoved the lordlings out in front of the wagon, stripping off his mask and theirs.

"They're here!" he shouted as Pa cursed and yanked on the reins. "I did what you wanted—"

An arrow sank, soft and immediate, into Hangdog's eye. He crumpled to the ground.

The world went silent. Fie stared at the impossible heap of black fabric and limbs that ought to have been Hangdog.

Another arrow whistled past, carving a stripe of searing pain above her elbow before it clattered against marble. She cried out.

A bellow echoed down the bridge like thunder: "*The queen wants him alive!*"

"Get behind the wagon!" Pa shouted, scrambling out of the driver's seat. Another arrow struck one of the oxen. It screamed and leapt forward, crashing into the other ox and sending the wagon skidding over the stone as Barf screeched inside.

Someone seized Fie's arm and hauled her behind the shuddering wagon. Another scream ripped through the air. This time it sounded like Wretch.

Pa emerged, fist locked around his string of teeth.

"This wasn't—He must have gone over to Rhusana—" Tavin's arm still wound round hers. The other kept Jasimir kneeling on the ground, where arrows couldn't reach. "We have to get out—"

Pa shook his head.

"I'm a marked man," he said, cutting his chief's string loose with a chilling calm. "Those Vultures could follow my witch-sign through all twelve hells. There's no 'we' here, Lord Hawk."

Pa threw the string over the wagon and closed his eyes.

Two Phoenix teeth roared to life in Fie's senses. There was a terrible crack and a blast of heat. A wall of fire swept around the bridge, circling the Crows.

"There's only you," said Pa.

When, not if.

Fie finally, terribly understood.

She found her voice. "Pa—no—"

"You get out, get as far from here as you can." He thrust the broken sword to her, and she hated it, hated the weight of it, hated the sudden flash of two deadly edges now in her hands. "Stay out of sight. Burn as many teeth as you have to." His bag of teeth fell into her arms with a horrible thud.

They were Pa's teeth, they were his sword, he was the chief, this was all wrong—

He gripped her shoulders. "You have to keep the oath, Fie."

"No—Pa, I'm no chief, I can't!"

"You have to keep the—"

An arrow pierced the flames from behind, striking Pa in the shoulder. He dropped to a knee as the fire sputtered.

Beyond the golden flames, Fie saw a towering shadow, crowned in a helmet ragged with notches.

"Get them out," Pa spat.

Fie shook her head, frantic. "No, *no*—"

Tavin dragged Jasimir to his feet, wrapped an arm around Fie's waist, and said, "Yes, chief."

She'd forgotten how damned fast he moved.

Fie saw walls of gilded fire. A break in the flames. A saw-edged Vulture helm. Pa's face cracking into desperation.

And then she saw naught but blood-soaked sunset as the prince, the Hawk, and the Merciful Crow tumbled over the side of the bridge, down to the black water below.

PART TWO

TRAITORS

— AND —

CHIEFS

CHAPTER NINE

— IN THIS LIFE OR THE NEXT —

FIE HAD NEVER EXPECTED TO DIE QUIET.

Young, maybe. On the end of a sword, also likely. And doing what she did best: picking a fight over something easier left alone.

She did not expect to die swallowed whole. But the Fan River had done just that.

The river churned with thrashing limbs and arrows like viper strikes, gurgling through the sides of her mask. Yet beyond her glassblack eyes lay naught but the bottomless dark of the reservoir sucking at her heels.

Then Pa's bag of teeth floated past.

Something snapped. She fought to catch at the leather—but Pa's sword slipped free—she couldn't lose it, she had to get them back to Pa, back to the chief—

The blade bit into her palms and fingers, and red bloomed in the water. She didn't care. She'd return Pa's sword or die sinking to the bottom of this damned well.

Someone yanked at her hood, dragging her up until she broke the surface. The silence of the river shattered into howling alarm horns and a roar of falling water.

"Hang on!" someone shouted before a wave slopped over Fie. The river wouldn't give her up easy, stuffing watery fingers through the mask and into her teeth, into her nose, drowning her in wet mint leaves. The current twisted her round and round until one hip slammed into a rough stone edge.

And there the river changed its mind, flinging her away, down into a slick blur of blue tile and reeling red sky. Some ironclad panic kept her bloody arms locked around the tooth bag and the broken sword, not caring that one wrong twist could gut her like a fish. She couldn't lose Pa's teeth, she couldn't lose the chief's blade, she couldn't, she couldn't—

Fie tumbled into one of the boys' backs with a solid, wet smack.

Tavin swore and yanked her to her feet on startling steady ground. She gulped for air but only choked on more water trapped in her mask's beak, doubling over. Hands pushed her hood back and worked about her hair until the mask fell loose.

The world spun tipsy around her as she fought for breath and bearings alike: bright tile, bewildered faces, bare skin. Bathing steps. The current had pushed them into one of the reservoir's drainage chutes, down to a plateau where the chutes broke across bathing steps. A mosaic of a dead Swan god frowned elegantly down at her from his perch on a mother-of-pearl moon.

Another chorus of alarm horns shrieked to life somewhere above.

"Here." Tavin tossed her mask aside and reached for the blade and the bag. She jerked back, blood threading her fingers. He winced. "You're hurting yourself—"

"I don't care."

"Please, Fie." He glanced over his shoulder, and if it weren't wholly impossible, she'd think he sounded something near desperate. "You don't have to let go, just let me help you tie them down. It'll be a lot harder to help your father without fingers."

Help Pa. She had to help Pa. She managed a stiff nod and let him pull the cloak from her shaking shoulders, then handed the sword and bag over, blood dripping down her wrists.

"I'll heal you once we're in the clear," he muttered, tearing off a strip of crowsilk and wrapping it around the blade, then knotting it at her belt along with the tooth bag. "If we're lucky, you won't pick up an infection . . . and here's company. Go."

Shouts and the stamp of Hawk boots rattled the air as Tavin pushed her and Jasimir into the next water chute. Fie plummeted down tile and stone worn smooth beneath years of water, rooftops and brick walls flashing by, alarm horns droning above the crash of water.

The chute spat her out into open air. For a tripe-twisting moment, tile and sea and upturned faces reeled below—then she plunged into the waters of Third Market's canal. Her head missed the edge of a cargo barge by a finger-span; her breath erupted from her all at once in a bubbled wheeze. One bloody hand grabbed the edge of the barge. It rocked and veered more than it ought to. She broke the surface and squinted up.

Tavin had landed on the barge's crates. The Gull sailor swung his barge pole up, yelling about bone thieves on his goods. In turn the Hawk tossed his sodden cloak in the Gull's face, grabbed the other end of the pole, neatly pushed the man into the canal, and slid down to the barge's deck.

"Where is he?" Tavin asked as he pulled Fie up. He didn't mean the sailor.

"Here." Jasimir climbed aboard at the barge's other end and darted to put the crates between himself and Third Market. "We can't stay on—"

"I know." Tavin took Fie's hands in his own and closed his eyes. A dreadful sharp itch rolled through every gash. She gasped, shuddering, and Tavin let go. "I'm sorry, I can't do more than stop the bleeding right now. Jas, cloak." Tavin tore the crowsilk into yet more strips and wound them around Fie's hands as alarm horns split the air anew. He twisted to look around, frowning. "On my signal, we jump to the street and—"

An arrow cut off the end of his plan, thudding into the crate by his ear.

He stared. "Consider that my signal."

They scrambled off the barge and into Third Market, Fie's wet sandals crunching against uneven brick. Alarm horns wailed through the tents. Shoppers halted in place, peering about for the cause. One man found it when Tavin shoved him out of their way and into a plantain stand. Curses and shouts trailed in their wake.

Then sun caught steel again, flitting through bodies at the end of the market ahead. Screams burst in the air like fireworks. Fie looked behind and found more Hawks closing in, barreling through a panicking crowd.

Tavin grabbed her shoulder. "You have to hide us."

"No," Jasimir cut in. "If we get separated, we'll lose one another."

Fie couldn't think. Help Pa. She had to help Pa.

Tavin muttered a curse, looking wildy about the market. His gaze lit upon a tent. "Watch Jas," he barked, and lunged.

A moment later a chorus of shattering ceramic scraped, dissonant, against the alarm horns. Fie caught the acid tang of flashburn and lantern oil.

So did everyone nearby.

The crowd's brewing panic boiled over into a full-blown stampede, sending a tidal wave of human flesh into the oncoming Hawks. One table tipped, then another. The deadly avalanche smashed and splattered across the street as people fled, as Fie's eyes ran, as her lungs burned, as she stumbled back.

Then—then, the sparks.

A blue phantom hissed across the oil and flashburn faster than a heartbeat. Forks of blazing white fire exploded from the streets, waves of heat stripping the river from Fie's face in puffs of steam.

Tavin burst from the flames. "The alley—go, *go*—"

The three of them bolted into the cramped back street. A moment later Fie heard a sound like breath being sucked through a flute.

The bricks beneath her feet leapt and shuddered as white light and thunder rocked the alleyway.

The tent. The whole tent of flashburn and lamp oil had gone off.

Dead gods be kind.

Tavin towed them farther down the alley, sheltering behind a cold communal oven. His hands were shaking. Adrenaline? Fear? Both, like her? Her blood still streaked his palms. "This is our chance. We can throw them off the trail."

I have to look after my own.

All of Fie's own were still in the Floating Fortress.

All of Fie's own might have died on that bridge—

"Fie." Jasimir's voice brought her back. "Could you create a diversion with a Peacock tooth?"

"Blowing a smoking crater in half of Third Market isn't enough of a diversion?" Tavin asked.

The prince shook his head. "Not like that. An illusion they'll chase instead. Can you do it?"

Could she? Fie pressed into the cold plaster wall. Peacock witches were a naka a dozen; she had enough of their teeth in her string.

She had more than that.

You're going to be a chief.

She saw Pa, holding out the sword to cut her first throat. She still wasn't ready. Pa, holding out the bag of teeth.

Look after your own.

"Fie?"

Tavin's voice dragged her back again. He looked at her like he had a thousand things to say, things like *I'm sorry* and *I know* and *Please* and, above all, *I need you.*

But only the strongest survived: "Can you do it?"

In answer, she pushed a Sparrow tooth free from her string with aching fingers. "Stay here."

Fie ducked into what remained of the street, shrouded in smoke and soot and a Sparrow Birthright for good measure. Mercifully, she saw no bodies, only flames dancing fitful across the broken bricks like Lovely Rhensa and his fallen foes. Had Tavin timed it so? Or had the lack of casualties been a solitary scrap of good fortune?

Hawks had started braving the dying fire, pushing at the edges of the flashburn. Fie swerved away from one particular bold guard, prying a Peacock witch-tooth from her string, then slipped behind a charred tent and let the Sparrow tooth go.

The Peacock witch-tooth kindled as it rolled betwixt her palms, a vivid song of whim and majesty. A grandfather, a storyteller, weaving legends of the ancient heroes to chubby, wide-eyed children by the hearth. The tooth's echo of him laughed with glee at the tale Fie passed on.

With a flick of her wrist, she tossed the tooth into the canal.

And with a twist of her will, three figures flickered into sight: a prince, a Hawk, and a Crow girl, clambering atop the barrels of a cargo barge. Shouts rose up from the guards. The three ghosts started like frightened deer, leaping from one barge to the next.

Boots and steel rumbled past. The Hawk guards were on the hunt. And thanks to the Peacock tooth leading the illusion down the canal as the current bore it along, they'd follow those ghosts until they learned better.

Once the guards had passed, she slipped back through the smoke. A pillar of fire still clawed at the darkening heavens where the oil tent had stood. A few paces off, a Gull woman watched it burn, tears cutting tracks through the soot on her stricken face.

The lordlings appeared from the hazy alley and motioned for her to follow, then set off for the stairs to Fourth Market. Fie couldn't say whether they knew the damage they'd done to get away; only that as they left Third Market behind, neither looked back, not even once.

———◆———

They took a long, halting way through Fourth Market, veering from guards as the afternoon's pack of bodies scattered into smaller crowds. Fog rose as night swallowed the sun, and a sluggish bay breeze wormed through Fie's hair, damp and warm as a drunkard's breath.

Tavin led them down through the market, pausing at each water-lift and drain chute, then finally stopped at a chute behind a shuttered stall. "Wait here."

He hopped onto an empty barge moored near the stall, then pressed his hand to a tile on the canal's far wall. It sank into its grout with a deliberate click. As he pulled his hand back, Fie caught the faint outline of a hammer engraved there.

The water cascading down the chute thinned to a trickle, then to a steady drip. Tavin pushed on the tiles below the chute's spout. A citizen-size panel swung inward with a grinding, sandy grate, revealing pitch-black within. Tavin held up a hand—*wait*—and climbed inside.

"Maintenance tunnels," Jasimir said. "Of course."

Firelight sparked in the dark, and a moment later, Tavin motioned for them to follow. Fie hopped onto the barge and let him pull her into the tunnel, mindful of the sword and tooth bag still knotted secure at her hip. Once Jasimir joined them, Tavin pulled a chain dangling by the entrance. The ceramic panel slid back into place, and with it fell a brutal quiet.

Tavin plucked a burning torch from the wall and lit another that he passed to the prince. Then he led them down a corridor, emerging in a round room where broad terra-cotta banks bracketed a course of slow dark water.

"The reservoir drains into irrigation channels for the Fan," Prince Jasimir said, swinging his torch about to survey the area. "They'll look for us to make a break for the gates, not shelter in the city. We should be safe here."

"That's the idea." Tavin dropped his torch into a sconce jutting from rumples of yellow fungi, let out a long, heavy breath, and then sank to the floor. A week ago, the prince might have turned up his nose at the slimy brick and suspicious puddles. Now he joined Fie and Tavin as one more exhausted heap, shoals in a sea of torch-lit gloom.

"May I?"

Fie blinked and found Tavin pointing to her tattered hands. "Aye," she croaked. He took one and began peeling away the stiff makeshift bandages, murmuring an apology each time she flinched at threads snagging on her wounds.

She'd never been tended to by a Hawk before today. She'd expected healing to be a relief. Instead when Tavin closed his eyes, an awful heat like nettles spread across her broken flesh.

To distract herself, Fie plucked at her string of teeth, over bones of Peacock and Sparrow, Phoenix and Crane. Then her fingers stalled on two milk teeth knotted side by side.

One tooth sat cold, a distant shade where its spark had been an hour before.

That tooth belonged to Hangdog.

The other still simmered with life.

That one belonged to Pa.

How long did he have? How long did any of her kin have?

"Once we're ready, we can take the tunnels out."

Tavin's voice bulled through the quiet. Fie and Jasimir both started.

"What?" Fie asked.

Tavin let her hand go. "Done with this side. Let's see the other. And the graze on your arm."

She rolled up her sleeve, wincing at the crackle of blood. "What do you mean, 'out'?" she asked again.

"The city gates will be buttoned up tight for days," he said, unwinding the rags from her fingers. "And most of the merchant ships are moored across the bay, so—"

"No. What do you mean, 'out'?" Fie jabbed her free thumb up. Stinging rolled up her fingers once more. "I'm getting my kin back."

Tavin's face stiffened. "Fie . . . there may not be much to get—"

"Pa." She pinched his tooth between her thumb and forefinger until it ground against her own knuckle-bone. "He's . . . he's still alive."

The hush that followed ached near as much as Fie did.

"He swore an oath," Tavin said at last.

It was Fie's turn to stiffen. She turned a hard stare on the Hawk. "What," she hissed, "does *that* mean?"

"I think you know what it means."

Fie did. She was a Crow; she knew a Money Dance when she heard one.

Jasimir sat up. "Tav——"

Fie jerked her arm free. It started to bleed again. "If you think I'm going to leave my family with some monster——"

"Your father told me if anything happened to him——" Tavin began.

"You two happened to him."

"So did your oath."

Her heels dug into the earthen floor. "We said we'd get you two to Cheparok——"

"Your father swore a Covenant oath to get Jasimir to his allies, in this life or the next." Frost slivered through Tavin's voice. He wouldn't look at her.

That only maddened her more. A Money Dance worked only when you knew your worth. When you knew what you were owed.

But they both knew what she owed him and his prince: nothing.

"We told her we—*I* had allies in Cheparok." Jasimir broke his silence. "The Crows kept their end of the deal."

"Really?" Tavin slashed a still-shaking hand at the moldering walls. "Does this look like the Floating Fortress to you, Jas? Did I miss you somehow mustering an army in the last ten minutes?"

The prince recoiled, cheeks darkening, but his jaw stiffened. "It doesn't matter. They got us this far. I can't ask for more."

"We don't have a choice." The wire around Tavin's words pulled taut. "The Oleander Gentry are about to own the throne. We all know how that ends."

The prince had no answer for that.

Fie did. "Pull that 'we' out of your mouth. My kin got you to the allies you asked for. And your damned *allies* shot arrows through——" The words turned to gravel on her tongue.

Hangdog's tooth stayed cold and quiet. Gone.

All of it was gone.

She had to get it back, she had to get them out, she had to get out—

"I'm sorry." Jasimir's hands tangled together, eyes scanning the dirt as if searching for words. "We . . . He said he'd take us in. I don't know what happened, why . . . If I just had my fire, I could have—"

He meant it to be an apology. Something to pacify her. Instead, a snarling tiger in Fie roared free.

"*I don't give a damn,*" she spat. "Those are my people, and I'm supposed to be their chief. And now *I'm* supposed to abandon my kin, *I'm* the one who has to save royals who haven't lifted a finger to protect me or mine?" She tottered to her feet.

"Get scummed." The ground swayed beneath her. She staggered toward the corridor anyway. "Both of you can get scummed."

"Fie—"

"Look after your own," she snarled. "And I'll look after mine."

Her hand closed around the bag of teeth.

Tavin's hand closed around her good arm. "You're going to get yourself killed."

"I'm going to get my pa," she shot back. "And I'm getting what's left of my people. And I'm getting my damn cat. Let go before I make you."

Tavin did, but only to slide past, planting himself between her and the way back.

"Move," she snarled.

Tavin had that look on his face again, the one that left a thousand things unsaid. A hard edge cut through his voice. "None of us want this, Fie. Not for you, not for us. But Jas and I don't have a chance against Rhusana without you. And neither do your people."

Pain shot through Fie's bloody hand as she snatched up Pa's rag-swaddled sword and pointed the broken end at Tavin, loose threads trembling. "Don't you dare. *You* brought my people into this. Don't you *dare.*"

He didn't stir, watching her. This time the look on his face said a solitary thing:

What do you want, Fie?

She knew full well how fast he could move. That if he wanted, Pa's sword would be on the bricks and she'd be next to it. But he knew how many Phoenix teeth were in that bag. And if she wanted, she could light him ablaze, light this city ablaze, light Sabor ablaze from mountain to coast, all before she hit the ground.

Almost all of her wanted to. Wanted out, out of this city, out of the deal, out of the oath she'd danced her way into.

Crows had one rule. *Look after your own.*

Her own were on that bridge—

Her own were scattered across Sabor.

"Your father said to keep the oath," Tavin said, staring down the broken end of the sword.

"*Damn you,*" Fie screamed.

He stepped away from the corridor.

What do you want, Fie?

She wanted to throw Pa's sword so far, she could forget she'd ever seen it saw at a throat. She wanted to kick Tavin's teeth out and use them to heal herself of everything Hawks had done to her today. She wanted to teach the lord-governor of the Fan the price for crossing a Crow witch.

Fie lurched forward. Caught herself. The hallway gaped two paces ahead. Her hand burned, bled on the hilt of the sword. She stumbled one more pace.

Give them fire, hissed the Phoenix teeth.

Get out, her gut hissed back.

All of her wanted to.

But it wasn't her oath to break. It was Pa's.

It wasn't just her price to pay. It was every Crow's.

She could burn it all down and run. But that was the way of dead royals who got what they wanted and didn't have to give a damn who paid for it.

Fie stood, motionless, for a long moment.

Then she stuck the sword through her sash, slumped against the wall, and stuck out a bloody hand.

And at that moment, Fie found what her Chief voice sounded like.

"Fix my hand. And tell me where in the twelve hells we're going."

CHAPTER TEN

— CHIEF VOICE —

"The marovar."

"What?" Jasimir straightened. "We'll never make it in time. And Aunt Draga hates me."

Tavin carefully took hold of Fie's arm once more. "She doesn't hate you," he said, brow furrowing. Heat burrowed into Fie's muscles again. "She's master-general of the King's Legions. She doesn't have enough time in the day to waste it on hating you."

"Last time she made the march to the palace, she called Father gilded dung."

"So she doesn't like the king," Tavin amended. "She serves him anyway. And that doesn't mean she hates you."

"She said I was so soft, they must not have gilded me yet."

"See? She likes you. Besides, she's sworn to the Hawk code. Rule number one is 'I will serve my nation and the throne above all.' If you're looking for loyalty, the master-general would roll across a league of rusty nails before she refused a royal command."

Fie gnawed on her free thumb-tip, chewing the notion over. What would Pa say about this? Walking direct into a Hawk nest?

Worse than walking into the queen's trap? Which part of it would get Pa killed? How many of her Crows had it killed already?

She swallowed hard. Pa's tooth still hummed on her string. He was alive, and she would have to be a chief for him. She could dance in the hells of her own moods later.

Hawks. The Marovar. The easy answer. That alone bode ill. "There anywhere else we might try?"

Tavin donned his blank face, the one that said he paid great mind where he treaded. "The regional governors are all Peacocks, except for in the Marovar. If even Jas's cousin has fallen in with Rhusana . . ."

Jasimir's face dropped. "That means we can't trust the Peacocks. Any of them."

"Oh no, not the Peacocks," Fie drawled, "they've been *such* a boon."

Tavin pretended not to hear. "And their Hawks answer to regional governors. So that rules out both castes. And Rhusana came from the Swan caste, so they'll back her——"

"Fine, fine," Fie interrupted. "I get it, we're rutted, it's the Marovar or nothing. But what's to keep Tatterhelm from puzzling that out himself and beating us there?"

Jasimir flinched. "She's got a point."

"She usually does," Tavin said under his breath.

"*She's* right here," Fie snapped.

"Apologies. You're right, he'll expect us to go straight to the master-general. But we can use that to throw him off. Markahns run every fort in the Marovar, so any of them will take us in and send word to Draga.

From here the nearest fortress is Trikovoi, in the southern end of the mountains. If we make it, we'll be safe."

"We?" she asked. "Or you two? I've dealt bad with enough Hawk scummers for one moon."

Tavin's mouth twisted. "You'll be fine while you're with us," he admitted. "And Draga. Draga hates unpaid debts."

"That makes three people I can trust, out of every fort in the Marovar." Fie gave him a long, cold scowl that said plain how much faith she put in those three. "What of the rest?"

The look Tavin gave her said even plainer that she was right to doubt. "The rest know what happens if you cross Draga." He stood. "We need to get as far from Cheparok as we can tonight. Are we ready to move?"

"Lead the way," Prince Jasimir said, collecting his torch.

Tavin held a hand out to Fie.

Something hitched in her gut.

I did what you wanted. Handog'd yelled that and taken an arrow in the eye in payment. It didn't take a scholar to square out who he'd been serving on the bridge instead of the Crows.

Yet she was the one walking away from her people now.

She forced her fist to uncurl and let Tavin help her up.

The three of them worked their way along the dark channels, through winding corridors and down crumbling stairs. Sometimes curious rat-shrills pierced the dark ahead, but they left only bones and dung by the time Fie arrived. Finally they reached a long drainage channel scarce as tall as her waist.

"This is the last," Tavin promised behind her, dousing his torch. "Then we're out."

Out.

Pa wouldn't make it out of the city tonight.

Pa wanted her to keep the oath.

Fie steeled herself and eased into the water.

And so the three of them left Cheparok the way they'd arrived: crawling on hand and knee.

Fie didn't know how long she splashed through the empty dark before a slivery silver glow sliced over the water's surface ahead. She crawled faster and faster—

And found herself below a square of iron lace. Tavin reached up to the middle of the grate and turned some unseen panel. The iron creaked and shuddered. With a heave, he shoved the grate aside.

For a moment, Fie could only stare at the night above, dusted in a belt of stars, buckled by a newborn Peacock Moon. She'd seen it near every night of her life, yet . . .

Her people, her home. If they could see the moon now, it would be through a cage of rooftops and plaster.

This was not like any other night of her life.

Tavin's hand jabbed into her sight. "Fie?"

She let him pull her up one more time.

———◆———

The walls of Cheparok loomed colossal behind them, skirted in a sour, briny fog. Blots of lantern-light singed holes in the mist, dotting an outdoor market along the eastern bank of the Fan River, just like the one before the western side's gate for Common Castes.

Fie's belly churned, half from nerves, half from hunger. Her frown dug deeper as she followed the lordlings into the haze.

Even if they could keep one step ahead of the Vultures, it would take near three weeks to get to the south end of the Marovar. And all they had were the boys' blades, Pa's broken sword, and a bag of very inedible teeth.

Jasimir had said days ago that the king could be dead before the end of Peacock Moon. Fie wasn't sure they'd make it that long, either.

Fie's stomach growled again as they passed slabs of spiced shark and onion searing on a griddle, kettles of honeyed maize-meal, stacks of buttered panbread, and more, all meant for those with coin. She tried not to look. Her nose, however, could not be leashed in.

A Crow shrine. They'd find a Crow shrine outside the city and see what could be foraged from the viatik stash. Fie had managed on an empty belly plenty of times.

A woman guarding a griddle cracked an egg over sizzling lentils, then rained a pink glitter of sea salt and paprika into the pan.

Fie bit her lip.

Tavin paused at the stall a moment, then hurried on. A few steps later, a calamity erupted at their backs, pots and pans clanging to the ground amid a flurry of swearing.

"Don't look," Tavin mumbled to them and sidled behind a stall, then turned his hands out. Three dumplings sat in each palm. "Found us some dinner."

Fie's eyes widened. "Did you steal those?"

"Borrowed," Tavin said. "Relieved. Liberated."

"So stolen," the prince said, flat. His hand paused halfway to a dumpling.

"Academically speaking." Tavin waggled his fingers, straining for his old humor. "But I have it on good authority that they taste exactly like dumplings obtained through more orthodox means."

Fie knew square how Pa felt about thieves.

She didn't know if the hunger did it, or the wear of the long day, but either way her Chief voice came back. With a vengeance.

"You ken me, aye?" Fie jabbed a finger at him. "See how I walked through that whole market without taking a damned thing? The last thing we need right now is an angry merchant bringing Hawks down on our heads."

"Only if they catch you," Tavin said with a haggard grin.

She didn't smile back. "If you're fixing to keep me along as your stand-in for chief, then you'd best act like it. Steal what you please when you're not mumming as a Crow. But if you're going to keep rolling our fortune-bones over something slight as an empty gut, I'd rather turn around right here and go try my luck with the Floating Fortress."

Tavin raised an eyebrow. "There are shorter ways to say 'I don't want a dumpling.'"

"How about 'don't steal, bastard boy'?" she shot back. "Is 'steal again and I'm out' too many words for you?"

His grin faded. "No, chief."

She gave a stiff nod. And then she swiped two dumplings. "Rule number two: don't waste food."

Prince Jasimir had the decency to look faintly disapproving as he also took two.

Before Fie could take a bite, she caught splinters of torchlight on steel in the corner of her eye. A pair of Hawks strolled down through the market, spears tipped against their shoulders.

She shoved her thieved dumplings into her bag and jabbed an elbow at Tavin. He blinked up around a mouthful and sighed, resigned. "It's that sort of day, isn't it?"

He stuffed the second dumpling into his mouth and led them away from the road, into the great swells of grass-studded sand betwixt them and the bay. Fie couldn't say how long they stumbled through the dunes, sharp seagrass whipping at her legs, only that the walls of Cheparok had shrunk too far and yet not enough by the time they stopped.

"Here." Weariness sapped the expected lilt from Tavin's voice as he gestured to a copse of squat sandpines at the edge of the beach. "This is . . . this is good."

Jasimir didn't say anything, just staggered to a patch of seagrass and dropped. Fie cast a last look behind her, then found her own sandy hassock and allowed her legs to give out. The hilt of Pa's sword jabbed into her ribs until she laid it aside.

Then, finally, she pulled the dumplings from her bag and took a bite.

Pa should have salted it for her first, as a Crow chief did.

Pa wasn't there.

The pastry dough was dry, the maize and tripe gooey. It glued to the inside of her mouth and stuck there as she chewed, a thick wad that hurt as she gulped it down. A faint snore said Jasimir had already fallen asleep.

Through the bottlebrushes of sandpine needles, she saw the pale streak of sand, a gray blur of ocean, and, too far away, the unyielding walls of Cheparok.

The next bite was harder to chew, harder to swallow.

A faraway part of her wished for a drink of water. Then the absurdity hit. She'd had plenty of water today, from the gentry's freshest reservoir to the canals of Third Market. She'd just been drowning at the time, was all.

A bubble of broken laughter turned to a shuddering cough, then a sob, and then Fie curled in on herself as she drowned again, this time in salt and fire running from her eyes, from her nose, from her mouth.

She wanted a campfire, she wanted a kettle of stew, she wanted Madcap's jests and Swain's nebbish sneer and Wretch's scoffs. She wanted walking songs and salt. She wanted Pa's voice.

She wanted her damned cat.

Fingers brushed her quaking shoulder, then vanished, a misstep corrected. Sand shifted at her right as someone sat.

"I'm sorry," Tavin said.

Part of her shriveled with shame at weeping like this before him. The rest was too raw and furious to give a damn.

"I'm sorry about my cousin in the market," he continued. "I'm sorry about my . . . about the Hawks, how they treated—how—how we treat you. And I'm sorry for making you keep the oath. I didn't—I don't—" His voice hitched, and he cut himself off a moment. "Rhusana gave the Crows over to the Oleanders, but Jas and I brought your family into this mess ourselves. I'm so sorry."

She wanted to hit him. She wanted him to stay. She wanted him to be speaking true.

But the weeping didn't go away. Neither did he.

The words spilled out like her tears, burning, unstoppable. "I hate it. I hate how, how we're always the ones who have to keep our mouths shut and take it and keep doing our job, because we're *Crows*. You can kick us around anytime because we all know if we kick back, you'll just put on some white powder, call yourselves Oleanders, and cut every one of us down."

She couldn't stop.

"And even if you don't, you just look the other way, and when they're done you say we provoked them, we brought it down on our heads, *we're* the ones who ought to hold our tongues, *we* ought to shut up and take the high road, *we* always pay so you don't have to."

Everything burned saltwater.

"And now *I* have to abandon my family, *I* have to save someone who didn't give a damn for my caste until it was convenient. Your prince's crown is coming out of *my* hide." She hated herself for dancing up the oath. She hated Pa for making her the one to keep it. She hated Tavin for his silence, for not leaving, for driving her to spew up the sickening fire in her heart instead of letting it break her down to ash.

"I'm sorry," he said again.

It made her angrier, somehow. "You're just as bad," she snarled. "It's easy, isn't it? Believing whatever the prince tells you to believe. You keep telling yourself he has to be right because otherwise you're dying for someone who isn't worth it. You see how we're treated on his family's watch, and you still tell yourself he'll be a good king."

"I . . ." His voice cracked. "I can't answer for—for Jas. But I swear if we make it out of this, I'll do everything I can to help you. And yours."

"Why should I trust you?" Her knees near swallowed her words. "Why should I trust *any* of you?"

A long wind dragged through the needles of the sandpines before Tavin said, bleak, "I don't know."

Then he stood, one more shadow tearing edges into the night sky.

"I'll take watch." He stumbled toward a break in the trees. "Get some rest."

Emptiness curdled where he'd been. Fie swallowed, then scrubbed her face dry with tight fists and coiled down in the lukewarm sand.

Sleep dragged her off despite the hurricane in her head and her heart, and didn't let her go until day broke across her face.

Fie woke to a mouthful of sand, a sliver of dawn slicing through the sandpines, and a strange sound drifting through the cool air. The tide had come in, pushing waves up only a score of paces from their camp. At the copse's edge, Tavin sat, eyes on the sunrise, humming. If it was a song, she didn't know it, halting and uneven, a melody meant for one voice alone.

Fie rolled to her knees. Tavin looked to her, the song halting. Something flashed through his eyes, something neither of them had words for, still somewhere between *I need you* and *I'm sorry*.

Then his head whipped about to stare at Cheparok. He shuffled back into cover. "Someone's coming," he muttered, and shook Jasimir's shoulder.

Fie crept to the edge, peering through the brush. Two figures emerged from the dunes, looking to and fro before settling on the sand-pines.

The sand at Fie's back hissed as the prince sat up. "I think the one in gray is a local," Tavin whispered. "The other is Viimo. She's one of Rhusana's best trackers."

Fie guessed Viimo to be the ruddy-faced skinwitch with a cap of pale curls who looked a few years older than them.

A skinwitch. A Vulture. Fie's heart began to pound.

The woman shushed the man at her side, then reached for a belt of narrow iron cylinders.

A Vulture. One of Tatterhelm's trackers. One of the queen's best.

Jasimir inhaled sharp. "That's a flare. She's calling for—"

They never found out. Tavin thrust out a hand, and Viimo and her guide fell to their knees, frozen.

Fie stared. She'd forgotten the Hawk blood Birthright meant more than healing.

"Hurry," Tavin gritted through his teeth, and she saw red blooming in his eyes as vessels burst. "Knock them out, tie them up, whatever you do—hurry."

Fie's heartbeat roared in her ears.

Jasimir started to climb through the copse. Fie beat him to it.

She hurled herself at Viimo, knocking her to the sand, a furious scream rising above the roar of the sea. Fie clawed and scratched and rained blows upon any flash of skinwitch she saw. Her own fists split at the knuckles, but she didn't care, spitting curse after curse through the blood and the pain until Jasimir pulled her off.

She'd been in a handful of scrapes in her life; she'd lived a handful of scrapes through the teeth of the dead. She wasn't a particular gifted fighter, for that did not a long-lived Crow make.

However, she found it cruelly easy to hit someone who couldn't hit back. Perhaps that was why the other castes liked it so.

"Not what I had in mind, but close enough." Tavin pinned Viimo facedown in the sand, one knee on her back. Jasimir tossed him a length of hemp rope from the other man, lying bound and unconscious nearby. "Viimo. It's been a while."

"Choke on horseshit, you little bastard," Viimo spat back, face scored with scratches.

Fie yanked Viimo's head up by her blond curls. "How many Crows did you kill?"

Viimo frowned. "As in today? The last year? Got to be a mite more specific."

"Fie left you both your eyes," Tavin said, mild. "All things considered, I'm fairly sure she's willing to revoke that decision if you don't start talking."

Viimo snorted at him. "You ain't got the tripes for it, Hawkling. And even if you did, you ain't got the time. How long you reckon before Tatterhelm comes crawling right up your—"

"Then we cut to the point." Fie let go and pried a tooth from her string. A Crane witch answered her call, an ancient magistrate whose righteous fury resonated with Fie's own wrath, ready to ring the truth in Viimo like a bell. "Sit her up."

Tavin pulled Viimo to her knees. The skinwitch's face soured when she spied the tooth. "Ugh. Cheater."

"How many Crows survived your ambush yesterday?" Fie asked.

The Vulture fought at first, her eyes burning, lips twisted shut. But the Crane Birthright of honesty would not be denied, and neither would Fie, and so the truth flossed through Viimo's clenched teeth: "Ten. Not counting your dead traitor boy, o'course."

Fie's heart sank. She'd lost one Crow. "There should be eleven. Who . . . who died?"

"Dead gods if I know." The skinwitch shrugged. Fie near went for her eyes again. "But it'll be nine soon. One's well on her way to wolf-feed."

"Who?" Fie's voice came out higher than she wanted. The Crane tooth slipped. "Is she wounded?"

Viimo gave Fie a look of disbelief. "No, just pining for her home-lands." Fie yanked the tooth tighter, and Viimo grimaced. "Of *course* she's wounded. Oldest woman in your kin, caught a few too many arrows from us on the bridge. She'll take water, but she ain't got much more'n a week left in her."

Wretch. It had to be. Wretch, who'd helped Fie practice all her whistle signals, who'd schooled her in laceroot and counting days and moons, who'd been the last one to cut Fie's hair before this terrible oath. And she was dying among Vultures.

". . . brought her water?" Tavin asked at the edge of Fie's ken.

The skinwitch looked away. "Aye. Dead hostage's no good."

The Crane tooth had slipped from Fie, but she rallied it again.

"Why take my kin hostage?" Fie demanded.

Viimo cracked a bloody, split-lipped grin. "You're the girl with all the teeth. And we already talked over one Crow chiefling. Maybe we can deal with you, too."

Tavin reached for her elbow, then caught himself. "Fie—"

She ignored him. "What did you promise Hangdog?"

Viimo shook her head. "You don't want it, chiefling. Help me bring these boys in and—"

The skinwitch had wormed out of the Crane witch-tooth's hold. Fie bore down with every scrap of rage in her bones. "*What did you promise him?*"

"He didn't want to be a Crow no more." The words burst from Viimo in a wheeze. "One of our scouts caught him a few nights back. Promised him he'd be spared, that he'd never have to burn another body again, never deal with Oleanders no more. All he had to do was give up the prince, and we'd forget he was a Crow."

The Crane witch-tooth slipped from Fie's hold in the stunned quiet. For a moment all she heard was the rush of the sea, the whine of the gulls kiting about overhead.

Viimo spat a bloody wad in the sand. "Guess he ain't a Crow no more now he's dead."

Fie sucked in a breath. She reached for Pa's sword.

"Wait—" Tavin threw a hand out.

She flinched back.

It was habit, really, old as her bones. A Hawk was a Hawk, and she jumped at any sudden moves. Even one who said he was sorry.

Even one who stared at her now, horrified, as he kenned true what that meant for the first time.

He swallowed. "Please . . . just . . . keep using the tooth. If you can. We need to know more."

All Fie could manage was a stiff nod. The tooth droned for her once more.

"Where do you think we're going?" Jasimir asked.

Viimo's look was pure venom, but the Crane tooth reeled the words from her regardless. "To the master-general. To Dragovoi."

Tavin and Jasimir traded looks. Dragovoi was the ancestral seat of the master-general, days north of Trikovoi. An opportunity.

"What about Tatterhelm's forces?" Tavin asked. "What are we up against?"

"Tatterhelm," the Vulture cackled, "who's enough on his own." Fie gave the tooth a push, and Viimo coughed. ". . . and me. And the queen's other three trackers. Six more skinwitches by special commission. A dozen grunts. And—" She cut off. A grimace stretched the scratches on her face farther. Her cheeks turned red, then purple.

The Crane witch-tooth squealed in Fie's bones. Viimo meant to fight, to outlast. But the tooth burned on Fie's wrath, and that well ran deeper than the reservoir of Cheparok.

She thought of Hangdog throwing them to the wolves and fed the tooth.

Viimo doubled over.

"*Ghasts,*" she choked out. "The queen raised ghasts for us."

"What are ghasts?" Jasimir asked.

"And how many?" added Tavin.

Viimo didn't fight those questions at all. Instead she grinned up at them, a little spit dribbling over her split lip. "You'll see soon enough."

To that, the Crane witch-tooth gave not a single hitch.

The lordlings looked to Fie. She shook her head. A queasy pinch gnawed at her gut, like she was back in Dumosa, staring at a gilded door. "She's telling the truth."

"Splendid," Tavin sighed. "Anything else?"

Jasimir fidgeted. "Has there . . . Have you seen a cat?"

Viimo squinted at him.

"She was in the Crows' wagon," he mumbled. "Her name is Barf."

"No, Highness," Viimo said in the slow, strung-out way of one scenting a joke they weren't in on, "I ain't seen a cat."

Maybe Barf had got lucky again. Fie wouldn't roll shells on those odds, though. "We done?" At the lordlings' nods, she let the Crane tooth fade.

"Last chance, chiefling." Viimo stuck her chin out. "Swear on my pappy's skin. You want your kin back? Covenant knows you're toting enough teeth to take these boys to Tatterhelm. Easy as that. Don't even have to turn traitor like your dead lad."

"Enough," Prince Jasimir snapped, arms folded. "What do we do with her?"

An awkward silence followed. Then Tavin drew a short sword. "I'll handle it."

Viimo's eyes flashed. "All right, Hawkling, let's get it over with."

Fie thought of Wretch, draining away under Tatterhelm's watch.

And then she thought of hostages.

"Wait," she said.

"Now here's a twist." Viimo grinned up at her. "Fancy a trade, chiefling?"

"Don't be absurd." Jasimir's voice faltered the tiniest bit.

Fie worked a tooth from her string, stone-faced. "Five skinwitches on the queen's hire, six more by commission, aye?"

"Aye."

"Eleven's enough to bring the lordlings in?"

"Aye."

Fie worked a tooth from her string, stone-faced, and dropped to a knee before the skinwitch. "See this? It's a Hawk tooth. You hold this, and I'll heal you. You'll stay bound, mind. I won't deal with Vultures without my own hostage."

Viimo rolled her eyes. "Aye, I suppose that's fair."

"*Fie.*" Tavin sounded as stranded as the prince.

Fie pushed the tooth between the skinwitch's bound palms. "There. Don't drop it."

"You're turning on us, too?" the prince demanded.

Fie stood and stepped back. "No."

Pa had had her wake up Hawk teeth before, but never a witch-tooth. Blood was a fearsome Birthright; he'd told her Hawks took years to master it, that even one slip could burst a vein she'd meant to mend. A handful of older chiefs like him could call on those teeth to heal, but only with enough practice to know what they were doing.

Fie did not know what she was doing. But she knew what she wanted: a Vulture's blood.

She would never forget the scream. One moment Viimo's hands were hands; the next they were a tangle of raw red flesh and tattered skin. Viimo curled over them, sobbing.

"What are you *doing?*" Jasimir stared at Fie in horror.

"Making sure she can't track us," Fie said, grim. "She needs to touch something of ours to pick up our trail. And Tatterhelm can't leave one of Rhusana's best to starve. Probably."

"But—"

"*This,*" Fie said, tucking another tooth into a pouch on Viimo's belt, "is also a Hawk tooth. If Tatterhelm wants to make use of you again, then he'd best collect you quick, and he'd best give that tooth to Pa. Once Wretch is sorted out, perhaps Pa will have time to heal you."

"You could have had your kin," Viimo snarled.

"And the queen could have had eleven skinwitches." Fie stood. "Now we're both down to ten."

This road had caught her the way only terrible roads could. The way back lay thorny and short, and the way forward lay thorny and long, and worst of all, she knew which way Hangdog had chosen.

But Fie's own were in Cheparok, her own were all across Sabor, her own were bound up in every word of the oath. Being chief meant leaving what she wanted behind, and the Covenant didn't give a damn if she hated that, too. By daylight she could see it all too clear. And if that meant dragging the prince all the way to the feet of Master-General Draga, she'd do it.

If it meant being a chief, even of a band of two false Crows, then that was who she'd be.

When she turned to the lordlings, she found Prince Jasimir studying the sand at his feet as if it held the answer to some great trial.

Then the crown prince of Sabor drew his dagger, pulled his topknot down, and cut his hair.

"I'll be right back," he said, hollow, and strode to the surf. When he returned, his hands were empty. The last sign of his lineage was gone.

Fie's belly growled. It only sharpened her head more. Food, new cloaks, new masks. They'd need to find the nearest Crow shrine for help. And by every dead god, Fie wasn't going to march all the way to the Marovar without some damned soap-shells.

"Hawk boy." Fie donned her Chief voice. "You took watch. Are you good to put some distance down? We'll stop for rest in a few hours."

Tavin looked from the prince to her and nodded, running a hand over his face. "Yes, chief."

Fie thought of traitors. And chiefs. And the oath. And Pa.

Then she wet her lips and whistled the marching order.

CHAPTER ELEVEN

CROSSROADS

BY THE TIME THEY FOUND A CROW SHRINE, FIE HAD GNAWED through the better part of three mint plants. Like Maykala's shrine, this one lurked in the safety of trees and teeth, shrouded by both fat-leaved shrubs and Sparrow magic.

At first, Tavin and Jasimir just gaped when Fie plucked a vine from the trunk of a massive red flaybark tree and began climbing. Not that she blamed them; their hair wouldn't stand on end like hers did here, on the burial grounds of a Crow god. To most of Sabor, this would appear as one more stretch of forest.

"We're dead men, Jas," Tavin said. "She's abandoning us after all."

Fie briefly contemplated whether scalping a member of her band would make her a bad chief.

"If you're just going to laze about, then aye, I'm abandoning you." She hoisted herself up to a branch thicker around than she. "Shrine's this way."

There was a pause, then she caught, "We're *definitely* dead men, Jas. She's completely addled."

Fie ignored him and kept climbing.

Once she broke through the wards of Sparrow misdirection and a touch of Peacock glamour, the shrine itself showed clear enough. Wooden rafts coasted on swells of smooth red boughs, staggered like a poppy-sniffer's notion of Cheparok. Palm thatches tented over low walls and woven screens. A wood-carved figure twice Fie's height perched above the platforms, lashed to the tree by thick vines that wound round its crossed legs and the four wings it had in place of arms. Four faces stared her down with eyes carved like four-pointed stars, each mouth twisted into a mask of fear, wrath, mirth, or sorrow.

"Cousins." The voice struck from beneath a palm thatch like a viper, thin and swift. "What brings you to the shrine of Crossroads-Eyes?"

It was an innocent question by the ear of any other caste. Fie knew better.

"The dead gods' Covenant led us here." She'd learned the words at Pa's knee. "And the dead gods' mercy will call us onward."

A woman emerged from the shadows of the highest thatch. A faded crowsilk tunic hung loose from her wiry frame, and a twist of rag looped to cover one eye and knotted in short gray curls. The other iron-hard eye fixed down on Fie as she pulled herself onto the lowest platform.

"You're young for a chief," she observed.

Fie got to her feet. "You're old for a Crow."

The shrine-keeper's mouth cracked into a smile more tooth than humor. It skewed toothier when the boys climbed up behind Fie. "And who're these, then?"

"My band." Fie jerked a thumb over her shoulder. "Mongrel and Pissabed."

"You leave your packs below?"

"Haven't got any. We're here for a restock."

The woman's eye narrowed. "What happened?"

"Oleanders," Fie said. It was enough of the truth to stand. And any Crow knew sore well how much awful possibility could be stuffed into just that one word.

Sure enough, the shrine-keeper waved her up. "I ken that, little chief. Let's get you lot kitted out."

Fie scrambled over the broad shallow arch of a branch, following a path chewed by scores of other nail-studded soles. Her breath caught as she scoured for footing. The tree's meat flashed green in too many patches to be the recent work of one woman.

Vultures. One more trap—

Fie stomped her panic down. The shrine was hidden, the shrine was safe—there was another answer, it couldn't be another ambush, Crows had one rule—

And Hangdog had tossed that rule over the bridge with her and the lordlings.

"Other Crows been through today?" Fie did her best to sound nonchalant. Crossroads-Eyes snarled and grinned and wept above, the wooden faces uncanny human under dapples of sun.

"You're the second band this morning," the keeper answered. "Something got Crows spooked of Cheparok?"

"Wouldn't know." That was a barefaced lie this time. Fie's head steadied anyhow. Lies were more familiar territory.

The shrine-keeper hummed as she retreated into the shade of the platform. Fie stepped up and blinked until her eyes cleared of the roof's shadows.

"Packs." The woman pointed to heaps of oiled canvas. "Salt over there. And the barrels got all manner of food that'll keep. Last band left a bounty. Seemed to think it'd be needed."

Fie could feel the woman's eye on her like a fingertip trailing down the back of her neck. She just handed packs to Jasimir and Tavin, who had the sense to keep their mouths shut for once.

"How's your string?" asked the keeper.

"Full enough." Fie could knot new teeth into the gaps when they made camp. "I've more teeth for the shrine if they're needed."

"They're not."

"It's all I have to trade for," Fie said, blunt.

The shrine-keeper weighed a small, battered cooking pot by hand, then passed it to Fie. "No trades. Take what you need. You know how it goes, little chief. Feed the Crows."

Fie tried not to wince as she watched the prince and the Hawk pile salt, dried meat, and strips of pounded fruit into their packs, wiping out more of the stash than they ought. "Aye."

"Sleeping mats." The woman handed over three straw rolls, then added a fat, clattering sack. "And soap-shells."

Fie claimed those with particular relish—then froze as a wail rose from another platform. Tavin and Jasimir too went still. The cry turned high and tremulous, murmurs chasing it, and Fie let out a breath. Only a baby, and judging by the lungs, a healthy one at that.

The shrine-keeper waved a gnarled hand as the wail turned to gurgles. "That tot's bound to scream down the sky itself," she groused. "Every hour, he tries."

Fie paused, counting up turns of the last moon. She was about to spend three more weeks dragging the lordlings about the hills. That made for a different sort of challenge. "Can you spare any laceroot seed?"

The keeper's gray brows rose. She flipped the latches on a worn trunk and dug inside. "You a-feared of getting with child, too?"

Tavin knocked over a pot of sandal-nails and swore under his breath.

Fie tried to ignore the pointed look the keeper gave him. She did not succeed. A flush nipped at her ears and neck. "I've no time for bleeding, let alone rutting."

The keeper sifted a fistful of black seed into a palm-size pouch, enough to keep this moon's bleeding at bay a few weeks. If Fie ran out before they made it to Trikovoi, she had bigger problems.

"Which way do you head now?" the woman asked, passing the pouch over.

"North."

"Other band went west, so the north's clear. You'll need cold gear past Gerbanyar. I got none of that here." She handed Fie robes, masks, a map charred into goat-hide, a flint, and a jug of flashburn. "There. Ought to set you until your next viatik."

"Thank you," Fie said.

"Thank Crossroads-Eyes," the shrine-keeper said dryly, jerking her head at the dead god. "Sees all your choices. Seems they wanted you to choose your way here."

"To be sure."

"Watch your back out on that road. Other Crows this morning, they said something odd." The woman's voice hardened. "Said Hawks ran through their camp last night. Not Oleanders—Hawks. Said they were looking for a girl chief and two false Crows." Fie froze. "And said there's a high price on those heads now."

Somewhere in the shadows of the shrine, the baby's cry rose again.

Fie heard a faint, deliberate rustle behind her that said Tavin was one wrong word from showing how false a Crow he was.

"Now I figure, we're Crows, we got one rule. I'm looking after my own, aye? And any chief, well, she's got to be following that rule, too. You strike me as a chief too sharp to break it." The keeper's eye drilled into Fie's. "Not a girl caught up in two mummers' troubles. If you see that girl out there, you make sure that trouble doesn't come down on all our heads. You hear?"

Fie didn't blink. "Aye."

"Then Crossroads-Eyes steer you safe. Go deal the dead gods' mercy."

They left with nary another word, picking their way down a lattice of vines and chittering tree-rats. Once they were earthbound and far enough from the shrine, Fie swung her pack off and dug for a fistful of dried panbread. Jasimir's shoulders sank with relief as he and Tavin did the same.

A hand full of panbread thrust into her sight. Fie looked up. Tavin held his breakfast out to her. Jasimir blinked, a strip of his own pan-bread still outstretched for his Hawk to taste. After a moment, he held the rest out to Fie as well.

Fie's throat closed. She fished out a pouch of salt and sprinkled it over their food. Her voice cracked as she said, "Go ahead."

"Thank you, chief," Tavin said quietly.

They returned to merciful silence, birdsong and rustling breezes washing through the air. Over and over, Fie repeated the shrine-keeper's words in her head: *A girl chief. Two false Crows. Trouble on all our heads.*

Look after your own.

This was the road Pa wanted her to take. The road Crossroads-Eyes wanted her to choose. And she couldn't fuss either of them now.

A question curled up as she chewed. "That skinwitch said the queen raised ghasts. Never heard of witchwork like that. And the queen's no witch anyhow."

Tavin and Jasimir traded glances. "I had . . . a theory," Jasimir began, hesitant. "You've heard of the ceremony to marry into the Phoenix caste, yes?"

Fie nodded. "Seen something like it in Swan teeth. You lose your Birthright, aye?"

"Correct." Jasimir frowned. "Wait—what do you mean, you've seen it in Swan teeth?"

"Swans don't rut inside the caste," Fie said around a mouthful of panbread. "At least, not to conceive. They find a willing partner outside the caste, and there's a ritual, and the partner loses their Birthright until the next new moon. Meanwhile they try real hard to make a baby Swan."

Tavin let out a long, exasperated sigh. "Of course. All this time we wondered how Rhusana pulled it off, and we could have just asked a Crow."

"Not the first time, won't be the last," Fie muttered. "So what'd she pull off?"

Jasimir ran a hand through his ragged hair. "The Phoenix ceremony is supposed to be permanent. Even witches lose their Birthright, and it never comes back."

Fie sorted it herself. "You think Rhusana did the Swan ceremony to herself, so her Birthright came back."

"And I think she's a Swan witch," Jasimir finished.

At that, Fie put down her panbread and stared.

"She has no witch-sign," Tavin added hastily. "And the odds of a Swan witch being born are—"

"I know what they are." Fie's voice had gone frigid. The Swan caste had only three dead gods. Three solitary witches in over a thousand-score people.

Any more than that, and they'd rule Sabor.

There was a hard reason why their witches weren't allowed to leave the Swan island even after coming of age. A hard reason why their Sparrow servants were clothed crown to foot, finger to toe.

In a Swan witch's hands, the desire Birthright became more than a way to command attention. When they caught hold of even a single strand of another's hair, they could seize that person's desire and twist it—and them—as that witch pleased.

All it would take was one stray hair from Fie's head, delivered to Queen Rhusana, and one scrap of hate the queen could seize on. Then Fie could wake one night to slit the boys' throats without a flinch.

"You knew," Fie accused, stacking up every horrid piece. "That's why you ran."

Jasimir shook his head, adamant. "It didn't sound possible until now. All three Swan witches are accounted for, she has no sign, *and* Tavin and I witnessed the marriage ceremony ourselves. We didn't know she could lose her Birthright for only a moon. I swear, I came to your band for help because Rhusana allied with the Oleanders, and for that reason alone."

Fie scowled, baleful, at the dirt. "Aught else you want to tell me? Tatterhelm's got a meaner cousin? The king's really two asps in a fancy robe?"

"I still don't know what Viimo meant about ghasts," Tavin said.

"Me either." Fie's gut twisted. Pa had taught her how to call Swan teeth just on principle, for they had but a largely useless few. Still, in the handful of times she'd blinked through the life in a dead Swan's spark, she'd heard no whisper of ghasts. And that, like so many things, bode ill.

Grim silence settled over them once more as Fie plaited a whole new set of troubles into the ones on her head.

Then Tavin's voice broke in. "I really have to know: Which one of us is Pissabed?"

He didn't want to be a Crow no more.

Fie had rolled Hangdog's tooth between her thumb and forefinger since they'd made camp by the flatway at sundown, so long that it had pressed trenches into both fingers. She didn't stop as she stared into the campfire now, a half-eaten heap of dinner cooling in the bowl beside her.

Hangdog had been born to be a chief like Fie. But he'd been willing to give it all up to get what he wanted.

She couldn't help but wonder what that was like.

"What if . . ." Jasimir's voice rattled her from her thoughts. "What if we went to the Hawks? Before Trikovoi, I mean."

Fie closed her eyes. She knew why the prince would ask; she knew the sense it made in his head. But ten hostage kin and one dead traitor had dragged on her heart all day, and all she wanted was to eat her dinner and not fight until dawn.

Then, to her surprise, Tavin spoke up. "We can't trust the Hawks."

Fie blinked at him.

So did Jasimir, his face darkening. "Then why are we even going to the Marovar?"

"Because the Hawks in the Marovar answer to the master-general."

"They *all* answer to Aunt Draga. If we find a league marker, I can just put my hand in the fire to show I'm a Phoenix, and—"

"We'll never get that close," Tavin said, terse. "We look like Crows. The best-case scenario is that they laugh us away. The worst case . . . You saw what they did in Cheparok."

Fie knew he didn't just mean the bribes. It rattled her, though, to hear him say it.

"Not all Hawks are bad," Jasimir argued. "For the dead gods' sake, *you're* a Hawk."

Tavin shook his head. "It doesn't take all Hawks to get us killed. It just takes one. I'll sent a message-hawk to the master-general once we reach the Marovar, but out here, I don't trust—" He cut off, caught his breath, and closed his eyes. "I—I don't trust other Hawks to protect us."

A stiff silence fermented over the campfire.

Fie rolled Hangdog's tooth in her fingers until it hurt. *Never have to burn another body, never deal with Oleanders. We'd forget he was a Crow.*

"Fine," the prince said eventually. "Knowing Rhusana, she'll want to take the throne in about two moons, on the summer solstice like a true Phoenix would. That leaves a moon and a half for her to . . . to remove Father." Fie tilted her head at that. "One week for Father's funeral, one more for the full coronation ceremony. She won't settle for anything less. So if we don't make it to the Marovar by the end of Peacock Moon . . ."

"King Surimir has a hunting accident," Tavin finished.

Peacock Moon yielded to Crow Moon; then Phoenix Moon began the new year at solstice. Crow Moon meant roadside vendors peddling charms to ward off sin, a month to cast off the year's follies and misfortunes, shorter viatik, shorter tempers.

Crow Moon was ripe for tragedy, like a king tumbling down a long set of stairs. Fie's brow furrowed. "Rhusana goes straight to the throne after him? Thought the king had a brother."

"Hunting accident," Prince Jasimir said, grim.

"But didn't your uncle have a daughter?"

"Hunting accident."

Fie gave the prince a long, narrow look. "How'd the queen first try to off you, again?"

Tavin coughed into his fist. It sounded strangely like "hunting accident."

"Maybe you lot ought to lay off hunting awhile," Fie said.

Tavin laughed outright at that. Jasimir, surprisingly, covered a smile with a hand. Fie couldn't recall the last time she'd seen him smile.

Fie couldn't help grinning back. Maybe it would be all right, at least for a little while. They weren't her kin, but the sharp edges of their pomp had worn off enough to abide for now.

Then Jasimir set his empty bowl down. "I'll take watch."

"No," Tavin said, swift as a gate slammed shut. "Leave it to Fie and me."

The prince frowned. "You know Mother wouldn't want me to be deadweight."

"She'd want me to do my job," Tavin said, stiff. "And that's keeping you alive."

"You managed it fine in the palace."

"We're not in the palace."

The prince's gaze shifted to linger on Fie. His frown deepened. "Suit yourself." He rolled out his sleeping mat and lay down without another word.

Fie couldn't fault Tavin's reasons; it'd be too easy for the Vultures to snatch the prince up if he alone kept watch. She was also dead sure this wasn't the last time they'd have this quarrel.

She rolled Hangdog's cold tooth betwixt her fingers again, over and over. Tavin broke the quiet soon enough. "Is there any chance you can sustain a glamour until the Marovar?"

Fie pursed her lips and reached for Pa's bag of teeth. Peacocks had plenty of witches, but they had an even more abundant desire to pay as cheap as possible. "Pa may have, eh, underestimated our stock," she allowed. "You want to look like the prince again?"

"We don't know what we're up against. And I'm his body double for a reason."

"That wasn't an 'aye,'" Fie noted. Tavin didn't elaborate. She fished a Peacock witch-tooth out of the bag anyhow, then sat on her knees before him.

The spark tittered as she called it to life, a Peacock gentlewoman who'd spun fanciful illusions for the royal nursery to gain favor with the queen. The older she'd gotten, the more cruelty and ambition had rotted her away, leaving battered servants, cheated merchants, and swelling coffers. When the plague came for her, she wove her own delirium dreams, giggling at the sights right up until Pa's blade touched her throat.

"What do you see?" Tavin asked.

Fie opened her eyes. "A Hawk full of sauce and nonsense," she answered, and handed him the tooth. "Keep this on you until the glamour breaks."

"I meant when you—I don't know—wake up a tooth? Is that what you do?"

"I see their lives." Fie squinted at the prince's sleeping face, tallying up the differences to paint onto Tavin. "Their choices." A straighter nose; a rounder eye. "How they died." Ears set a little lower. "What they did to Crows. I've seen how every other caste lives. Hold still."

Though Tavin had tucked the tooth up a sleeve, it hummed yet in Fie's mind, clear as a bell. She traced a path for the Birthright along Tavin's face, fingers skimming a breath away from his skin. The nick on his brow vanished; the arch of his nose shallowed; the curl smoothed from his hair at the nape of his neck.

She tried not to think on the heat that grew beneath her fingertips, or whether it came from him or from her.

She also tried not to think on the fact that she'd have to do every bit of it again when the tooth burned out two nights hence.

Tavin watched her hand pass in quiet until she reached for his burn-scarred knuckles. Then he twitched back. "Leave it. Please. I'll . . . cover it up."

Startled, she only nodded.

"Is there anything else?" he asked.

Fie studied Jasimir's face, then turned back to Tavin. Something was amiss. She frowned, searching for the flaw. "Aye. Hold on."

Tavin exhaled. "We've never thanked you, have we? For any of this."

"Crows don't get thanked. We get paid. Sometimes."

"I'm serious." He'd stopped watching her weave the glamour, gazing dead-on at her now. "You could have taken Viimo's deal. You could have had your family back. But you didn't give us up. Thank you."

Fie went still.

She scrabbled about her head for a scrap of wrath, anything to carve another line betwixt her and the Hawk. But all she could think of was Pa and Wretch and Swain and Madcap and every Crow she'd lost, and the hateful wisp of hope that she might find them again.

Fie's own words failed her, and his still raced about her head, and to her dismay the knot in her throat broke open. The camp's firelight blurred with tears.

"Oh—oh no. I'm sorry. I didn't mean to make you cry. Twelve hells, I'm bad at this." Tavin fumbled his sleeve about his thumb and reached for her, then caught himself. "Er . . . may I?"

She managed a wordless nod. Hawks didn't ask. Fie had no notion how to deal with one who did.

Tavin dabbed at her face. "I promise you, when Jas is safe, I'll help you get them all back. I'd swear to the Covenant, but I suspect you're getting tired of that."

Fie gave him a weary look. "Don't try to sell me pretty words, Hawk boy. We both know you'll be nailed to the prince until one of you dies."

He glanced sidelong at Jasimir. His answer did not come as quick or easy as she thought it would, nor as loud. "I have to disappear. After . . . the Marovar. It's a divine mandate when a Phoenix prince survives the plague. It's a cheap hoax when his guard conveniently lives, too. Taverin sza Markahn died a quarter moon ago; I'll be trapped in the palace's shadows if I go back. And I will not live as a ghost."

The words spilled before Fie could catch them: "Not anymore."

Something sudden and starving flashed through Tavin's face then, flames tearing through silk. "Not anymore."

He sounded too alike Pa, only a week ago: *We need this deal.* Only Tavin didn't need to cut any oath; he needed to cut himself free.

Fie refused to feel sorry for a Hawk, even a pretty one mopping up her face. Instead she said, "Well, we'll have to live through this mess first."

"They're all short lives." He bent a shallow smile. "The cleverest girl I've ever known told me that, so it must be true."

"The cleverest girl you've ever known got her family captured by a monster." Her voice hitched. Tavin shook his head and caught another tear, then another, a slow thumb trailing down the side of her cheek.

"The queen did that," he said. "And the governor. And Tatterhelm." Then, quiet: "Jas and I did that. I'll do everything I can to make it right." His hand dropped to graze her knuckles, still battered from when she'd split them on Viimo. "I can fix that, if you'd like."

She nodded, her voice failing her.

Tavin gathered her hands in his, brow furrowing. The same needling heat flared about her fingers as new skin swallowed the scabs. She couldn't help a sharp breath.

His gaze flicked up to her. "Sorry. I'm not all that good at healing."

Fie saw it, then, the flaw in his façade: the campfire lit his dark eyes closer to gold than Jasimir's flickers of gray.

How did she know that?

She couldn't ken why she couldn't bear to change it. She hated him for trying to give her hope. She hated herself for hoping at all.

And then, with horror and fury, she found she hated her traitor heart, for burning quiet with something that was not hate at all.

A sick frost rolled down her veins. Hawks didn't fancy Crows, they used them. Tavin had wooed her kin well enough when he needed their help. This was naught more than another round of that dance.

And even if it *was* more—no. That road wasn't meant for either of them, not a Hawk, not a Crow—

Didn't want to be a Crow no more, the memory of a skinwitch hissed.

Hangdog hadn't wanted it.

Did Fie?

Enough. None of it mattered anyhow, not with the oath still at all their throats. She yanked her hands free and turned away. "You want to help me? Fix your head on your own job."

"What do you mean?" Tavin asked, but his tone betrayed him: He kenned her clear. And he wanted to be wrong.

All more of his mummery, she told herself. It was a mercy she couldn't see his face.

"You know what I mean." Fie unfurled her sleeping mat and lay down, waiting for an answer.

None came. "Wake me for second watch," she muttered, and closed her eyes.

———◆◆◆———

When Fie took up second watch, the prince waited until Tavin's breath had evened out and only then eased himself up on an elbow.

She'd expected it: he'd gone to bed far too prickly to stay there. Her voice stayed low, skimming through the campfire sparks. "Aye?"

To her surprise, Jasimir scooted closer, one eye yet on Tavin. "Why can't you read?"

"Why can't you keep your own business?" Fie snapped back, ears burning. "You really got up to rub that in my face?"

"No—I—I apologize." Jasimir grimaced. "That came out wrong. I just don't understand—couldn't you have asked Swain to teach you, if it bothers you this much?"

Fie scowled into the dark; she knew square why she hadn't asked. "Crows use our own marks. We don't need to read."

And she hadn't minded the difference right up until a day ago, when a pretty Hawk boy accidentally carved that line between them.

Jasimir picked up a stick of kindling and wrung it in his hands. "I thought . . . if you wanted to learn, I could help." When Fie stared at him, wordless, he stumbled on. "I have to do *something* to be useful or I'm going to go mad. And you're going to be a full chief someday, and my mother always said a leader needs to be as skilled as anyone they lead, and . . ." He jabbed the kindling in the dirt. "And if there's anything I've learned, it's that you want to be the best chief you can."

Fie almost burst into a bitter laugh at that. What she wanted would make her a terrible chief. But the prince was a roundabout sort of right: she wanted to be a capable chief.

And she wanted to not shrink inside each time Tavin carefully read out a flatway sign now, pretending he was thinking aloud and not fooling anyone for a moment.

"When can you teach me?" she mumbled.

Jasimir snatched up the kindling, sitting straighter. "During your watch, while Tav's asleep. Then he can't tell me I should be resting instead."

Fie mulled it over. This wasn't about her, not really; he wanted to play charity at a Crow, and more likely than not he wanted to do something without his Hawk's go-ahead for once.

Besides, Fie knew her Crow marks; she knew scores of walking songs; she could recite the histories of their chiefs and their gods. That was good enough for Pa.

Fie studied the trees twisting beyond the firelight, and for a moment, she thought the forest watched back. Patches of night yawned in something like an uncanny face peering from the bushes.

Then a passing breeze ruffled the brush. The face broke into naught more than leaves.

Fie pinched at Pa's tooth. He hadn't needed more than Crow marks to be chief, but that was before lordlings and skinwitches and queens had crashed down on all their heads.

Maybe, to keep the oath, she needed to be more.

Fie let the tooth go and looked at the prince. "Where do we start?"

CHAPTER TWELVE

— THE BEACON —

"Is that edible?"

Fie resisted the call to sigh. "No."

"You're not even looking," Tavin accused.

"Because you're pointing at the mushroom." Its vivid orange cap had jabbed into Fie's sight like a thumb as she trudged past, a nub of brightness in the gray-green hillsides. And by now, she'd kenned too keen to how Tavin took interest in that which stuck out.

Four days had broken since leaving Crossroads-Eyes' shrine. Since then, Fie had settled into as near a routine as she could manage: Follow the main flatway north. Hide from the sound of horses or Hawk patrols. Try not to miss Madcap's walking songs.

Ignore the hollow sting in her gut every other night, when she glamoured Tavin's face away with a new Peacock tooth. Catalogue a new way she could tell him apart from the prince: a tilt to his brow, a stray freckle by the corner of his mouth. How the slightest gesture seemed weighted with motive.

How the weight of his gaze shifted on her.

Sleep half the night. Chew a few bitter laceroot seeds. Trade out watches with Tavin. Scratch out a few new letters with Jasimir. Trade dark for a dawn the prince still prayed to.

Follow the flatway north, as squash fields bled into sprouts of maize, then orchards and rocky pastures. North, toward the Hawks, toward the Marovar, toward a Covenant oath kept.

Fie had moments of anger and moments of doubt, and worst of all, moments of terrible peace. Moments to wash up alone, to watch the sunrise in silence, to sharpen the chief's blade by herself.

She ought to have hated it. She surely hated that she didn't.

"Fine. Is *that* edible?"

But not as much as she hated Tavin's way of passing the time.

This time she had to turn to see what he'd found. It appeared to be a rock.

"The moss," he clarified as her face darkened.

She couldn't bite back the scowl anymore. He'd asked the same question of dozens of plants in the last few days. "If you want to soil yourself for three days, aye."

"That sounds useful." He grinned at her and the prince. "You two are making the same face again."

"Because neither of us wants to know how that's supposed to be useful," Fie said. "And—"

A rumble beneath her soles cut her short. She sighed and started toward the bramble at the roadside. "Riders. Come on."

The boys hadn't tried to fuss her like they'd fussed at Pa; it seemed they'd been cured of that in Cheparok. They hurried into the bushes, crouching to peer through the leaves as Fie called up a Sparrow tooth just to be safe. A few breaths later, a few horses trotted by, their riders cowled in the faded lavender hoods of young Owl sojourn-scholars. They had the deeper brown skin of Owls from the western coastal academies, darker than Fie and much darker than Vultures.

Jasimir let out a sigh of relief as they passed, and shifted to stand. Fie yanked him back down.

The tremors only grew. The sojourn-scholars twisted to look at their backs—then cursed as more horses cantered into sight. Dust billowed up from the road, wheeling into one more ring about the Owls as the new arrivals surrounded them.

"What is the meaning of this?" one Owl scholar demanded, coughing.

As the dust settled, one jagged silhouette stood apart from the rest. Four lines of new-cut steel shone brighter than the older notches carved into a helm crowning a mountain of a man.

Tatterhelm.

Her kin's killer, not twenty paces away. One Phoenix tooth, maybe two, and Fie could take him down—

And lose the prince, the oath, everything Pa had trusted to her, because she couldn't also take down the rest of the skinwitches riding with him. A sick kind of wrath paced in her heart, rattling its bars; for now, Fie kept it caged.

"Business of the queen," Tatterhelm boomed. "You see any bone thieves on this road?"

"The Merciful Crows?" Another Owl cocked his head. "Whatever for?"

Tatterhelm pressed his mount closer. "*Business of the queen,*" he repeated. "Looking for three of 'em. Won't ask again."

The scholars traded looks. "We didn't see three," the first Owl said, slow. "We saw a band yesterday, perhaps a score? They were bound northwest, I believe to Livabai."

"They could've fallen in with another band." That Vulture's voice scraped all too familiar; last time Fie had heard it, the skinwitch had been huddled in the bloody sand. When Fie squinted, she could make out bandages swaddling Viimo's hands. She'd survived Cheparok after all. "To throw us off, since we figured out where they're headed."

A grunt echoed from the ragged helm as it swiveled about, slowing when the eye-slits turned Fie's way.

She lit another Sparrow tooth swift as she could, snapping it into harmony. The twin teeth showed her each beacon of a gaze, as before. This time, some gazes fractured into spidery branches picking at the tracks on the road—skinwitches sniffing for their marks. None stuck.

Glee flashed through Fie at that. Skinwitches were like hounds: they needed to know a scent to track it. Without something that belonged to her or the lordlings, they couldn't sift their footfalls out of the flatway. So far, the Vultures had their wits alone to lead them, and those were about to lead them astray.

Tatterhelm let out a harsh cry and lashed his horse into a gallop. The rest of the Vultures followed, leaving three Owls in the dust and three fugitives in the brush.

Fie tallied them up as they left: less than a score of Vulture riders, fewer than Viimo had numbered, all carrying naught but a few packs and furs. She thumbed Pa's tooth: the spark flickered yet.

Once the Owls had shaken off the dust and carried on down the road, grumbling about the indignity of it all, Fie sat back. "They've a caravan."

Tavin rocked on his heels. "How can you tell?"

"The horses," Jasimir answered for her. "They're packing just enough supplies to camp a day or two. They must have a supply caravan trailing them. I suspect that's also where they'll have the . . ." He faltered. "The hostages."

That sick wrath shook its cage once more. Fie stuffed it down.

Near three weeks left in Peacock Moon. That'd be time aplenty for other castes to ride to Trikovoi, but for Crows with beacons to answer, that'd be cutting it close. Too close to waste any lead they could scrape up.

Fie picked at Pa's tooth the way the Vultures had picked at the road: angry with what it couldn't tell her. Then she pushed herself to her feet. "We keep moving."

She felt Tavin's eyes on her as she shoved her way back to the road, but all he said was "Yes, chief."

———◆◆◆———

"Now you write it."

Fie took the twig from Jasimir and fumbled about for a grip that felt right. None did. Her fingers shook as she carved a tremulous line in the dirt, then another, and another.

They looked nothing like Jasimir's tidy letters; hers were overlarge and tilting like a drunk. Her ears burned.

"This is nonsense," she mumbled, and dropped the stick.

Jasimir scuffed out her first attempt, then handed the twig back. "My mother said my letters wobbled like colts when she first taught me to write," he said. "It's like anything else: it just takes practice. Try again."

"Do you miss her?" Fie began to scratch out another line.

"Every day," he sighed. "Mother made sure I never ran out of scrolls to read or strategy games to work through. She said a sharp mind did more on the throne than a sharp sword. But Father would have preferred me to be"——he blinked through the campfire, where Tavin stretched on a sleeping mat——"someone different."

"You know it's his job to die for you." The second the words flew out, Fie silently cursed herself. Tavin scarce needed her to fight his quarrels.

"It's his job to keep me alive," Jasimir corrected, stiff. "Just like it's my job to keep the country alive. Mother raised us both to know our duty."

"Oh aye, he's supposed to take an arrow for you, and you're supposed to suffer a crown for him. It all evens out."

The jibe sailed clear over the prince's head. "Exactly. Besides, when he's not on duty, he gets to do whatever he wants. And unlike me, he can go right back to doing that once we return to Dumosa."

"And if he doesn't want that?" Fie's writing stick stalled in the dirt. "To go back?"

The prince let out a baffled laugh. "As opposed to——to this? Cowering in bushes, washing in puddles, and eating scraps? He's a Hawk. He has no business living like a——"

He cut himself off, but not near soon enough.

A log popped in the campfire, spewing up sparks in the silence.

"Like what?" Fie asked, just to make him say it out loud. Her hands shook.

"I didn't mean——"

"Like a Crow?" She threw the stick down across the half-scrawled letter. "You palace boys, you're too good for this life, aye? You don't deserve to be treated like *me*."

Jasimir held up his hands, voice rising. "I don't know! There has to be some reason why the Covenant lets this happen to you——"

"You mean your pa," Fie spat. "There has to be a reason your pa lets this happen."

Tavin rolled over, yawning, and Fie's gut lurched. She scuffed a foot through her letters swift as she could.

"What . . ." Tavin sat up. "Why're *both* of you awake?"

"It's naught," Fie answered, at the same time Prince Jasimir said, "I was teaching her to read."

Fie's very skin crawled with fury and humiliation. "Was *not*."

Prince Jasimir stared. "What is the matter with you? We've been at it for five days now."

"*Shut up,*" Fie hissed, desperate. Maybe if Tavin went back to sleep, he'd forget he saw anything.

You reckon he'll take you away and polish you up so much that the gentry forget what you came from? Hangdog sneered, a shadow on a creek bank long gone.

"You ungrateful little—"

"Jas." Tavin cut the prince off. "Be quiet."

Jasimir drew himself up, looking wholly betrayed. "*Are you—*"

Tavin held a hand up, brow furrowed, searching the dark. "Do you hear that?"

Fie sifted through the noises one by one: the creak of smoldering firewood. Leaves murmuring in a weak wind. The soft trill of faraway cicada song.

Just beyond it all, a thin, uneven whistle.

Not the sort Fie issued for marching orders or the steps of the Money Dance, nor even the sort Swain half hummed under his breath while he tallied inventory. The nearest thing Fie could recall was a hunched-up poppy-sniffer she'd passed in an alley years ago, a forgotten reed pipe resting on his slack bottom lip. Every wheeze had skimmed off a faltering note.

And somewhere beyond their campfire, it sounded as if scores of those poppy-sniffer whistles were closing in.

"Trees. Now. Grab what you can." Fie had started keeping a few bowlfuls of earth near their campfires for moments like this. She threw the dirt over the flames, smothering them in an instant. Then she blinked away the deeper dark and shoved as much as she could into her pack.

The whistles whined louder.

Mercifully, the prince was not barefoot this time. He and Tavin had scaled a sturdy oak, and Fie followed them up, calling two Sparrow teeth. She settled on a thick bough, teeth alight, and tried not to think on all the supplies still left below.

The whistling rose to a soft shriek, mere paces from camp.

Fie had seen her fair ration of terrible things in her sixteen years: scummed sinners, long-dead Oleander victims, the aftermath of a plague beacon gone unanswered. She'd heard campfire tales of monsters, devils, ghosts of wretched souls even the Covenant refused. All stories, she'd told herself. The only monsters she'd seen were humans with something to hide behind.

But by every dead god, she was starting to believe now.

Fie heard the dull clang of a pot overturned, a flap of a sleeping mat, strange wet leathery sighs, and above all, the whistles. But the dark hid the camp below too well. She could see shifting ripples of piecemeal moonlight and no more.

Worse, the twin Sparrow teeth ought to have shown her gazes peering about camp, so she might turn them away as needed. The teeth burned steady as they always did, and yet—

Fie saw naught below.

No searching looks, no scouring beacons, no Vulture gazes prying about the dirt. Only shifting, slippery night.

A brief sizzle drifted up, chased by a whiff of something rancid and burnt. Then the whistles shifted, flowing out of the camp, away to the north.

Fie didn't let out her breath until long after the final quiet shrill seeped away.

"Anyone see what that was?" she whispered.

"No." Tavin's voice shook. "Jas?"

"I've no idea."

Fie rolled Pa's tooth about, half to think, half to comfort herself with the familiar spark. What would he do, hunted by the night itself?

Same as he ever did: keep them safe.

"We'll stay up here until sunrise. You two try to sleep. Tie yourselves to the branch if you can." It would be a long, cold few hours. Fie resigned herself to spending it thinking on what had passed through camp and flinching at every twig snap. "I'll finish out my watch."

———— ◆ ◆ ◆ ————

The dawn gave them no answers.

It did, however, allow them a small mercy. The supplies they'd abandoned were knocked about the clearing as if a drunkard had bumbled into them, but near all of it was salvageable. Beyond that, the visitors had left only two signs of their arrival. The first were strange, writhing drag marks all about the dirt.

The second was a thin film of something sticky and charred, left behind on the campfire's now-dead coals. The outline was too plain to deny: a flat wedge with five dents at the broad end.

"It's a footprint," Tavin said. "Who steps in hot coals and doesn't scream?"

"If we're right about Rhusana being a witch, maybe those were people under her thrall." Jasimir glanced at Fie, cautious.

She ignored him. If the prince thought a raid from an unseen nightmarish beast was enough to make her forget what he'd said, he had sore underestimated the depths of her spite.

Instead she cinched her pack shut. "We can ponder it on the road. Daylight's wasting."

Jasimir sucked in a breath. She ignored that, too.

Then Tavin pointed over her shoulder. "Fie, look."

She twisted round. Above the treetops, a thin column of orange smoke coiled in the air to the north.

It seemed the Covenant had a long day in store for her. With a sigh, she yanked her pack back open.

"How far is it?" Tavin asked.

"Plague beacons start black." She rummaged about for the goat-hide map. "Every league marker nearby lights up purple smoke. Then every league marker that sees purple lights blue, and then it goes green, yellow, orange, and red." Sure enough, a new red curl rose from the south, where they'd passed a league marker the afternoon before. "So five or six leagues." She spread the map out. A web of rivers and roads scrawled across the leather in seared lines and Crow signs, mottled in forests or hills.

"Is it Livabai?" Tavin peered over her shoulder. "Because that's bound to be a trap."

His breath caught her hair in a sore distracting manner. Fie gritted her teeth and tried to focus on the cities. Livabai sat on the shores of a lake, and she didn't see one within seven leagues. "No."

Her finger traced the flatway line, prodding out the beacon's probable sources. The answers were not kind. "We know it's north of here. If we're lucky, it's due north. If we're less lucky, we'll need to head west at the next crossroads. Worst is if it's east."

"Trikovoi's northeast," Tavin said. "So why is east bad?"

"Because then the plague's more like to be in Gerbanyar." She read out the city's Crow signs. "'Cold.' 'Don't stay overnight.' And best of all, 'Oleanders.'"

Tavin's frown cut sharp as Hawk steel. "That's too risky."

"They're all too risky," Fie said. "Pa told you: Crows go where we're called."

"And if you're being called into a trap?" His frown didn't budge. "Vultures passed us yesterday, then our camp was overrun by the world's worst band of pipers, and now suddenly there's a plague beacon from the same direction they *both* headed. Even if this one is fine, how long do you think it'll take Tatterhelm to figure out that's how he can lure us in?"

"He'll have to find a town that lets him first. Hate us or no, people know what happens when they attack Crows in the open." Fie pointed to a vale on the map near Trikovoi. The lone Crow mark there said *"ashes."* "There was a village here once. They decided the chief asked too much for viatik and cut down her husband and child. The band carried word out, and next time that village lit a plague beacon, no one answered until after the whole valley rotted. Saw it burn myself. Any town that lends Tatterhelm their plague beacon knows they'll meet the same."

Tavin stood, arms crossed. "He may not give them much of a choice in the matter."

"I still have to answer," she fired back. "It's my duty. I don't get to only do it when it's easy, any more than you get to guard the prince only when he's safe. And if you think the rest of the region won't lash out at Crows for a shirked beacon—"

"I won't risk thousands of lives to the plague," Jasimir said, abrupt. "She's right. Besides, we need more supplies or we'll never last in the mountains. The only way we'll get them is the viatik."

"Easier to say when your caste hasn't caught the plague since Ambra," Tavin grumbled. "But fine, I'm outvoted."

"I'll handle the body." The hilt of Pa's broken sword prodded Fie in the side. "All you two need to do is hope it's not Gerbanyar."

———◆—◆◆———

"I suppose I could have hoped harder," Tavin admitted the next morning.

A black serpent of smoke writhed into the sky above, whelped from the signal post of Gerbanyar.

"Masks on," Fie ordered, unhitching hers from her pack. "From here on out, keep your mouths shut and your eyes sharp, ken me?"

Tavin glanced sidelong at her. It was one of his many-sided looks, saying *we're walking into trouble*, saying *none of us are ready*, saying *none of us can walk away*.

But what won this time was "Yes, chief."

Fie strode to the post and rang the bell. The Hawk guard leaned out from the platform long enough to give her a curt nod. A whistle pierced the air as the plague beacon sputtered out.

A man strolled through the gate in Gerbanyar's plain stone wall. He matched his city well enough: his face was the grayish sort of brown, and the painted stripes of his hide vest matched the stripes of granite and basalt stacked into nearby house walls. Those stripes marked him for a Pigeon and a courier; the twitch of his gaze marked him for a man Fie wouldn't trust at her back anytime soon.

"This way," he announced, a smirk tugging at his lips.

For a moment, Fie couldn't make her feet work. It reeked of a trap.

"Right behind you," Tavin said under his breath.

"I said mouths shut," she mumbled, and headed for the gate.

The Pigeon courier led them down the main road, where mismatched stones sank into usurping moss. Gerbanyar was nowhere near as large as Cheparok, and though it too spilled across a hillside, the gray stack-stone houses jutted up as they pleased.

But the messenger's path didn't curve toward the houses. Instead, he took them past an open market, where merchants laid one hand on the purses at their belts; past pens of goats and chickens and cattle and the flint-faced shepherds who stopped to watch; and at last toward a stone-lined channel at the lowest ground within Gerbanyar's walls.

Fie's gut sank. "You scummed the sinner," she said flatly.

"You took too long getting here." The courier no longer bothered hiding his smirk. "So we took matters into our own hands."

She strode over to the channel's edge. Gutter-mouths punctured the rim of a far wall, their contents plopping into murky water padded in yellow algae. Scant paces below Fie, fetid waters lapped sleepily at the breast of a man lying in the waste.

The marks of the Sinner's Plague burned clear enough on him: lips dark with bloody tracks, skin bruised with the Sinner's Brand, eyes pasted shut in crusts. Flies clotted his air, crawling in and out of a mouth agape. A dirty sleeping mat carpeted the rough hewn steps nearby. Fie wondered if the sinner had started on the mat and rolled into the cesspool in his fever dreams, or if the scummers had tossed him in, mat and all, not caring where either landed.

Sometimes sinners got scummed because they'd earned their plague at their neighbors' expense, and those trespasses had come home to roost. And sometimes sinners got scummed because their neighbors wanted Crows to wade around in filth while they watched.

From the collection of onlookers Fie found when she turned round, she wagered it was the latter.

But that body wasn't about to drag itself onto a pyre. She'd wrapped her arms hand-to-elbow in rags, yet she hadn't wagered on fishing a corpse out of a sewer. "We need a cart," she announced. "And firewood. That's our viatik."

"You've got his mat," another man said, sporting a Sparrow

butcher's pattern-work apron. "Drag him out on that. Firewood's at the gate. You can have his teeth for viatik."

She gave the man a snide look before remembering it was wasted behind her mask. "Aye, I'll drag a leaky sinner all the way through your city, right on by all your livestock and all your markets, and then I'll wait for that plague beacon to light back up for the rest of you. I want a cart."

"I see one sinner and three bone thieves. Carry him out."

Fie bit her lip. She couldn't risk the lordlings touching a plague body. A gate to the eastern road yawned on the other side of the channel. Maybe she could haul the body that far herself.

Then the Pigeon man nodded to the Sparrow and jogged off. The Sparrow butcher hid a smirk behind a hand.

Something else was coming.

"Fie—" Tavin started.

"I'll handle it," she interrupted. There was no time for lordling nonsense. She had to get them out before the Pigeon courier came back.

"On your own?" Tavin whispered.

"Aye, *Pissabed*," she said, "on my own. Stay up here."

She marched down the steps. The mint in her mask's beak couldn't overpower the foul stench of plague and dung, so she sucked each breath through her teeth.

"There she goes," someone laughed above. "Told you. Crows are right at home in the scum."

Fie set her pack down on the steps, pulled the filthy sleeping mat to the sinner, then took hold of his nearest arm and yanked. The man didn't budge.

Instead, he screamed.

Fie dropped him faster than a hot coal. A cloud of flies spewed up. A terrible chill swept down her own limbs, fingertips buzzing; the broken sword swayed at her side like a noose.

Still alive. Somehow, the sinner was still alive. And that meant one thing.

When, not if.

A needle-thin rasp faltered from the man's bloody mouth:

"Mercy."

CHAPTER THIRTEEN

—— DEAD GODS' MERCY ——

THE FIRST TIME FIE TRIED TO TAKE HOLD OF THE BROKEN SWORD, it slipped free and clattered down the stone steps, resting against the sinner's side.

The second time, she kept her grip, but daylight shivered along its chipped blade, the rag-bound hilt locked in her shaking fist.

"Think her hands got more use than that under those rags?" a Sparrow man jested at the top of the channel.

She heard the scrape of sandal-nails and whipped round. Tavin had half turned toward the Sparrow, one white-knuckled fist drifting to where his own short swords were belted below the Crow cloak.

If he were a Crow, she could tug at her hood to signal, *Don't make trouble.* If he were a Crow, he'd know better than to make trouble here to start with.

She cleared her throat. Thunderously. It served well enough: he turned back to her, arms folding tidy and harmless. For the time being.

The sinner spasmed at her feet.

Fie's gut was a nest of vipers, ready to betray her at one wrong move.

What had Pa done? The memories shied from her like mice in dark corners. He'd taken off his mask. Twelve hells if she'd take hers off and let her face show plain now.

He'd used his Safe voice. He'd had her for a helper. Here, she had neither.

All she had was mercy in her shuddering grasp. And it was time to deal it.

She knelt by the sinner.

"I'm a Crow," she told him. Her quiet voice shook as much as the rest of her. "I'm here for you."

The sinner smiled.

She wanted to run from the road that had trapped her so. She wanted to leave the man to die in the scum. She wanted to cast the chief's blade behind her and never look back.

You have to keep your eyes open.

Fie laid one hand on a salt-rimed forehead and lowered the blade against the sinner's throat.

And then she did what Pa had done.

The flesh parted all too easy. Fie choked on her own breath, fumbling the sword as the man jerked. Blood splashed over her hands, over the sinner, over the stone steps—had Pa's sinners all bled so? Had she done it right?

Blood burned in her mouth—no, no, the salt of tears rolling down to her quivering chin, tears she couldn't fathom, tears she couldn't hold off—she'd been merciful, she'd done what Pa would, she'd given the sinner what he wanted—she was a chief, she was a chief, she was a chief—

Far away, the Sparrow butcher said, "You lot'll be lucky to go that easy with the Oleander Gentry."

The viper-nest in her gut thrashed. She couldn't say if it was the threat or the blood that did it. They had to get out of this mess before aught else fouled up.

What came next? Get the dead sinner out. Was he even dead yet? He'd gone still. Flies crawled about his face once more. The grim necklace of red bubbles popped one by one. His eyes were closed, just like in sleep.

Sleep. The sleeping mat. Get him on the mat.

Fie tried to grab a handful of bloody shirt. Crimson greased her slipping hands. The dead man slid a little deeper into the scum.

"Fie—you need help—"

Tavin's voice rang much too close. She whirled round again and found him halfway down the steps, halfway to the sinner, halfway to her.

This close and he'd catch the plague. This close and she'd watch his mouth crack and bleed, she'd hear him cough up soft bits of his lungs, and if she was a real chief, she'd be the one dealing him mercy before it got bad. Her hands, his throat, his blood, her mercy—

The blade fell to the stone again.

Look after your own.

"Get out," she hissed around a traitorous sob. Her empty hands rattled at her sides, shaking blood off in shivering droplets. She had no mercy left in her, not for him, not now. "Don't touch me, don't touch the sinner, just watch the damn pr—Watch your cousin, aye?"

"Fie—"

"Get out!"

No mercy, only blood on her hands, and fear of the part of her that wanted him to stay.

Another cackle from the crowd. Mostly Common Castes, they'd

cozied up to the edge of the channel, too far to hear her, too close for her guts to settle. At the front stood that Sparrow butcher.

Too close. All of them were too close.

"Oleanders won't snuff you so swift." The butcher's voice was flat, matter-of-fact. "We know there's nowhere to spill that filth blood but the sewers when we're done with you."

"Ignore him and get back to your cousin," Fie rasped. Light sliced across the glassblack eyes of Tavin's mask. He didn't move. "They just want to flash their steel because we *sure* don't have any, aye, Pissabed?"

All it'd take to go sideways was one glimpse of Tavin's short swords.

The Sparrow man licked his lips. "The sewers'll run red for moons. Look at them. They know what's coming. Aren't even going to bother running, are you?"

Tavin uncrossed his arms.

"*Ignore him,*" Fie ordered, desperate. One fly, then another landed on her blood-soaked hands.

"Oh, noisy tongue on that one," the Sparrow laughed. "How about your lads there? They got mouths worth using, too?"

A Crow would know how this game played out. Let them say what they will. Let them kick and curse and keep moving on, because the cost of cursing back wasn't yours alone to pay.

But Tavin was a Hawk, not a Crow, and the high castes never bothered with who paid for their folly.

"Best get used to that scum, bone thief," the courier laughed. "You'll be drowning in it with the rest of the filth when the White Phoenix gets . . ."

He trailed off, looking at his hands. Then he let out a short yip as his fingers purpled and curled like pill-beetles.

And that was where Fie had fouled up: she'd forgotten that war-witches needed no steel to kill.

The butcher crumpled, screaming, as blisters boiled over his blackening flesh.

Panicked shrieks ricocheted off the paving stones. In seconds the throng of onlookers had dissolved to a jostling rush shoving away from the sewage channel. Only the Sparrow remained, a twitching heap of limbs and smoking rag.

The air in Fie's mask savored of mint and pig fat. Like burnt sinner.

Get out. She had to get out.

"Fie—"

Tavin swayed at the edge of her sight. One hand reached for her.

Then he crashed to the stone, and moved no more.

The prince stumbled down the stairs as she froze. Hangdog had fallen just so—the bridge was behind her, the Floating Fortress was behind her, Hangdog was behind her—no, he lay on the steps now, as good as dead—not again—

Jasimir shook Tavin by the shoulders, again and again. He didn't stir.

Look after your own.

She was their chief.

Some stony part of her broke through the fear and fury. Cold reckoning ratcheted through her head. The Pigeon courier would be back any moment with some ugly surprise. She couldn't leave the sinner. Or Tavin. The sinner was dead. Tavin was—

Silent.

Jasimir stripped off Tavin's mask. Blood trailed from the Hawk's nose and shuttered eyes.

Terror sucked Fie's cold reckoning under.

"He breathing?" Her own voice rang pitifully high and strangled in her ears.

Jasimir held a trembling hand over Tavin's mouth, then nodded.

The flood ebbed. Still alive. She had to get them out.

"Flashburn," she barked, pointing a bloody finger at her pack.

For once, the prince didn't argue. Maybe he distrusted his voice as much as she'd doubted her own. He passed the jug to her without a word.

Fie gritted her teeth and turned her back on Tavin. She knelt by the dead sinner, forced her fingers into his mouth, and upturned the jug. Clear ooze slid over her knuckles and down the man's throat, its bitter reek running roughshod through the air.

"Water." She snatched up her stump of a sword, spun on a heel, and held her arms out to the prince. "Hands and blade." He emptied a water skin over her palms and sword until the wet rags on her hands ran near clear.

Cloth scuffed over stone behind her—but neither Jasimir nor Tavin had moved. Where had the sound come from?

Another scrape gave her the dreadful answer.

Still alive. The Sparrow butcher was still alive.

His shriveled hand convulsed, the same shiny red-black as a strip of smoked pig. One bloodshot eye wandered to her broken blade.

"Crow," he whined.

Fie's throat closed. She knew what came next.

"Mercy."

Not again, she couldn't cut another throat again; only sinners could ask for mercy from Crows—that was the way of it, right? But perhaps the Covenant had sent her instead of waiting for the plague, and if she didn't send them on it'd bring a hell down on their heads—

"*Mercy,*" the butcher begged.

"I'll do it."

Tavin groggily shoved himself up, blood smeared from cheek to jaw where he'd tried to wipe it off. The blood vessels in his eyes had burst, dyeing their whites bright as poppies.

"Don't push yourself," Jasimir protested.

Tavin ignored him, staggering to his feet with a spit-weight of his usual grace. For a moment he looked near ready to collapse again. Then he drew one short sword from a hip, and the weight of a hilt in his hand seemed to tip him into focus once more.

"I'll do it," he said again. His gaze reeled to the street leading to the sewer. "Oh. That's a . . . problem."

Fie followed his gaze, even as a hollow clatter on paving stone told her what she'd find. Greggur Tatterhelm rode for them, the Pigeon courier pointing the way.

She'd been right about the sinner.

Tavin had been right about the trap.

A bell pealed. No, not a bell—the scraping toll came from Tavin's blade. The Sparrow gaped at the sky, any last dregs of life emptying from his eyes. The Hawk had dealt mercy for her.

Tatterhelm was nearly upon them.

But she still had a sinner to burn—still had a duty to the Covenant—

She still had an oath to keep. And to keep it, she needed to get them out.

Then Fie saw the flashburn sheen spreading across the sewage. It had leaked from the red split in the dead man's throat.

She pried a Phoenix tooth from her string. It lit in her hands, burning away the rag in a flash of steam as she bolted for Tavin.

Tatterhelm was only paces away, sword raised.

Fie hurled the tooth toward the dead sinner, feeding the strength of her own bones to that hungry spark, then threw herself at Tavin. He fell beneath her with a startled wheeze.

White flames blasted from the channel with a fluty, ear-shattering howl.

The fires clawed at the sky, rolling past the sewer's walls to lick at the city's stones. Tatterhelm's horse screamed and danced back, and a cry rose from the market as thatch roofs caught sparks.

Fie held fast to the tooth-spark of Phoenix Birthright, reminding the flames who had called them forth, and breaking them round her and Tavin as best she could. Bright yolk-gold plumes of Phoenix fire roared from the sinner's charring corpse as Fie's eyes watered again. A poorer pyre than the sinner deserved, but if it burned hot enough, it would do.

They only had a few moments before the flashburn ran out and Tatterhelm blocked their way once more. "The gate," she cried to Jasimir, who stood unbothered by the fire. "Go!"

He grabbed her pack and leapt up the steps as she pulled Tavin up and followed. More hoofbeats rumbled a tattoo down the road.

They scuttled over the uneven ground, rounding the edge of the stone pit. Two Hawk guards planted themselves between them and the gateway, arrows trained on them.

Fie didn't think, just called two Gull witch-teeth in her string and whipped them into harmony. A vicious wind howled down the road, picking up the guards and slamming them into the stack-stone walls. She almost laughed at how easy it was.

Aye, and now you're down two witch-teeth, her colder voice reminded her. But hadn't Pa said to burn as many teeth as she needed?

She glanced back and saw the flashburn-white fading away, though the gold Phoenix fire had swallowed the sinner whole.

"Welcome to our roads, cousin," she whispered, and kept running.

Hoofbeats clattered off the rock at their back.

The road was too clean, too easy for riders. She called after Tavin and Jasimir and veered off the flatway, into sparse trees and yellowing grass, aiming for a rocky hillside thick with trees.

The nails in her soles scraped and slid on more and more stone as the ground climbed and dirt thinned. The thunder in her ears could have been hoofbeats, could have been the boys behind her, could have been her own heartbeat; she didn't dare stop to find out. Branches whipped at her face, withered vines catching at her feet. Her lungs burned. She couldn't suck in air fast enough to drown their fire.

The rumble in her ears could only be hoofbeats now.

Up. *Up.* She scrambled up and onward, tracing the worst path for riders to fight through. The trees gave way to a sharp crest capped in a slide of broken slate. Only a few thumbs of basalt boulders kept it moored to the hillside.

The dead gods had at last granted her a kindness.

Fie shot straight into the slate. Shards rattled free, slipping beneath her sandals.

Good. She needed that.

"Are you mad?" Jasimir demanded behind her, hoarse. "There's no cover."

"Horses," she wheezed between breaths, fighting for another foothold, then another. Each step set off a cascade of tumbling slate. She angled for the steepest path and pushed on, taking each step twice, sliding back and hissing a litany of curses through her gasps for air. Broken stone bit into her palms every time she tried to steady herself.

Then one foot scraped on softer earth, sole-nails biting down hard. Every muscle screamed as she shoved herself up, up, up to steady ground, up to the hill's summit. Her knees wobbled as she turned about.

Sure enough, a handful of Vultures had stalled at the base of the slate slide, their horses tossing their heads. If Fie's sandals had struggled, hooves had no chance at all. She'd bought them time—

A glint caught her eye, just in time to see the arrow loosed direct at her.

Something knocked her clean off her feet. The arrow whizzed over her head, streaking across the sky in the brief moment before everything went dark.

For a heartbeat she thought she'd fainted—but shouts and sliding slate still rattled in her ears. A hand kept her head tucked down, and arms anchored her to crowsilk and flesh as impact after dizzying impact shuddered through them both. Soon they fetched up against a boulder.

Fie took a moment to ken that they'd stopped, her brains still skittering about. Then the grip on her loosened. She raised her head and found Tavin sprawled under her, gray-faced and wincing. He'd taken the brunt of their fall.

He'd taken it for her. To save her life. To save *her*.

Fie didn't know why the notion gutted her so.

Jasimir skidded down to them. "Is he hurt?"

"No," Tavin grumbled.

Fie rolled to her feet. "Are you lying?"

He shot her a sour look. "Yes."

"How bad?"

"I'll live." He let her help him up, one hand pressed to his side, leaning askew to keep the weight off a leg. Fie winced at an ugly burn over one shoulder. She hadn't kept all the flames off him after all. "How long do we have?"

"Ten minutes at most. But we'll never outrun them on foot." Prince Jasimir peered up at the hill's summit for any sign of Vultures.

"So we don't outrun them. We hide." Fie pointed to the trees below.

The prince pursed his lips. "These are the best skinwitches in Sabor."

"And I'm the worst Crow they'll ever cross," she snapped. "They have my family. They're lucky all I aim to do is hide."

She slung Tavin's arm over her shoulders and set off, not bothering to wait for royal permission.

"We'll hole up and you can fix yourself," Fie muttered, as much to Tavin as to herself.

"If I didn't know better, I'd think you're worried."

"Worried I'll have to hide your body." That was a half-truth.

Tavin forced a crooked smile around clenched teeth. "You're getting sentimental on me."

"Aye, and that sentiment is 'don't leave a trail of bodies,'" she said, grim.

"That's"—he sucked in a breath as they slid down a tricky bit of path—"touching."

Fie waited for him to keep chattering off his sauce and nonsense. He didn't.

"We'll hole up," she mumbled again. "Don't go leaving a trail."

"Yes, chief." His voice scarce rose above the rattle of stone.

She half dragged Tavin past the first few trees sturdy enough for them. "First place they'll look, likely," she grunted in answer to the prince's sprouting question. "Too easy."

The tree she settled for was a cedar sheathed in bark ragged enough to swallow the marks of nailed soles. This time the prince helped push Tavin up and followed on his own. No sooner had Fie steadied herself on a branch than the slow pound of hooves dripped into the air.

These weren't night-bold Oleanders looking for a scapegoat. She wasn't crawling past bribe-fattened gate guards anymore, either. The queen's own Vultures, the best skinwitches in Sabor, were out for her hide.

Fie drew two Sparrow teeth from her bag, rolled them between sweat-sticky palms, and closed her eyes.

CHAPTER FOURTEEN

——— OFF THE ROADS ———

*H*armony.

The two Sparrow teeth flickered to dissonant life. Fie wrestled with both until the chord struck and prayed it would be enough.

Fie saw the gaze before she saw the Vulture, lit up by the Sparrow teeth. The skinwitch's attention flicked and pried about the trees like a forked tongue, lingering on any snapped twigs or traces of nail-lined soles. This was the true face of the Vulture Birthright, the hunger of a predator stalking a scent. The jingle of bridle and creak of saddle leather slid into a creeping dirge, measured in the drumbeat of hooves.

What had Tavin said of the queen's Vultures a week past? Tatterhelm wasn't the best of the trackers. He was all twelve hells to cross just the same. He had Rhusana's favor.

And likely he had Fie's family.

Fie didn't know if she wanted to see Tatterhelm, or a Vulture who was a few less hells to cross.

The branch shivered as Tavin shifted. She caught a muffled hiss—and then quiet. The Hawk alone knew true how bad he'd been wounded. But if healing himself burned as much as when he'd healed her, for once, she didn't envy him.

He'd be fine. He'd be back on his feet soon enough, armed with his short swords and his smiles deadlier still, back to vexing her at every turn.

He'd saved her life. Broken her fall.

He had to be fine.

The skinwitch rode into sight, below ragged curtains of needled boughs: Tatterhelm.

For a heartbeat Fie was back in another tree a week before, watching an Oleander lord try to smoke them out. Where the lord had shouted and cursed and threatened, though, Tatterhelm spoke not a single word. Instead he paced, studying the forest about them with the patience of a man certain of victory. And with good reason: she could see his gaze alight upon one track after another, drawing closer to their tree.

One of Tatterhelm's fists stayed clenched tight around a strange fistful of dried leaves.

The string of teeth twitched at her throat. Fie started. Her own fingers had already plucked at a Phoenix molar.

Give him fire.

That voice didn't even sound like a Phoenix's anymore.

Tatterhelm dragged on the reins. His mount grunted and stopped, pawing at the needle-strewn ground. Sharp pine resin wafted up the warm air.

Now, her own damned head urged. *Give him fire. Teach them you're not to be crossed.*

Give him fire and you bring the whole rutted lot of them down on you, her Chief voice snapped back. *Pick that fight when your Hawk isn't in pieces.*

And a dreadful mutinous part of her yet wondered when she'd started calling Tavin *her* Hawk.

The Sparrow teeth squawked and slid out of tune.

Harmony, Pa's voice chided as she scrambled to push the teeth back into order, fingers digging into the uneven bark.

The skinwitch's searchlight crept up toward her.

She ground her teeth, holding the harmony as steady as she could. It wavered as the Vulture picked and peeled at the slippery edges of the Sparrow teeth's refuge. Panic simmered in her gut and clawed finger by finger up her spine. They'd already been caught, Tatterhelm only meant to toy with her, hiding was no use—

Bitter fury boiled up with the fear.

She was so, so sick of hiding. Just once—

Teach them how you look after your own.

Her Phoenix teeth warmed on their string.

No. Fie swallowed, fighting for a steady head. Tatterhelm wasn't the best, but he was good enough to break through her teeth, and that was aught that mattered. Two weren't enough to hold off his gaze.

Pa sometimes used three teeth.

But Pa hadn't taught her how.

Pain shot through Fie's index finger as a sliver of bark burrowed beneath the nail, yet her hold on the branch only tightened. Forget three, she'd need a lone Phoenix tooth and then she'd have vengeance for Pa, for her kin—

It could be so easy. The Sparrow-tooth harmony began to fray.

Tatterhelm reached for a hunting horn at his belt.

Their branch shuddered—Tavin had tipped off-balance—

She seized his hand, rough with dried blood and slate dust.

And a third Sparrow tooth sparked awake on her string.

Fie's bones didn't just hum, they *sang*, an awful drone that felt like it might shake her straight into the next life. It took all her focus to pin the tooth into harmony, into balance, and to keep it there—but then there it stayed, each tooth steadying the other two in turn like the legs of a stool. Tatterhelm's gaze sloughed away like an old scab.

And after a long moment, he rode on.

Each dwindling hoofbeat was an accusation. He had dead Crows to answer for, and Fie—she had enough fire teeth to light Sabor from mountain to coast.

But what she wanted didn't matter.

Tavin, too, had steadied out. She pulled her hand free of his and looked away.

Three Sparrow teeth. Fie let her senses roam, prodding at what the triad could reveal. Nearer to Gerbanyar, she half saw, half sensed something like distant cobwebby nets casting about over the treetops. The nearest one already trailed dreamily toward them, just half a league off.

It had to be the rest of the trackers aiming to sniff them out. One thing was sore sure: she didn't want to be any nearer those webs than she had to be. Tatterhelm had ridden on far enough now. It was time to move.

Fie let the third Sparrow tooth go and slipped off the branch, intending to dangle from her fingertips.

Instead every bone in her hands dragged like iron. Her fingers slipped off the branch. She hit the ground in a flurry of pine needles and crowsilk, knocking the wind clean out of her gut.

She gasped as cedar boughs and silvery sky spun dizzily above. A thin whine rang through her ears, the only sound until a thud said one of the boys had made it down as well.

Tavin lurched into view. He looked much better. At least she thought he did. Less blood, less flinching. Maybe no limping now. That meant he was better, right?

His mouth moved, but she caught no words, only a dull ringing. He really had a nice mouth. Even with a little blood streaked at one corner.

She almost believed the fear on his face. He'd gotten hurt for her today. Almost died. A lot. Kin might do that. Caste might do that. Not some near-royal lordling. It made no sense. He made no sense.

He crouched by her side, and as Fie's thoughts slipped and wobbled about in her rattled skull, one thought drifted, dreadful and plain, to the surface: she wanted that.

She wanted him to stay at her side. Not for the day, not for the moon. She wanted him with her even after the oath. She wanted it more than she knew how to want someone. She wanted it more than fire or steel or teeth.

And she wholeheartedly hated it.

". . . hear me?" Tavin's voice seeped in past the ringing in her ears, rising with worry. "Fie? Are you hurt?"

She blinked up at him as her head began to clear. Then she laughed.

It was not a happy laugh.

A raid from monsters. A scummed sinner. The first throat she'd ever cut. A war-witch boiling a man in his own blood before her eyes. An ambush from the queen's pet Vultures. That same war-witch near snapping his own neck on her account. Tatterhelm walking away in one piece. Falling out of a stupid tree.

And a traitor heart that refused to listen to sense.

She hated it. Hated all of it. Hated him. Hated herself.

"Anything else?" she croaked, waving a shaky, blood-flecked hand at the sky. "Covenant? Got any more disasters you're keen to spit my way? Day's still young."

Tavin let out a breath, then brushed her hair aside to rest calloused fingertips on her brow. "Let's not go giving the Covenant any ideas. Can you move your—"

"Let's not go telling me what to do." Fie swatted his hand off and made herself sit up, a peculiar wrath aching in her bones. He had no right to her, to any part of her, least of all her heart. "You damned *fool*. We could have been in and out of Gerbanyar before Tatterhelm caught up, but you just had to lose your head, didn't you?"

Tavin jerked back, shamefaced. Part of her curled with guilt. He'd felled that man on her account.

But she hadn't asked for it. Wanted it, perhaps, in the ugly way she'd wanted Tatterhelm to burn before her. But wanting and asking were beasts of two wholly different names.

"We're lucky the Gerbanyar Hawks didn't stuff us all full of arrows on the spot," she spat. "The queen would've liked that, aye? You'd have done her work for her."

Tavin stared at the ground. Maybe if she pushed him far enough, this nonsense of theirs would be over. He'd stop pretending a Crow and a Hawk could share a road as aught but strangers, and she'd keep pretending it didn't matter to her.

The razor edge of anger glittered in his eyes again. The set of his mouth said it wouldn't be turned on her.

Somehow that only infuriated her more. "What, Vulture got your tongue? You couldn't keep quiet when all our hides were on the line, but *now* it suits you? You've mummed as my kin for nigh a fortnight now. When are you going to understand that being a Crow means you can't just do what you want?"

"*Don't try to tell me I do what I want,*" Tavin snapped.

He rocked back on his heels. One hand ran over his mouth, fingertips pushing down into the sides of his jaw. Then he stood and looked away.

In the startled silence, Fie wondered if she'd meant her words for Tavin or for herself.

The prince's voice cut through the air. "Enough. It's not his fault."

"If by 'not his fault' you mean 'square his fault,' then aye."

"He saved your life not ten minutes ago." Jasimir's tone soured on *your*. "Haven't you been berating us since day one for not standing up for the Crows? Make up your mind whether you want our help or not."

"You call that help? Your Peacocks and Hawks listen to crowns, not Crows. Deal with them when you're not hiding behind our masks, and I'll call that help."

"I already swore an oath to do just that, and if you think that won't cost me dearly—"

"Oh aye, such a trial," Fie sneered. "Poor little princeling has to treat us like people."

Tavin spoke before the prince could fire back. "We need to get moving."

"To where?" Fie lurched to her feet, wearing a scowl. "The Vultures know we're headed northeast. They'll block the flatway to the Marovar."

"We don't have anywhere else," Tavin said shortly. "They can't go too far from their supply caravan, which slows them down in bad terrain. We can keep ahead of them if we stay off the roads."

Fie sucked in a breath. "I won't be able to see plague beacons."

"No," Tavin agreed, "you won't."

He didn't know what he was asking. Lordlings got to look away when they wanted to. Fie'd never had a choice in keeping her eyes open.

"You won't be able to walk us into another trap," the prince muttered.

"Jas." Tavin shook his head.

Fie waited for the rest of what he ought to say: *I know we're asking more of you. But your Crows need you. We need you. I need you.*

She knew it all already. Believed some of it. The rest—the rest she wanted from him.

But he didn't offer another word. And she would not ask.

Perhaps she'd pushed him far enough after all.

Perhaps she'd pushed too far.

But going off the roads . . . She'd already turned her back on her kin. What would the Covenant think of her turning her back on sinners?

Didn't want to be a Crow no more.

Fie's hands curled into dust-lined fists. The Covenant knew the oath she carried now. And Pa wanted her to keep it. It was plain as that.

She shifted her pack and squinted for where afternoon sunlight needled through the cedar boughs. "We go northeast," she said finally, and set off through the trees, back to the sun.

———◆———

Fie's hands burned with salt in a hundred tiny scrapes, and yet she kept scrubbing.

The sun had long slunk below the horizon before they'd stopped for the night. They'd pushed up in thick silence through the bristling hills, up into rockier ground, onto thinner game trails, always searching the growing dark for skinwitches closing in. When they'd staggered to a halt by a pond in the crook of a steep hillside, she'd waited for the boys to refill the water skins, then burned the remains of her arm-rags on the campfire and took the salt and soap-shells to the pond.

She couldn't wash up proper here, not a few paces from the campfire. Even though Tavin had been badgered into sleeping while dinner cooked and the prince didn't shine to girls at all, stripping down in front of lordlings didn't sit right.

But scrub as she might, she couldn't shake the memory of Pa's sword sliding through flesh. By firelight, the salt and suds on her arms might as well have been blood. Even a string of bubbles on the pond's surface reminded her of the gash across the sinner's throat.

"Was that your first time killing someone?"

Fie started. The prince had perched by the campfire, stirring a mash of maize and salt pork, one eye on Tavin's sleeping back.

"Aye," she said.

"I'm sorry."

"For what?"

Jasimir frowned at the mash. "You . . . your family should have been here to help."

Near a week had passed since she'd left them in Cheparok, yet a hot lump still rose in Fie's throat. She splashed cold water on her arms. "Have you ever killed someone?"

He shook his head. "Tavin has. Before today, I mean. One of Rhusana's assassins went down fighting, and another fell on her own poisoned dagger, so Tavin put her out of her misery."

"That's . . . nice of him?"

"It's how we were raised. The Hawk code requires you to treat an enemy with dignity, even in death." Jasimir let the campfire roll around his fingers.

Fie straightened and scoured the hillsides, calling up two Sparrow teeth she'd kept simmering, then working in a third for just a moment. The only Vulture signs the triad showed were those gauzy webs still near Gerbanyar.

She let the third tooth go and returned to the fire, stretching her arms out to help them dry. "Pa never said if it got easier."

"It shouldn't." Tavin sat up, rubbing his eyes. "It does."

"Go back to sleep," the prince said at once. "You need to recover. I'll take your watch."

"I'm fine. Besides, how could I sleep through a feast like this?" He flashed a smile Fie didn't buy for a second. Neither did she miss how his eyes swept the dark.

She salted their paltry dinner anyhow, trying not to fret over their dwindling rations. Four days without viatik made for thin fare, and she wasn't about to march back into Gerbanyar to collect pay.

She wasn't alone in her worries. "We're not going to make it to the Marovar like this," Jasimir said around a mouthful of maize. "Even if we had enough food, we'd freeze on the first mountain."

"We'll cross that bridge when we get to it," Tavin said.

"No, we need to come up with a plan." Jasimir pushed a strip of dried panbread about his bowl. "We're farther north now. Maybe—"

Tavin shook his head. "Not again, Jas."

"The Hawks could escort us there faster."

"Or they could hand us over to Tatterhelm for an early solstice present." Tavin tried to make it sound like a joke. The strain in his voice hamstrung any levity. "The Gerbanyar Hawks weren't exactly throwing themselves between us and the Vultures."

"Then we find other Hawks."

"No, Jas."

"They're Hawks, they have a *code*—"

"I said no." Tavin's voice flattened from amiable to unmovable. "It's my job to keep you in one piece. Let me do it."

Fie knew an order when she heard one. Even if it was aimed at a prince.

A faint howl silenced them, rising and falling with the breeze. Wind on rocks, that was all, yet Fie waited to be sure before she took up her dinner again.

She chewed her maize, glancing between Tavin, who stirred the fire, and the prince, who stared at the coals. "You can have my watch, cousin," she offered, half-jesting.

Tavin wasn't taking any chances. "No he can't."

Jasimir's fists tightened to knots on his knees. He picked up his empty bowl and the cooking pot and stalked off to wash them at the far side of the pond.

"Fie, when you're done . . ." Tavin tossed a burned-out Peacock tooth into the grass. "The glamour's nearly gone."

She picked out a Peacock witch-tooth from the bag, then scooted over. Tavin took the kindled tooth from her with a ghost of a flinch.

"How are you doing?" he asked. At Fie's puzzled look, he ducked his head. "The first time I took a life, I threw up. On the corpse, in fact."

She wrinkled her nose. "Don't you Hawks have some high-minded rule about respecting the dead?"

"This may shock you, but it turns out Hawks don't always follow our own rules," Tavin said, dry. His eyes followed her as she swept the glamour over his face. "But I was trained to kill people and I still felt awful. Are you all right?"

"I don't know," she admitted, cursing in her head. She knew it was best to finish the glamour and be done with it, but her wretched tongue kept wagging anyway. "My job's to cut throats, so what does it matter? I'll get all right by it. Someday."

He started to answer, just as her fingers trailed to that wretched distracting freckle by the corner of his mouth. They both froze a breath too long.

"I think I should teach you to use a sword," Tavin blurted.

Fie jerked her hand away before it made a fool of her. "*What?*"

"Everyone needs a hobby." He rubbed the back of his neck, as if trying to scrape together another jest. "And an appalling number of Saborians seem to have picked 'murdering Crows' for theirs." Tavin pointed to Pa's broken sword. "I guarantee fewer people would try to stiff you on viatik if they thought you could use that for more than mercy."

"You've seen how your kind feel about Crows carrying swords. How do you reckon the Hawks'll like Crows knowing how to use them?"

"I'm not teaching all the Crows, I'm teaching you. And if we get Jas on the throne, the Hawks will be so busy escorting your people around that they might see the wisdom of teaching them, too."

She pursed her lips. He could have offered this anytime in the last fortnight. Anytime before now. He hadn't. This had naught to do with hobbies. "You don't think we can outrun the Vultures?"

Tavin looked to the prince, guilt flashing through his face. Jasimir was still on the far side of the pond. "I should know better than to try slipping anything past you. I don't know when we'll cross them again. But it's still a long way to the Marovar, with or without roads. And after today . . ." He faltered. "I just—I want you to be able to protect yourself."

And the pieces fell together for Fie. This wasn't wholly about the Vultures either. It was also about the Sparrow crooning death threats, and it was about the crowd who'd cheered him on. "I'm carrying enough Phoenix teeth to burn us a road clear to the Marovar and back. You know why I let that scummer yell as he pleased?" she asked. Tavin shook his head. "Because he wanted an excuse to do worse. That's the game, get it? They've naught to lose by playing with us. And there's no way for us to win."

"So you let them talk and cut your losses." He shook his head again. "That's . . . You shouldn't have to live like that."

"Aye. And that's why I asked for Hawks." She staggered to her feet, ignoring the ache of weary muscles and the warning clamor of her own head. "But until I get them, I suppose it's worth knowing how to use a sword."

What was she playing at? Pa's tooth rolled in her fingers. Crows weren't allowed steel.

Nor were they allowed fire teeth and abandoned roads. She'd taken on both to keep the Covenant oath, and if it helped get them to Trikovoi in one piece, she'd take up a sword, too.

Tavin stood, then looked about. Alarm shot through his face. "Where's Jas?"

Fie twisted. The prince's shadow had vanished from the pond.

"Right here." Jasimir emerged at the other side of the fire, pot and bowl in hand. "What's the matter?"

Tavin ran a hand over his face. "Nothing. It's fine. I'm teaching Fie to use a sword, if you want to help."

The prince looked from Tavin to her then, tallying up a sore kind of sum. He sat, slow. "I'll . . . keep a lookout." He glanced up. "Since we *are* being hunted by Vultures. In case anyone forgot."

Tavin forced out an uneasy laugh. "If only." He gestured to a patch of level ground a few paces away. "Let's be clear of the fire."

They were also clear of the prince's earshot. Fie didn't think that to be chance.

It would be naught but practice. Plain and easy as a game of Twelve Shells, and no more to it.

Fie knew a lie when she heard one. Even one she aimed at herself.

Tavin unsheathed his swords but set them in the grass near his feet, much to Fie's relief. Instead he passed her an empty scabbard, then used the remaining scabbard to draw two marks in the dirt, dim by firelight. "Keep your feet on those. Now look at me." She did. "Keep looking at me." He circled to her right side, so her chin near lined up to her shoulder. "Hold up your, er, sword. Elbow loose. There. If you remember anything, let it be this."

"Standing like a dolt?" Fie asked. Everything about it felt unnatural and foolish. The Vultures couldn't possibly be watching, or she'd have heard their laughter.

"I know it doesn't feel right." A shade of Tavin's normal grin flashed as he turned square to her and tapped one of his shoulders. "Here, try to hit me." She took an awkward step forward and jabbed the scabbard into his shoulder easy enough, then retreated to her footmarks.

Tavin shifted, mirroring the stance he'd set her into: scabbard held out between them, the rest of him angled to the side. He tapped the same shoulder. "Again."

She tried, but he all but brushed the strike aside. Now she saw: even if she got past his own weapon, she had to travel within his arm's reach and then hit a shoulder still tilted askew from her.

"That's why," he said. "If anything will keep you alive, it's this: be as small a target as you can. And always keep your weapon between you and your foe." His mouth twisted. "All things considered, that will probably come naturally to you."

She gave him a dark look. "Aye, and I bet hitting you will, too."

"I wouldn't be surprised." The grin that followed flashed more than a shade of his usual humor. "Short swords don't have much range, but you have the element of surprise. Your best shot will be knocking a hit off course and using that opening to go for their hands, eyes, anything you can. Try to hit me, slowly." She did. He brushed her strike off again, but then in a blink, he was closer, his scabbard tapping her forearm.

Fie narrowed her eyes. "What just happened?"

Tavin shifted back. "Watch. Block." He pushed her scabbard away slow, firelight slipping along the lines of his scarred wrist. "Step in." He stepped into the void. "Strike." His scabbard completed an arc it had begun in the block, landing at her forearm again. "Now you—"

She moved before he finished. He automatically sprang out of her range, then sighed. "I knew I should have put off teaching you how to hit me."

"You said to use the element of surprise."

"Yes, on people who are trying to kill you!" He gave an exasperated laugh, a little too loud, then glanced to the prince.

Jasimir was listing sideways, chin propped on a palm. A snore betrayed him.

Relief flickered through Tavin's expression.

Fie lowered her scabbard. "Why are you dragging it out?"

"I'm not," he said, setting himself back into the sword stance. "I am fully prepared for you to hit me. Have at it."

She scowled. *Block.* "You know what I mean." Her scabbard pushed his aside. Her voice lowered. "You're not going back to the palace." *Step in.* "And he thinks you are." *Strike.* She went for the throat. "You'll die for him, but you won't tell him the truth?"

Tavin's face was unreadable; he did not move away. "What does it matter to you?"

"It's a pain in my ass," she hissed. Yet another half-lie. "And yours. He keeps harping on the Hawks because he needs to believe you're all squeaky-clean and selfless, married to your duty."

"What does that have to do with me?"

Fie stepped back. "What's your duty to the prince?"

"To keep him alive." Tavin nodded slowly. "To . . . to die for him."

"Aye." Fie shrugged. "So he needs to believe you'll do it, and he'll keep up that nonsense the whole way to the Marovar, just to prove it. Unless you tell him the truth."

"It's not that easy." Tavin stepped back. "Again."

Annoyance made her hasty. *Block.* "Twelve hells it isn't."

Step in. "It's not about me," Tavin said, "it's the king." *Strike.* "Again."

"What's the king to do with it?" Fie returned to her footmarks.

"King Surimir has a . . . a shine for Hawks." Tavin frowned. By dark, Fie could pretend she hadn't polished away his scars. "He's the sort of king who travels with half an army just to remind people he commands their blades. He wants people to think he's dangerous. To treat him like he is."

Fie remembered the first time she'd held Phoenix fire. She hadn't wanted to burn the world down; she'd wanted the world to know she *could*.

"He's a Phoenix witch," she mumbled. "He's a king. Isn't that enough?"

Tavin shook his head. "Again." *Block.* "He married Queen Jasindra mostly to add her to his armory. I was given to Jas so he could start his own Hawk collection." *Step in.* "But Surimir wants an imitator, not a son. Jas has no interest in throwing himself parades or yanking half the Splendid Castes into his bed. The queen raised him to be a good ruler. I was raised to be a good Hawk. You can guess which of us the king thinks is useful."

Strike.

She knew what he meant, yet she couldn't help another jab. "And how does you tumbling all those palace waifs help the prince, then?"

Fie hid her delight when he actually slipped. Then she tripped on her own snare: he righted himself, all fluster and fumble, and Fie discovered she found that disturbingly close to charming. *Damn* him. Of course he'd find a way to make stumbling about attractive.

"It—it would have been cruel to ask for more," he said, blunt. "To try to make anything last." She lowered her scabbard, feeling as though she'd waded into waters deeper than she'd thought. "I'm a bastard, an heir to nothing. For ten years, I've been told my only purpose is to keep Jas alive. That the best thing I can do is die for him. Of course I met people I wanted, but how could I ask them to stay mine when I couldn't truly be theirs?"

Any sneer or jest had long withered on Fie's tongue. "You're still going to disappear once we're out of this. What are you going to tell him then?"

"The truth. Fie, I promised I'd do everything I can to help you. I brought this on your family. I owe you a debt. And my life will be my own to give, as long as you would have it." He raised his scabbard, and something frighteningly near hope rose in his voice. "Again."

Fie tried to order her whirlwind thoughts and couldn't even see where to start. Tavin's arm moved through the dark.

He truly meant to vanish.

Block.

He meant to help her. To do everything he could. But she'd thought—

Step in.

She'd told herself he only had a tourist's interest in her. That he found her at best a useful ally to woo, at worst the makings of a lurid boast to scandalize the other Hawks.

Not someone worth everything he had to give.

Some distant side of her unspooled Jasimir's words short hours ago: *He saved your life.*

Strike.

Tavin did not step back. Neither did she, lingering too close, far too close, locked in their makeshift duel.

"When you said you don't do what you want . . ." She trailed off, knowing stark what she asked, too unsteady to say the words aloud.

He bent his head to her, near enough that his hair dusted her brow. Fie didn't mean to turn her face up, but her chin had a mind of its own.

"You know what I mean," he whispered.

Fie's traitor heart thundered its assent, even as her mind rattled through its protests. She ought to run, to cool her head, if only her feet would cooperate—she had to run, she couldn't have what she wanted—not the way she wanted him—

Yet Tavin moved first. His breath caught; she felt its absence on her cheeks.

And then he stepped back.

Something old and familiar slid across his features easy as a paper screen, hiding any sign of the unpolished, unpracticed boy of a moment ago.

"It's late," he said, voice fraying at the very edges. "You should rest. I'll take watch."

CHAPTER FIFTEEN

—— WOLF COUNTRY ——

Tᴴᴱ ʜᴜᴍᴍɪɴɢ ᴡᴏᴋᴇ ꜰɪᴇ, ᴀs ɪᴛ ʜᴀᴅ ɴᴇᴀʀ ᴇᴠᴇʀʏ ᴍᴏʀɴɪɴɢ sɪɴᴄᴇ Cheparok.

Tavin sat with his back to her, humming quiet into the dark. She couldn't tell if he meant to rouse her by it, or if he'd been at the song awhile. He never seemed to be at the same place when her eyes opened.

Gray-blue gnawed at the eastern horizon. Her watch had come.

Fie rolled up onto her knees, yawning. Tavin glanced back at her, nodded, and folded himself to the ground near the prince.

She stretched and fished the laceroot seeds from her pack, letting their bitter pulp prick her awake. The pot went on the coals with a fistful of wild mint for tea. She settled beside it, running a hand through her dusty hair, and tried not to dwell on how she welcomed the quiet in the mornings now, with her two false Crows fast asleep.

Instead Fie's mind circled round the moment, not long enough past, when she'd near done the unthinkable.

But this time, Tavin was the one who'd run.

Her face warmed, whether with humiliation or something else, she couldn't say. Perhaps he'd thought twice on distraction with Tatterhelm on their trail. Perhaps she'd pushed his mummer's bluff too far.

Perhaps he'd remembered she was a Crow.

She didn't know what she'd hoped for. Oh, there were tales to be sure, songs of Sparrows and Hawks struck apart by caste law, beggars and queens, lords who gave up their caste for love of a Swan . . . but her faith in songs had long run dry. Only the gentry found happy endings in those songs. Only a fool would believe them true.

Only a fool would believe, for even the scarcest moment, that she'd walk a happier road with a Hawk.

She didn't realize her stare had snagged on his sleeping face until a crackle from the embers drew it away.

Fie lost track of time as silvery light seeped into the dark overhead. Cricket-song trickled up through the grass. She sipped her mint tea and watched a lone wolf trail a cluster of shaggy goats, threading through a distant hillside of stone and brush and yellowing bramble. She'd no call to fear wolves in summer, not with fresh kill in their belly. The wolves of winter, though . . .

Pa'd taught her to watch the starving wolf. When beasts go hungry too long, he'd said, they forget what they ought to fear.

Now, in the dry chill of a gray dawn, Fie thought of the wolf, and then she thought of Hangdog's tooth hanging cold on her string, and an arrow shot through an eye as the Peacock lord watched.

A twig snapped behind her.

Fie went still, every nerve flaring. When no sound followed, she let out a sigh, put down her tea, and picked up the pot.

Then in one swift twist, she flung its boiling water into the tree-barred dark at her back.

A man's scream shattered the quiet.

A shadow broke from the trees, only to stumble straight into Fie swinging the scalding pot. He dropped. Six more shades erupted from the dark, flashing blades and teeth, but they struck too late: they'd already woken the prince and the Hawk.

The rest was a frenzy of noise, steel, and blood. One body fell, then another—and then, curiously, the last four assailants whipped back into the thinning dark.

A chorus of sick whistles trailed in their wake.

Fie stared after them, belly churning. In the fray, they'd looked the same as any other Vulture, yet—

"Eyes," Prince Jasimir croaked. "They had no—no eyes—" He doubled over, retching.

Tavin braced Jasimir's shoulders. "They saw us fine, Jas. It was just the dark."

A laugh gurgled through the camp. Fie wrenched about and found one of the Vultures clutching his spilling tripe.

"Aye, Highness," he giggled. "Just the dark."

Fie stalked over and knelt. The Vulture was fading. She snatched up a Crane tooth and called it to life. It wasn't enough to force truth, but enough to smell a lie. "How did you find us?"

A bloody grin split his face. "We have something that belongs to you."

Fie felt as if someone had unraveled her with one sharp yank.

So that was how the Vultures had caught their trail. Whatever they had—a loose hair, an old shirt, a worn ragdoll—it meant any Vulture would see a path to them as long as it sat in their bare hands, witch or no.

By rights, the Vultures should have shown up hours ago. Something had to have broken the trail.

Three teeth. She'd burned the trio of Sparrow teeth.

So three could shake even the best of the Vultures. Pa would be proud—

Pa.

"How many of your Crow hostages are still alive?" she demanded, suddenly horrified that it hadn't been her first question.

The man convulsed, choking.

"*How many?*" she demanded. It was no use. In moments, the Vulture had gone still.

Tavin crouched by her side. "The scouts that ran will bring Tatterhelm as fast as he can ride. We need to get away."

"There's at least a week's worth of food here." Jasimir had pried a pack from a dead Vulture. "Tatterhelm must have sent them to search ahead of the main party."

Fie stood. "Take anything of use from the dead—provisions, gloves, furs. We need cold gear and food more than they do. Then we move out."

Jasimir looked up from the pack. "We have to give them final rites."

"That better be a royal 'we,' cousin." Fie set about dragging the bodies together. "If these scummers were dying of thirst in the desert, I wouldn't give them a single drop of my piss."

"If we leave them like animals, we're just as bad as they are," Jasimir insisted. "You'll give sinners final rites, but not them? Is that what you call mercy?"

"No," Fie answered, looking pointedly at the distant hill, where a bloody goat carcass painted a red smear in the grass. Three dead Vultures. Easy prey. "This is what I call wolf country."

"Tav." The prince gave his Hawk a look. "The code *says,* 'I will not dishonor my dead.'"

Tavin's shoulders stiffened. "It also says, 'I will serve my nation and the throne above all,'" he said, sounding tired. "And that one comes first."

On the first day after Gerbanyar, they changed the watch.

Fie lit three Sparrow teeth once they set off, and tried to shake the singing from her bones. With three teeth she could weave the refuge round herself and the lordlings, slipping them from the Vulture's notice but letting them yet see one another. Then she kept three alight all through the day and through a cold, starless first watch, until Tavin shook her from her red-eyed fog.

She let the Sparrow teeth go and slept a fitful few hours, knowing every breath left them all exposed to the Vultures on their trail.

On the second day, a headache roosted in Fie's skull. She kept her three teeth burning anyhow and practiced swords again with Tavin and wiped his face into the prince's once more. When she slept, Tatterhelm stalked her dreams, and he cut oath after oath into her palms until they were as useless as Viimo's.

On the third day, she found she missed waking to Tavin's humming. She didn't tell him.

On the fourth day, her every bone ached as they picked their way across a vast field of black rock bubbled like foam, hard and sharp as hunger. Thin, curling grass sprouted between stone, and halfway through, they found a pool of steaming water as vivid blue as a peacock plume's eye with no bottom in sight.

Prince Jasimir reached for it, and Fie wondered for a terrible moment how easy it would be to let him go, give the Vultures what they wanted, and bring it all to an end.

Instead she yanked him back and threw a rock into the pool. It dissolved almost immediately.

Jasimir spent the rest of the day clenching and unclenching the fist he'd near lost.

She took Tavin's face again that night. He pretended he didn't see how her hands shook, and she pretended not to see how he ground his teeth, and after, they kept their distance to practice swords. She kept her watch beneath a dead Vulture's elk pelt, watching a storm drum thunder across the plain, three teeth burning, burning, burning still, her bones singing so loud it felt like screaming.

Late in the night, copper stung her nose. When she touched her fingers to her upper lip, they came away red.

The skinwitches had drawn near enough that she could sense their spidery hunting veils on a far horizon. They wouldn't catch up while she slept, but they would gain ground all the same.

The storm moved on, and the bleeding stopped before Tavin woke for his watch. She didn't tell him about that, either. In the morning, for the fifth straight day, she lit the teeth.

On the sixth day, she fell.

Gray patches had drifted through her vision all morning. She'd wanted to believe it was only from Vultures scavenging at her sleep, but she knew better. Her bones sang no more, ached no more, only shuddered and howled. Still she kept the three teeth burning.

The skinwitches had drawn too close. A day behind them, maybe less.

And every time she slept, she let them close in.

They'd made it across the plain, into the kind of country where crags and cliffs jutted up from dark forests like teeth of a beast bent on devouring the sky. By Fie's guess, the summer solstice was only a moon and a half off, yet snow still lingered in the shade of impossibly tall pines. Every so often, when the boys' backs were turned, Fie would scrub a fistful of slush over her face to sting herself awake.

It didn't work. Midway through the afternoon, gray choked her vision off. Fie stopped, bones screeching in protest as she fought to keep upright. They had to keep moving. The Sparrow tooth triad showed her

Vulture webs prowling at the horizon, waiting for her to foul up. Keep moving. Keep your eyes open. Keep the oath—

Her knees buckled. Someone called her name, once, twice—then nothing.

She'd no notion of how much time passed before Tavin's face swam into view. His voice followed a slow heartbeat later.

". . . too much. We need to get somewhere safe so she can rest."

"You managed in Gerbanyar," the prince argued. "What if she just walks—"

"No." Tavin cut him off. "It's not the same. I lost control. She's been burning herself out for days."

"Have not," she tried to grumble. Instead what she said was "Hrmmgh."

The world tipped. Tavin had shifted her in his arms. "Easy now," he said in something uncomfortably close to a Safe voice, dabbing at her nose with one sleeve. Red spotted the cloth. "You'll be fine, you just need to sleep it off."

She didn't want to sleep it off. The Vultures were coming.

"Hngh," she protested before gray clouded her sight again.

Everything spun as Tavin stood, gathering her to him. "We need to get to shelter."

No, she tried to say, but couldn't manage even that. *You have to keep moving, you have to keep your eyes open*—

"Are you sure?"

"She's the only reason the Vultures haven't rounded us up already," Tavin said tightly. "Yes, Jas. I'm sure."

Gray faded to black and took Fie with it.

She woke to the scratch of stone.

"Let me." That was Tavin.

Scratch. Scratch. "I can do it."

"Jas—"

"Just—just let me . . ." *Scratch-scratch-scratch.* ". . . give me a moment. It just has to catch—"

"Go wash up, Jas," Tavin sighed. "We probably won't have another chance before we reach Trikovoi."

"If we don't get captured by Vultures first," Jasimir muttered amid a scuffle of sandal-nails.

"We won't." Tavin went unanswered. Footsteps echoed and dwindled. Fie caught the rattle of flint, then a hiss and crack before orange light bloomed beyond her eyelids.

She forced her eyes open. The blur of color and shadow sifted into jagged stone walls, a meager fire clambering up dried brush, a kneeling shadow with his back to her. The rest of the world filled in slow: air warmer than it had any right to be this far into the mountains, ground harder than dirt, furs heaped heavy and soft over her, copper in the back of her throat.

Tavin had found them shelter after all. Groggy, she watched him add kindling to the fire and wondered if she could reach him from where she lay, what would happen if she ran her fingertips down his spine.

Then Tavin turned to check on her, his face for once raw and open with worry. It softened into a smile when he saw she was awake. She couldn't help but smile back, too tired, too far off the roads to hate herself for it.

"How long was I out?" Fie asked.

Scratch-scratch-scratch. This time the scrape came from the prince's return.

"Not nearly long enough." Tavin fumbled for the pot, dumped a few fistfuls of rice and dried peas and salt pork inside, then poured water over the mess and set it by the fire. "My turn to wash up. If I'm not back in an hour, assume cave ghosts got me and make a run for it. But eat dinner first."

Jasimir took Tavin's place, frowning, as the Hawk strode away. Fie sat up, every muscle fighting back, and took a second look at their home for the night. Her pack had been repurposed as her pillow; the other packs sat nearby. She saw neither beginning nor end to the cave, only walls bending out of sight. A cooler draft wafted from the passage opposite of where Tavin had gone off to, yet their camp stayed balmier than the fire alone ought to have managed.

She cleared her throat. "How's it so warm in here?"

The prince glanced at her, brief as a static shock. "There's a hot spring farther in."

That explained it. The notion of washing up in a proper spring near made Fie weep. The notion of Tavin washing up in a hot spring had an entirely different effect on her.

"You should leave him be."

Fie stared at the prince, heat rushing up her neck. "What?"

"I'm not *utterly* oblivious." Jasimir almost looked shamefaced. "But you're only going to get hurt."

The fire in Fie's skull had little to do with her notions of Tavin now. "You don't know what you're talking about."

"You're just distracting him," Jasimir said, flat. "And I'm trying to help. Maybe it seems like he's serious now, but he's never been with someone for more than a moon."

"Keep your own damn business," Fie snapped. "I'm not here to warm my bed. I'm busy keeping you both alive."

"Why?" She'd set Jasimir off good and true this time. "You're not bound to anything. You could go any time, collect your kin, and leave us be. But you're not doing this for the oath anymore, are you?"

Fie's fist knotted in the stolen fur. Her voice shook. "If I didn't care about the oath, *cousin*, I'd have gladly handed you to Tatterhelm myself."

"Your friend Hangdog certainly seemed to care about keeping the—"

"*Enough.*" Tavin emerged from the shadows behind them, startling Fie and the prince both. "You should be ashamed of that oath, Jas. It means both our castes are failing to protect our own people."

Prince Jasimir's mouth opened and closed. He looked as mortified as Fie felt.

She yanked a change of clothes and the bag of soap-shells free from her pack. "I'll wash up," she mumbled, tottering to her feet. Tavin reached to steady her, and she didn't know if she wanted to veer away or stumble to him.

She settled for neither, slipping past and into the dim passage, head a-whirl. Sure enough, the air thickened with steam the farther she went, soon yawning into a broad, clear pool. Waning daylight curled in the air, streaming from a gap far above.

Fie took a moment to try her three Sparrow teeth. They only lasted a breath, just long enough to show wisps of Vulture tracking spells sloughing off. They must have latched on the moment she fell.

She made a Vulture tooth last longer, searching for Tatterhelm's supply master with one hand on a belt she'd taken from the dead skinwitches. The trail stretched far beyond the cave, distant enough to buy them at least a night.

The thought of the oath perched on her shoulder while she stripped out of her clothes and brought them with her to wash in the stinging-hot water, cracking a handful of soap-shells with relish.

What sort of Crow turned her back on the roads the Covenant bound her to walk? What sort of Crow practiced at swords? What Crow would cross a skinwitch, threaten a prince, and think folly over a bastard Hawk?

A traitor like Hangdog, part of her said.

A chief like Pa, another pushed back.

And a third whispered, *One too hungry to remember fear.*

She hadn't any answer by the time she climbed out of the pool, scrubbed near-sore and happier for it. She didn't know if she'd have an answer before she reached the Marovar, or even after.

They were close. They would beat Tatterhelm to Trikovoi, and Pa would be her chief again, and the prince would be someone else's problem, and Tavin . . . she couldn't dwell on Tavin.

She wrung out the sodden clothes and pulled on her dry spares, then padded back, sandals in hand. A bowl of dinner sat by the campfire; Prince Jasimir brushed past her, wordlessly bearing an armful of dishes and dirty clothes to the spring. Tavin was nowhere to be seen. She scowled. That meant he'd taken her watch.

The glamour still needed to be pasted on again, no matter how tired she was. Fie laid her wet clothes out to dry by the fire, then plucked the bowl from the ground and went in search of the Hawk.

She found him near the mouth of the cave, a handful of pelts at his side to ward off the frosty night ahead. Indigo pines carpeted the valley below them; threads of lightning stitched a sky plush with storm clouds.

Tavin glanced back at her, and something like the lightning flickered through his eyes. Then that old, practiced paper-screen look walled it off once more.

Fie decided the glamour could wait until after she'd eaten. She sat beside him, shoveling rice and pork into her mouth with dried panbread. The air's chill slid down her waterlogged hair, clinging to her scalp. "This is my watch."

"How far off are they?" he asked quietly.

Fie put one hand on a stolen fur, then called the Vulture tooth back to life. It showed her a clear path through the trees this time, somewhere beyond the storm. Less than a day off now. Creeping closer.

She pointed to the ridge. "Out there. They won't reach us tonight, but . . ."

Tavin nodded. She waited for some new foolery: a jest about cave ghosts, a jibe about his cooking, anything. It didn't come.

"I can hide us again," she offered.

"They already know we've stopped here. Save your strength."

"Then let me take watch." A cold wind buffeted her, chased by a soft rumble of thunder.

Tavin winced. "It's fine. You deserve a—"

"Talk plain," Fie interrupted, chewing over another mouthful of dinner. "You don't want to deal with the prince. What's got you so riled up? None of what he said was a surprise."

Tavin studied the horizon a long while before he spoke. "You remember the game I showed you? Twelve Shells?"

"Aye."

"Remember how I said the palace plays its own versions?"

"Aye. What's it to do with the prince?"

"How many castes are there in Sabor, Fie?"

Twelve. Twelve castes, all told. She began to see where he was going. "How does it work?"

"Each shell has a caste, and a value."

"Let me guess," she said. "The Crow shell is worthless."

"And if there's a draw . . . whoever has the Crow shell loses the game."

Fie shrugged and set her empty bowl aside. "I got rough news for you: they act even worse about Crows outside Twelve Shells."

"But that's just it." His face stayed steady; his hands couldn't stay still, running over stone, picking at a loose thread, knotting together until his knuckles paled. "It's everywhere. It's *everywhere*. The Oleanders, the markets in Cheparok, everything. You're right, you've been right the whole time, I know it, and Jas knows it, and the reason I don't want to look at him is because we both told you we'd fix it and . . . and I don't think we can."

Fie watched the storm, thunder rolling about her head as the wind picked up.

"You can't," she said finally.

"We said we would."

"You said you would help me after this," she corrected. "And the prince swore to grant us Hawk guards, because that's what I asked for."

He gave a short, bitter laugh. "We both know Hawks can't be trusted."

"Aye, I'd fancy it if they'd treat us like people," Fie said. "I'll settle for them following royal commands, like it or not. It won't change your Twelve Shells, it won't stop towns shorting viatik. But it'll say we're part of Sabor, that the boy below the crown thinks we have worth. And royal opinions tend to catch on." She settled back. "So why didn't you say aught sooner?"

His throat moved; the screen slipped back. "I . . . I never know what to say to you," he admitted. "It's usually wrong."

She couldn't help a thin smile. "You've got a few things right."

"Not enough. I want . . ." He trailed off, then cleared his throat. "You're here for the glamour, right?"

"Now?" She reached for a Peacock tooth.

He ducked his head, resigned. "It's not like Tatterhelm's turned around and gone home."

A tooth had never felt so heavy in Fie's hand. She let it go. "He's not at our door, either. It can wait."

"No," he sighed. "Please. Let's get it over with." Tavin closed his eyes, like he awaited a magistrate's sentencing. One she would hand down.

She reached for him—then, for the first time, let her fingers brush his jaw, turning his face to her. The words fell before she could catch them. "What do you want?"

He wore the thousand-sided look once more, but this time, in a thousand different ways, it said only one thing:

You.

"It doesn't matter," he said instead, voice cracking.

Thunder shook the sky.

She'd known, she'd known, she'd known all along. Every look, every touch, every stray unpracticed smile, it had all said as much and more. And her own head had been dancing round it, insisting no Hawk could want her, searching for angles and motives, spinning lie after lie to cocoon the fearful truth.

Heartbeat after heartbeat rattled in Fie's ears, the seed of another fearful truth unfurling, working its way to the surface of her thoughts. It didn't matter what they wanted. She knew that too well. She was a Crow chief, he was the prince's Hawk; until this nightmare passed, they had to look after their own. The oath, the prince, they came first and naught else.

What do you want, Fie?

The first shoots pierced through: she wanted him more than fire or steel or games, hungered for him in a way she couldn't fathom, couldn't reconcile, couldn't stop.

It didn't matter.

She thought of the wolf in winter. She thought of hunger greater than fear.

And the terrible truth took root:

If it didn't matter what they wanted, it wouldn't matter if—just once—they got it.

When, not if.

Fie took Tavin's face in her hands and kissed him.

At first he hardly stirred, and for a horrid moment she thought she'd made a mistake, that she'd misjudged it all, that he'd think her a fool—she pulled back—

Then a strange, slight shiver passed through him, and a breath later, she found that meant the last of his restraint had snapped.

He didn't kiss her back so much as drown himself in her. His fingers wound themselves in her hair, mapped out the bones and planes of her back by touch, fitted her hips against his; his mouth sought hers like a cure, starving and fierce, only to wander down her throat until she could scarce breathe.

A light scrape pricked at her collarbone—and then her head flooded with heat, with need, with dizzying awe and fear and desire, all anchored to thoughts of—her?

Oh. She drew Tavin back to her mouth. "Mind your teeth."

"Yes, chief," he murmured, and set about doing just that.

She didn't mean to slide her hands below his shirt, yet she found them there, roaming along scar and muscle and rib and finding her hunger only growing, a fire that sparked from skin striking skin and burned without mercy. Soon the shirts were an afterthought. One rasped question and granted permission later, the rest of their clothing followed suit, forgotten even faster in the crash of thunder and the fire driving them both.

Before, when she'd lain with Hangdog, it had been matters of urgency, a hasty exchange of services. Needs met and dismissed with one eye still at watch, one ear still pressed to the ground, ready to flee.

Now Fie didn't know if she could tear herself away, caught in a way that felt like binds breaking, lost in a way that felt like being found. Tavin too moved with urgency, but it was a curious kind, a need to discover every place that made her shiver or gasp or bite her fist to keep from crying out. And then he found them again, and again, and again; Fie knew only the fire arching through her, through him, again and again, until it finally left them both trembling and tangled in the dark.

After, as she lay in his arms under their ragged cloaks and stolen furs, she told him: "You know this won't be easy."

In answer, he pulled her closer and kissed her one more time. Then he told her: "You make me believe I can do something better with my life than die."

"Oh." She did not know what else to say besides "Well. You should." Then she wriggled farther away from the cold of the passing storm. "Wake me for second watch."

It was a strange thing, to fall asleep feeling safer for the warmth at her back. To fall asleep feeling safe at all.

Where her dreams went that night, no Vultures followed.

CHAPTER SIXTEEN

— THE FOOL —

TAVIN DID NOT WAKE HER FOR SECOND WATCH.

Fie roused on her own anyhow. The humming did it, quieter than before, and somehow familiar by now. She pushed her head out from the pelts and found him sitting up beside her, eyes on the dark valley below.

"What's that song?" she mumbled, resting her chin on his stomach.

He smiled down at her in a fashion Fie would have called revolting a moon earlier. *Damn* him, making a foolish sap of her. "It's an old watch-hymn my mother used to sing. It's supposed to help you keep awake."

"Seems like it works."

"Well enough." He threaded a lock of her hair through his fingers. "How . . . how are you feeling?"

She knew a question behind a question when she heard one, sleepy as she was. "You surprised me. Figured you'd know all there was to tumbling, but . . ."

He tensed. "It's . . . complicated," he said, an edge of uncertainty in his voice. "Gender's never mattered to me, but I—I didn't want to get anyone with child. So if that was a possibility, we just did other, er, activities. Was it—were you—"

"Aye. You did right." She relented and gave him a crooked grin, and was secretly tickled when he relaxed, his breath settling into an easy rise and fall. "But I won't mind if you want more practice."

He huffed a laugh at that, one that rumbled through her, too. His fingers curled tighter in her hair, his thumb resting just below her ear. "I wish I could do it all right. Flowers, poetry, awkward conversations with your parents. You know . . . courtship."

"Told you I don't truck with those," she said through a yawn. "Can't even read poetry."

"I'll read it to you. I guarantee it will be terrible." He grinned. "There will be nineteen verses. Your eyes will absolutely be likened to starless skies. So will your hair. I'm not very creative."

"Stick with flowers." Fie wrinkled her nose.

"Or knives. Weapons. That's what Hawks give one another, anyway. Half of Dragovoi's armory comes from the year the master-general chose her spouses."

"I've already go half a sword." She traced the shiny lines of his burn scar, curious. "Who gave you this?"

She felt his breath catch, the skin beneath her cheek stilling for a heartbeat or two. Then he said, "Someone who didn't know what they were doing."

The old bitterness in his voice reminded her of Hangdog.

She didn't ask more, only twined her fingers with his until the rise and fall of his chest steadied again.

Then she pushed herself up and reached for her clothes. "I'm getting my laceroot. And then I'm taking watch."

Tavin opened his mouth to argue and yawned instead. When Fie returned, she settled beside him and shifted his head onto her lap.

"I don't suppose I can convince you to sleep more," he sighed, weariness bleeding his words together.

"Maybe when you stop slurring." She couldn't scrape the wry smile from her voice. "Now quit fussing and get some rest."

Fie took his disgruntled grumble as surrender. The rhythm of breath on her knee evened out as she turned her eyes to the dark beyond the cave.

Somewhere, beyond the quiet, beyond the heat of her and her Hawk, somewhere she couldn't see—the Vultures waited for her.

For a moment, the weight of the unreadable dark crushed in all about Fie. The best trackers in Sabor hunted her. The queen had sold the Crow caste to a prey-beast's death. And her family lived only as long as their monstrous captor found them useful.

Fie ought to have rolled Pa's tooth in her fingers. Instead they twisted in the hair at the nape of Tavin's neck. It shouldn't have comforted her; it did anyhow.

The peculiar Hawk at her knee believed they could put it all to rights. Believed in her. Believed in a life with her after this.

Perhaps he was a fool after all. Or perhaps he'd gotten something else right.

Fie kept one hand on her Hawk and both eyes on the ebbing dark.

A few hours passed before shuffling echoed from deeper within their cave. The prince had woken. Fie's gut twinged. Jasimir was bound to ken what her absence meant. The question was how he'd take it.

The hue of the cloud-dusted horizon said she had another hour or two before they had to face him. Maybe less, if the skinwitches had made good time tonight.

She called a Vulture tooth to life and gripped a stolen fur. The trail lit up—

And stopped a bare league off, in the valley below.

Fie sucked in a breath and shook Tavin's shoulder, trying to keep her head steady. "Tavin—*Tavin*—"

He jerked awake. "What's wrong?"

"The Vultures." She staggered to her feet, swaying as blood rushed down her numb legs. "I just looked—they're—they're too close—"

"How far?"

"A league, maybe."

Tavin swore and shouted for the prince. He and Fie scrambled about for clothing and blades, stumbling into each other in the dim. Cold guilt thudded about Fie's belly. If she'd held out longer with her three teeth; if she'd taken first watch; if she'd checked sooner—

Calloused hands cupped her cheeks, stilling her. "This isn't your fault."

"Twelve hells it isn't," Fie spat. "I'm the—"

"The only reason we've made it this far. We're all in over our heads." Brute honesty chewed a ragged edge in his voice. "You're the only one treading water. We can vanish once we clear the cave, and they'll lose us again, all right?" She didn't answer. He pulled her close, leaning his brow on hers. "Fie. They've been closer than this twice now, and we've still outrun them thanks to you."

"But we have to keep doing it, *keep* outrunning them, all the way to the Marovar," she whispered. "And they only have to catch up once."

At the grate of a throat clearing, Fie and Tavin jolted apart. Jasimir stood a few paces away, face ironed blank. "What's wrong?"

"The Vultures are a league off," Fie blurted.

Jasimir's eyes widened, then landed on her. "How did they get so close?" he asked, frosty.

"We all needed to rest." Tavin strode past the prince. "And now we need to get out."

Fie followed him, furs and cloaks bundled under an arm. Behind her, she could have sworn she heard the prince mutter, "'*Rest.*'"

A flush ran up her neck. She did not look back.

They left minutes later, Fie dragging three Sparrow teeth into harmony as sunrise ripped the dark seam of the horizon. Spindly fingers of Vulture tracking spells pried all about the cave behind them, fumbling over rock and tree like a drunkard who'd dropped his purse in the dark.

All through the morning they hurried on, through beech and spruce and bristling pine, as the trees thinned and yielded to snow-patched black stone. A hushed murmur through the leaves swelled to a full-throated roar once they reached the gnashing river.

"It's the Fan," Tavin said as they paused at the top of the banks. He hadn't spoken since they'd left the cave. None of them had. Instead they'd glanced over their shoulders again and again and rushed ahead. "This is where it starts, from the glaciers."

It looked nothing like the sedate ribbon Fie recalled from Cheparok. But the river was far, far from the southern deltas now, and so were they.

Tavin sat and unrolled one of the stolen pelts from his pack, then cut two wide strips and handed them to Fie. "Wrap your sandals. We'll be crossing snow and ice soon."

"Where are the Vultures?" Jasimir asked over the water's rush.

Fie reached through her triad of teeth and grimaced. "League and a half? We've gone northeast. They're going due north."

"They must think we're trying the Sangrapa Pass." Tavin waved at a dip between two gray peaks leagues north, then handed two more hide strips to the prince. "It's the fastest route to Draga. But Trikovoi is beyond the Misgova Pass." He pointed to a toothsome, winding slope to the east. "We can clear it tonight. And if we make it through Misgova without them catching on . . ."

It could give them the lead they needed. Fie still heard the question behind the question. She dug a fistful of Sparrow teeth from her bag. "But if they catch on, they'll know we aim for Trikovoi, and then we're rutted." Tavin nodded, grim. She fed the teeth into gloves she'd stripped off a dead Vulture days ago, trapping them against her palms. "So I'll make sure they don't."

"You fainted yesterday," the prince said. "Are you certain—"

"Aye," Fie snapped, and pushed on the hide binding her sandals until the nails poked through. "We done dawdling?"

They were done dawdling. Tavin led them along the river, following a game track drawn with a toddler's shine for nonsense curves. Trees shrank to thorny scrub, and scrub to grass and wiry lichens. Shaggy goats paid them no heed, nibbling daintily at any sprouts of green.

On they climbed, on and on and up and up, and with every breath Fie marked the path of the skinwitches, the searching talons of their tracking spells, the distance between them. It did not grow fast enough, but it grew, enough to keep her weaving tooth after tooth into her triad.

That old headache grew as well, starting as they picked their way over a rope bridge strung across a great ice-mottled ravine. Fie fought it off as best she could. The pain was only another note in the harmony that, by all the dead gods, she would hold until they'd cleared Misgova Pass.

Then as the noon sun crested above, dizziness struck, sending Fie to her knees. She retched up bile and just barely caught herself before the Sparrow teeth slipped into discord.

"Is it the teeth?" Jasimir asked.

"It's the height," Tavin answered as she scoured her mouth with clean snow. "Mountain sickness. Some people aren't used to climbing this far up."

"Aye," Fie croaked, and let the Hawk pull her back up, his hand lingering in hers. "Just . . . keep going. We have to clear the pass."

"I can carry you." Tavin's grip on her tightened.

"Not with that pack you can't." She forced her feet into an aching stagger again. "Come on. We clear the pass tonight, or we don't clear it at all."

They pushed on, picking a switchback trail over ground that tilted ever steeper. Only plain rope bridges marked the passage of any life here, lashed between boulders, over ravines, along cliff faces. They had just set foot on one when the wind whipped at them, clawing at her cloak and tearing through the rags and fur beneath. Fie turned her face to the rock only to stop the sand pushing into her clenched eyes.

"*Keep going!*" Jasimir shouted as the bridge bucked.

Fie fumbled along the quivering rope, sliding on her knees. Another blast of wind meant her eyes stayed shuttered. She scrabbled about until her fingers caught in the gap between frosty planks, then pulled herself forward. One plank. Two. Four. She lost count, dragging herself through the howling wind.

At last her hand scraped on solid stone. She heaved herself onto the blessed steady earth, crept into the shelter of a boulder where the prince already huddled, then curled into a shaking ball. A moment later something heavy and warm flopped over her. She had a notion who that was.

"Let's never do that again," she wheezed.

"I have bad news for you," Tavin said into her shoulder, voice muffled in cold and rag. "We have to do that again. A lot." Then he straightened with a groan. "How are you doing?"

She pushed herself to her knees. "I'll hold up."

"I'm fine," the prince said sharply behind her. "Let's go."

Tavin pulled Fie to her feet again. Her bones felt hollow and sick with a three-tooth song. She swayed until he steadied her. "We're almost at the summit," he told her. "Almost there. Just hang on."

This time he did not let go of her hand, anchoring her as they stumbled on through the cold.

Fie's sight dimmed with each step, her skull pounding. A chant, half a prayer, sifted from the haze: *Keep the harmony. Keep your eyes open. Keep the oath. Look after your own.*

The world bled into blinding white ice and hard black stone, into one footfall after another, into blurring peaks and burning lungs and belly acid on her tongue.

Keep the harmony.

On, on, on they climbed, higher and higher, into snow that buckled and swallowed them to their waists, through wind that near stripped them from the earth.

Keep the oath.

The sun had sunk near halfway to the horizon when Tavin stopped. "There." He pointed to a shallow rise ahead. "The summit. After this we'll clear the pass in no time. Then I'll send Draga the message-hawk for Trikovoi's plague beacon, and all we have to do is walk from there. Just a little more, Fie."

She tried to nod. Tried to keep her eyes open. Tried to hold the harmony.

She couldn't.

Look after your own.

Her knees buckled. The teeth snapped into screaming discord, then drowned beneath the roar in her ears.

As everything faded away, part of Fie whispered, *They only have to catch you once.*

When her eyes cleared of shadows, the world was a-tilt, rocking steady and even. Tavin's taut face above drowned in a sky that had begun to lose its light. He'd wound up carrying her after all.

Shaking, Fie called three Sparrow teeth to life, but she already knew what she'd find. The webs of skinwitch spells peeled away from her and the boys, but the damage was done. The Vultures had changed course for Trikovoi. She'd cost them their lead and betrayed their destination in one swoop.

Look after your own.

She'd failed to keep the only rule Crows had. Tears rolled down her face and froze there.

"It'll be all right," Tavin said quietly.

Her whisper broke halfway through. "I'm sorry."

Jasimir jabbed into her line of sight, pausing at Tavin's side. "So what now? The Vultures know—"

"We keep going." Tavin did just that, passing the prince.

Jasimir strode to catch up. "You keep saying that, but that isn't working, is it? We're going to keep doing precisely what Tatterhelm thinks we're going to do? What's the point if *she's* going to keep giving away our location?"

"Leave it alone, Jas." For the first time, Fie heard an open warning in Tavin's voice.

"It's time to go to the Hawks. If she can't throw the Vultures off—"

"Leave. It."

"This is my life, *our* lives at stake here!" Jasimir shouted. "My condolences if that conflicts with who you want in your bed this week!"

Tavin stopped. His grip on Fie shook, anger rolling off him like a heat wave.

"Put me down," Fie said, partially to head him off from saying some fool thing.

Tavin set her on her feet. "Can you walk?"

"Aye." Fie wobbled a moment before planting herself sturdy in the snow.

Then she slapped the prince.

A resounding *crack* bounced off the stone as he gaped at her, hand on his jaw. His eyes flicked over to Tavin's face before flinching back to Fie's.

"First of all," Fie snarled, "you keep your voice down out here, unless you fancy an avalanche. Second. *Aye.* I fouled up. Likely I'll do it again. But Ambra help me, you leave who's bedding who out of it, or I swear to every dead god I'll—"

"You'll what?" Jasimir spat. "Leave me to die out here? Let the Oleander Gentry ride down your caste?"

"The sad thing," Fie hissed, "is you really think you're better than Rhusana."

Jasimir's whole face tightened, then crumpled. Wind shrieked through the comb of the summit behind them.

Eventually Tavin spoke, softer now. "Changing course now does nothing. Trikovoi is still the closest fort in the Marovar. And we still have to clear this pass tonight."

He took Fie's hand and headed down a snowbank.

"If you're wondering," he said after a long moment, "that is what it's like to deal with the king. And every one of us knows Jas is better than that."

Fie wasn't so sure. She kept that much to herself. "The king throws a tantrum when his Hawks stop doting on him for an hour?"

"The king throws a tantrum when someone else wants his toys. Jas takes after his mother more." Tavin grimaced. "And you were right. He's afraid I'm abandoning my duty."

Fie tilted her head. The prince looked fair alive to her. "How?"

He squeezed her hand and gave her a strained smile. "For you."

"Oh." Fie couldn't stave off a smile of her own.

"I didn't expect to find meaning and purpose and all that when I faked my death, but here we are."

"Here we are," Fie echoed. "*I didn't expect all this trouble when I thought we were picking up two dead lordlings.*"

"Two exceptionally handsome and charming dead lordlings."

"I should have burned that quarantine hut down with you both inside."

"And here I thought you didn't have a romantic bone in your body."

"Don't get used to it," she returned, and realized that she wanted this: his jests, his laugh, his hand in hers as they traveled on. Even with the skinwitches haunting each step, the notion of walking the roads of Sabor with her kin at her back and him at her side . . . that was something to want and to have.

If they made it out.

Ahead of them, mountain upon mountain scraped at the sky; at their backs, the prince ground his teeth.

Somewhere out there waited Trikovoi. Somewhere much, much too far from here.

———◆———

They pushed on.

After the sun tumbled below the horizon, the waning Peacock Moon lit their way, ghosting off sheets of snow and ice and wet rock. More than once, Fie looked back at the ragged trail they'd carved and cringed. The Vultures needed no spell to follow them this far.

Through the night they stumbled. Snow yielded to stone, and stone yielded to gravel and thin, spiteful moss. The slopes rose and fell in sharp crags and shallow basins, bridge after rope bridge spanning the only way onward.

Finally they reached the trees, whip-thin pines clustered as if huddled for warmth. Black boughs choked the moonlight until they had naught to see by. She slept a few brief hours curled in Tavin's arms, then made him trade the watch to her and rest, her head tucked beneath his chin. When the sun crested the horizon, they split cold, greasy strips of dried beef three ways and set off again.

By noon, if she looked back to Misgova's summit, she could see Vulture riders picking their way down the pass.

They pushed on.

By midafternoon her bones gave out, run too dry to carry her and the teeth both. Tavin picked her up once more and didn't set her down until the mountains grew too dark to continue.

She insisted on taking first watch. When he woke for the second, he asked for a Peacock glamour.

Through the dark, and through her tears, she gave him as close to the prince's face as she could manage.

When she woke, only half a league remained betwixt them and the skinwitches.

They pushed on.

Briars knotted about the slopes, digging thorns into their arms. After the bramble trapped the prince a fourth time, Tavin led them clear of the forests, into plain sight but free of snares. They chased the rising sun east over rattling slides of slate and through a gnarling canyon spiked in great fingers of stone.

By noon, between heaving breaths and the scream of her three teeth, Fie could hear the faint clip of hoofbeats on stone.

Tavin tried to steer them from the open plains now, aiming for

ravines or slopes ragged with boulders and outcroppings. The nails studding Fie's soles near wore down to toothless nubs as they bit paths over
barefaced rock.

Then, with the sun prodding the western horizon, the rough terrain wore out. The three of them stopped behind a boulder, weighing
their choices: a broad shallow ravine below, or a stretch of shattered slate
ahead. Tavin took an experimental step into the slide. A rock slid free
and set off a small cascade. He looked over his shoulder. Fie followed
his look and saw no Vultures, but that meant naught to her.

"The ravine won't give us away," she said.

"This is faster," Tavin said shortly. "We just have to cross before they
notice."

"Fine." The prince strode into the slide, not looking back.

Fie followed, uneasy. The rocks slipped and rolled beneath her feet
as she struggled to keep up, keep her balance, keep the harmony. Wave
after wave of broken stone tumbled down the hill in their wake. Even if
the Vultures couldn't break through her triad of Sparrow teeth, this
spectacle all but begged to betray them.

Pa's broken sword banged at one hip, the bag of teeth swinging at
the other.

You have to keep the oath, Fie.

Halfway across the shattered stones, the prince fell.

It all happened faster than Fie thought possible:

In one heartbeat, Jasimir teetered ahead of her.

In the next, he'd slid yards away, rolling in a tangle of slate and rag.

He skidded to a halt and staggered to his feet, bedraggled but whole.
Below him, the ripple of falling rock grew, and grew, until stones the
size of Fie's head toppled down the hill in a cracking cacophony.

Then a mournful hunting horn swelled above the falling rock, sweeping from the valley at their backs.

The Vultures had found them.

"Get to the ravine!" Fie bolted down the hill, half sliding as the footing buckled and shifted. The roar of blood and adrenaline clashed in her ears with the clatter of plummeting rock. Then they slowed and stopped at the edge of the gorge, and she realized half the noise came from hoofbeats upon hoofbeats.

They hurried toward a steep game track winding into the canyon but had made it just a few paces when Tavin yanked both Fie and Jasimir to a stop. Not a half league downhill, riders cantered into the gorge's mouth.

"Bridge," Jasimir gasped, pointing to a rope bridge farther down, spanning the narrowest neck of the gap. "If they don't notice us cross—"

"Done." Tavin turned on a heel. Fie cursed the dead god who'd invented hills, legs burning as pure adrenaline carried her back up the game track. Something coppery stained each agonizing breath. They reached the bridge a minute later, squinting down the canyon. Riders thundered toward them, just a quarter league and a few bends of the canyon walls away.

Fie lurched toward the bridge. Tavin caught at her arm.

"Wait." He touched two fingers to her lips. They came away bright with crimson. "Fie. You're—you have to let the teeth go."

"They'll find us," she gasped, mountain and sky spinning in her sights.

"They'll absolutely find us if you're dead." His hands wrapped around her shoulders. "Let them go."

"But—" Jasimir's eyes locked on the Vulture riders.

Look after your own. She shook her head. Not Misgova. Not again. She was a chief.

"*Let them go.*" Tavin's hold on her tightened.

Her vision blurred before she could muster a retort. Only adrenaline had kept her moving this long, she kenned it as well as he did. One moment of fraying focus was all it took.

Fie buckled.

A tooth slipped away, then a second, and the third.

"Bridge. Now." Tavin waved the prince on, then guided Fie onto the swaying planks, one hand braced on her spine.

Another hunting horn howled down the stone.

The canyon floor heaved below, not even thrice a man's height away. Fie near vomited.

"Hang on." Tavin's fingertips pressed in a steady half-moon between her shoulders. "Just have to get over the bridge."

Jasimir looked back. "We can't outrun them. Not like this."

"Keep going," Tavin barked.

A horse's scream ripped down through the gorge.

Fie tried to train her eyes on the end of the bridge, on one fixed point. Make it off the bridge. Keep on your feet. Keep going.

The hoofbeats rose like a tide.

"We won't make it," the prince called. "Maybe we can negotiate—"

"They negotiate using arrows, Jas. Keep going."

"We've already lost!" Jasimir stopped and spun around, a few planks from the end of the bridge. "It's over. She's too weak—"

"Fie," she interrupted, hoarse.

"What?"

"You know my name." She spat blood into the canyon below. "If I'm about to die for you, you can damn well use it."

Jasimir looked from her to Tavin and took a deep breath. "They . . . they aren't after you. If I give myself up, the two of you can escape."

Wind and hoofbeats and hunting horns crashed around the rock walls.

THE MERCIFUL CROW

Tavin's face tightened. He looked at the canyon and at the bridge, and then he looked at the prince.

"Yes," Tavin said, "you can."

He pulled Fie to him and pressed a swift, soft kiss to her mouth.

"It'll be all right," he whispered.

And then he shoved her back.

Fie crashed into the prince. The two of them fell not onto rickety plank but steady ground, over the gorge at last.

Steel clattered and flashed. Fie scrambled to her knees. Something dropped from her arms onto the ground beside her—Tavin's pack, and something cold and heavy—

A scabbard. A short sword. Unbroken.

Tavin knelt on a plank, wrapping one hand around a cord, the other holding his remaining blade aloft.

His voice rang hard as iron. "Keep the oath."

And in one terminal sweep, he cut the ropes of the bridge.

It happened faster than Fie thought possible:

In one heartbeat his eyes held hers.

I can do something better with my life than die.

In the next, he was gone.

259

PART THREE

BASTARDS

—— AND ——

GODS

CHAPTER SEVENTEEN

LITTLE WITNESS

WHERE HORNS AND HOOVES AND HOWLING WIND HAD RAGED, now reigned silence.

Fie did not hear Tavin hit the ground. She did not hear the prince cry out beside her. She did not hear the triumphant yips of skinwitches scenting their victory at hand.

She heard naught a thing but the horrified roar in her skull.

Jasimir crawled over to the edge of the canyon, his mouth moving in the fading sunlight. Shouting? Was he calling down to the Hawk? To the Vultures?

Keep the oath.

Tavin's last words sent the cogs in her head grating into a mad spin. The gates opened; noise and fear and wrath flooded back in.

Gone, he was gone—

You have to keep—you have to—

She had a screaming prince and a broken bridge and a pack of Vultures coming for her head. And she had an awful cold part of her that knew no matter what, getting caught by Tatterhelm could bring naught but hell on their heads.

With a ragged sob, she drew Pa's broken sword. Then she hurled herself at the prince.

He didn't see her coming. She slammed into his back, knocking him flat to the ground. Something crunched in his pack.

"What in the twelve hells are you *doing*?" he gasped.

"Stay down," she growled through her tears. "You'll give us away."

Jasimir thrashed, trying to toss her off his back. "No, we have to help him—he can't—we can't just—"

The hoofbeats slowed below. If the prince kept yelling, they'd all be rutted.

Fie flipped the broken sword and leveled its jagged, trembling point to Jasimir's right eye.

"Stay down and shut up, or else," she said, ice in her voice, ice in her spine, ice in her gut. "You can still be a king with one eye."

Jasimir went still. For once, he'd taken her at her word.

". . . don't understand!"

Tavin's voice drifted up from the ravine.

"I'm not—you—you're after the prince, right?" he whined. "He abandoned me, him and that Crow girl—they cut the bridge—"

"Shut him up." A gravelly bass rolled off the stones. Fie had heard it before: *Business of the queen.*

Fie heard a *crack* and a brief yelp. If she strained, she could peer just over the edge. . . .

The Vultures surrounded Tavin, trapping him against the far rock wall, their backs to her. Tavin had yanked his sleeves around his hands and wrists, hiding his burn. His left shoulder sagged in a way that made

Fie queasy, and blood painted his mouth and chin bright in the dying light.

"No, you've got it wrong," Tavin said, piteous as Barf begging for scraps. "I'm the *double*. The prince took off with that girl. They tricked me, they cut the bridge while I was crossing. I'm just a decoy to slow you all down."

Jasimir squirmed beneath her. Fie twitched the sword's jag closer. Tavin always had some scheme up his sleeve, she had to believe in him—

And if that scheme meant dying for the prince?

Her fingers slipped a little on the hilt.

She inhaled through her nose, imagining cold iron running down her backbone, keeping her steady.

"If he's right, we're losing time." A third skinwitch twisted about to scan the canyon. Fie ducked from sight.

"It's a bare-assed lie." Viimo's drawl echoed up. "Princeling doesn't fancy girls. He ain't running off with one. The double's the one with a shine for the Crow."

"No," Tavin pleaded, "they left me, *they left me*—"

Fie knew it for a ruse. She kenned his game now: let them chew over the half-baked lie and never know they'd swallowed another whole.

The words still tore at her heart without mercy.

She'd abandoned him just like she'd abandoned her kin in Cheparok, in the hands of murderers, all for the sake of this damned oath.

"This one's noisy for a Hawk," another skinwitch observed. "I'm with Viimo."

"You have to believe me," Tavin babbled. "They're getting away—"

"Pipe down." Another crack and cry. Fie's gut wrenched.

She wanted to set the canyon ablaze. She wanted to wipe the blood from his face. She wanted to leave naught of the skinwitches but scorched earth.

Broken steel shuddered in her hand, less than a finger-span from Jasimir.

"One way to know for certain," Tatterhelm rumbled. "Test him."

Test him? She didn't dare try for another look. She caught a jingle, a thin *scratch-scratch-scratch*—then a hiss. Murmurs swept through the Vultures.

"Aye," Viimo said. "It's over. That's our prince."

"Pack him up," ordered Tatterhelm. "We'll send a message-hawk to the queen after we get back to the caravan."

The air clotted with shuffling, grunts, and whickering horses. Fie kept still, kept steady, kept the broken blade trained on the prince's eye lest he ruin it all, kept thoughts of Tavin at arm's length.

She shivered. Tears streaked down her chin, landing in Jasimir's dusty hair. She told herself she would not grieve.

Part of her knew she didn't. Grief scarred over wounds. This, now— all this meant was she still couldn't stop the bleeding.

A horn shrieked the marching order to a chorus of victory whoops. Slow and unstoppable, the hoofbeats and horns drained from the ravine, until only the howling wind remained.

Tavin was gone.

Fie rolled off the prince and, for a long moment, stared at the sky purpling like a bruise above.

She wanted Tavin's smile. She wanted his arms around her, the warmth of him at her back, the moment not three days past where she believed, really believed, that perhaps they two could put things to rights.

But it didn't matter what she wanted when it was far, far from her grasp.

In the long, fearful months after she'd found the ruins of her ma, night after night, she'd kept watch with Pa. Madcap, newer to the band than Fie, had called her Little Witness: the dead Crow god, a beggar girl who saw all misdeeds and recorded them for the Covenant's judgment. Likely Fie looked the part, staring out into the dark from under Pa's cloak with her wide, solemn, black eyes, her hair in ragged tufts that she wouldn't yet let Wretch tidy.

It wasn't long before someone told Madcap what had happened to Fie's ma, and they never called her Little Witness again. But Pa told no one the truth of it: Fie only kept watch because she couldn't bear to dream.

Instead, Pa told her stories.

He told her tales of tricksters and queens as they sat and watched the roads for strangers in the night. He told her of heroes who fought monsters from beyond the mountains and seas. He told her of Ambra and the tigers she rode, the villains she conquered, the fires she burned through Sabor. He told her how every witch of a caste was one of their dead gods reborn, even him. Even her.

And when Fie at last fell asleep, she did not see her mother. She saw adventures grander than her world of dusty roads and shrouded dead. And she wanted to believe Pa: once upon a time, she could have been a god.

She did not feel like that god now.

She felt like Little Witness. She'd done nothing but watch.

The sky above swam and marbled with tears.

This was all her doing. She'd chosen this road. She'd brokered the oath herself. And if she'd been stronger, if she'd been a better witch, if she'd kenned what Tavin meant to do—

No. A stronger witch still wouldn't have made it all the way to Trikovoi. Tavin had known this day would come; he'd planned it for near ten years.

That's the game, get it? They've naught to lose by playing with us.

Her own words echoed back, cold and hard.

And there's no way for us to win.

It was always going to come to this.

She wasn't a god or a hero on a grand quest to slay some beast from beyond the seas.

She was a chief. And her monster sat on a throne.

So you cut your losses, Tavin had said.

It was harder to believe when every loss had a name. Tavin. Pa. Wretch. Madcap. Swain. All her kin.

Even Hangdog.

The oath, the oath, that damned oath had eaten them all whole.

That damned oath was all she had left.

By every dead god, she was going to keep it. There was one way off this road, and that was to walk it to its end.

Fie took a deep breath and closed her eyes. If she didn't think of him, think of any of them, she could do this.

She sat up, aching from crown to toe, then crawled over to Tavin's pack. Jasimir didn't stir from the ground, eyes clenched shut, mouth moving in something like a prayer. She only caught snatches of words:

"*. . . not dishonor my blood . . . a Hawk who . . . not forsake . . .*"

Her hands shook as she worked at the knots cinching the pack shut.

The words came clearer now. "*. . . follow until I must lead. I will shield until I must strike.*"

She cut through the ties with Pa's sword.

"*By my blood, I swear, I will serve my nation and the throne above all.*"

She did not look at Tavin's sheathed blade still lying in the dirt.

The prince's mumble cut off. Jasimir pushed himself up to glower at her. Clean tracks ran down his face from red-rimmed eyes. "That— that isn't yours."

"Aye," Fie said dully. "You'll have to carry some of it, too."

"It belongs to Tavin," Jasimir said. "It's his."

Fie's mouth twisted. She turned back to the pack and pulled out the cooking pot. "He knew what he was doing."

"We have to go after him. Hawks don't forsake their blood."

"He wanted us to keep the oath."

"Stop that. Stop saying he *knew* and he *wanted*. He's not dead."

The pot fell. She didn't answer.

Even if they didn't catch the fading Peacock glamour, sooner or later, one of the skinwitches would spot the scar tangling about Tavin's wrist, a burn that a fireproof Phoenix prince would never have. Fie just prayed they caught on while they still had use for hostages.

"He's not dead," Jasimir repeated, angry.

Fie just pulled a spare cloak out of the pack, winding it around her shaking fist. Her silence only seemed to stoke his anger.

"He only gave himself up so you could get away," Jasimir railed on. "He did this for *you*. And you didn't even—you won't even go after him. You don't care."

Fie bit her tongue hard, hard enough to taste blood. Then she looked at the modest heap of Tavin's supplies and decided she'd carry them on her own after all. Anything to leave this damned canyon faster.

"You could have saved him. You have every Phoenix tooth in Sabor. Why didn't you do anything? You just let them—"

Finally Fie picked up Tavin's sword and stood.

"Where do you think you're going?" Jasimir demanded, scrambling to his feet.

"We have to leave," she croaked.

"Twelve hells we do!" Jasimir's voice cracked. "We're getting him back."

"Shut your mouth." She needed him to stop talking about Tavin. She needed to cut her losses and move on, move out before anything else fouled up.

"You did *nothing*, it's your fault—"

She spun around. "Aye, to be sure it's all my fault, it's not like you kept harping on *Hawks* and *duty* and how *he* had to keep you alive—"

"You didn't stop him, you let him go—" Jasimir sputtered back.

"—and it's my fault your rat-heart cousin turned on us in Cheparok, and I'm sure it's my fault your rotten pappy let the Oleanders grow strong enough to sway a queen, aye—"

"Don't talk about politics you don't understand—"

"—and of course, when this all goes guts-up because no one in their right mind will buy that *you* have a drop of Ambra in you, that'll be my fault, too, aye?"

"How much more will you let them take from you?" The prince's hands balled into fists. "They have your father, they have your family, and now they have Tavin. What *else* are you going to give up?"

Fie turned, half to get moving, half because her lip quivered. "We have to keep the oa—"

"*Fuck* the oath!" Jasimir shoved her from behind. The sword tumbled from her grip and clattered to the earth.

Fie stood a moment, breathing hard. Then she collected the sword and turned, slow, to face Jasimir. His chin jutted out, eyes burning in the bloody dusk.

"Say that again," she rasped.

He glared dead at her, tears cutting fresh lines down his face. "Fuck. The. Oath."

The iron in her spine yielded to murderous fire.

A curious thing happened then: the crown prince of Sabor looked at Fie, and for the first time, fear crept into his eyes.

Perhaps it was the sword that she had and he didn't. Perhaps it was the memory of what she'd done to Viimo and the knowledge that more Hawk teeth waited in the bag at Fie's side.

Perhaps it was the fact that to most of the nation, he was good as dead.

For the first time, both of them kenned he was wholly at her mercy.

Fie cocked her head, eyes glittering sharp. Some part of her had been ready for this from the moment he tried to duck cutting the oath. He could spout his high-minded hogwash all he wanted, but she'd waited for what happened when it stopped being easy to keep his word. And here they were.

What's your word worth, Hangdog asked on a night too far away, *when you're good as dead?*

Nothing, it turned out. It was worth nothing.

It'd be so easy. She could march the prince into Tatterhelm's camp at sword point. She'd barter all the hostages back. She'd buy them time.

She'd look after her own.

You're the girl with all the teeth, Viimo said on a faraway dune. *Maybe we can deal with you, too.*

Just like they'd dealt with Hangdog.

A dull despair smothered that merciless fire. Aye, she could hand Tatterhelm the prince. Then he'd fill her kin with arrows because he could.

And even if she could get them all away, she'd still have one moon at most before Oleanders turned the roads red with Crow blood.

All the fire and steel in the world, and she'd still always be a Crow. Aught else was one of Pa's stories, a child's game of pretend, a little girl riding a goat, hoisting a stick, and calling herself Ambra.

"That oath," Fie forced through a choked sob, "is all I have left. And it's cost me everything. *Everything.* So spare me your noise about what I've given up. You didn't care when I lost all my kin, as long as you were safe. As long as *I* kept the oath. You know why I made you swear before the Covenant? Because I knew the second that oath started to pinch, you'd run."

Jasimir's eyes flashed in the gloom. "It turns out you're better at abandoning your family than I am. Leave if you want. I won't forsake my blood."

Fie regarded him for a long moment. The frost reclaimed her voice. "Aye. I'm going to Trikovoi. I don't have a choice. And neither do you. You're coming with."

Jasimir stared at her, fists clenched. Then he sat in the dirt, back to her. "Go ahead and try."

The last of the sunset bled out, and a chill settled on the mountainside like a fog.

Fie scrubbed at her face with a rough sleeve until the tears smeared away.

She marched over to the prince, wrapped both hands around the straps of the pack on his back, and began to walk.

"Hey—*hey*—" Jasimir squawked in protest as she yanked him along. "Stop—!"

"No." Fie sought the horizon for the lingering stain of sunset past. Trikovoi lay to the northeast; the sun and moon would have to be her compass.

Then she staggered and fell on her rear. Jasimir had slipped his arms from the straps.

Fie shot to her feet before he did. In one savage lunge, she snatched a handful of his collar. And she began to walk again. The dull nails in her soles crunched against the rocky earth.

Jasimir half stumbled, half dragged behind her. "Let—me—*go*," he wheezed. "You faithless—I order you to—I *order you*—"

Fie let go, then gave him a spiteful push to the ground.

"Ken me," she grated out. "You *will* keep your oath. That's what Pa and Tavin gave themselves up for and you know it. So you and I can walk to Trikovoi nice and quiet, just like they asked. Don't even have to pretend to like each other. Or, by every dead god, I will drag you to Trikovoi myself."

She turned to the northeast and pointed to the crescent winking above. "One week left in Peacock Moon. Choose quick."

She began to walk.

For a moment, she heard the scrape of her own footfalls, alone.

Then she caught a scuffle. The prince's footsteps gritted behind her.

Not another word passed between them as they marched in silence, stiff and hollow, into the swelling dark.

CHAPTER EIGHTEEN

— SKIN DEEP —

THEY STUMBLED OVER RIDGE AND PLAIN, THROUGH THE NIGHT AND the dark, stopping only as dawn pushed a questioning thumb of light along the eastern ridge. For a short half hour they rested, gnawing dried grapes and long-stale panbread that lumped up in Fie's gut, hard as the silence between her and the prince.

He did not pray to the dawn this time.

As they chewed, Fie called up two Vulture teeth, one hand on the hilt of Tavin's sword. She told herself she just needed to know the skin-witches hadn't resumed their hunt.

They hadn't. Tavin's trail led into the forests they'd left behind, farther from her than ever.

A knot in her throat tightened. Suddenly Fie couldn't abide sitting quiet anymore. She stood, checked her pack, checked her map, checked the dawn. Once the prince was on his feet, they set off again.

She couldn't stop herself from tracing Tavin's path near every hour as they carried on beneath the stare of a cold sun. The fifth time, his trail stretched beyond the crest of Misgova Pass.

She let the Vulture tooth go and did not call on it again.

Early in the afternoon, they passed within eyeshot of a handful of scattered huts nestled in the crook of a steep valley. Herds of goats and cattle wreathed the village. If Fie squinted, she could spy children picking snow figs. A narrow roughway road trickled out of sight, rolling down to what had to be a flatway.

"We should go back on the roads."

Fie jumped at the prince's voice. "What?"

"The Vultures aren't following us anymore," Jasimir said. "So we can afford to take the roads. They'll be faster."

She bristled. The notion was solid enough, aye. But the way he said it . . . he made it sound as if she ought to have thought of it hours ago. "No," she said. "If we hit a plague beacon, we're rutted."

Jasimir scowled. "Don't play naïve. You're passing them anyway."

If Tavin were here, he'd spout some nonsense to settle both their hackles. Instead, they only had empty air for a buffer, and it did not measure up. For a moment Fie wondered if Tatterhelm would accept the prince's corpse for trade. She might have tested it if she weren't so tired.

But the prince was right, and they had but a week of Peacock Moon left.

"Fine," she sighed. "Skirt the village. No going to the Hawks. Don't look other travelers in the eye."

"Yes, *chief.*" He said the title like a curse, just like he'd done with Pa. Fie took that as an endorsement and set off down the hill.

An ugly thought crossed her mind as she plowed over hassocks of wiry grass. They had planned on Tavin signaling Draga for them. Now they would be approaching Trikovoi unannounced and uninvited, a pair of battered, road-worn Crows. And she had a keen notion of how they'd be received.

Perhaps she ought to burn Pigeon teeth for luck before they arrived. And she'd surely need to pray the Hawks at guard had open minds.

Returning to the roads should have felt like a homecoming. Part of her did steady once her worn sandals touched ground on the roughway. But the rest of her felt the stares from Hawks as they passed league markers, the lingering glances from Sparrows in the pastures. Three Crows had made a small band. Two made an oddity.

The roads were her home. That didn't make them less of a trap.

They staggered on through the twilight until they at last reached the flatway. A road marker stood at the crossroads, brandishing signs for every direction. Crow marks had been scratched into each, but naught told her which way led to Trikovoi, and Fie had forgotten her letters by now.

Jasimir said nothing.

Fie didn't know if he meant to be difficult or if he truly didn't remember. She didn't want to find out which. Instead she just cleared her throat and said, "Which one's Trikovoi?"

"Oh." He leaned forward to peer at the letters, face rigid and blank, then pointed to the right. "This way."

They carried on past another league marker. Jasimir eyed the Hawks pacing about the brazier at the top but kept his mouth shut.

Eventually he broke the silence as they trudged into a twisting forest. "We should stop."

Fie stuffed down a protest. A distant part of her knew she couldn't walk straight to Trikovoi, but by every dead god, she wanted to.

"Fine," she said dully, and sat at the roadside. "Here's as good as anywhere."

That was a lie: she'd in fact sat on an uncomfortably angular rock that she remained on out of sheer belligerence. But Jasimir only nodded and joined her.

She fished out her bag of laceroot and counted out a few seeds, blinking away the stinging in her eyes. No sense in stopping now, with or without Tavin there—not with Trikovoi still so far off.

"Don't tell me you're worried *I'll* get you with child," Jasimir scoffed.

"Don't flatter yourself," she shot back. "And learn how bleeding works. I don't need any *more* pains in the ass."

The tyrant silence reigned cold betwixt them. Jasimir started rummaging in his pack. "I still say we should go to the Hawks. They're honor bound to—"

She couldn't hide her irritation. "I still say no."

"Because I said it and not Tavin."

That hit closer than she'd own to. "Because it's a fool notion. They'll never believe us." Jasimir rolled his eyes. Her temper flared. "And if we're going for the cheap hits, when Tavin told you no, you listened."

"This is different."

"Keep telling yourself that," Fie said.

"Tavin was trying to protect us. You're just—" He cut himself off, shaking his head. "Never mind."

"I'm. *What*."

The prince would not look at her. "You're no Tavin," he mumbled.

"Neither are you," Fie said, prying a few pelts from her pack. Jasimir flinched. She heaved one in his general direction. "Enough. Sleep in that. I'm taking watch."

He wrinkled his nose as if the pelt was still attached to a rotting doe. "You're joking. I know what you two did in these."

"Oh aye?" Fie asked with nasty, sugar-bright cheer. "You sorted out what rutting is? You're such a grown-up little man!"

His lip curled. "Don't be vulgar."

"And you grow the hell up." She didn't feel like pulling punches anymore. "Stop whipping me because your Hawk did *square* what you wanted him to."

Jasimir recoiled like she'd struck him. "Don't you *dare*. I didn't want him to—to—I just wanted him to do his duty—"

"Which is to die for you—"

"It's to put *me* first!" Jasimir slammed a palm over his heart. "He's the closest thing to a brother I have! He had his pick of the court, did he tell you? Every week he brought back a different Hawk sword-maid, a different Peacock lord-in-waiting, a new Swan apprentice, and he still put me first. He was *never* going to parade around a little Crow half chief for a wife."

"Did he tell you he never meant to go back to court?" Fie snarled. Jasimir's jaw dropped. "Aye. *Never*. He said it'd blow your story if both of you survived the plague. He said when I left Trikovoi, it'd be with him at my side. And he said the only reason he never stayed with a lover before was because he thought he'd have to die for you someday. So I hope you feel real damn kingly about every time you've thrown that in his face."

Jasimir stared at her, aghast. She wasn't done.

"I knew I wasn't the first," she hissed. "And I know who I am. Now you tell me. Is your problem that you came second to me? Or is it that you came second to a Crow?"

Jasimir froze.

"Which is it, palace boy?" she demanded.

The answer came out in a ragged rush. "*Both.*"

Fie caught her breath. To her astonishment, her eyes pricked with tears. She hadn't expected the prince to own to it. To fight her, to whine, to dodge, to deny—all likely. She didn't know why hearing him admit it shook her so.

Jasimir ran his hands over his face. Then he got to his feet and stalked off into the trees without another word.

When he came back, it was with an armful of fallen branches. Some had dried out enough to hold a flame, but others still showed green at the heart of their splinters, the leaves barely wilted. "I need the cooking pot and a fire."

Fie blinked at him, hackles rising again at his imperious tone, but she kept silent and yanked open her own pack, pulling out the cooking pot.

He snapped the larger branches in twain and set about stacking them with methodical precision into the tidiest pyramid of firewood Fie had ever seen, a feat double impressive considering she burned bodies for a living. Jasimir rocked back on his heels and looked at her, impatient.

He'd built the green branches into the stack. Amateur. "That wood won't light with just a flint," Fie said.

"*You're* the one who can start fires out here, remember?" the prince snapped. "Not me."

"I don't have Phoenix teeth to waste on every little thing," Fie said. "I won't squander one on a campfire. Find better firewood, or we don't get dinner."

"You go find it. You're the one who won't burn a tooth."

Sparks caught on a different kind of tinder. Fie threw down the cooking pot. "Apologies if I won't give up *more* on your account—"

"Apologies if extorting me had consequences," Jasimir retorted. "You knew I was vulnerable, and you took advantage of that to drag me into an oath that could very well tear this kingdom apart."

Fresh fire spiked up Fie's backbone. "Don't act like you didn't invite this. If your scum-hearted father had done his job—"

"Don't talk about my father like that." Jasimir glowered. "You have no idea what it's like."

"I see it every time I use one of your miserable teeth!" Fie's empty belly rumbled. "Aye, I've seen how you Phoenixes live. All the food you want, all the clothing, the wisest scholars to tutor you, the strongest Hawks to watch your walls, and the prettiest gentry to kiss your asses."

Jasimir got to his feet, livid. "You don't know what you're talking about. I can't just force the nobility to do what I want. They're already going to try to beggar their towns with new taxes and claim that it's to pay for your Hawk escorts. I can't fail my people like that."

By every dead damned god, Fie was sick of bartering for her right to exist. She stood to face him down. "And who in the twelve hells do you think Crows are? Someone else's people? Someone else's problem? Because you already made my oath with the rest of Sabor: you protect your people and set our laws, and we pay for your crown. That's your oath as king. You just don't want to keep it with Crows."

He took a step back, shaken. "It's—it's not that simple—"

"*I* don't get to look away from the throats I have to cut. Why should you?" Wrath roared in her ears. "You can't even admit—"

Fie cut herself off. The ground trembled beneath her soles.

The shaking was more than wrath, more than hunger. When she whipped about, she found torchlight closing in on them from both sides of the road.

"Oleanders," she whispered. Jasimir cursed and snatched up his pack, then froze. The torchlight was too near for Sparrow teeth to save them.

Wrath turned to sick panic. How had she missed it? How long had she been off the roads, running from being a Crow, that she'd foul up this bad?

Fie's head scrambled for a plan. Pa would have known what to do—a Peacock illusion—no, no time—Phoenix teeth?

Flame couldn't stop steel, though. Moreover, she carried every Phoenix tooth in Sabor. If she called on them now and even one Oleander made it out to report back to Rhusana . . . if they saw Jasimir unscathed by fire . . .

Her time ran dry.

Within heartbeats, the Oleander Gentry had them surrounded. A dozen or so riders, all armed, all on horseback, clogging both sides of the road.

She'd have to scrap another way out.

"Now this is odd, eh?" A man dismounted, the oleander blossom shivering on his breast as he angled a bronze-tipped spear at Jasimir. He wore a crude mask: just two eyes gouged in a pale leather rag. "Two bone thieves. Made enough noise that we thought you were a proper mess of the rats."

Fie sucked in a breath, eyes darting about the road. Most of these Oleanders had cloaked themselves in undyed cotton and linen. No fine lords this time. Behind the riders lurked another half-dozen people on foot. Too many to take on herself.

"Look at this." The ringleader strolled over to Fie and drew Tavin's short sword from its scabbard at her side. "Little one's gone and stole steel teeth."

She had to get them out.

No, her Chief voice said. *Just the prince.*

If she bought the prince a chance to get away . . . she could sort herself out after.

"We found it." Fie didn't feel like concocting a tale when the Oleanders didn't care for the truth either way. All she needed was a distraction. She caught Jasimir's eye, then sent a pointed look to the forest.

"Oh, they found it," the Oleander man laughed, dropping Tavin's sword in the dirt. He leaned so close, the rawhide drape of his mask brushed her nose. "Where'd you find it, dirty little thief?"

Silently she called two Sparrow teeth to life on her string, anchoring them to her weary bones. By now, finding balance was easy as a whistle.

A subtle shift rippled through the Oleanders: heads tilted and eyes shifted until they were all decidedly *not* looking at the prince. Jasimir's face dropped as he caught on. Fie flicked her eyes to the forest again, then stared the ringleader down.

"Found it up your ass," she announced, voice carrying clear over the road. Hisses swept about the Oleanders. They'd expected her to beg. Now they'd make her pay.

Fie shut her eyes. Whatever came next—it had to be enough to cover Jasimir's escape. It *had* to.

But nothing came.

When she opened her eyes, the ringleader still stood before her, chuckling. Worse, Jasimir hadn't moved, his face clouded with uncertainty.

"Two bone thieves," the Oleander mused. "So peculiar. Not the only peculiar thing this moon, either. A friend, a very kind lady, sent along a message this way, you see. Look for bone thieves, traveling in three, maybe two. And she sent us . . . oh, some help."

Fie caught a horrid slippery whisper, like a sinner's last wet breath.

Two men appeared behind Jasimir and seized his arms, forcing him to his knees.

No, not—not quite men. The torchlight made ghouls of all the Oleanders in their masks and scarves, but something about the figures seemed . . . wrong.

"Let—*go*—" Jasimir thrashed.

Then she saw it. The men's arms coiled about Jasimir's elbows like asps, like rope, boneless and wrenched tight. Their clothing—Vulture make—slipped in odd places, slumping below shoulders and hips.

An arm slithered about Fie's throat, a weight pressing against her back like a cold sweat. She gasped and jammed Pa's broken sword into the place where a gut ought to be.

It sank to the hilt without a sound, but the flesh round her throat stayed iron-solid. She twisted until her captor swam into view.

She knew his face.

The skinwitch who'd ambushed them a week and a half ago. The one they'd left for the wolves.

His slack face had turned a sick gray. His mouth gaped in a silent, toothless hole; limp skin flapped like a flag where a nose belonged.

He had no eyes. Instead, torchlight slicked off a dark maroon paste where a skull ought to be.

If she'd had the breath to scream, she would have. All she could do was claw at the arm about her throat. The skin bent and stretched about her fingers, like it was filled with naught but air, yet the grip on her stayed crushing as stone.

"Skin-ghasts got no bones for you, little thief." The Oleander man ruffled Fie's hair hard enough to rip strands out, then whirled to face Jasimir. "Special present from the White Phoenix herself, since her pet Vulture's taking too long. Wanted us to find someone very important to her and help him come home."

Jasimir went still.

"The White Phoenix said if we find him, tell him he can come back, that they'll sort it out with his father, and it'll all be fine." The ringleader came to a halt one pace from Jasimir. "Of course, this *important* person, he's a prince. Not a Crow, just mumming as one. Risky business to be sure, since we've our own way of dealing with Crows here. But all that prince would have to do is come forward, and we'd get him back to

Dumosa, safe and sound. Easy as that. It's just been one big misunderstanding, hasn't it?"

The skin-ghast's arm tightened, crushing the last of Fie's breath.

Jasimir looked from Fie to the ringleader. Then he bowed his head. "What about . . . the Crows?"

Fie almost started laughing.

Hangdog had been right. She'd dragged the prince this far, she'd given everything she had and more, all for an oath he'd never meant to keep.

"Don't you fret." The Oleander flicked his hand. "We'll handle them, Highness."

Fie's sight dimmed.

"Let's get you back to Dumosa." The Oleander waved off the skin-ghasts holding Jasimir, then reached out to help him up. "Your father's waiting."

Fie took some wretched comfort in the fact that even if she died here and now, the Covenant would not forget the oath. The prince could run from her, from Pa, from every Crow in Sabor, but he'd carry that oath to the grave and beyond.

It would have to be good enough.

Jasimir straightened. He took the Oleander's hand.

Then he yanked the man closer. Steel flashed, a thorn darting through torchlight.

The Oleander man gaped, dumbfounded, at the dagger in his belly.

"There's been a misunderstanding." Jasimir jerked the dagger free. "I'd have sworn that prince is dead."

CHAPTER NINETEEN

— THE CROW AND THE HEIR —

O F ALL THE SIGHTS FIE EXPECTED TO SEE BEFORE SHE CHOKED TO death, Prince Jasimir vomiting on the corpse of an Oleander hadn't made the list.

The world went dark, shouts fading from her ears—then the weight at her back abruptly slackened. She staggered forward, the skin-ghast's arm still locked about her throat. Someone grabbed her, and then with a jerk, the arm fell away. She gasped and coughed, eyes watering.

The prince knelt beside her, pinning the skin-ghast's arm to the ground with Tavin's sword. Scraps of gray skin littered the ground around them, wriggling and unfurling still. The skin-ghast's head flattened out like raw dough, then swelled again. Just beyond it lay the dead Oleander.

He still had a few strands of Fie's hair clenched in a fist. Enough to make a new puppet for Rhusana, once they'd finished with her.

"*Now* can you spare a Phoenix tooth?"

Trust Jasimir to get petty at a moment like this. Fie shot him a glare and scrabbled for her string.

The Oleanders had drawn their steel, the other skin-ghasts lurching toward them with a faint whistle. Still too many to fight.

Not too many to outrun.

The Phoenix tooth answered Fie's call.

A dead witch-king roared in her bones, and golden fire bloomed in a shrieking arc. The Oleanders' horses crashed into one another as their riders swore. Yet they didn't flee, as if they doubted her.

As if they doubted the wrath of a Crow.

Fie fed the fire her fear and her fury; the ghost of the Phoenix led the charge. Flames turned into a wall, into a wave, into the jaws of a terrible beast crashing down around them.

The Oleanders fled then.

"Grab what you can," she wheezed. Jasimir pulled her to her feet and lunged for their packs.

Fie tossed the Phoenix tooth at the dead Oleander, burning every last strand of her hair in his hand. A golden wall stretched along the road, keeping the Oleanders at bay. The tooth wouldn't last but a few heartbeats more, but Fie prayed that'd give them enough of a start.

She and Jasimir fled into the trees.

She didn't know how long they ran, only that golden fire waned to more mundane orange that shrank behind them. Hoofbeats drummed through the forest, chased by shouts, taunts, torchlight. More than once she and Jasimir huddled in the brush until a pale rider or a slithering skin-ghast passed and the quiet dark returned.

Eventually they cleared the woods. A sickle midnight moon gleamed above, its weak light catching on the mellow slopes of a pasture studded with goats and cattle.

Fie pointed. A few dozen paces away, a crude wooden structure sheltered great heaps of hay. "There."

Jasimir nodded. They hopped the pasture fence, then the one around the hay, and crawled into a discreet hollow.

For a long moment, neither of them stirred. Fie simply blinked at the sky, breathing in the dust-honey smell of the hay, trying to think of anything but the horror of what hunted them now. From the pounding of her heart and the shivers still rattling her ribs, that was a lost battle.

"Bronze," Jasimir croaked. "The man I killed. He had a bronze-tipped spear. For Hawks at village outposts."

"Aye," Fie said.

Another creaking pause. Then: "I killed someone."

"Tavin said . . ." Fie's voice broke. "He said it gets easier." Jasimir didn't answer. She forced herself to sit up and dig in her pack. "Also said he barfed on the body the first time, too, so you've that to bond over later."

Jasimir made an odd sound that turned into a wavering, desperate laugh. He covered his eyes. "What in all twelve hells did we just . . . What *was* that? What were *those*?"

Fie gulped. She could reckon with skin-ghasts the way she reckoned with sinners: distant enough to blunt the horror. Or at least she could try.

"Never heard of a Swan witch as could do that." Fie pulled out strips of dried fruit and jerky and passed half to him, ignoring her trembling hands. "Looked like just . . . skins. But I never heard of a skinwitch as could do that, either." The memory of clammy, empty skin clung too tight. She made herself bite off a chunk of meat and chewed awhile, too belly-sick to swallow but a little at a time. "Likely that's what ran through our camp before Gerbanyar. You saw one close-up, aye? When the Vultures tried to jump us."

"We thought it was a trick of the dark."

"But half the group ran off once the others went down," she mulled. "The fleshy ones. And the skin-ghasts only ran through our camp before, naught else. So they won't attack on their own; they need people to follow. That's good for us."

Jasimir choked on his dried fruit. "How is *any* part of this good for us?"

"Oleanders don't ride by day, not yet, and the Vultures are off our trail for now. We stick to the roads until nigh sundown, hole up somewhere off the track for the night, and likely we can skip their ken." Fie uncorked a water skin and took a swig. "We can still make it to Trikovoi before the end of Peacock Moon."

Jasimir let out a long breath and drew a new one. "How . . . After everything I've done, everything you said about my father . . . why do you still care about saving him?"

"I don't." She tilted her head back, letting her eyes close just a moment. If ever Fie had felt like mincing her words, it wasn't now. "He's been a bad king to me, and he doesn't sound like all that good of a father to you. But it gets worse if Rhusana takes his place. And I can't save *any* of them alone. Not Tavin, not my kin, not even the king. Not without the master-general's help."

"Aunt Draga will get your family back," Jasimir said. "She already has to rescue Tavin, since they're blood relatives. The master-general will follow the Hawk code."

Part of her dared to hope he was right. The rest of her called it foolishness. She couldn't think on which one hurt more. Instead she said, "I'll take watch."

"We should split it." Jasimir sat upright.

She shook her head. "If the Oleanders come round, I'll need to set off Sparrow teeth soon as I can."

Jasimir rubbed his face. "Then I'll help you stay awake. We can take turns sleeping around dawn."

If Fie was too tired to argue with that, then she needed the help. "Do what you like," she sighed.

The night returned to quiet, broken only by muffled lowing of cattle and the iron toll of slaughter bells.

One of Fie's untamable questions broke loose: "Why didn't you go with the Oleanders?"

Jasimir didn't answer for so long, she wondered if he'd fallen asleep anyhow. "I had a tutor," he said at last. "A scholar on the ethics of ruling— everything I need to weigh when I make decisions for the good of the kingdom. She's written dozens of scrolls on political power and rulers who succeeded and rulers who failed. There's a wing in the royal library named for her. She was one of my mother's best friends before . . . before."

He blinked, as if searching the stars for answers to a question he couldn't ask aloud yet.

"She said exactly what you did. That people pay me, in loyalty and in blood and in coin, because if enough people do, then I can repay them by making their lives better as their king. But . . ." He shook his head. "She didn't say anything about the Crows. Not that the nation would collapse without you. Not how the other castes prey on you anyway. Her life's work is the architecture of countries. She—she *has* to know. But she didn't even talk about it once." He swallowed. "There's . . . no real reason for *me* not to know, is there?"

"No," Fie said quiet. "There isn't."

He buried his face in his hands again. "I don't know what I'm going to do," he said. "The most powerful people in the kingdom can't even say the problem is real."

"They know it is," Fie said grimly, scanning the dark for torches. "Otherwise they wouldn't be so hell-bent on pretending it isn't."

"I don't know how to fix it."

And I don't think we can.

Fie's eyes burned. "Tavin said that, too," she said, hoarse. "You can't fix it, not everywhere and not all at once. But you can begin by keeping the oath. By telling the Splendid Castes and Hunting Castes that we're part of Sabor."

"I hate it," Jasimir admitted. "I hate being the heir. Nothing can ever be simple or easy. Most of the time it just feels like . . . like choosing which finger to cut off that day." He glanced over at her and sighed. "And here I am whining about hard choices to the girl whose family is being held hostage by my enemies."

Fie laughed.

It was not a happy laugh.

But nor was it an angry one this time.

"Now you're catching on," she said wearily.

Iron bells clanked soft across the pasture. A thin cloud smeared the moonlight across the sky. A rider passed down the distant road, and both of them held their breath, listening for the whistle of skin-ghasts, until the hoofbeats faded.

"I'm sorry," Jasimir said. "I thought . . . I thought I knew who I had to be, to deserve the crown. But all that's done is brought you pain."

Before Fie could answer, a flicker of torchlight kindled in the woods at pasture's edge. She and Jasimir both went still, then shrank into the hay. A Sparrow tooth sparked to life.

A woman strode out of the trees, flanked by two hollow-eyed skin-ghasts. Her linen cloak flapped like the skin-ghasts' lank arms as she swept her torch about; the skin-ghasts' empty faces followed that flame.

The Oleander woman's gaze passed over the hay heaps. She took a few steps closer.

Please, Fie begged the Sparrow tooth, the dead gods, the Covenant, aught that was listening. She was so, so tired of monsters at her door. *Please, just let her pass.*

A goat grazing nearby raised its head and bleated, the slaughter bell clanking at its throat. Another goat joined in.

The woman hesitated, then turned back to the woods. Soon enough the shadows swallowed her and the skin-ghasts both.

Fie let the Sparrow tooth go, eyes blearing. A long, long watch lay ahead. But at least she wasn't keeping it alone.

"I . . . owe you another apology," Jasimir said, twisting straw round his fingers. "You were right. I thought all Tavin saw in you was company in his bed. I thought that was all he could possibly want with . . . with a Crow. But you were more."

The stars above blurred and burned with tears. Fie squeezed her eyes shut again.

"He looked at you the same way you look at roads." Jasimir's voice cracked. "Like where they go frightens you, and you love them for it."

"Tavin told me you'd be a good king." Fie's voice stayed rough and low. "He believed it enough to give himself up. So maybe you earned the crown after all."

Jasimir attempted a wan smile. "You can't start being nice to me. It's terrifying."

Maybe they could make it like this. Fie didn't want to let herself hope, but she hadn't wanted to get attached to a mouthy Hawk, and that hadn't square worked out, either.

Maybe they could make it to Trikovoi and get her kin back, get her Hawk back, save the Crows.

Maybe they could change Sabor.

"You get Nice Fie until sunrise," she told the prince. "Then I am never letting you forget that you barfed on a corpse."

The moon hung at an hour past midnight.

"Was your ma like the master-general?" Fie scraped the question from the exhausted fog in her skull.

Jasimir hesitated. "She . . . she was and she wasn't. The army called her and Aunt Draga the Twin Talons for a reason, but in private, they were very different. Mother had more of a mind for diplomacy and court games. She could ruin anyone in one breath if they crossed her. Most of court quickly figured out not to." His voice hitched. "Fie, I think—I think Rhusana murdered my mother."

Fie straightened. "*What?* How?"

"Father uses Swan pavilions to host smaller events of state. He started going to Rhusana's more and more one summer, then bringing her to the palace itself, and then by winter solstice . . ."

Fie remembered that day in cold Hawk Moon, when every beacon in Sabor lit up in black smoke. "What happened?"

"The doctor said Mother was ill, but they wouldn't let anyone see her until . . . until the pyre. There were marks all over her throat, I saw them. And two moons after they burned her, we had a new queen."

"So Rhusana poisoned her?"

"I don't know." Jasimir stared into the cold night. "No. I do. I just don't know how she did it. I . . . I haven't told anyone. Not even Tavin." Jasimir shivered. "Maybe I should have sooner, but . . . he would have thought I was . . . weak for doing nothing."

"Tavin or your father?"

His mouth twisted, bitter. "Both."

———◆———

Almost daybreak. Fie wasn't awake, not truly, just staring into the hazy dark.

Jasimir's mouth moved, forming words scarce above a whisper. He'd muttered the chant to himself enough times that Fie had lost count. ". . . *I will not run from my fear*," he mumbled. "*I will not forsake my blood. I will not dishonor my dead. By my steel, I swear.*"

It wasn't a watch-hymn, but Fie supposed the pretty words of the Hawk code worked near as good.

"*I will follow until I must lead. I will shield until I must strike. I will fight until I must heal. By my nation, I swear.*"

Another pinprick of torchlight pierced the night. Jasimir jostled her elbow.

They watched it bob and weave through the woods, finally fading from sight.

Jasimir started up again: "*I will serve my nation and the throne above all,*" he recited. "*I will not dishonor my blood, my nation, or my steel. And I will not abide a Hawk who does. By my blood, I swear.*"

Pretty words. Words of a prince.

At the eastern horizon, the weight of the night began to ease.

The dawn broke.

When Jasimir told Fie to sleep, she didn't fight, curling in the hay. She woke with the sun square in her eyes a few hours later. Not near enough rest, but it'd tide her over.

They split more dried fruit, shook off the straw, and staggered to their feet.

"Here." Jasimir held out Tavin's sword.

She sheathed it, then bit her lip.

"Where . . ." Fie's voice came out a squeak. She cleared her throat. "Where did we leave off with reading?"

"Ta . . . Trilo . . . ?" Fie scowled at the flatway signpost. "Is it Trikovoi?"

Jasimir moved his finger along the symbols. "*Ta*, then *ri*, becomes *tri*. *Ka*, then *o*, becomes *ko*. *Va*—"

"With *oi* is *voi*. Trikovoi. Aye. I know." The prince had shoved letter after letter before her nose for the past four days, even carrying about a scrap of slate and a soft, pale rock to write with. This far northeast, the flatways wound quiet round the mountains, their dry dust only stirred by wandering Owl scholars and Sparrow farmers carting vegetables and livestock to the markets of the Marovar. By day, there were precious few distractions from Jasimir's academic zeal.

It hadn't been easy. The first evening, they'd tussled when she told him to be stingy with their dwindling dried meat. He'd stormed off into the firs again, carrying a length of rope and his dagger. Dinner had been thin and their words short, and after sundown the whistles of skin-ghasts had driven them into the trees once more.

Then she'd woken to grouse roasting on an improvised spit, a dead pheasant lying in a rope snare nearby, and the prince kneeling to the dawn.

Jasimir had straightened and held up a scrap of slate. A few plain letters were scrawled across it. "Let's try this again."

And from there they'd slowly jostled each other into a routine. She still felt it, the hard ache of silence where Tavin's laugh ought to have been, the cold absence of fingers that had brushed against hers, the longing to catch him watching her again. The prince didn't hum any watch-hymns; she didn't wake to find that someone had covered her with a spare pelt. In all the small things that ought to have been there and weren't, she missed Tavin the most.

But she had an oath to keep. So did the prince.

And so they did. They shared the quiet as Oleander torches lit the woods, as skin-ghasts prowled beneath the trees they'd climbed. And when the danger passed, silence filled in with letters on slate, stories of the court and of the road, memories traded and admired and mourned.

He said foolish things sometimes, asked questions only someone who'd grown in a palace would have. And when Fie told him as much, sometimes he frosted over again and kept quiet awhile. But more and more often, he simply nodded and listened to why.

"Next challenge," Jasimir said. "How many leagues to go?"

Numbers. Those were even worse than the alphabet. Fie squinted at the end of the sign. "Two tens and . . . five?"

"Four. But you were close."

"So are we." Fie added up the distance. "Three days' walk."

"That's the end of Peacock Moon." He rubbed the back of his neck, mouth twisting.

Fie pointed to the nearest league marker. "You know what happened when they lit the plague beacons for you? They sent up colors like ordinary round the palace, all the way out to red. Then every other league marker in Sabor burned black. Last time they did that . . ." She faltered. ". . . was nigh on a half-dozen years ago. For your mother. So if aught happens to the king, we'll know."

"I didn't know about that," he said, quiet.

"Aye. Madcap told me it was a thousand-thousand royal ghosts." Fie scowled. "Scared the piss out of me."

Jasimir laughed at that. Then he sobered. "Any change with . . . with the Vultures?"

Like Tavin, he had a shine for questions beneath questions. She rested a hand on the unbroken sword and called on a Vulture tooth. "The trail's too far off to read all the way out," she answered, then reached for a different tooth on her string. Pa's spark burned there. "Could be past Gerbanyar by now. And Pa's still alive. That's all I know."

No telling how Tavin was keeping. Dead or alive, the skinwitches had stolen him farther than she could see.

"Three days," Jasimir said after a beat. Then he produced the scrap of slate. "We have a lot of reading practice to do."

———◆◆◆———

They made it another day and a half before the Covenant caught up.

Seven days since they'd lost Tavin and returned to the roads. It was a generous stretch, but one Fie had always known would end.

The sun was hanging low at their backs, and the prince blushing through the third verse of "The Lad from Across the Sea," when she saw it waiting down the road.

The dead gods' mercy called them onward: a string of bloodred smoke needled the sky.

CHAPTER TWENTY

ROYAL GHOSTS

"HOW FAR OFF?" JASIMIR ASKED, SQUINTING AT THE PLAGUE BEACON. It near blended into the sundown-soaked sky.

"Seven leagues. A day." Fie squinted at the angle of the sun, the lines of the mountains. "Due east, so could be close to Trikovoi. Could also be another trap."

"We would know if the Vultures passed us, right?" Jasimir rubbed his chin. "Do you suppose the Oleander Gentry have gotten clever?"

"Maybe." A curl of unease twined in her gut. If she didn't answer, the Covenant would stack every one of the plague-dead on her head alone.

If she did . . . Tatterhelm could be waiting.

"Let's keep going," Jasimir said. "Either we reach the beacon first and can look for signs of a trap, or we reach Trikovoi first and I'll ask Aunt Draga to loan us an escort."

"'Us'?"

"My caste hasn't caught the plague since Ambra," he said firmly. "I'll just wash up after to be safe. Didn't I tell you? A leader should be skilled as any of their followers."

"Aye. And then you said you were too good to live as a Crow."

Jasimir cringed. "Right. Well. Let's say my perspective has shifted."

Fie allowed herself a strained laugh as they started walking, but her heart wouldn't settle. *Always watch the crowd.* She hooked a finger around a Vulture tooth on her string, then reached for Tavin's sword.

His trail rolled south, on and on down the flatway, just as it ought. Fie let out a breath.

Then the trail stopped. She stopped as well.

"What's wrong?"

"The Vultures have come north," Fie answered, brow furrowed. Tavin's glamour had to have burned out days ago, yet only now did they move north. "Can you get the map?" Jasimir freed it from her pack, then unfurled it on the thin roadside grass. Spring had ended dry and hot in the Marovar, turning green shoots yellow even before the solstice.

Fie knelt and tried to reckon Tavin's trail against the line of the flatway burnt into the goat-hide. One fingertip traced the road until just north of Gerbanyar. That yielded no good answers. "They're riding toward the crossroads."

Jasimir tapped the map. "They could be aiming for the flatway west. That's the fastest route back to the capital." He grimaced. "Or they could be coming after us."

She pinched at Pa's tooth. His spark hadn't gone out. He lived yet, but who else? She knew Tatterhelm had taken one of her own on the bridge; she knew he'd shot down Hangdog the moment he could. The skinwitch had ten hostages when he'd left Cheparok. How many had he bothered to keep alive?

Fretting wouldn't keep her oaths, though.

"We're a day from Trikovoi. They're too far to catch up before we make it." Jasimir leaned back on his heels. "Let's follow the beacons until they split from the road and see how close the Vultures are by then."

Uncertainty coiled around his words. Part of Fie felt better for hearing it there. "That's sound enough. We can cover at least another league before we stop tonight."

They camped in the ruins of an old watchtower that night, one they'd found thanks to Crow marks on a signpost. It held a bounty: a clean well, a long-feral vegetable garden, and, best of all, a hearth. For the first time in days, they could light a fire and not betray their camp.

Jasimir watched Fie scrawling out *Ta-ri-ka-o-va-oi* in the ashes. "And then Tavin passed the governor the platter of Hassuran steak and said, 'I didn't think your son could make it.'"

Fie collapsed into giggles, the weary sort that came of late nights.

So did Jasimir. When the laughter died down, he said, "Gods, I miss him."

A knot blistered in Fie's throat. "Aye," she whispered. "So do I." *Ta. Ri.* The letters blurred. She needed a distraction, anything to leave that wound alone. "He said the king has a shine for Hawks."

"Hawks and women. At least he and I have the Hawks in common. Hopefully for different reasons." Jasimir's voice scraped with something almost like hunger. "But that's why he married one of the Twin Talons. I don't think Aunt Draga ever forgave him for it." He reached for the fire, letting it harmlessly thread his knuckles. "All he wanted was a son like a Hawk. When Tavin arrived . . ."

Fie knotted it all up herself: How the prince had demanded Tavin's duty, not understanding what it would mean to be fulfilled. How he'd rankled as Tavin's loyalty slipped to her. The tremor in his voice when he'd claimed his Hawk had one job alone.

"The king put Tavin first," Fie said.

Jasimir closed his eyes and nodded like it hurt. "My mother spent so much time training him, right until she died, and Father would always . . . light up when he watched. I've barely seen him since he married Rhusana." He let out a bitter laugh. "He couldn't even be bothered to watch my funeral march."

Beyond the ruined watchtower walls, a reedy howl coasted on the wind. They both knew the whistle of skin-ghasts by now; they both fell silent until it faded.

Then Jasimir glanced at the ashes and brightened a little. "Your *vois* are getting better. Keep it up and when you see Swain again, you can help him with his scroll." Jasimir stared into the fire. "I can't believe everything Crows carry in your heads. It's incredible. All that history, all your traditions . . ."

"That's what walking songs are for. We hear them nigh as soon as we're born." Fie pondered a moment. "The teeth feel like that, too. Like each one has a song, and when I call them, the dead sing through me."

"Were either of your parents a witch?"

Fie shook her head. "No. Wretch said Ma met my blood-pa when both their bands stayed in the same shrine. She fancied him, and then I happened nine moons later. Pa's my real one. He took me for his own daughter when Ma died."

"Do you still miss her?"

The slate slipped a little. Fie licked her lips and smudged her name off the surface. "I was four," she said, frowning as she began writing anew. "I don't remember much before . . . Oleanders got her." She closed her eyes a moment, plucking the dim memories like crowsilk from branches almost too high to reach. "Ma kept her hair long for a Crow. She liked to pick dandelions and blow all the fluff off, and we'd see who could do it faster. Pa said she was so dead-set to give me my name herself that she sent off anyone who couldn't keep their mouth shut while she birthed me."

"Why would she do that?"

"Crows name their babes for the first cross word sent their way. It's luck. That word can't hurt you any if it's already your name. She said I howled like a devil when I came out, like I was born vexed with the world. Ma couldn't abide the noise. That's how I came to be Fie." She swallowed. "So aye. I suppose I still miss my ma, too."

Jasimir stared through the decrepit roof, up to the stars. "I'm sorry. I'm sorry Father didn't stop the Oleanders sooner. I'm sorry I haven't done anything about them, either."

Fie turned the scrap of slate over. "They're the same, in the end. Different heads on the same monster. The Oleanders. Rhusana."

"My father."

Fie threw a sharp glance at the prince. His eyes were fixed on the stars, his face hard as iron.

"You wanted to save him," she said.

"I still do." His mouth quirked, too alike Tavin. "If he's someone I can save."

Fie knew he didn't mean to save the king from just Rhusana.

"People get drunk on crowns," she warned. "Think they can do as they please because they know we'll catch twelve hells if we hit back. But by every dead god, one day I will. And so will you."

"Let's make them pay," Jasimir whispered.

"Let's burn them down," she answered.

A look shuttled between them like the weft of a loom. The threads of their terribly different worlds gathered, crossed, and pulled taut.

They didn't speak the words aloud; they cut no oaths into their palms. But a promise took root in them all the same.

She didn't want to burn Sabor down. Neither did the prince.

But, by every dead god, one day Sabor would know that they could.

◆

In the morning, Tavin's trail stopped north of the crossroads—but not so far north that the skinwitches stood any chance of closing in.

"It doesn't make sense," Fie said peevishly, squinting at the map. "They're not moving fast enough to be hunting us, so why come north?"

"Let's figure that out once we reach Trikovoi." Uncertainty lingered in Jasimir's tone.

They carried on, following beacon after beacon. By noon, Fie could see the stone fangs of Trikovoi's towers jutting from the crest of a stone ridge and looming over a field of maize ahead.

"Almost there." Wariness dangled each word at arm's length. The next beacon could lead them down some roughway, giving the Vultures time to cover ground.

Fie opened her mouth to answer—then froze.

A soft, dangerous shiver crept up through the soles of her sandals from the road below.

She knew it. She knew that tremble like the voice of kin.

And in that moment, she knew exact where they'd fouled up.

Jasimir stopped dead, eyes widening as he too read the signs.

"The trail," he whispered. "We weren't tracking the skinwitches, we were tracking Tavin—"

The shiver swelled to a rumbling high tide. Fie heard a scream just beyond the bend of the road at their backs.

"Run—run—!" Jasimir bolted off the road, Fie at his heels.

They scrambled over a splinted fence and plunged into maize stalks near as tall as Fie. A dark border of firs waited at the field's end, and beyond it, not one league off, lay Trikovoi.

She couldn't run a league straight. Not with a pack weighing her down. They weren't going to make it—

Fie thought of the starving wolf and ran.

Maize leaves bit at Fie's face and hands as she and Jasimir stumbled over furrows of crumbling earth. She didn't waste time trying to call on Sparrow teeth: the sway of stalks betrayed nigh every step they took.

They only have to catch you once.

A Vulture whoop streaked the air. Moments later, the drumbeat of hooves muddled into the wet crackle of breaking stalks.

Almost there—almost out—they were only a few paces from the woods—

Something splattered at her feet, speckling the back of her legs. She caught a whiff of acid and burnt wool—then pain burst across her calves.

Jasimir crashed into her, knocking them both to the ground. She swore, bewildered, and tried to shove him off. He rolled back to his feet and dragged her up. "Your legs—fire—" he wheezed.

Fie twisted and saw scorch marks burned into the backs of her wool leggings, the flesh beneath red and welting. A scattering of small white fires speckled the maize behind them, each no bigger than a fist.

An arrow whistled eerily through the air, then thudded into the trunk of a fir nearby. White fire sprayed from its shaft like syrup.

"Flashburn." Fie sucked a breath through her teeth. "It's flashburn."

She had to hand it to the Vultures: if you wanted to kill a Crow and keep a Phoenix, fire was the way to do it.

Jasimir's horror said he, too, had pieced it together. "Come on. They won't have a clear shot in the forest."

They raced into the firs. Any sign of Trikovoi vanished behind heavy, needled boughs. Shouts and cursing echoed behind them. The horses weren't built to weave through the thickets here, but they'd catch up sooner than later.

"We just—have to get—to Trikovoi," Fie panted, staggering up a heap of rocks. The plague beacons would have to wait, and the Covenant would have to forgive her, and the dead gods would have to be kind if she and the prince were going to make it out of this damned—

The forest stopped.

That was false; it didn't so much stop as empty out. The ground at their feet clogged with rocks and broken wood and old caked mud. Hundreds of trees stood before them, gray and clean, stripped of their bark and needles but for tufts near their dead crowns.

Pa called them ghost forests, stretches of trees that a mudslide had smashed in the pass of a few breaths. Right now, all Fie saw stretched ahead of her were a thousand-thousand royal ghosts, and the teeth of Trikovoi in the slopes less than a league away.

Hoofbeats pounded behind them.

She and Jasimir took off into the ghost forest, aimed dead for the fortress. The ground bucked and slipped beneath their feet, branches rolling, dried mud buckling, stones tipping every which way. Fie prayed that would foul up the riders even worse.

Then an arrow sailed over her head and into the trunk of a ghost tree.

Flames leapt from every drop of flashburn, spreading in a trice. Jasimir yanked her back as the tree groaned and splintered into a pillar of white fire.

Shielding their eyes, they veered round it, still pushing on toward the fortress. Almost there—they just had to get away from the Vultures, just had to clear these damned ghosts—

Another arrow hit, and another, sinking into the dead trees. Fie twisted but saw no riders. A war cry shrieked from the dark woods to her left, and its match echoed back from her right.

The Vultures had them flanked.

Arrows rained down around them, sending up belches of white fire wherever they hit. The earth beneath their feet began to hiss and steam. Flames outran her and the prince until the world was white-streaked fire, waves of blistering heat, air that reeked of flashburn and smoke, and a roar that near drowned out the skinwitches' cries of triumph.

They'd run headlong into the Vultures' trap.

A ghost tree screamed as it crashed to the ground not ten paces off. Fie swore and hid her face from the shower of embers, choking on air that scraped vicious at her lungs with every breath.

Jasimir wrapped an arm around her and barreled on. His voice barely sounded above the maelstrom. "Use a Phoenix tooth!" he shouted. "You can put out the fire like you did with the Oleanders."

It had taken near everything she had to bring that tiny campfire to heel nigh a moon ago. But even if she wanted to argue now, she hadn't the breath for it.

Fie called up a Phoenix witch-tooth. The one that answered gave her a song of battles and glory, a prince convinced his name would resound through history. Fie drew the power through her, then bent it to the fires ahead.

She might as well have bent it to an ocean. Wherever she pushed, the fire only flowed round. Fie cursed and tried again, tried to shove enough away to let them pass, but the white flashburn flames scratched and pried and slid about no matter how she willed them away.

Get out. You have to get out. You have to keep the oath—

But everywhere she looked, she saw only burning ghosts.

The seed of a notion sprouted. Fie licked her dry lips, tried to take a breath, couldn't. The world began to flood with gray.

She closed her eyes and called up a second Phoenix witch-tooth.

A queen answered this time. And she fought furiously with the dead prince, circling and spitting like cats. But they were neither a match for Fie, the worst Crow they would ever cross.

She wrenched the teeth into harmony without mercy and let them burn together.

Roaring gold fire erupted about her and the prince, fire that answered to Fie alone. It wheeled and shrieked, a blazing storm tearing through the flashburn-white flames, clearing a ring for her and Jasimir to pass.

The wider their halo grew, the more it sucked in clean air, leaving scarce enough to choke down. And with every breath, the twin teeth fought like no others had, thrashing for discord and, more dangerously, for release.

If Fie let them, they would burn Sabor from mountain to coast.

"Trikovoi," she gasped instead, and staggered into a run once more.

The towers of Trikovoi carved at the sky ahead, creeping closer with each step, rimmed in the golden fire she kept leashed. Almost there. The teeth howled and twisted in her hold.

She tripped, stumbled, shoved herself back up.

Almost there.

Everything dissolved to flame and scorching air, breath after agonizing breath, ground that shifted with every step. She didn't run so much as half fall, again and again, snatching her balance back each time, lurching forward through white fire and smoking earth and trees smashing down around them.

Vultures wailed beyond her sight, furious. Arrow after arrow dashed against the wall of golden Phoenix fire, only to be torn apart when its own flashburn exploded in the fiercer heat. The flashburn fire pushed back, thunderous. She could feel it, acid-born and starving, snapping at their halo of gold—that white fire was a wolf, and those jaws were hell-bent to close on her—

The oath, keep the oath, keep going, she had to keep the oath, she had to look after her own, she was a chief, she was a chief, she was a chief—

Fie staggered as the ground steadied and hardened beneath her feet.

The flatway. They'd burned a path straight from one bend of the flatway to another. And the gates of Trikovoi waited only a hundred paces away.

Jasimir let out a laugh like a sob behind her. This time it was pure relief.

Then hooves rattled the wind at their backs once more.

Fie spun round. For a dreadful moment, she was back on the bridge of the Floating Fortress; above golden flames, she saw a rider crowned in a jagged helm.

She didn't feel the arrow when it buried itself in her thigh.

She dropped. She couldn't help it; one moment her right leg bore her weight, and the next it folded and dumped her on the road. This arrow bore no flashburn, only a shaft of steel, and so the fires hadn't troubled it in the slightest.

Pain ripped up and down Fie's thigh, the kind that she felt in her teeth, the kind that twisted in her gut and turned her bones to water. Her fingers scrabbled at the arrow's stem before she could fight the instinct, sending searing agony through her leg.

The teeth screeched into discord. Fie let one go, kept the other alight, sweat rolling down her face as she forced her bloody hands to clench in the dirt instead. A wall of golden fire bowed across the road. The Vulture riders kept their distance.

She didn't realize the prince had been calling her name until he knelt at her side. "We're almost there, Fie, just a little more to go."

He looped her arm over his neck again. She tried to stand—slipped—

One wrong step put all her weight on her right leg. She screamed, red flashing through her sight. Jasimir swore and lowered her to the ground again.

"I can't believe this," he said with a strained smile, too alike Tavin. "You're supposed to drag me into Trikovoi, not the other way around."

Fie winced, propping herself up on shaking arms. So close—they were so, so, so damned close—

She shook her pain-addled thoughts down as blood pooled beneath her leg. She could heal herself with a Hawk tooth—no, healing was risky work to do on its own, let alone while injured and rushed. She could call Gull winds to blow the arrows off course—but she'd need two teeth, maybe three, and she'd have to hold them—

More red fog chewed into her vision. Paces away, the Vultures' horses pawed at the earth.

The starving wolf had come for her. And she had no way to run.

Her heart thudded in her ears. So close—she'd almost done it— Wretch said they'd tell her story for centuries—

The story of a chief.

Her red-stained fingers shook too much to undo the knot on the bag of Phoenix teeth. She pushed it at Jasimir. "Get this open."

"What are you planning?" His face blurred and swayed back into focus. She was running out of time.

Fie looked dead at Tatterhelm. Then she looked back to the prince.

"Leave your pack here and make a run for the gates. I'll hold the road."

Another arrow sighed in passing, ringing off the dry earth.

Jasimir's face hardened. "Not an option. I'll carry you."

Fie blinked away patches of red as she shook her head. "I've got one waking minute left, maybe two. The second I black out, they'll ride you down."

"I won't—"

"You *have* to," she yelled, voice cracking.

"No one else is dying for me," he spat back.

She seized a fistful of his shirt, smudging dirt and blood on the crowsilk. "You get caught and it's all rutted. It's all a waste, everything you've given up, everything I've given up to get this far. All of it. You get caught and Rhusana wins. You have to be king. *You have to keep the oath.*"

Even as she said the words aloud, the last lit Phoenix tooth slid from her grasp.

The flames sputtered into thin air, revealing a line of skinwitches across the road, dim phantoms in the haze. Tatterhelm rode at their heart, the notch-cut helm carving an unmistakable crown on his hulking silhouette; behind them swayed the drooping shadows of even more skin-ghasts.

Tatterhelm nudged his horse into a deliberate, unhurried stroll. Each ambling hoofbeat fell like the slow toll of a slaughter bell.

"Go," Fie hissed. If she pulled together, she could light one more tooth, one more fire—she couldn't burn it all, but by Ambra, she could burn her name into history—

The crown prince of Sabor got to his feet.

And then he planted himself between Fie and the Vultures.

"No," he said. "They have to go through me. Rhusana wants me alive. So we'll see how many of them it takes."

Tatterhelm paused, the helmet's eye-slits betraying naught. Then he flicked his reins and rode on.

Fie wanted to fight. She wanted to drag Jasimir to the gates of Trikovoi herself. She wanted to tell Tavin she'd done it, she'd kept the oath.

She wanted to see Pa again.

The earth shuddered.

At first, she thought thunder had rolled off the mountainsides. But that was wrong: the blue skies were only mottled with smoke.

Then she thought it might be more skinwitches. But that too was wrong: Tatterhelm dragged on his reins less than five paces from the prince, and twisted in his saddle to peer into the murky road behind him.

And then Fie saw the tusks.

They broke through the billowing smoke like warships through fog, a landslide of muscle and coarse fur. Weak sunlight picked out the steel spikes bristling the deadly bone arcs of each tusk, the plates strapped to every massive skull and trunk and leg, the razor-sharp lances lashed in clusters within reach of their riders.

Fie had seen mammoths before. At a distance. In a pasture. She had never seen them ridden to war.

She couldn't tell if the Vultures had, either, but at least they had the sense to scatter when the mammoth riders charged.

Tatterhelm's mount reared and whinnied. Fie heard a growled curse. He kicked at the horse's sides until it dropped and shied toward them. Fie's heart lurched as his hand swiped for the prince—

And a spear thudded into the road one hair away from his fingers, its shaft reverberating like a warning rattle.

Tatterhelm cursed again, turned his mount, and fled into the cover of dust. In a heartbeat, every Vulture rider and skin-ghast vanished from the road.

Fie slumped back with a broken laugh, red swimming in her vision. She didn't know if the lightness in her chest came from relief or blood loss.

She'd done it.

She'd brought the prince to his allies.

A mountain of a shadow rumbled nearer, fading in and out of sight. A mammoth. A rider, spear still in hand.

"Master-General Draga," the prince said stiffly from somewhere above her. "How did you know?"

"You lit a fire the size of Gerbanyar, *Highness*," his aunt answered from even higher. Fie could scarce pick her form out of the blur, but she sounded like the sort of woman who enjoyed riding mammoths full tilt at a pack of Vultures. "And even if you hadn't, I was warned to expect your arrival."

She pointed her spear to the gates behind them.

Fie reeled about, heart in her throat. Had she missed it? But Tavin hadn't—he *couldn't* have gotten the message out—

A black thread of smoke spooled into the sky, lit from Trikovoi's plague beacon.

"Oh," Fie said.

And then, eyes shuttering, she fell to the dirt.

CHAPTER TWENTY-ONE

— CROW MOON —

"**S**HE'S COMING AROUND."

"Am not," Fie grumbled into unyielding dark.

"I, for one, am not convinced," another voice said, dry. Fie had heard that one before, grating through dust and smoke . . . Jasimir had called her Draga—

Her eyes flew open and saw only stone.

Fie blinked and craned her aching head about, tallying up the surroundings. Stone walls, stone floors, stone ceiling, diamond-shaped windows letting in near-sunset light. Dark figures at a desk. Another figure crouching by her side.

The weight of her swords was gone. Fie threw a hand to her throat and found the string of teeth untouched, Pa's tooth yet humming.

Trust Hawks to take her steel but leave her teeth.

"Stay still," the first voice ordered, the one who'd announced her awakening. A little sting of pain darted through Fie's right leg. She blinked once more and found herself sprawled on a low wood bench. A bloody arrow lay on the ground nearby. Someone had cut gashes through her wool leggings—likely the Hawk woman at her side, who was frowning at the gore. Fie felt naught but a faint unpleasant tickle until the woman rocked back and stood. "All done. It'll be stiff for a day. Expect flashburn scars."

The healer didn't address Fie, instead directing her report to the woman across the room. Now that Fie could see her plain, it was clear the master-general did not need the mammoth in order to loom. Draga hadn't bothered changing out of her dusty leather armor; the only concession she'd made was a discarded helmet, which was leaving a rim of sweat on the parchment scattered across the desk. Fie saw the family resemblance between her and Jasimir at once: same dark gold skin, same sharp jaw, same lean build.

Where Jasimir fidgeted in a chair before the master-general, however, his aunt all but lounged against the desk, the picture of ease. "Good work, Corporal Lakima." Draga nodded to the healer, who saluted and posted herself at the door.

She'd dealt with Fie's wounds faster and more painlessly than Tavin ever had. He'd been right about being a middling healer after all. Fie sat up and stretched out her sore leg. "Where are we?"

"Inside Trikovoi," Draga answered. "The fort's commander has generously lent us his office. Corporal, please arrange for food and water to be sent up. The children look rather peaked."

"I can escort you to a location more . . . suitable for the master-general," Corporal Lakima said with the kind of delicacy that suggested the commander's office had not been lent so much as commandeered.

Draga glanced at her, something metallic tinkling in her gray-streaked black hair. Her smile showed a few too many teeth. "I find this office suits me, corporal. I'd hate to refuse the commander's generosity. Oh, and if you would? Send wine, too."

Once the door shut, Draga shed the smile like a winter coat. "You two reek of questions, among other things. Yes, Taverin got the message-hawk through. Half the north's league markers are staffed by Markahns, so don't look so impressed."

Taverin sza Markahn. Bastard or not, Tavin's name had been good for something after all. Fie swallowed.

Draga's voice roughened. "The Hawks who took his message said he appeared to be injured at the time, which tells me he was still pretending to be the prince. Clearly that didn't last long enough. I can't tell you if he's still alive, but Tatterhelm would be a fool to throw away any of his bargaining chips. Scouts are sweeping the mountains nearby to see if we can pin down his location as we speak."

"What of Father?" Jasimir asked.

Draga looked as if she'd stepped in dung. "What of him?"

"Is he . . . Has Rhusana . . . ?"

"Ah. No." Draga leaned back. "For better or worse, he's still on the throne."

A knock at the door interrupted them. Draga straightened, and Fie saw that the tinkling came from finger-length steel feathers dangling from a tight knot of dark hair at the back of her head. Hawk custom. One for each battle won. Draga wore more than Fie could count. "Enter."

A cadet near about Jasimir's age walked in, bearing a platter of fresh panbread, soft goat cheese, figs, and smoked meats. A second cadet followed with one sweating pitcher of water and another of rich red wine. They both snuck fleeting, sidelong glances at Fie and Jasimir. One's lip twitched into a curl before flattening out.

Fie almost laughed out loud. Between the prince's grime, his ragged clothes, and his lost topknot, the cadets had taken him for a Crow.

Draga cleared her throat. "Give my gratitude to the commander," she said pointedly. After the door shut she rolled her eyes. "Prissy little things. Eat up, I'm certain you're famished."

Draga poured two brass goblets of water and handed them to Jasimir and Fie, then poured herself wine. "So. Highness. The last time I heard from Taverin, Rhusana had just arranged to have ground glass dumped in your wine, because I suppose that harridan needed a hobby. He mentioned you might be paying a visit to your auntie soon. Then the next thing I know, a Phoenix has conveniently died of the plague for the first time in five hundred years, and just as conveniently, so has Taverin sza Markahn."

"I didn't know he was in contact with you." Jasimir's knuckles tightened on his goblet, though he'd schooled his face into granite.

"Markahns. We're dirty gossips to the bone." She grinned that toothy, sharp grin again, and Fie suddenly kenned where Tavin had learned to make the slightest gesture look lethal. "As my blood, my protection is yours, and as my prince, my loyalty is yours. But if you've got more in mind than taking up residence in the Marovar, you'd best lay it out for me."

"Tavin's original plan was to claim I survived the plague through the strength of Ambra's bloodline," Jasimir elaborated. "I'd return to the capital with the regional governors rallied behind me. The lord-governor of the Fan said he'd aid us, but we walked straight into Rhusana's ambush."

"So you came to me instead." Draga eyed her goblet and sighed. "Only Taverin would come up with a scheme that ludicrous in the first place. I'm going to need more wine." She tipped the glass at Fie. "And you, Lady Merciful. I can't believe you shepherded the boys across the whole wretched nation out of the goodness and charity in your heart. I also can't help noticing you're missing your flock."

"Tatterhelm took my kin hostage in Cheparok." Fie sipped her water, a show of ease as deliberate as Draga's choice of stolen offices. "I'm here because Rhusana allied herself with the Oleander Gentry."

"Can't say I'm surprised," Draga muttered into her wine.

"So I swore the prince to a Covenant oath," Fie said.

Draga winced and took a swig of wine.

"We'd get him to his allies, and in exchange, the Crows will be guarded against Oleanders. By Hawks."

Draga spat out her wine.

"*What?*" she demanded. "What kind of—never mind. Forget Taverin's scheme, *that* is the most ludicrous thing I have ever heard and will ever hear again, in this lifetime or the next."

"The ludicrous thing is that it hasn't happened sooner," Jasimir said. "I've seen Oleander rides with my own eyes. And I've seen how the rest of the country thinks they can treat Crows because there are no repercussions. It's going to end."

Draga's brow furrowed. "Let me be plain with you, *Highness*. You need the cooperation of the Hawks. You won't get it, not when you're asking them to roll shells with the Sinner's Plague."

"Is the plague the problem, or is it the Crows?" Jasimir met her gaze steady and hard.

"I won't pretend that's not part of it," Draga returned.

"They need to get over it," Jasimir replied. "I'm not asking the Hawks to take any risk Tavin and I didn't take, and survive, ourselves. If you want to look at it as a general, we're preventing a takeover of the throne. I have to look at it as a king. The Crows are my people. Our people. They're part of Sabor. It's long past time to act like it."

Draga gave him a long, heavy look and poured herself more wine. "You're right. But it's not enough to just be right. I know my Hawks. You force this on them, and they'll turn on you. The answer is no."

Fie dropped her goblet with a clang of brass. Water spilled across the floor, flashing peach from the reflected sundown.

She hadn't heard right. Tavin had said Draga was loyal, that she'd follow royal commands. And the prince—

"He swore an oath," she said, furious. "And my end's kept."

Jasimir's hands balled to fists. "Fie's right. I made a vow to the Covenant."

"That's not how it works," Draga interrupted, iron in her voice. "I could swear to the Covenant that I'll leap mountains in a minute, but that won't mean I can. Did you explicitly promise you'd assign Hawks to guard the Crows?"

Jasimir blinked. "I . . . I said I'd ensure the Crows' protection as king."

"And I asked for Hawks," Fie added.

"That doesn't sound like you're sworn to give them anything of the sort, then." Draga frowned at the desk, hunting for a place to set her goblet down, but found none. "Once the hostages are recovered, I'll parade you back to Dumosa. While I'm there, I can personally encourage Rhusana to retire quietly to some country manor before I find a lawful way to send her to her choice of hells. After that, we can discuss more . . . *reasonable* measures to keep your oath."

Fie laughed out loud this time, burying her face in her hands. Of course the Hawks would turn their backs, even on their own prince. They'd break every code they had to keep from helping Crows.

All she'd done, all she'd lost, all she'd borne to bring the prince down her road . . . it wasn't enough. The next laugh came out a half sob. "You should have left me to Tatterhelm."

A hand braced her shoulder—Jasimir. His voice hardened. "What if I'm not asking, master-general?"

Draga tossed aside her empty goblet. Then she drew herself up to her full height, steel feathers whispering a warning. "Your mother taught you the Hawk code, Highness. What comes first?"

Jasimir licked his lips. "'I will serve my nation and the throne—'"

"Correct. 'I will serve my nation.'" Draga folded her arms. "*Before* I serve the throne. I agree that the Oleanders pose a significant threat, but I don't consider alienating allies good for my nation. And that is what I serve first."

Every Phoenix tooth in Fie's string wanted to burn Trikovoi to the ground. She knotted her hands to keep them still. If the Hawks thought her teeth a threat, they'd take them, too.

Jasimir sent Fie a look that said, *This isn't over.*

Fie wished she could believe it. She might yet get her kin back, but without the master-general, the oath lay hollow as a skin-ghast.

"Tomorrow, we'll work on rescuing the hostages." A shadow crossed Draga's face and vanished. "You two will be quartered in adjacent private rooms. I'll arrange for baths and meals to be provided. Open the door only if you hear four knocks, understand?"

The last comment ought to have been aimed at the prince. Instead, the master-general's steely gaze pointed at Fie.

Of course. Draga didn't trust her own troops to guard Crows on the road. Why would a fortress be any different?

"Aye," Fie said, matching her stare, steel for bitter steel. She'd get Tavin and her kin back. She'd stop the queen. But the fight for the oath— for Crows to walk more than a murderous road—was nowhere near over. "I understand."

Fie was not sure what to make of the bed.

In her sixteen short years, Fie had slept indoors, outdoors, on sun-warmed dust, in shady tree boughs, on the tiles of shrine floors, through sweltering heat and relentless rains and sometimes creeping frost. She'd slept on mountain and plain and in city and marsh.

But she had never slept in a fortress. The room itself was peculiar enough: plain stone walls lined with heavy tapestry, more diamond-shaped windows barred against intruders and the moonless dark, a cold brazier, oil lamps dangling in the corners. Fie had been surprised to find both her swords left in a plain rack. Then she kenned why: the Hawks had decided they didn't pose any true threat in the hands of a Crow.

A puddle glossed the floor where a copper tub had waited for her alongside a change of clothing and an array of soaps and ointments. Stone-faced cadets had borne the tub away after she'd scrubbed off the smoke and road dust, and they'd returned with a finer dinner than she could conquer. Even now, a lukewarm skin dried over leftover chunks of goat and squash swimming in a rich cream sauce. Draga had even sent them with a small bowl of salt, a thoughtful touch that Fie despised.

But she still wasn't wholly sure of the bed.

The mattress seemed to be stuffed with down and straw, resting on a net of hempen rope. A soft sheepskin spread out over more woolen blankets, a luxury Fie found excessive until the temperature plunged after sundown.

It was all so soft. Too soft. And quiet.

She ought to be on watch. She ought to be counting her teeth. She ought to be eyeing what lurked in the dark, wrapped in a stolen pelt, trying not to think of Tavin or Pa or Wretch or her ma.

She ought to be doing something, *anything* to bring them back.

Instead she lay under a suffocating heap of blankets, weighty and near sick on lordling grub, leagues and leagues from sleep.

Her gut ached with more than a heavy dinner. Aye, she'd done it. She'd brought the prince to safety. She'd kept her end of the oath. And she'd be able to save them—Tavin, her kin, the king. Draga would see to that.

But her caste . . .

She knew in her bones that when Pa had sent her over the bridge, when Tavin had cast himself into the ravine, neither of them had done it to settle for Oleanders riding only by night.

Maybe in a year, or two, or five, Jasimir would sit on the throne, and he'd craft some law to banish the Oleanders, and the Hunting Castes and the Splendid Castes could call it good enough. And the Oleanders would carry on like always, the Crows would die like always, and like always, the law would not weep for Crows.

Somewhere beyond the window, in the chill of Marovar night, a Hawk at watch began to hum.

Enough.

She could make use of her time finding a way out of this damn stone maze for when the Hawks' charity inevitably ran dry. She rolled from her bed, reached for her sandals, then thought of the nail scratches she'd left in the stone floor and pulled on sheepskin slippers instead.

Fie kept one blanket wrapped about her shoulders as she slipped into the hallway, away from the nagging hymn. Oil lamps marked the turns in the corridor, and more windows let in whispers of the first night of Crow Moon.

For a moment she stilled. Crow Moon. The final moon of the Saborian year.

All across Sabor, Crows would be gathered at one of their greater shrines—in Little Witness's watchtower, the groves of Gen-Mara, the ruined temple of Dena Wrathful. If not there, then any haven shrine. If they couldn't find a shrine, they would find a crossroads. There would be ceremonies: new witches hailed, new chiefs declared, an empty pyre for faces newly missing. Wedding vows for those who wanted to swear them. Bands cobbled together from stragglers and survivors.

A proper Crow would be with her people tonight. A proper

chief-to-be would line up with the other trainees, wearing wreaths of magnolias, and wait. One by one, the old chiefs would cut their own strings of teeth, tie them round the throats of the new, and hand off their broken blades. Magnolia crowns would be cast to the pyre, and then . . .

Then, if Fie were a proper Crow still, she would have been a true chief.

A watch-hymn drifted through the window. Fie fled.

A Sparrow tooth slipped her past the guards tossing shells at hall's end. The farther she went, the more she lost herself in the craft of Trikovoi, mammoth ivory rails wrought in angular pattern-knots, a fine-carved snow lion grasping a bundle of lit juniper incense in its marble jaws, mahogany columns and rafters carved for purpose, not pomp.

Tavin had only said his mother rode mammoths in the Marovar, not which fortress she rode for. Was that why he'd been so adamant to come to Trikovoi—he'd hoped to find her here? Had she been watching, waiting when Fie and the prince staggered into the road, only to find no sign of her son?

Or was she asleep in some other cold stone fortress, unaware that Tavin lived only as long as Tatterhelm allowed?

Fie's gut knotted. She ought to be claiming her own from the skin-witches. She ought to be burning her magnolia crown on a pyre. She ought to be able to stop thinking of Tavin, even for a moment.

Instead, she hunted for her way out.

Then, as she passed the entrance of another grand hall, something snagged her eye: a figure that belonged behind ranks of soldiers.

She let the Sparrow tooth go and slid into the hall. Jasimir glanced up and raised his eyebrows at her, unsurprised.

"How did you get past the guards?" Fie whispered as she walked over.

"Practice." Jasimir shrugged. "Sometimes I'd need to attend a state dinner or the like, but we'd get wind of some potential threat. Tav took my place, but I usually snuck out anyway. Mother only caught me the first few times."

He gave a strained smile, and with a start, Fie saw what had drawn him into this hall: a fine painting over his shoulder. Two women, nigh identical in their armor, their flinty stares, even the hands resting on their saber hilts. Twin Talons.

Fie stepped closer, studying the portrait. After a moment she pointed to the figure on the right. "That's your mother?"

He nodded.

She could see it, now that she'd met Draga. Jasindra's dark eyes sparked nearer to gray than gold, like Jasimir's; Draga's nose arched in a way neither her sister's nor her nephew's did; all three shared a narrow jaw and lanky build. But Jasimir's sharp-cut mouth and broad cheekbones had come from the king to be sure.

Something curled in the back of Fie's skull, like she hunted a word she'd forgot. She frowned.

"I think Mother would have liked you," Jasimir said.

Fie's frown went taut. "Cousin, I don't think her road and mine ever could have crossed unless she caught the plague."

His face fell a little. "I . . . I suppose that's true."

Fie stepped back, looking about the hall. More portraits hung on the walls: simple, familiar, lavish, stern. Dynasties of Hawks. Most, oddly, had a cat somewhere in the painting—a ball of striped fur on a background balcony, a shadow on a wall, a pair of eyes in the grass. A small tabby sat betwixt Draga and Jasindra, the picture of fluffy disdain. "Why the cats?"

"Legend says a Markahn helped Ambra tame the first tiger she rode to war. Cats are something like a patron of the clan." Jasimir grimaced.

"There's a reason Rhusana wanted to pay you with a stray tabby for taking two dead Markahns."

"Let me guess," Fie drawled. "Same reason she drags that tiger pelt by the tail." Jasimir nodded. "Is that why you saved Barf?"

"I saved her because I could." Jasimir pursed his lips. "I keep thinking about that Crane arbiter, the one who almost let Barf out. How do you get squeamish over burning a cat to death when you're there to do worse to people?"

"You know how."

Jasimir sighed. "You think the people are less than animals." Silence waxed, then waned. "I swore an oath. I don't care if I have to personally beg every Hawk in the Marovar. The Crows will have guards."

Pretty words, pretty words. She didn't doubt Jasimir, not after the last week, but she had precious little faith in the mercy of Hawks.

"Aye," she lied.

"Something's bothering Aunt Draga. She's not . . . like this." Jasimir picked at the sleeve of his sleeping robe. "I'll make my case again after we've got your family back."

"And if that doesn't work?" Fie couldn't help but ask. Somewhere out in the night, Crows were supposed to be celebrating their moon. And that meant that somewhere out there, Oleanders were preparing to ride.

"Then I'll make it again, to as many Hawks as it takes, as many times as it takes," Jasimir said. "I swore an oath."

How long would the Crows have to wait?

The prince's own words echoed from the ravine, more than a week past. *How much more will you let them take from you?*

She'd get her kin back. She'd get Tavin back. She'd stop the queen. And someday—someday she might fall asleep feeling safe again.

For tonight, it had to be enough.

Twin Hawks stared down at her from their portraits, imperious. Fie wished someone had bothered to paint her mother before the Oleanders tore her to pieces. The peculiar itch wormed about the back of her head once more.

Somewhere in the hall, a muffled hum of a watch-hymn threaded the quiet. Fie knew that, wander as she might, she'd never outrun it. There was no way out of Trikovoi for her until the Hawks let her go.

"Thank you for saving my cat," Fie said, stiff. "I should try to sleep."

⬥

Four knocks came at noon, ringing through the prince's room.

Fie set down her practice slate as Jasimir answered the door. Corporal Lakima stood outside, stony-faced and tight-lipped, gaze shifting from the prince to Fie and her wobbling letters. "The master-general calls for you." Jasimir and Fie traded looks. Lakima coughed. "There's a message."

Lakima scarce had time to clear the way before Jasimir and Fie flew out, half running down the hall.

When they burst into the commander's study, Draga didn't even glance up from the sole parchment on the now-cleared desk, her face gray and hard as Fie's slate.

"Close the door."

Lakima pushed it shut.

"They're in the Fallow Vale, an hour's ride north from here," Draga said. "Tatterhelm walked out to meet my scouts himself."

"Did they attack?" Jasimir asked.

"No. He . . . he brought Taverin with him. With a knife to his throat. And then he handed the scouts this." Draga began to read aloud. "'*To Master-General Draga Vastali szo Markahn: I, Greggur Tatterhelm, acting*

⚘ 324 ⚘

in the name of Her Majesty the queen, order you to surrender the traitor Jasimir Surimas sza Lahadar.'" She licked her lips. *"'Should you fail to comply, you will share his charges of high treason, conspiracy, fraud, and criminal blasphemy. Moreover . . .'"*

Draga trailed off. The parchment rattled beneath her fingers, and suddenly Fie saw red-brown flecks on the sheet. Something cold hooked into her belly and dragged down.

The master-general cleared her throat and continued. *"'Moreover, we have custody of the prince's accomplices, including ten Crows and the Hawk Taverin sza Markahn. If you wish to recover them alive, you will send the prince and no more than one escort, unarmed and on foot, to the Fallow Vale at dawn. Any sign of additional reinforcements or attempts to free the hostages will result in their immediate execution.'"*

The cold hook dragged harder.

Draga sucked in a breath. *"'Finally, for every day you delay, we will consider it an insult to the justice of Her Majesty and will submit an accomplice to the appropriate punishment. You will find the queen's justice'"*—Draga leaned back and twitched the parchment—*"'attached.'* I . . . I don't know who . . ."

A crooked, brown-gray worm rolled onto the desk, trailing a smear of red.

For a moment, Fie saw not a desk in a stone room but a dusty dawn road of years ago. That time, she'd been too young to know the bloody-tipped twigs for aught but a curiosity.

Now, near a dozen years later, she knew a little finger when she saw one.

Sometimes the drag of horror hit a low so deep in Fie that she couldn't even begin to reckon with it, only wait for the rest of her head to catch up.

She blinked. Inhaled. Took stock of the buzzing in her ears, the words of the letter, the gray of Draga's face, the silence of the prince, the sluggish thunder of her own heart.

There wasn't much time before the sickness would hit. Before wrath choked every drop of reason from her thoughts.

Before Tatterhelm sent another finger to point at her.

She hadn't much time.

Fie forced herself to step forward, reach out, and touch the spur of bone jutting from the flesh.

The spark stung when she called it out.

"Pa," she gasped.

And then the sickness caught up.

Jasimir hurried her to a wash basin just in time. When she finished retching, he handed her a goblet of water, looking back to Draga. "We can ambush them. I'll go in with one Hawk—"

"It's a trap."

"I can try to hide your riders," Fie coughed, then spat into the basin.

Draga shook her head. "Did I stutter? This is a trap." Her eyes had gone cold and dark. "They're going to kill all the hostages, no matter what."

"The letter says—" Jasimir started.

"The letter is bait. All he wants is for you to walk into the Fallow Vale unprotected, thinking you can save them."

"I have to try."

Draga gripped the desk chair. "No. Rhusana wins the moment you walk into his camp. If you care for the Crows, *all of them*, you can't give yourself up. Not without forsaking the whole caste. You have to cut your losses."

Fie's belly-sick passed, wrath flaring in its wake. "Easier said when it's not your loss to cut."

"Don't tell me about my losses," Draga snapped.

"Don't pretend you give a damn about my caste," Fie hissed back. "If Tatterhelm had a dozen Hawks—"

"Tatterhelm has——" Draga cut herself off, running a hand over her hair. "This is why he takes hostages: he wants us shaken, he *wants* us making mistakes. If we give him the prince, it's all over. I could follow him all the way back to the royal palace with a mammoth army, but as long as he keeps that knife on—on Jasimir, there won't be a single damned thing any of us can do."

"Your song'll change when he starts sending pieces of a Hawk," Fie spat.

Draga stared at her. Jasimir inhaled sharp at Fie's side but said naught.

"It will not," said the master-general in a voice that sliced high and razor-thin.

"Aye? Maybe the first day it won't, when it's just Tavin's little finger." Fie's own voice rattled with fury. "If Tatterhelm gets impatient, maybe he'll just send the whole hand."

"Tavin's your blood," Jasimir added, voice rising. "What about the Hawk code? What about 'I will not forsake—'"

"I know the code!"

Draga's shout shattered over the stone walls. In the stunned quiet, she strode to the window, staring out through the crossed iron bars. Steel shuddered and clinked in her hair.

"Taverin has always known his duty. We serve the nation first." A crack in her voice filled in with granite. "When you act in anger, you've already lost. Jasimir, being a king means sometimes you choose who to sacrifice. Today the choice is ten Crows and a Hawk, or the Crow caste and Sabor. Do you understand?"

Jasimir didn't answer.

Draga didn't turn from the window, but her spine pulled stiff as Pa's little finger on the desk. "Do you understand?" she repeated, harder than before.

Silence stretched thin as spider silk, then snapped when the prince whispered, "Yes."

Fie felt the sucker punch in her bones. He wouldn't look at her.

"Consider yourself lucky, because today I'm going to make this choice for you," Draga said, facing them once more. "Corporal Lakima, return these two to their own rooms. I want a watch posted to make sure they stay there."

As before, Draga should have looked to the prince. Instead her eyes burned on Fie.

"Yes, master-general." An iron grip settled on Fie's shoulder.

"You *can't*—" Fie protested.

"Shut the door," Draga muttered, dropping into the commander's chair. "And tell someone to bring me some gods-damned wine."

At first, Fie screamed.

She cried out with fury: fury with Draga for sentencing her family to a wretched death, fury with Jasimir for letting her, fury with Pa for sending her to safety in Cheparok, fury with Tavin for stealing into her heart and tearing it asunder, and, most of all, fury with Sabor, with the Covenant, with the dead gods.

Then she crumpled with shame: shame for giving up her own, shame for failing to keep her one rule as a chief, shame for not scratching and clawing her way out of Trikovoi.

Then, at last, she wept with grief, and when she did, she grieved for more things than she could count, than she could name, but most of all, she grieved for the brief thread of hope that had sparked when she saw Tavin's beacon burning in the gate of Trikovoi.

When she was done weeping, she slept without dreams.

And when she woke, it was by the light of the Crow Moon.

For a while, she lay in the dark on her foul, soft bed in her foul, safe room, her thoughts winding up and spinning out like a spindle. Would Tatterhelm send a piece of someone else in the morning? Or would he cut off more of Pa?

Would she let him?

Every heartbeat in her ears was an accusation.

Draga was right: the whole Crow caste hung on Jasimir reaching the throne.

Jasimir was right: he understood what was at stake.

Tavin was right: he could have done something better with his life than die.

Fie searched the dark for answers and found none.

But that made sense. She had no right to expect answers here in this safe, quiet, too-damned-soft room, not with her people caught in Tatterhelm's hell.

If she wanted a way out, she had to hunt it down herself.

Slipping out was easy enough: a Peacock-tooth illusion crafted a second Fie to stumble from her room, startling the guards long enough to let the true Fie sidle behind them. Once she'd rounded a corner, she sent the illusion back to her room, then traded the Peacock tooth for a Sparrow's.

And then she hunted.

Fie wound through hall after darkened hall, some narrow, some yawning, some guarded by grim-faced Hawks, others empty as a gambler's oath. Her slippers left no mark on the stone as she passed.

All she needed was a way out, she told herself. Then she'd take up her teeth and her steel and bring down as many Vultures as she could before—

Before they killed her. Or worse, kept her alive. Tatterhelm had more skinwitches than she had Crows, and he had grunts, and he had skin-ghasts. All he would do was start sending pieces of her to Jasimir.

It was always going to come to this.

Tavin had always known. So had she. Ever since she'd crawled out of Cheparok. No——ever since she'd fallen from the bridge of the Floating Fortress.

No——ever since Pa had thrust the chief's sword into her hands.

What do you want, Fie?

Her caste, or her kin. Thousands of Crows, ridden down by day and night. Or ten of her own, dying by pieces.

That's the game, get it?

The road had trapped her, and she couldn't see which way was right. Every hope, every oath, every scrap of faith she'd had in Hangdog, in Tavin, in Jasimir, one way or another, they'd turned to arrow after arrow in her eye.

She stumbled. Smacked into a wall. Sagged against it.

One way or another, she would lose everything.

Fury howled in her heart. This was all wrong. She'd learned to fight like a Hawk. She'd learned to read and write like a Phoenix. She'd kept her head steady, burned her teeth, broken the only Crow rule. She'd near killed herself day after day, road after road, mountain after mountain, to keep the damned oath.

And she would still lose.

There was no way for her to win. There never had been.

How much more will you let them take?

She slid down the wall and curled there, shaking. This was the game. This was the true Money Dance: the rest of the castes could spin and whirl and scream at the Crows, take what they wanted, as long as they wanted, knowing that the Crows couldn't do a gods-damned thing to stop it. Sabor had never once intended for her to win.

They didn't believe a Crow could.

Far away, a watch-hymn eased into the silence. Fie ignored it.

Then the hymn wandered into a lonely trickle of notes. One she'd heard nigh every morning.

Fie scrambled to her feet, heart pounding. It couldn't be Tavin—yet her unsteady legs pushed her forward, following the sound. He'd said his mother sang it—maybe Fie would never see Pa again, but at least she could make this much right—

She shadowed a Hawk through a door and stepped into the frigid Marovar night. Stars sprayed over the brutally clear sky above, crowned in the circlet of Crow Moon rising.

Dead ahead of Fie, a Hawk woman leaned on a watch post, staring into the mountains, humming a watch-hymn that sometimes splintered around a choked breath.

Dark as it was, Fie could still mark the razor flash of steel feathers in her hair.

She's a mammoth rider in the Marovar, Tavin had whispered by a camp-fire a moon ago.

The question in Fie's skull unwound.

Twin Talons. But how—

She knew what it meant.

For a moment she swayed in place, still cloaked in the Sparrow tooth, her head a-riot with a thousand threads that suddenly knotted and pulled tight.

Stitch by stitch, the tapestry unfurled, stretching on and on until she saw not a weaving but a wrathful way out.

How much more, the prince had asked, *will you let them take?*

This was the dance. This was the game. The one she wasn't meant to win.

But now—she had fire. She had steel.

She knew her road.

The prince had sworn to protect her caste. He had sworn to make the Oleanders pay.

She was a chief; he was a prince. And one of them was a liar.

Fie waited for another guard to crack the door, then flitted back into the halls of Trikovoi, bound for her room, her swords, her teeth.

Bound for the prince.

Bound for the Fallow Vale.

Whether or not she burned her crown on a pyre, she was a chief. It was time she looked after her own.

CHAPTER TWENTY-TWO

THE SLAUGHTER BELL

FIE DIDN'T INTEND TO STIR THE ASHES WHERE SHE TREAD, BUT SHE did all the same.

Fie didn't intend to feel bad for Jasimir, either, but that happened, too, as he stumbled on the hobbles round his ankles. She yanked him upright, none too gentle, and prodded him on with the point of Tavin's short sword. Her pity had only extended to a stolen—*liberated*—Hawk cloak about his shoulders to ward off the predawn chill.

He shot her a dark look but kept walking, hands bound before him. Fie suspected the prince had choice words for her.

That was partly why she'd gagged him with a twist of rag before dragging him into the Fallow Vale.

She'd been here before, or at least near enough to watch it burn. Once, the valley had held a village. Once, that village had cut a chief's husband and child down. And once, a plague beacon went unanswered. Now all that was left was blackened earth, and a mark on her map that read *ashes*.

As she marched the prince on, a fretful wind picked at long-cold cinders and scraped grit over crumbling stone walls and barren fields. Every hut, every corpse, every field had been put to the torch; everywhere the plague had touched. That alone could halt an outbreak: burn all to ash and leave it be for years, for generations, until the grass at last grew green over the remains.

Fie had to give Tatterhelm his due: with a shifting haze of windborne cinder and myriad walls to shelter behind, he couldn't have picked a better place to hole up.

Especially if he had untold numbers of skin-ghasts to hide.

Gray light leached into the dark over the valley's eastern wall, warning of a sunrise the prince wouldn't see today. Fie's throat knotted. All this had begun in the Hall of the Dawn; so, too, would it end with the rising sun.

"Faster," she muttered to Jasimir. Tatterhelm might not wait before taking another piece of Pa. The prince gave her a look of pure disgust, but she pushed him on. They slowed as they passed the first burned-out house, peering for any slip of the skinwitches or their skin-ghasts.

It's a trap, Draga rasped in her memory.

Fie's sandal-nails crunched through something black and brittle. A whisper of escaping bone-sparks told her what she'd trod upon.

"That's far enough."

Tatterhelm's voice clapped like thunder ahead. Fie started and gave Jasimir's shoulder a sharp jerk.

The Vulture rounded a scorched corner, one hand locked about the back of Tavin's neck. The other held a dagger to Tavin's throat.

Still alive. Fie froze. Tavin was still alive. They'd bound his wrists before him. A lattice of dried blood streaked the side of his face, and bruises darkened his jaw, his arms, nigh everywhere she looked. Why hadn't he healed himself? Had they simply beat him until he couldn't keep up?

But he walked yet, breathed yet. He was there.

She hadn't really believed she'd see him alive again. Not since he'd cut the bridge.

A heavy ring tolled with Tavin's every step. It took Fie a moment to find the culprit.

Tatterhelm had knotted an iron slaughter bell round Tavin's neck.

Tatterhelm stopped. The tolling didn't. More shadows split from the blackened bones of the ruins: ten Vultures, ten Crows, ten more slaughter bells ringing dull at ten more throats.

Tatterhelm's meaning cut all too clear. But this was the way of one who'd been a hunter all his life; he wanted her rattled and scattered.

Instead, Fie spat in the ashes. Her anger was a curious thing, sometimes jagged and broken as Pa's sword, sometimes heavy and storied as the bag of teeth. She'd left them both behind to reckon with Tatterhelm. He would not shake anger from her here.

She counted each Crow's face, every one her home. Madcap, their chin stuck out. Pa, rag bound about the knuckles of his right hand. Wretch, her lips moving frantic as Viimo kept a dagger at her throat.

She did not see Swain.

Tears boiled into her vision before she could wrest them away. Swain, with his scrolls and figures, his dry jests, the trench that dug in his brow when he pored over maps or coin. No matter where they were in Sabor, he'd managed to find posies for his wife's birthday, year after year, even after the roads had claimed her.

Tatterhelm had taken him from Fie in Cheparok.

He would take no one else. Not one Crow more. She was a chief. She would look after her own.

"Fie, *get out*—" Pa started. His Vulture captor seized Pa's right hand and squeezed. Pa choked off a sharp cry. New bright red stained the bandage.

Give them fire, whispered the Phoenix teeth on Fie's string.

Fie fouled up when she looked Tavin's way. He didn't speak, eyes burning through her. Of course he'd known she would take the deal. Maybe, for a moment, he'd believed that she'd choose another road. But they both knew better; Fie only hoped he hadn't fooled himself for too long.

Once more, his face said a thousand things, full of fury and desperation and guilt and, worst of all, betrayal.

Maybe one day he would forgive her for this. But she'd always known it wouldn't be easy.

Tatterhelm shoved Tavin to his knees, knife still at his throat, one hand digging into Tavin's scalp. The northman hadn't even bothered to don his favored helm to reckon with a little Crow half chief; he wore just a chestplate and heavy boots over his grubby yellow tunic and wool leggings. His pork-pink arms bulged bare and stark with valor mark tattoos in the gloom, his wild straw hair coiling about his shoulders. A beaked Crow mask swung from his belt like a prize scalp.

"You've been a pain in my ass," he rumbled. "Making me hound you across the damned nation all on some fool's notion."

Fie spat in the cinders again. "You here to deal or not?"

"Y'know what the problem is with you people?" He pulled the mask free of his belt and tossed it into the dust at Fie's feet. "You forget what you are. Queen's comin' for your kind, won't be stopped by some bone thief brat."

Long-dead mint sprigs spilled from the beak.

We have something that belongs to you.

The Vultures had trailed *her* the whole time. Not the prince, not Tavin. They'd known to follow *her*.

"Maybe the prince learns his lesson about trusting Crows," Tatterhelm grunted, "but I'd say that lesson'll be . . . eh, short-lived."

He wanted her rattled. Fie knew a Money Dance when she heard one.

"Enough," she snapped. "I did what you wanted. Now let them go."

"Settle down." Tatterhelm's knifepoint scratched at Tavin's throat. "Viimo."

"Aye, boss?" Viimo answered from Wretch's side, one fist holding fast to the older woman's bonds. Wretch's mouth moved, too quiet for aught but Viimo to hear. The skinwitch ignored her.

"These two bring any company?"

Viimo closed her eyes a long moment. Her brow knotted, then untied. Her free fist curled. "I see nothin', boss."

Draga hadn't yet noticed their absence, then. Or she had cut her losses like Fie couldn't. Either way, Fie was on her own.

On her own and in too deep to get out now.

Tatterhelm narrowed his eyes at her. "Drop the cloak."

She let go of Jasimir. "Move and I'll gut you," she warned him, and pulled her ragged robe over her head.

Tatterhelm squinted at her shirt and leggings, searching for any hint of hidden weapons. She knew he'd find none. He jerked his chin. "The teeth."

Fie clenched her jaw, then lifted Tavin's sword and sliced through her chief's string. It fell to the ash with her robe.

"Now the sword."

Fie let the Hawk blade drop. When it struck the earth, she'd have sworn she'd stripped herself bare. Thin wool wouldn't stop arrows. No teeth, no steel. Easy prey.

Pa had said she was a dead god reborn. She did not feel like one now. Not even Little Witness.

Her pulse beat a funeral march in her ears.

She did not look at Tavin.

"Bring the prince closer."

"Let them go," she returned.

Tatterhelm pressed a red line into the side of Tavin's throat, just below the shade of a bruise. Tavin jerked; his slaughter bell tolled.

"I ain't askin' twice," Tatterhelm said.

The cold hook in Fie's guts winched tight. She forced a breath through her nose and marched Jasimir onward, unarmed. Empty-handed. Toothless.

Every heartbeat echoed what burned in every Crow's eyes:

Traitor. Traitor. Traitor.

She fouled up and looked to Tavin again. What burned in his face was much, much worse.

She didn't know why she'd ever fooled herself into hoping for forgiveness.

He would live. That had to be enough.

When they drew within a few paces, Tatterhelm barked, "Hold up." They stopped. "Prince goes the rest of the way himself."

This was it. Fie licked her lips and let Jasimir go. He shook his head and tried to protest around the gag. It sounded something like "You can't."

"Trust me," Fie said, "it's too late for that, Highness."

She shoved him to the Vultures.

"*No!*" Tavin shouted, wild-eyed.

Jasimir stumbled through the dust—one pace, two—and Tatterhelm seized the scruff of his neck.

Now. Fie licked her lips, drew breath to whistle—

And the ashes erupted at her feet.

Gray, flat hands slapped about her ankles. Another pair roped round her throat. She screamed, half fear, half fury, thrashing like an animal in a snare.

She'd forgotten the skin-ghasts, and now—it had all fouled up.

Fie choked out a furious scream before the clammy hands yanked tight.

Cinders rained from two skin-ghasts as they swelled from below, slick gray hides gorging like water skins. The one grasping her ankles yanked them up with him as he rose, until she hung by both her neck and feet.

And then the skin-ghasts' faces filled in, hollow, dreadful. Known.

Hangdog's eyeless face yawned at her, narrowing his hold on her throat.

The thing that had once been Swain began to drag at her ankles.

Panic shrieked through her veins. She flailed for—for aught, a rock, a scrap of bone, even a handful of hide. But the skin-ghasts simply folded out of the way, pulling like they meant to tear her apart.

Pain ripped along her jaw, up and down her spine, at her ankles. She heard screams that weren't her own. Some sounded like they might be her name. One sounded like it might be Tavin.

The skin-ghasts said naught, for they had no tongue, no bones, no teeth to speak with. Only Hangdog's slack face. Only Swain's.

The queen had, in the end, turned even Fie's dead to her ends.

How much more, Jasimir had asked, *will you let them take?*

She'd never expected to die quiet. Young, maybe. But not like this.

She'd not come here to die.

She'd come to look after her own.

Fie wet her lips and forced the last of her breath into an earsplitting whistle.

If Tavin were a Crow, he'd know that whistle signal. It meant *drop*.

If Tavin were the prince, he'd know what was coming.

And if Tavin were only a Hawk, he would have died when Fie loosed the Phoenix tooth that had burned, hidden, in Jasimir's bound fists all along.

But Tavin wasn't only a Hawk.

And so when the cyclone of Phoenix fire swallowed Tavin, his prince, and his captor in one starving snap of golden teeth, only the skin-witch burned.

The Crows flattened themselves to the earth in a chorus of iron bell-song. Phoenix fire swept over them, scattering the skinwitches like sparks.

Greggur Tatterhelm rolled from the fire, skin blistering over his valor marks, and leapt for her. The plain, brutal knife swept down——

And jolted away as Jasimir threw himself into Tatterhelm's side. They toppled into the skin-ghast at her feet, knocking its grip loose.

Fie's feet hit the dirt. Hangdog's hollow hands dug into the flesh of her throat. Through watering eyes, she saw more skin-ghasts bursting from the ash, grasping for the Crows—she had to get free—she had to look after her own—

The Phoenix tooth burned yet in Jasimir's fist. She called it once more.

Golden fire rushed round her, devouring empty skin with a horrid crackle. Swain crumpled like paper, shriveling in an instant. The other skin-ghast let her go.

Fie crashed to the cinders, gasping air stained with old grease.

Hangdog's skin-ghast staggered, peeling and charring, until he collapsed. The dark sockets of his face warped as flames ate him whole.

Why? she wanted to ask. *You sold us to them, and this is what they made of you. Why?*

He crumbled away, into the ash.

"Fie—!"

She wrenched about on her knees. Jasimir crawled toward her. Fie yanked the prince's cloak aside and freed Pa's broken sword from where it dangled along Jasimir's backbone. The weight of it steadied her as she reached for Jasimir's bound hands.

The prince's eyes snared behind her and flew wide. She couldn't turn fast enough.

A fist like a hammer smashed into her jaw, knocking her back into the dust. Pain shot through her teeth. She heard another crack and cry paces away.

"*Get up!*" She'd know Tavin's voice anywhere, even raw and hoarse.

A steel-toed boot thudded into her ribs. She tumbled through ash again, slipping and choking on a mouthful of grit. Pa's sword slipped from her grip.

"Cute trick," Tatterhelm grunted. "You oughta've run."

Blistered fingers locked around her throat and hefted her to dangle before the skinwitch. The world reeled in Fie's eyes, painting a streaking picture: the fire fading, the Vultures and their skin-ghasts circling the Crows, Jasimir slumping against a wall paces away, one ankle bent awful wrong. Tavin kneeling at his side.

Fie saw a fistful of dwindling flame in Jasimir's palm, the remnants of Fie's grand plan. Tavin's mouth moved. Then he reached for Jasimir's hand.

She squirmed, clawing at Tatterhelm's fingers. He squeezed tighter, crueler even than the skin-ghasts.

"Coulda just walked away," he said dully. "Had to go and cause a mess. You thought you could *fight*?" He shook her like a ragdoll, voice rising. "You thought you could take *me*?"

He slammed her into another wall. The stones shook, a few black chunks falling.

"You forgot what you are," he snarled.

Fie's sight fogged, her lungs howling like a skin-ghast for air. Tatterhelm hefted his knife.

Suddenly, Tavin's arms whipped over Tatterhelm's head, his bound wrists yanking tight against the Vulture's windpipe. Fie dropped free.

She ducked under the swing of Tatterhelm's arm and snatched up the chief's sword, rolling to her knees in time to block the Vulture's knife.

"Reckon I know what I am," Fie answered.

Tatterhelm stumbled from Tavin's weight. She sprang to her feet in his range, too fast to catch.

The skinwitch had never thought she would take this road.

Fie struck like the Covenant's own judgment, blade crashing down on Tatterhelm's forearm. His hand split free with a meaty *thunk*, still clutching his dagger, and landed in the ash.

Tatterhelm stared, stupefied, at the bleeding stump where his hand had been. And then he screamed. Tavin slipped off him and darted to Fie's side.

"Tatterhelm's down!" shouted another Vulture, and pointed his sword at Pa. "No prisoners but the prince!"

Tavin shoved teeth into her hand: First, the burning Phoenix tooth he'd taken from Jasimir.

Then—the two she'd yet to light.

Fie closed her eyes. *Harmony.* One tooth alight. *Harmony.* She struck a second, and the gold flame piped and howled. The Vultures slowed, fearful. *Harmony.*

She struck the third.

Phoenix fire blasted through the valley, greedy and ruthless, tearing over ash and ruin and long-cold bone and showing mercy only to the Crows. The golden blaze swelled like a flood, dwarfing the dawn, until the Fallow Vale burned end to blackened end. Tatterhelm stood no chance so close to her; he vanished in roaring flame. The skin-ghasts too crumpled in place, sloughing into smoke or dribbling into boiling puddles.

Every other Vulture shrieked and bolted for shelter. They would find none.

Fie clenched a raised hand into a fist, reaping the fire. It spun into great wheels about the Vultures, caging them in.

Fire-song raged in her bones, in her heart, in her teeth. One dead queen. Three milk teeth. She'd hunted for near an hour to pick out Phoenix teeth that wouldn't fight one another. Now they balanced as one, burned as one, and answered to her wrath alone.

Tatterhelm had never once believed a Crow could best him.

Pa might be right about witches and dead gods; perhaps she'd been one, and perhaps so had Tatterhelm, once. But right or wrong, it hadn't taken a god to strike him down. Only a chief and the element of surprise.

She had business to settle before she dealt with the surviving Vultures. She strode to Jasimir through the flames, Tavin trailing behind her.

Jasimir had pushed himself up on one leg, clinging to the wall. His eyes landed on Tavin and the telltale flames nipping harmlessly at his arms. "You're . . . you're a Phoenix."

Tavin flinched, eyes on the ground. "I'm a bastard."

"He's your brother," Fie finished, hoarse, and sawed at the bonds about Tavin's wrists. "Half, at least."

Tavin looked at her then, as the rope fell free.

She wanted to burn away the awful anger and shame in his eyes. She wanted him to heal himself as he had before. She wanted his hand in hers.

She wanted him to forgive her for risking his king, for laying his secret bare, for letting him fall to Tatterhelm to begin with.

But she was a chief, and her own were not out of the valley yet.

"It'll be all right," she lied, and cut the slaughter bell from his neck.

An open hand reached into the space between them. Tavin blinked at the prince, then took it. Jasimir wobbled—and embraced his brother.

"I should have seen it," Jasimir mumbled. "I . . . didn't want to. I'm sorry."

Tavin didn't answer, but neither did he let go, and in his own way, that was answer enough.

Fie's breath came hard and harsh as she turned to the Vultures, trying not to choke on the reek of burnt hair and foul cooking flesh. Blood sizzled in the back of her throat, a sign she kenned too well by now. Easy harmony or no, the dead queen was fading.

Fire prowled round the remaining Vultures, keeping its distance, waiting for her command. One way or another, it was time they learned what it meant to cross the wrong Crow.

"Drop your weapons," she ordered. Most obeyed; a few stragglers hesitated until fire lashed at their elbows. Madcap took a spear and passed it to Jasimir to use as a walking staff.

"Now what, chiefling?" Viimo asked.

Fie swallowed, the burn of blood rising on her tongue. The fire rolled about her and the lordlings like a loyal beast. Three teeth of a dead queen and she could do anything. She could light them up, watch them burn, watch Sabor burn from mountain to coast if she wanted.

She was tired of pretending she wouldn't.

No—that was false, still, even now.

Just once, she wanted someone to treat her like she would. And the terror in the Vultures' eyes seemed to be a good start to that.

They'd hunted her for nigh a whole moon. They'd taken her family. They'd shed her kin's blood. Just because they never imagined they'd find themselves at her mercy.

Tavin's slaughter bell still dangled from her fingers.

Wind flushed through the vale, spraying ash and grit down the road, through the fire, as sunlight snatched at the edges of the valley walls. *Mercy*, it seemed to say.

And her teeth answered in kind: *Give them fire.*

"Fie." Jasimir's voice cut through the haze.

"Don't tell me to spare them," she hissed, half wishing he would.

"That's your choice to make," he said, face steady in the wash of gold firelight. "But it won't be for much longer." He pointed back down the road they'd walked.

A horn wailed off the gray hillsides, near buried in thunder as mammoth after mammoth stormed into the vale.

But Viimo had said—

Fie spun and found Viimo's face in her fiery cage. The skinwitch watched the mammoth cavalry pound down the ashen road, her dirty face grim—not surprised.

So Viimo had lied to Tatterhelm. She'd known the Hawks were coming. She'd betrayed her own leader, and her kin would pay. Why in the twelve hells would she turn on her own?

Maybe Hangdog could have told her.

If she let Viimo burn, she'd never find out.

Mammoth riders cascaded into the ruined village, surrounding them before Fie could make up her mind.

"You can let the fire go," Tavin said from behind her, resigned.

Fie winced. *A Markahn bastard. One more Hawk for the collection.* How long had Tavin known who he was? How long had he kept it secret? And now here he stood plain in roaring flame, unscathed, before scores of Crows and Vultures and Hawks. There'd be no running from the truth any longer.

Fie loosed the teeth. Mammoth riders circled the Vultures and dismounted, unwinding shackles. The master-general herself rode toward Fie through the ebbing flames, storm-faced. Fie couldn't say which loomed more menacing: the mammoth or Draga.

If Draga meant to have her head for this, though, perhaps Fie'd settle for dragging the Vultures into the twelve hells with her after all.

Then someone limped past, leaning on a spear, and planted himself between Fie and the master-general:

Jasimir.

Another dusty shadow followed him, standing steady in the road. Madcap. Another: Wretch. And more still.

Crow by Crow, they walled Fie off, and at last Pa's arm wrapped about Fie's shoulders as he took his place by her side.

For all her spite and cleverness, everything had emptied out of Fie, leaving her only with a knot in her throat and eyes that burned with tears. Pa pulled her in and let her bury her face in his shirt, just as he had for years. For a perfect moment, Fie didn't give a damn for Hawks or princes or skinwitches.

She'd done it. She'd kept the oath, she'd struck down Tatterhelm, she'd looked after her own.

Draga might execute her now, but at least she'd die a chief.

"Out of the way," the master-general ordered.

"You'll not lay a finger on her," Wretch answered, just as hard.

"She assaulted and abducted the heir to the throne so she could use him as bait. He could have been killed." Draga cleared her throat. "I cannot—"

"I commanded her to."

Fie raised her head and looked at Jasimir. This had not been part of their plan.

Draga blinked, which seemed to be as much surprise as she'd allow herself to display on a battlefield. "Think very carefully about what you are telling me, *Highness*."

"I commanded her to," Jasimir repeated, loud and plain. "Perhaps we should discuss this on the ground, master-general?"

To Draga's credit, she knew better than to let the prince shout within her soldiers' earshot about how he and a half-grown Crow had played the head of Sabor's armies for a fool. She climbed down from her mammoth and strode over, looking not the slightest bit appeased. "There were clear signs of a fight in your chambers."

Jasimir shrugged. "If there weren't, you would have searched Trikovoi for us first. We needed you to come after us at the right time."

That much was true. They'd left a clear trail of nail scratches all the way out.

"And if I hadn't followed? You couldn't just surrender to Tatterhelm."

"Oh aye, that they did," Madcap said, their voice bright. "Hoodwinked us all, head and heart."

"I carried Phoenix teeth in my hands," Jasimir clarified. "Tatterhelm didn't think to check the captive for any weapons."

Draga frowned. "The Phoenix teeth couldn't have been a surprise to him. Did he magically forget to bring a hostage you wouldn't burn, or did you just cut your losses?"

Jasimir glanced over his shoulder, then turned back. His voice dropped, though there was precious little point in subtlety now. "He brought Tavin."

Draga's face fractured as she found her son behind the Crows. For once, she couldn't frost it over. "And?" Her voice cracked.

"I'm fine," Tavin answered, stiff. "Tatterhelm is not."

"You're hurt—"

"I'll live."

Draga nodded, more a twitch of her chin than anything. Then she drew herself up and narrowed her gaze on the prince. "You're saying you thought of this all on your own? That she only followed your orders?"

Pa started forward, but Fie shook her head.

"Royal commands," she said, letting go of Pa to stand on her own. "Can't disobey those."

The master-general shot her a cold look.

"I take full responsibility," Jasimir answered. "Any punishment should fall on me alone."

Draga's mouth tightened. It was plain she didn't believe him for a heartbeat. But she couldn't exactly pass a reckoning on her own crown prince.

"This ploy could have destroyed everything you worked for," Draga snapped. "The fact that it worked is only a sign that the Covenant isn't done with any of you yet."

"It worked because Tatterhelm underestimated Fie." Tavin's voice cut through the crowd, straight to his mother. "And so did you."

Silence stretched taught as a wire until Draga's shoulders slumped. She rubbed a hand over her face, letting out a long-suffering sigh. "Anything else? Anyone have another grievance or five they feel compelled to air? Any new secrets to fess up?"

"Tavin and I slept together," Fie offered. "Since you're asking. Probably would've come out one way or another."

Pa turned a laugh into a cough. Madcap twisted about and crudely gestured their approval.

Draga stared at Fie a long, long moment, then muttered, "I'm getting back on the mammoth."

"That went well," Pa said under his breath.

"Corporal Lakima," Draga called, stalking away. "I want healers working through these people before we return to Trikovoi. And we're taking the Vultures with us. Spare hostages never hurt anyone."

"Wait." Fie pushed forward as Draga spun on a heel, scowling. "Keep Viimo separate. She lied to Tatterhelm and said she didn't see you coming. The other Vultures will know."

"Why would she do that?" Draga demanded, bewildered. Fie shook her head. "Fine. She'll have a nice cozy dungeon all to herself. Now follow me so we can patch you lot up."

The Crows hung back, looking from Fie to Pa, and with an odd lurch, Fie realized they waited for the marching order.

Pa raised his brows at her. "Well?"

Fie wavered. "I—I dropped my teeth," she said.

Pa nodded and patted her shoulder. "Catch up when you find them."

He whistled the marching order. The Crows moved out, peppering Jasimir and Tavin with questions.

Fie hung back to peer about the cinders, hunting for her tooth string. She also didn't favor adding a lost sword to Tavin's list of troubles.

As she turned, Tavin's iron bell swung on its rope. Fie hadn't realized she still clenched it in a sweating fist.

Hot, scaly fingers closed around her ankle.

She yipped and jerked free, stumbling in her haste. A blackened hand scrabbled through the ash toward her, leashed to a steaming mass of burnt flesh.

Tatterhelm somehow lived yet.

But not much longer: his blood turned the cinders about him to dull red paste. If he were fortunate, blood loss would fade him out before the burns could.

"*Mercy,*" he gasped.

She sucked in a breath that savored of ash and scorched hair.

Mercy.

They always wanted it, in the end. They wanted to hunt Crows, and they wanted to cut them to bits, and when they faced the Covenant's judgment, they wanted the Crows to grant them a swifter, cleaner way out.

Fie's hand slipped a little. Her chief's sword no longer steadied her.

This was her road, wasn't it? She was a chief. She was a Merciful Crow. Maybe the Covenant had skipped the plague with Tatterhelm and sent her to crop him instead. Maybe she was the Covenant's judgment now.

She thought of the sinner in Gerbanyar, the smile on his face, the blood on her hands. She saw the Oleanders beneath her tree, screaming for her blood. She saw the Hawks of Cheparok haunting her steps just for being a Crow in the wrong market. Because Crows had to let them. Because Crows would always be merciful.

She saw fire on a bridge. An arrow in an eye. Swain, sharing his scroll with a prince. Tavin, cutting through the rope bridge. Iron slaughter bells hanging about the heads of her own.

She saw a finger on a desk. She saw a trail of fingers on a dusty road.

She saw her own blood-soaked hands.

She was a chief; she looked after her own. Crows, sinners, bastards, kings-to-be; somehow, they had all become her own.

"*Damn you, Crow*," he begged. "*Mercy.*"

Greggur Tatterhelm suffered no plague. He'd chosen his own road, just as Fie had chosen hers.

The Covenant could have sent the plague to deal with him. Instead it had sent a Crow.

Fie dropped Tavin's slaughter bell in the ash before the skinwitch's dimming eyes.

"Some of us," she told him, "are more merciful than others."

The nails in her sandals ground on cinder and bone as she turned from the Vulture. Her teeth and Tavin's sword waited in the ashen road ahead.

She took them up again, and did not look back.

CHAPTER TWENTY-THREE

— SHORT LIVES —

"FIGURED I AIN'T SEEN THE LAST OF YOU."

True to Draga's word, Fie found Viimo alone in her cell. The Hawks at guard eyed Fie but said naught. Perhaps they'd learned her teeth made a better threat than any steel.

She'd slipped off while Corporal Lakima settled the Crows in guest barracks. Her kin were safe and whole, mostly; yet Fie had something more to settle before she could face Pa. Her head told her plain what would come of that talk. Her gut said she wasn't ready to own it, not yet. And her heart . . .

Her heart had ghosts to cast out.

The skinwitch propped herself up on an elbow, sprawled on a thin straw pallet. "You lookin' to make speeches, or you lookin' to whine about your dead traitor lad?"

"Your kin shot Hangdog down," she reminded Viimo, trying to sound imperious. "That's two counts of Vulture treachery to one from a Crow, so let's mind who we're calling traitors here."

"It's to be speeches, then." Viimo flopped back down on the pallet and closed her eyes. "Go on, get it over with. I got sleep to catch up on."

"What were you promised?"

No answer came.

Fie gripped the bars hard enough for cold iron to grate against bone. "*Why* did you turn on Tatterhelm?"

Viimo opened one eye. "And if I don't say, you'll use another Crane tooth, aye?"

"Maybe. Maybe I think you want to tell me."

Viimo opened her other eye.

"Stuck under a mountain, split off from your kin, and you just brought your own leader down," Fie continued, leaning into the bars. "I wager you want to tell someone, *anyone*, why, before they hang you for treason."

Viimo didn't speak for a moment. Then she sat up and folded her arms, tracing the valor marks there. "I found tots," she said. For the first time a bleak note sawed in her voice. "When I was younger. Lost ones, stolen ones. Could track them halfway 'cross Sabor if I wanted. And I'd bring 'em back. Got too good at it, and the queen heard what I can do, and next thing I know . . . Well, you don't say nay to a queen. But I liked bringin' the tots back. I liked who I was. Not someone who hunts brats and roughs up grannies."

Wretch. Fie remembered how the old Crow had spoken to Viimo, even with a knife at her throat.

"It don't take a master scholar to read the Oleanders' horseshit for what it is," Viimo sighed. "So nobody promised me nothin', chiefling. I didn't want to be that person no more."

Fie didn't know why the notion made her so angry.

No, she did.

The words flew out before she could stem the tide: "So you didn't do a thing until you decided you didn't *like yourself*? You didn't draw that line when your lot cut off Pa's finger? When you tried to burn me alive? When you tricked a boy into turning on his own kin by telling him you'd treat him like a person? Wasn't any of it enough for you to stop Tatterhelm?"

"It all was," Viimo said, exhausted. "I didn't."

"I hope you aren't waiting on my forgiveness," Fie hissed.

Viimo sighed and dropped back onto the pallet. "I ain't waitin' on aught from you. You asked me what makes a traitor, chiefling, and the only thing I got that crosses with your dead boy is this: we both didn't want who we were. That's all."

She closed her eyes and did not say another word.

Fie mulled over throwing pebbles at Viimo until she sat up again, but decided the Vulture had naught more worth hearing.

She'd come to settle her heart. Instead the ghosts lingered yet, and still she had to face Pa.

And Tavin, another voice nagged.

The thought of looking Tavin in the eye tonight made Fie burn like a sinner. It also made her want to run out of Trikovoi and not stop until she hit the sea.

She all but bolted for the barracks.

She found the Crows hustling in and out of the courtyard, sorting through heaps of gear and goods. Draga had conferred the entirety of the Vultures' supply caravans upon the Crows, a bounty that could very well last them until the end of summer.

As long as they met no Oleanders.

Fie let out a breath. She doubted duping the master-general into a rescue would make Draga reconsider her stance on the oath.

"I count six water skins here, Highness," Madcap called.

Fie blinked. Jasimir peered around a cart, marking a note on a length of parchment. "That makes a dozen even. Could you please add them to the others?" He pointed inside.

Fie walked over as Madcap bustled past. "What are you doing?"

Jasimir flashed a list at her. "Someone has to write all this down."

Swain had always scratched out their inventory. Fie supposed that would fall to her now. "I can take over."

Jasimir shook his head. "We're catching up. Did you know Tavin poisoned the Vultures?"

"Snuck some plant into their stew down by Gerbanyar," Wretch added, swinging a sack of rice over her shoulder. "Gave them the runs for three days."

He'd found a way to make the moss useful after all. Fie couldn't help a grin. "Did the prince tell you he barfed on a corpse?"

The Crows' laughter rose, then died when a Chief voice called. "Fie."

Jasimir pointed his charcoal stick over her shoulder. She turned. Pa sat at a table inside the barrack, gesturing to the seat across from him.

Fie unbuckled the chief's blade as she walked over and set it down on the lacquered red table before she sat.

Pa did not take it.

"The prince told me the Hawks are balking at the oath," he said. Fie's gut twisted, half-relieved she didn't have to break the news, half-miserable for failing him so. "Don't fret, Fie. It'll come. Maybe it takes longer than we hoped, but it'll come."

"Your end's kept, at least," she whispered, ragged.

"Aye. Remember what I told you about earning your string?" Pa hefted a cooking pot by the handle. Without a little finger to grip tight, it wobbled bad. "I can't deal mercy proper now. Could try with my left hand, but I won't be fast or sure."

"And that's no mercy at all." Fie swallowed, eyes on the broken sword. *We both didn't want who we were.* "Pa, I'm too young to be chief."

"You're too young for near all you did the last moon and a half."

I don't want to be chief.

Fie stared at the table's thick red lacquer.

"I didn't want it, either," Pa said, too quiet for the others to hear.

She looked up, startled. The confession burst free. "Pa, I—I carried steel, I learned to read, I left the roads. I *liked* it. I don't want to be chief. I don't know if I want to be a *Crow.*"

He reached over and took her hand. "No chief I've ever met looked down the road and wanted what they saw waiting for them. Hangdog never saw a way out for Crows. He gave up on us. But you, Fie . . . you changed that road. You made it one you *could* want. Learning your letters, carrying steel . . . Those don't make you less of a Crow. They open ways for the rest of us. And when any of us look at your road, we see you're bound to be one of the greatest chiefs the Crows will ever witness."

"Tell that to Swain." Fie's voice cracked.

"He said it himself the night we cut the oath." Pa gingerly tested his scarred, Hawk-healed knuckle. "Your ma said you were born vexed with the world, aye. And Swain said you were born vexed enough to turn it on its head."

She had no answer, only eyes that burned wet. Pa gripped her hand tighter.

"The Oleanders, they say we bring our troubles on ourselves, aye?" He leaned in. "Spend enough time biting your tongue instead of spitting back and you start to believe them. But there's good in your road. Aye, we walk a harder, longer way to get it, but it's ours. It's yours. You deserve it and more. Don't let them take that from you, too." He leaned back and sighed. "Where's your string? Don't need ten fingers to tie that, at least."

Fie pulled her tooth string from a pocket and brushed off the ash, then handed it over. Pa circled round to her back and looped it about her neck once more. A moment later, he let it fall, knotted tight.

"By the Covenant's measure and the dead gods' eyes, you're a chief," he recited. "Deal their mercy. And look after your own."

The string felt heavier than before. She'd looked after two false Crows; now she had a band of ten true ones. But she had Pa, and she had Wretch, and she had a prince's oath.

And she had a bag of Phoenix teeth. That helped.

Pa sat across from her once more and raised an eyebrow. "So. You and the Hawk lad?"

She hid her face in her hands. "I don't want to talk about it."

"Naught to be ashamed of, either," Pa said, treading cautious. "He saved all our lives on the road. Tatterhelm thought he had the prince and didn't care to keep toting spare hostages. Your boy blew his own ruse to keep us alive, knowing he'd take twelve hells for it. He's got his head on right."

"It's all a wash, anyway," she sighed, searching her hems until she found a thread to pick. "I near got his brother killed. *And* I paraded his biggest secret about before half of Trikovoi. He hardly even looked at me. Reckon we're done for."

Pa gave her a narrow look. "*I* reckon he started shining to you the moment you punched him. By the time Tatterhelm brought him in, that boy lit up like a torch anytime he caught your name. That's a dedicated kind of shine to be sure. I'd wager some faith on it."

For the second time that afternoon, she had no answer, no matter how she scoured the table for one.

"Excuse me." Jasimir's voice carried from a few paces away as he walked over to the table. "We found . . . this."

He held out Swain's scroll.

Fie took it in a shaking hand and spread the crackling parchment. For the first time, the letters ordered themselves for her: lines of a walking song, of lore, of lives here and gone.

"I was thinking . . ." Jasimir rubbed the back of his neck. "There are scribes in the fort. I could arrange for one to sit with the Crows and keep recording as long as you're in Trikovoi. And if you'll allow it, we could make a copy of this scroll . . . for the royal library."

Fie looked up at him and found her smile to be well-watered. "Aye. Swain would have liked that."

Jasimir returned her smile. "That wasn't the only thing we found."

Fie followed his gaze to the door, where Wretch had just walked in.

In her arms squirmed a very dirty, very grumpy gray tabby.

"Little beast trailed the caravan all the way from Cheparok," Wretch groused. "You've Madcap and your Hawk lad to thank for sneaking her scraps and keeping her out of sight."

Barf squirmed free and trotted over to Fie, sniffing at her sandals. After a moment the cat rolled on Fie's feet, squalling a reprimand. She only yowled louder when Fie picked her up and buried her face in Barf's dusty fur.

"Reckon she missed the cat most," Wretch said.

"Reckon she missed her pretty Hawk boy most," Madcap called from across the room.

Barf mewled in indignation when tears dampened her fur, and wriggled loose once more. Fie tried her best to scowl through leaky eyes.

"I miss silence," she declared, then relented, scrubbing at her face. "And I suppose I missed you lot, too."

Fie slipped away after dinner while her kin sang a rowdy camp song and danced about a fire burning in the courtyard's great brazier. A few of the morning's mammoth riders hung about, comparing scars and trading tales.

She just needed a fresh breath, that was all. She'd go back to the barrack and sleep with her kin, as she had every night of her life until Peacock Moon.

Or she could go back to her room. Her own room, quiet and private, where no one would ask aught of her, where she could wash off the ashes, curl up in a bed, and work at the knots in her head and her heart over the road that stretched before her now.

A treacherous part of her had loved the silence of the mornings, keeping watch over her tiny band of false Crows, the solitude and peace.

Perhaps Pa had understood that when he said no chief wanted their duty.

Perhaps she wouldn't have that kind of peace much longer.

Fie went looking for her room.

That turned out to be a feat easier intended than accomplished. Trikovoi's winding corridors swallowed her whole, sending her up stairways and down them again, round and round training yards and mess halls, circling like a hound settling to bed. At last a doorway spat her out onto a walkway between towers just as the last edge of sunlight sank into the mountains.

And there she found Draga and Tavin, leaning against the wall, heads bowed to speak quick and quiet. Tavin looked up when the door swung shut behind Fie. A raw shadow darted through his expression before he screened it off again.

Now she knew where he'd learned that from.

Draga saw what caught her son's eye and muttered something, then pushed off the wall and headed toward the other door.

Fie reckoned she hadn't really ever been looking for her room.

She steeled herself and walked nearer to Tavin, trying to ignore the rattle of her heart shaking its cage. "What did she say?"

"That she didn't raise a coward." Tavin's voice rang hollow to Fie's ear; his face stayed blank.

"What does that mean?" she asked, half to drive him to speak again. She wanted to hear his voice. She wanted to know he'd not suffered too much with Tatterhelm.

She wanted to know if he'd forgiven her.

Tavin levered himself onto his feet proper, still not looking her way. "It means we should talk somewhere better than here."

Fie followed him up a set of stairs that curled about a tower, lead dragging in her gut. At the top waited a cold brazier and a handful of benches.

Tavin held a hand over the brazier, then jerked it back, gaze flicking to Fie. His shoulders dropped.

He trailed fingers over the coals, and golden fire sprang up in their wake.

"When——" His voice cracked. He cleared his throat but did not pull his hand from the brazier. Flames curled and danced along the lines of his burn scar. "When I was seven, the king came to Dragovoi. Mother told me to stay out of sight, but . . . he saw me. I looked exactly like Jas. And Surimir knew that about eight years earlier, on his own wedding night, he'd been drunk enough to command Mother to his bed while Aunt Jasindra was still at the reception."

Fie's belly churned. Tavin had told her of Hawk loyalty to the crown, of Surimir's fondness for abusing it. Yet she couldn't fathom how one of the gods' favored Phoenixes could sink to that terrible depth.

Tavin wasn't done. "Mother never formally acknowledged me as her son and heir. It'd raise too many questions about my father. I don't know how many half castes there are, but . . . when you're half a Phoenix, you can't just play with fire, you have to deliberately *try* to not get burned. Mother could teach me only the blood Birthright. So. You asked where this"—he turned his burnt wrist—"came from. When Surimir saw me, he had a strong notion of what I was. And he held my hand in a fire until I figured out how to prove him right."

More than ever, Fie wanted her hand in his. She wanted to stay by his side, plant herself betwixt him and the king if they ever saw that monster again. She wanted to burn down Surimir's ugly palace and teach him the price of treating his people like toys.

Instead, she sat on the bench and watched the fire. "That was how you fooled the Vultures. They tried to burn you."

He nodded. "The rest of the Hawks just saw me as a bastard and a healer close to Jas's age, perfect for a bodyguard. Surimir knew I was . . . his. And perfect for Jas's double."

"What else did I miss?"

He let out a breath, thinking. "I . . . started the fire in the cave. The man in Gerbanyar—half of that was blood, half of that was fire. The campfire, back with the Oleanders."

"You put it out." No wonder Fie's Phoenix teeth hadn't stopped the flashburn fires outside Trikovoi. Phoenixes knew how to start fires; their bastards had to learn how to stop them.

A chill wind whistled over the tower, knocking sparks from the brazier. They blazed orange against the darkening sky, then winked out. Fie couldn't stave off her question any longer.

"Are you angry with me?"

Tavin gave her an unreadable look. "With you?"

"You've been hiding all this most your life. It's not like I asked before airing it out far and wide."

He pulled his hand from the fire and turned to her, brow furrowing. "You saved me from a slow, agonizing death, Fie. Twelve hells, you made it look easy. Anger is the *opposite* of how I feel. If anything, I'm lucky you're still voluntarily in the same fortress as I am." Fie cocked her head, puzzled. He rubbed the back of his neck. "Everything that—that happened with us . . . happened while I was keeping this from you. That's not right. You have every right to hate me."

"Why?" Fie asked.

"I pretended I was someone I'm not," Tavin said, the words falling almost too swift and heavy to catch. "I know what the king has done to you and yours, what he's allowed to happen. I know what my father is."

"And I know who you are." Fie met his gaze, steady and unwavering. It felt just like the night they'd met, when she'd stared down his steel. This time, he held the point to his own throat.

"That doesn't change anything for you?" He'd gone stock-still. "Anything at all?"

Fie pursed her lips, thinking. The fire crackled in the brazier, casting a rosier light over both of them as the sky steeped into indigo.

At last she said, "If I'd known I'd rutted a half prince, probably I would've bragged about it more."

Tavin stared at her in disbelief. Then his shoulders began to shake. He threw his head back and let his laughter spill into the night. Fie grinned up at him from her bench, feeling tension slip from her spine like a straggling thread pulled free.

They'd both been afraid. They'd both been wrong. She supposed that meant they both were fools, at least this once.

Tavin closed the distance, knelt before her, and pulled her to him, still shaking with laughter and relief.

"I missed you," he whispered into her hair. "Gods, Fie, I've known you a moon and a half, and I swear I didn't know I could miss anyone that much."

The hollowness in his voice had filled in.

Fie tried to answer through the lump in her throat. A sniffle gave her away before the tears did; Tavin only held her tighter as she buried her face in his shoulder. The weight of the last two weeks crashed in— every league she'd walked knowing it carried her farther from him, every hour she'd spent wondering if he yet lived while she kept watch in the dark, every time she'd waited for his laugh and nonsense only to remember where they'd gone.

She didn't wait to stop crying before she kissed him. Salt stung her tongue, then faded as he kissed her back, careful at first, then spiraling into dizzy, feverish glee that somehow, someway they had managed to find each other once more. She'd forgotten how much she liked the way his chin brushed hers, the feel of his back shifting beneath her palms, the sharp, quick breath when she pressed her mouth along his jawline. She'd forgotten how he could light her up like her veins ran with flash-burn, even with something as simple as fingertips tracing her hips.

Pulling back took more effort than she'd reckoned for; every time she caught her breath, he stole it from her again, and the worst part was that she didn't want him to stop. Eventually she found a moment to gasp, "My room."

She felt Tavin's too-pretty grin. "How do you like having a room to yourself?"

"I'm about to like it a lot more," she answered. "Once you help me figure out where it is."

He laughed again and scooped her up in his arms as he stood. "Yes, chief."

———◆◆◆———

Fie woke in the soft half shadows before dawn, still curled against Tavin, still marveling that he was there.

And, by the creeping morning light, she allowed herself to untie the most painful knot in her head and heart, made all the worse by the boy at her back.

He shifted, mumbling her name in his sleep, and that undid her entirely. She eased herself from the bed, pulled a robe over the shirt she'd stolen from him, and glided into the hall. The Hawks at guard just nodded as she passed.

This time she caught the familiar watch-hymn sooner and followed it up to the wall that Draga seemed to favor. The master-general stood there wrapped in a thick snow lion pelt, eyes on the west.

"Tavin hummed that at watch," Fie said. Draga's gaze flicked to her, then returned to the horizon. "That's how I figured out you were his ma."

Draga barked a quiet laugh. "He's right. It's truly impossible to slip anything past you. Here."

She drew a dagger from her sash and handed it to Fie hilt-first. The moonlight drew out waving bands across the blade.

"That's tiger steel," Draga said. "It's stronger than any other metal we know. This blade outlived my mother and her mother, and it will outlive me. But it takes a master blacksmith to forge."

"Aye." Fie passed it back. "I saw it once in a Hawk tooth. Rush, and it shatters." She leaned against the wall. "But leave the blade too long, and it's rutted all the same."

"I thought it would be like tiger steel," Draga said. "The oath. Because you're right, no Saborian should live as the Crows do. And if we forge something better, the nation will be stronger for it. But if we move too fast . . ." She sighed. "The fact is, we're already shattering. How we treat Crows is a liability. The queen's using it to net herself a throne. And you, a teenage girl, used it to fool the master-general of the kingdom's armies."

"No hard feelings," Fie said with a shrug.

Draga shot her a sharp look. "It's been a long day and night, Lady

Crow. Don't try me. *Especially* while wearing my beloved son's shirt."
Fie coughed, ears burning, and Draga continued. "I've had war scholars
digging through our libraries for anything on skin-ghasts. We've found
nothing. There's no knowing how great a threat we're facing, but we
know the queen means to wipe out people the Hawks are honor-bound
to protect."

Fie took a gamble. "Because no one's protected us."

"Because we failed." Draga nodded, jaw set.

"Pa says change always has a price." Fie stared at dawn's edge in the
eastern sky. "That even Phoenixes need ashes to rise."

A moment passed before Draga spoke. "A few hours ago, Corporal
Lakima came to my office with five other Hawks. They've volunteered
to accompany you when you leave."

Fie blinked.

"Other command posts have sent in reports of the skin-ghasts. I'm
going to order them to increase patrols by night. I'm also going to relay
that the Crows are being targeted and require them to report any Crow
casualties immediately." Draga turned about to face the east, same as
Fie. "It's not perfect. There are a thousand ways it'll be fouled up. But
it's a way to flush out the Hawks who are part of the problem, so that
once Rhusana is handled . . . we can keep the oath."

Fie's fingers dug into stone. "You'll—you'll give us Hawks?"

"Save your victory dance," drawled Draga. "First I have to parade
that boy all the way back to the royal palace with enough bells, flags,
and armed soldiers to really say, 'Auntie Draga loves you.' *Then* we have
to win over the king and sort out a gods-awful horror of logistics and
recruit volunteers and then . . ." Draga rubbed a hand over her face.
"Then, yes. You will have Hawks."

Fie couldn't breathe.

You will have Hawks.

She'd done it. She'd made the oath. She'd kept it.

For her ma, for Pa, for Wretch, even for Hangdog—she'd kept the oath.

"I . . . apologize," Draga said stiffly. "You should have had us sooner." She slid Fie another look. "You've already figured out the catch, haven't you?"

Fie nodded, throat tightening once more.

"Then I'm sorry for that, too." Draga's face softened. "He'll be waking up any moment now. I believe you have a better use for your time."

Fie mimicked the Hawk salute, much to Draga's ire, and returned to her room. Tavin rolled onto his back when the door shut, drowsy and smiling as he reached out a hand. She wound her fingers in his and climbed into bed beside him.

"Were you outside?" he mumbled against the side of her neck. "You're cold."

"Aye." She closed her eyes, letting herself enjoy his lips on her skin a moment more, but the longer she waited, the more bitter the words would be. She forced them out. "I know you can't leave with us."

He went still, fingertips pressing against her ribs.

"No," he admitted, "I can't."

It was one thing for the bastard of an unknown father to roam Sabor at her side.

It was wholly different for the king's bastard to do it.

"It's only while Rhusana is still in power." He pushed himself up to look her in the eye. "She'd use me against Jas the first chance she got. Mother would murder me if I set foot outside Trikovoi with anything less than a company of mammoth riders, and she'd be right to do it." His hand slid along her cheek. "Once the queen is gone, I . . . I'll find you. I don't care how far you are or how long it takes, I swear I'll find you again."

Fie closed her eyes. "Aye, and that could be one moon from now. Or it could be the rest of your life."

Tavin wove his fingers through hers once more and kissed them. "The girl I love said they're all short lives. So I won't make her wait long either way."

Fie wanted to fight, even with naught to win. She wanted to hear him call her the girl he loved again. She wanted to burn every Sparrow tooth she had to keep him with her, hidden at her side as they roamed from beacon to beacon, season after season.

But long ago he'd said he would not live as a ghost.

And she'd known this would never be easy.

They were all short lives. She'd just wanted to spend more of hers with him.

She'd just wanted more time. And for now, they only had until the dead gods' mercy called her onward.

The dead gods hadn't called her to the roads yet. Until they did, she would have that much of what she wanted.

Fie drew her Hawk to her once more.

On the seventh dawn of Crow Moon, a trail of crimson smoke scratched the horizon, and Fie knew her time had come.

The Crows gathered at the fortress's main gate, adjusting the straps of new sandals and checking the hold of the new cart while their new chief said her goodbyes.

Jasimir moved first, shuffling over with a thick scroll of parchment and charcoal sticks. "Here. Practice your letters. And write to me."

"Is that a royal command?" she asked, unable to stuff down a grin.

"Write to me, *please*," he amended. "And to Tav. He's already started pining and you haven't even left yet."

"I don't think '*Dear Jas and Tavin, today we only had to avoid twenty Oleanders trying to murder us*' will cheer him up."

"Then it's a good thing you're not going alone." He nodded to the supply wagon waiting beside the Crow's new cart, where Corporal Lakima and her five Hawks waited.

Fie couldn't say whether six Hawks could stop the Oleander Gentry in their tracks, but they were a sore good start.

Jasimir gripped her shoulder. "Don't die," he said, and only half of his tone said it was a jest. "I'm keeping the oath. You're not allowed to die until you've seen it for yourself."

Half of her grin said she believed him. "I'll try. So far I've been fair good at it."

"That makes two of us. But I think Tav's about to commit an act of treason if I keep you any longer."

Fie looked behind her. Sure enough, Tavin had gone fidgety, scowling at the road ahead. Coming from him, that was nigh a death threat.

She gave Jasimir a whole grin this time, then went to her Hawk.

"Do you want your sword back?" she asked him, reaching to unbuckle the scabbard from her belt.

He opened his mouth, shut it again, and, without a word, pulled her into a long, hard kiss. Madcap whooped somewhere at her back; Fie managed a rude gesture in reply before returning to more pressing business.

When they finally broke apart, he stayed near, cradling her face in his hands. "Please, please be safe."

"You just made a fair case for staying in one piece," Fie informed him. "But you should probably boot Rhusana fast anyway. Barf's bound to miss you."

That nudged a soft laugh out of him. "Only the cat?"

"Suppose I might, too," she allowed. "You want your sword back or not?"

"Keep it. Use it. Just stay alive, no matter what." Tavin traced her cheekbones with shaking thumbs. "I don't care if you burn down half of Sabor. And I don't care how long it takes, I swear I'll find you again."

"It won't take you too long." She kissed him one last time, light and quick. "Crows go where we're called."

And then she stepped back, knowing if she lingered any longer, she'd never let go.

But she was a chief with a beacon at her back. She had mercy to deal; she had an oath to witness; she had her own to look after. And her road had led her this far, down strange ways and to strange ends, taking her where no one thought a Crow would tread. She had no reason to doubt that even if Tavin couldn't share her path now, someday it could lead her back to him.

"We're moving out," she announced, as Pa had done a thousand times before.

A chorus of ayes resounded from her kin. And a new answer followed from Corporal Lakima and her Hawks: "Yes, chief."

She whistled the marching order, cast one more look to her lordlings, and turned away.

She had a chief's string; she had Pa's blade; she had a bag of Phoenix teeth. She had a king-to-be's oath; she had a Hawk's sword; she had a bastard boy's heart. She had a mask and a fistful of fresh mint.

A league away, a red trail of smoke called for Merciful Crows. It was time for a chief to answer.

Fie set off down the road.

Acknowledgments

When it comes down to it, all I did was write down the words; there are countless people without whom this book would not exist, and really they should get some of the credit.

First and foremost, the team of highly trained professionals who have made this whole business bearable. Thank you to my agent, Victoria Marini, for steering me through the shoals of this industry, and patiently handing me a life ring whenever I found myself determined to flail in water a mere two feet deep. A thousand-thousand thanks to my brilliant editor, Tiff Liao, who has championed a chief, raised the bar for a queen, and fast-tracked skin monsters with enthusiasm I had scarcely dared to hope for in such a wonderful human being.

A whole bag of thank you to the team at Henry Holt and Mac Kids, particularly the elite squad of publicity and marketing sorceresses

Morgan, Jo, Allegra, Melissa, Katie, and Caitlin—I want to lie down just *thinking* about the work you do, and I know I couldn't be in better hands. Thank you so much to Jean Feiwel and Christian Trimmer for opening the door to a strange, angry little story, to Kristin Dulaney for sending it overseas, and to Rich Deas and Sophie Erb for designing the perfect book to carry it out.

Thank you to my early readers and critique partners, Sheena, Sarah, Jamie, Paula, Hanna, Emily, Christine, and Rory, for helping me believe I just might have something decent on my hands, and thank you to Elle McKinney, my fellow Sailor Scout, without whom I never would have made it to the end of this road. Thank you for never letting me give up on Fie, or on myself.

Thank you also to so many facets of the YA community, large and small; to the Novel 19s for sharing the journey, to the 2015 Pitch Wars class that has been there for me for this entire roller coaster and beyond, and to the bloggers and bookstagrammers who have been boosting *TMC*. (Special shout-out to the incredible Hafsah Faizal for commiserating with me on design, merch, and all things Book Hustle.) And thank you to so, so many authors who have extended a hand, an ear, and/or a word to a very nervous debut, helping me with everything from major decisions to my first speaking gig. Without you, I would almost certainly be hiding under my bed for the next decade, which wouldn't be all that conducive to my career.

I also need to put in a good word for my circle of friends and family who have watched this whole publishing shenanigan unfold with occasionally baffled, but always supportive, delight. My Portland friends (and London and Boulder auxiliary chapters), for whom I would walk a minimum of five hundred miles, and quite possibly five hundred more. Gaby, you always took my writing seriously, which is doubly impressive considering how little I take seriously. Megan, can you believe I actually didn't kill off the love interest in this one? (It's fine, there's a sequel.) Marie, this is my thank-you for driving me everywhere; I can only assume this has guaranteed me another five hundred free rides. Sarah V, I hope you know how your steady stream of cat GIFs has sustained me. Codino, I owe you a beer for putting up with my rants and conspiracy theories. Regan, I owe you a beer pretty much constantly, but in particular for refusing to let me calcify into a permanent installment in my apartment.

And finally, to my parents, who had the grace not to question your daughter's sometimes-volatile career choices, in particular when I was using my BA to wash dishes part-time while working on my manuscript. (You could say that one . . . panned out.) You kept me knee-deep in books as a kid, so really this author thing is all your fault, and when I'd set out on my own, you kept me afloat when safe harbors were few and far between. Thank you for letting me find my own way.

(And of course, if I've neglected to mention you here, you can have my cats' allotment of gratitude. They certainly don't need it; they've been no help whatsoever.)

Rhunadei

Jawbone Gulf

Teisanar

THE HAVODII FLATS

Nisodei

THE LASH

DOMAREM

THE JARIDEI COAST

Karostei

THE SPROUT

ZARODEI

THE HEM

THE VINE

THE FAN

DUMOSA

Shattered Bay

CHEPAROK

MOREISAR

YIMESEI

Silk Cove

Parilai

Jobelii

Sea of Glass

Map of